Dear Reader,

The editors at Harlequin and Silhouette are thrilled to be able to bring you a brand-new featured author program for 2005! Signature Select aims to single out outstanding stories, contemporary themes and oft-requested classics by some of your favorite series authors and present them to you in a variety of formats bound by truly striking covers.

We want to provide several different types of reading experiences in the new Signature Select program. The Spotlight books offer a single "big read" by a talented series author, the Collections present three novellas on a selected theme in one volume, the Sagas contain sprawling, sometimes multi-generational family tales (often related to a favorite family first introduced in series), and the Miniseries feature requested previously published books, with two or, occasionally, three complete stories in one volume. The Signature Select program offers one book in each of these categories per month, and fans of limited continuity series will also find these continuing stories under the Signature Select umbrella.

In addition, these volumes bring you bonus features...different in every single book! You may learn more about the author in an extended interview, more about the setting or inspiration for the book, more about subjects related to the theme and, often, a bonus short read will be included. Authors and editors have been outdoing themselves in originating creative material for our bonus features—we're sure you'll be surprised and pleased with the results!

The Signature Select program strives to bring you a variety of reading experiences by authors you've come to love, as well as by rising stars you'll be glad you've discovered. Watch for new stories from Janelle Denison, Donna Kauffman, Leslie Kelly, Marie Ferrarella, Suzanne Forster, Stephanie Bond, Christine Rimmer and scores more of the brightest talents in romance fiction!

The excitement continues!

Warm wishes for happy reading,

Marsha Zinberg

Marsha Zinberg
Executive Editor
The Signature Select Program

COLLECTION

FIONA HOOD-STEWART

SHARON KENDRICK

JACKIE BRAUN

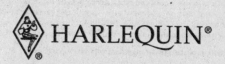

TORONTO • NEW YORK • LONDON
AMSTERDAM • PARIS • SYDNEY • HAMBURG
STOCKHOLM • ATHENS • TOKYO • MILAN • MADRID
PRAGUE • WARSAW • BUDAPEST • AUCKLAND

ISBN 0-373-83665-1

EXCLUSIVE!

Copyright © 2005 by Harlequin Books S.A.

The publisher acknowledges the copyright holders
of the individual works as follows:

HOLLYWOOD LIFE OR ROYAL WIFE?
Copyright © 2005 by Fiona Hood-Stewart

MARRIAGE SCANDAL, SHOWBIZ BABY!
Copyright © 2005 by Sharon Kendrick

SEX, LIES AND A SECURITY TAPE
Copyright © 2005 by Jackie Braun Fridline

This edition published by arrangement with Harlequin Books S.A.

® and TM are trademarks of the publisher. Trademarks indicated with
® are registered in the United States Patent and Trademark Office, the
Canadian Trade Marks Office and in other countries.

www.eHarlequin.com

Printed in U.S.A.

CONTENTS

HOLLYWOOD LIFE OR ROYAL WIFE?

Fiona Hood-Stewart

VICTORIA'S SECRET'S OUT

Film star Victoria Woodward has been spotted with Prince Rodolfo of Maldavina on several occasions this week at the Cannes Film Festival, fueling rumors that the pair are in the throes of a passionate affair. Victoria, who starred in the hit Hollywood movie

CHAPTER ONE

SHE HATED EVERY MINUTE of it: the hype, the flashbulbs everywhere she went, the ever-present expectations...

And now they wanted her to be on show yet again.

Victoria Woodward sighed. How she wished that the wretched movie, of which she'd unwittingly become the star, had not ended up as a contender to win the Cannes Film Festival.

But it was too late for regrets. Too late to wish herself back in the security and anonymity of Hetherington, the English village where she'd resided all her life, where everything was predictable and simple. To think she'd used to consider it boring, had longed for change and excitement. As though granting her wish, fate had changed her life overnight, swooping her into a Hollywood whirlwind of parties, private jets, paparazzi, and the not-so-easy-position of being dogged at every step by the press and the curious.

Now, as she exited the airport at Nice, another batch of eager reporters lay in wait.

'For goodness' sake, smile,' Anne Murphy, her agent, hissed. 'Ed'll have a fit if he sees more pictures of you sulking.' She pulled Victoria forward and hurried her out of the terminal. Immediately the press rushed upon them.

'Is it true you may win the Palme d'Or, Miss Woodward?' A reporter poked a microphone aggressively under her nose.

'Do you have a boyfriend, Miss Woodward? Is it true that you and Peter Simmons are dating?'

Victoria experienced that familiar and frightening tightening of her throat, followed by a paralysing rigidity that made it almost impossible to speak or move. Fear gripped her gut. She turned in panic to Anne.

'Get me out of here,' she muttered, her long blonde hair swinging wildly, her grey eyes glazed.

'The car's right there.' Anne held her elbow and manoeuvred her expertly through the crowd.

Two burly young men in grey suits and designer sunglasses kept the spectators at bay as they forged a path to the limo that represented her safe haven. Forcing one foot in front of the other, Victoria managed a brief smile, then plunged inside the vehicle, curling up in the corner, ignoring the eager faces pressed against the windows, the camera lenses seeking one last shot of her before the car glided off into traffic.

'Victoria, you're just going to have to get used to this,' Anne said sternly. Anne was short and sandy-haired, and the thirty-five-year-old New Yorker's tone spelled efficiency.

'I simply hate it,' Victoria whispered, stretching her long slim legs out before her. 'I think I must be claustrophobic or something.'

'Well, this is hardly the moment to make earth-shattering discoveries,' Anne replied tartly, sending her a significant look. 'You're on show, honey; that's what they're paying several million bucks for.'

'I thought that was for playing Xanthia in the movie,' Victoria said crossly, hair curtaining her face as she dropped her chin on her chest.

'Now, grow up, Vic. You know perfectly well that was just the beginning. I really don't understand what you're complaining about. Anybody else would be delighted to have reached stardom in such a short time.'

'I loathe it.'

'And I give up,' Anne exclaimed, rolling her eyes, wishing Ed Banes, the director, had chosen someone else for the role. For, although the girl was a natural, she had been nothing but trouble from the word go. Anne had warned Ed and the others that it wasn't going to be a smooth ride. But had they listened? No. And as usual she was left to clean up. She liked Victoria a lot—thought she was a sweet, sensitive kid and a great actress. But that wasn't enough. If she wasn't disposed to do the PR, and put up with the media, it was just no damn good.

Glancing sideways at her charge, Anne decided to let Victoria be until they got to the Carlton Hotel in Cannes. She leaned back against the leather seat and flipped through the Festival programme.

There was a dinner tonight. She supposed that would be another piece of work. A top fashion house was delivering Victoria's dress this afternoon. God only knew what she would do if there was a mistake in the fitting. Anne checked the guest list. Several other stars would be present. That would make Victoria less conspicuous.

A couple of heads of state would be there, a sprinkling of royalty, and some famous rock stars to help dilute things. She glanced at the table seating. Victoria was placed to the right of HRH Prince Rodolfo of Malvarina, the ruler of the tiny principality, an island not far off the coast of Italy.

Anne twiddled her pen a minute and thought about what the bankers had said regarding a change of residence for Victoria. Malvarina wasn't a bad option—one of the more attractive tax havens, easy to access, and with great banking laws. She wondered whether to mention it, then took a look a Victoria's closed face, grimaced and decided not to. Right now, all Victoria seemed to want was to return to this place—Hetherington, the small English village where she and her widowed mother had lived. It was all very cute, but not Anne's style. Malvarina, on the other hand, was smooth and sophisticated. Some of the world's richest and glitziest had moved there, seeking anonymity.

Hmmm. Anonymity. That might be just be the selling point, she reflected. After all, *everyone* in Malvarina was rich and famous. Another star would just blend in. Anne made a note on her Palm Pilot to mention the subject to Victoria at a suitable moment, then glanced at her watch. Time to make sure Victoria would brave the arrival at the Carlton and the inevitable pack of reporters awaiting them without a scene.

IN HER HUGE SUITE over looking the Croisette and the Mediterranean, Victoria sank down on the king-size bed and let out a sigh. She didn't want it to be this way, wished that everything could be as she'd imagined it would be when she'd been discovered and offered the role—before she'd rushed into all of this, so excited and thinking of nothing but the opportunity to act. She'd always wanted to be an actress and now, at only twenty, she'd been offered the break of a lifetime. So why was it so hard to do the other thing? Most people wanted to be famous, to be in the limelight, to be a star, seek fame and fortune. But to her the publicity and pressure were insurmountable obstacles that she found increasingly hard to deal with.

Time to take one of her pills, she realised, getting up and moving towards the bathroom. As she did so she remembered just how she'd discovered Dr Richard Browne, the man who kept her sane.

It had happened one night at a huge Hollywood dinner, when she'd slipped into the bathroom and leaned against the basin, closing her eyes and feeling desperate. The girl washing her hands at the next basin had looked across at her curiously.

'You okay?' she'd asked.

'Fine,' Victoria had answered, mustering a smile.

'You sure?' The girl had grimaced. 'I guess you're finding it hard to deal with all the crap. I used to be like that too. I ended up at a shrink. And thank God I did. It saved my life, man.' She dried her hands on a towel and dropped it in the basket next to the sink.

'Did he help you? The shrink, I mean?'

'Sure he helped me,' the girl had answered, laughing sympathetically. 'It was like I'd turned a corner. He gave me some medication that *really* did the trick.'

'That sounds wonderful,' Victoria had replied, her voice filled with longing. What she wouldn't have done for some assistance.

'Hey, if you want I can give you his number. He's really cool. Have a pen?'

'Yes. Here.' Victoria had rummaged in her evening purse and produced a pen and an old paper napkin, which she'd handed to her bathroom companion. Moments later she'd slipped the napkin back in her bag, determined to give the doctor a ring on the morrow.

'You'll like him. He's very experienced in treating people in the movie business who are suffering from stress. He'll have you feeling great in no time.'

And the girl had proved to be right. Dr Richard Browne had immediately understood her problem and had written out a prescription for a substantial supply of small capsules. He'd said they'd make her feel better very quickly, and she was to call his office when she needed more. They had, and she did—even though it was expensive. Not that money was in any way an impediment any longer. It seemed to flow in from every quarter

Now, for a long moment, Victoria hesitated, one of the capsules placed on her palm. Deep inside, she knew she shouldn't be relying on drugs. She had never enquired of the doctor what they contained. But if lots of actors took them they couldn't be harmful, she figured, eyeing the medication for a moment. Then, knowing she had to go back out there and face the crowd, a wave of panic overwhelmed her and she popped it in her mouth before she could change her mind.

Minutes later, it felt as though a black cloud had lifted. Suddenly she was relaxed and able to cope. But she'd have to take another one before she could face the dinner tonight.

Did Anne know that she helped herself with meds? Victoria wondered. She didn't think so. She'd been very careful not to let on. Anne disapproved of anything that might tarnish Victoria's reputation. So Victoria kept quiet about it, figuring that as long as no one found out it was okay. What mattered was that with the help of the meds she was able to produce the result they wanted. Surely that was what mattered?

She moved to the window and looked down at the people wandering up and down the promenade: the stargazers, the groupies, the wannabe actors and actresses, trying to attract the attention of the press and the movers and shakers of the film industry. For a moment she felt a rush of shame. What wouldn't those people out there give to be in her place? She had it all, yet she hated it. Not the actual making of the movie, she reflected— *that* she'd really enjoyed, even though the schedule had been relentlessly demanding. It had been wonderful, the film set her natural habitat. And when at last she'd seen the final rushes she'd been enchanted. It was the hype she couldn't handle.

A knock on the door made her turn sharply. It was all about to begin again. An afternoon programme of activities: interviews, the hairdresser, the make-up artist, a photo shoot. She swallowed. She *had* to face it.

'Come in,' she said brightly, plastering on a smile.

'How are you feeling, Vic?' Anne eyed her closely.

'Fine, thanks. Ready to roll.'

'Good.' Anne looked relieved. 'Then let's get going. The press are assembled in the main conference room, but we'll fix your make-up and hair first. Marci's got your outfit ready.'

Victoria nodded. She would do it. Could do it. Was determined to get through it, and maybe learn to hate it a bit less... She slipped her hand in the pocket of her designer jacket and was reassured by the feel of the extra capsule she'd slipped in as a precaution. Tossing her hair back, she went through the different expressions she'd practised in front of the mirror. Her masks, as she liked to think of them.

Soon they were making their descent in the lift, with Anne delivering last-minute orders on her mobile. The lift doors opened onto the main lobby and it all began again...

'OKAY,' ANNE SAID several hours later as they made their way to the Presidential Suite, where Ed was holding a cocktail party, 'you did great.'

Victoria rolled her eyes. 'There's still tonight to get through. I'm dreading it already.'

'It'll be fine. Everybody who's anybody will be at the dinner—it's an A-list event.'

'How reassuring,' she said dryly. 'Do I *have* to go?' she muttered, knowing the answer and lifting the skirt of her gauze embroidered gown to negotiate the stairs. Behind her two private detectives followed her every move, never taking their eyes off the one-hundred-and-fifty-thousand-pound diamond necklace and earrings that a top jeweller had lent her for the night.

'I guess that's a joke, right?' Anne queried, her brows shooting up.

Victoria made a face. 'I suppose.' She shrugged, and glanced at her bejewelled evening purse to make sure it was securely shut. She could always go to the loo and pop a 'lifesaver', as she liked to think of them, if things got sticky.

'Okay. Remember—be polite and charming and you'll do just fine. This is your big chance, Victoria—don't blow it,' Anne admonished. 'And, by the way, our financial people want to talk to you about moving residence for tax reasons. Have you heard of a place called Malvarina?'

Victoria frowned. 'It's some island somewhere in the Mediterranean, isn't it?' she said, still treading carefully so as not to step on the hem of her dress.

'Yes. And it happens to be a great tax haven too. In fact, tonight you're seated next to—'

But Anne's next words were lost as Ed's large bald figure appeared in the doorway of the Presidential Suite and he swooped Victoria away on his arm. Oh, well, Anne thought to herself. She'd done her best.

She stopped, checked out the room, heard the buzz of voices, high-pitched laughter and the clink of expensive crystal. Victoria would do okay, she assured herself, and with that thought she set out to chat up the reporters who were trying to get exclusives with her charge.

CHAPTER TWO

RUNNING A PRINCIPALITY WAS no different from running a large company, Rodolfo reflected, as he stepped out of the lift and headed towards the next event. The need to be present at a seemingly never-ending succession of social occasions such as the Cannes Film Festival bored him. Still, it was definitely bringing in the kind of business the island needed.

His grandfather, the late Prince, had ensured that life in the principality remained very closed and refined. While he was alive only the ancient aristocratic families that had centuries-old residences on the island had been allowed tax breaks. But his grandfather had been dead for three years now, and Rodolfo was doing his damnedest to help his small dominion develop into a modern, self-sufficient state.

Its people needed work which would allow them to stay on the island, instead of having to leave and seek jobs in neighbouring countries. Rodolfo was determined to offer them a better standard of living, and he was sure that it could be achieved by tapping in to the island's tourist and residency potential. Already many wealthy business people and movie stars, seeking seclusion and privacy, were moving to the island, thanks to the new tax laws he'd had passed.

Hence his reason for attending the Cannes Film Festival. For, like it or not, he, as the Prince, was Malvarina's best marketing spokesman.

Rodolfo had spent several years preparing for what he was now implementing. All the while he'd been at Oxford, and later when he was at Harvard, he'd known that he would never persuade his grandfather to change the old ways. Instead he'd bided his time, respecting his grandparent's views, but knowing exactly what he would undertake when the opportunity finally arose. In the meantime he had gained experience by working with major companies in London and New York and through living life to the fullest, aware that one day he would be the ruler of the small principality. And when the moment had come the people of the island had watched suspiciously as Rodolfo implemented his reforms and passed new laws.

However, little by little, he had won them over. Now there was a top-line tourism and hotel school where the islanders could train. Language courses and the possibility of exchange programmes with other countries existed too. Rodolfo wanted the best for his people, but he also expected them to provide the best possible service to those he was inviting to make the island their primary residence.

Straightening his bow tie, Rodolfo glanced critically at his tanned reflection in the glinting mirror in the corridor. He'd aged in the last couple of years. New responsibilities had brought tiny crows' feet around his dark eyes, and streaks of silver touched his temples. Par for the course, he reflected, fixing his cufflinks and wondering which film star he would be expected to be polite to tonight and how many ego trips he would have to endure.

Cannes and its glitz and glamour bored him. But it was here that potential clients hung out. People, it seemed, were drawn to royalty like bees to honey. His lips curved ironically. He'd lost count of the number of women who'd thrown themselves at him, hoping to share his bed and to be able to say that they'd had a fling with one of Europe's most eligible bachelors. Some may even have dreamed of another fairy tale *à la* Grace Kelly. But he was uninterested in the blonde-and-silicone perfection that was presently on offer, bored with the vapid top models he'd dated with no strings attached, and the inevitable publicity that accompanied his numerous affairs.

Of course the future of the principality was something he now had to take into consideration. Hence his introduction to several aristocratic European women whom the council of the island considered suitable brides. He sighed. Just thinking about them made his heart sink. To have to spend the rest of his life with a woman he didn't love seemed a lot to ask. On the other hand, since Giada had died in that plane accident seven years ago he'd never thought of giving away his heart again. So perhaps it would be easier simply to marry someone like the Spanish *duquesa* the council were so keen on, or that German countess, and forget about romance.

He glanced at the thin gold watch gracing his wrist.

Time for the show to begin. On his way out of his suite his valet had handed him a white silk scarf which he threw casually around his neck. Another black-tie event. How many could they squeeze into the space of one festival? he wondered with a grimace.

VICTORIA FIDDLED with the stem of her champagne flute and forced herself to appear interested in the dull story that a fellow actor was recounting about himself and his exploits in some obscure film which, he told her, was bound to win a prize at next year's festival in Sundance, even though it was not making waves in Cannes. She made all the right noises and caught Anne's eye, hoping she might be rescued.

It was only the beginning of what promised to be an interminable evening. Mercifully dinner was announced and she was able to escape.

'Mademoiselle Woodward…'

The elegant MC showed her to her place at the central table. Why did she always have to be stuck in the most conspicuous place? she wondered, thanking him. The tables were filling up. The large room was decorated with a sylvan theme: glistening silver leaves and branches were entwined with fairylights under glittering chandeliers. The effect was rather special. A woodland fragrance had been sprayed to give the room more atmosphere. They'd even managed a soundtrack of birds twittering in the background. She sat down, along with the other bejewelled women, and plastered on a plastic smile, her mind wandering. Behind the seated diners hawk-eyed bodyguards hovered, just out of sight of the ever-rolling cameras...

'*Signorina.*' A deep masculine voice to her right made her nearly jump from her reverie. She looked up. Next to her stood a dark, handsome man with the ghost of a smile hovering about his lips.

Victoria blushed. It was as if he'd read her thoughts, knew she'd been off in a world of her own.

'Good evening, *signorina*. May I?' He raised a quizzical brow, then prepared to sit next to her.

'Oh, please,' she murmured, realising that she hadn't checked the place card of her neighbour.

'Thank you.' He slid into the chair with a brief smile. 'Good evening. I am Rodolfo Fragottini,' he said casually.

'Hi. I'm Victoria Woodward,' she replied.

'Of that I am well aware,' he said smoothly. 'In fact the whole world is aware of your presence here tonight, *signorina*. May I congratulate you on your success? I have not had the pleasure of seeing your movie yet, but I gather that your performance is spellbinding.'

'Uh, thanks.' She flashed the ritual demure smile. Why had she not created a formulated reply for these compliments that she was so bad at receiving?

'You do not feel your performance was that great?' he queried.

She turned, caught a swift flash of humour in his eyes and lowered hers. 'Actually, I— Oh, I really don't know,' she muttered, embarrassed.

'You didn't seem to agree with me, that's all,' he said, eyes laughing as she looked up once more.

Despite her nervousness, Victoria smiled back. 'It's

difficult to judge one's own performance. People say it was good. I always feel it could have been better.'

'Ah! You are a perfectionist?' he teased.

'No,' she responded. 'It's my job. I want to do my best. I just don't see what all the fuss is about. Oops.' She bit her lip, realising she shouldn't have said that.

'How refreshing,' he murmured, glancing at her with new interest. Here was a superstar not obsessed with her own fame and glory. A novelty by any standard. Also, she reminded him of someone. 'Do I take it that you are not enchanted with having to keep up appearances on a permanent basis, Miss Woodward?' he asked, placing his white linen napkin on his knee.

'Well…' She shrugged, glanced at him sideways and caught the flicker of mischief in his eyes. 'It does become a bit heavy going after a while.'

'You amaze me. I thought this was what all actors and actresses dreamed of—fame and recognition. It does not please you?'

'Of course it does. It's just that...' She caught Anne's eye and quickly stared at her plate, hoping the pill she'd taken beforehand would keep up its effect for long enough to get her through the evening.

'Just that you don't feel at ease in this role?' he asked searchingly. There was something about her that struck a chord.

Their eyes met and her pulse missed a beat. 'How can you tell?'

It was his turn to shrug. 'I observe people. Like you, I am often subjected to the stares and curiosity of others. It can become extremely trying,' he finished dryly.

'Oh, my goodness, Your Royal Highness!' An elderly woman decked in diamonds and with several obvious face-lifts in her wake cooed across the table at him.

'Good evening, Madame Jensen.' He bowed his head in greeting.

Victoria blinked. Royal Highness? He'd said his name was Fragottini and, being her usual distracted self, she hadn't bothered to glance at the place cards. Now she really had put her foot in it. Anne would have wanted her glittering for royalty, she reflected wryly, eyeing her lobster cocktail with a glint of humour. She looked at it and sighed. She was so sick of all this rich food, of the wining and dining. What she wouldn't give for a good old steak and kidney pie at the Bells pub in Hetherington.

'You do not like lobster, *signorina*?'

Realising Rodolfo Fragottini was politely waiting for her to start, Victoria picked up her fork and smiled briefly. 'I'm sure it's delicious,' she replied, forcing herself to slip a forkful into her mouth.

'I doubt it. These large dinners rarely are. Would you consider me very pushy if I said I think you are lying?'

Victoria nearly choked. She hastily grabbed her water glass and took a long sip to quell her laughter.

'Better?' he enquired solicitously.

'Fine. Sorry.' She cast him an apologetic glance tinged with a smile. 'It's just I seem to have had so many different cocktails lately I'm a bit saturated.'

'I can understand that,' he sympathised, rolling his eyes expressively. 'Lobster cocktail, *foie gras, que-*

nelles. I too have to admit that I've had my share of rich food for a while to come.'

'But surely you eat things like this the whole time? I mean, you're a prince or a king or something, so I suppose you live in a palace and eat off gold plate?' she challenged.

'Not quite. Even we royals have had to adapt to modern times,' he replied, tongue in cheek, enjoying the banter. 'Actually, I rather like going to the supermarket, choosing ingredients and cooking myself.'

'Gosh, in the royal kitchen?'

'No. I have an apartment in the castle where I live, and I try to prepare my own dishes as much as possible. Nothing like a nice plate of spag bog,' he added with a wink.

'Spag bog?' she exclaimed, spluttering with laughter and trying to remember that he was a royal. She pressed the napkin to her lips to suppress a giggle. 'Where did someone like you learn to eat spaghetti Bolognese?'

'At Oxford. I'm really rather good at pasta, though I say it myself. You should come and try it some time. Do you cook? Or does your Hollywood schedule not allow for such personal indulgences?'

'You're right,' she sighed, 'it doesn't. But actually I love to cook. Or used to, until all this came down.' She raised her hand, then let it drop in her lap.

'And where was that?' he asked curious about this girl who jogged his memory.

'Oh, back in Hetherington. That's the village where my mother lives. I do quite a lot of baking too.'

'Where is this village?' he asked, picking up his fork once more.

'In England—Sussex. It's very pretty—cottages with thatched roofs and no lighting on the streets at night. We live in a manor house just outside.'

'It sounds wonderfully quaint. I can understand why you would want to return there.'

'Can you? I thought people like you were trying to transform their countries into havens for the rich and glitzy.'

'Really? Is that what you've heard?' She caught the edge to his voice.

'My agent has some idea that I ought to move to a principality called Malvarina. Apparently they have very attractive tax laws. Maybe you've heard of it?' she responded.

'Actually, I know it quite well. What have you heard about Malvarina?' He arched a brow thoughtfully.

'That it's another Monte Carlo—filled with rich tycoons flitting about on glitzy yachts. I suppose the local potentate is luring them in by the dozen. Personally I think it's criminal to spoil somewhere which up until now seems to have been preserved from an invasion by the outside world just for the sake of money. It sounds a bit like a theme park to me.'

'You don't say?' He raised an amused, quizzical brow and leaned back in his gilt dining chair, the better to observe her. Quite the little spitfire, Miss Woodward, if her conversation up until now was anything to go by. 'Let me get this right. You think that the Prince of Malvarina is some sort of exotic dictator, making a theme park out of what was once a beautiful, unspoiled Mediterranean retreat?'

'Something like that.'

'Maybe you should go and take a look at it yourself before forming such a cast-iron opinion. You never know. You might be agreeably surprised.'

'I suppose you could be right about that, but I doubt it,' she confided. 'I heard the Prince himself is here, flogging the place. That doesn't bode well, does it?'

'Definitely a bad sign,' he agreed.

'In fact, I was meant to be sitting next to him tonight. They must have changed the seating.'

'Really?' His laughing dark eyes met hers full on.

All at once Victoria's stomach lurched. 'Uh-oh,' she murmured, turning bright red as she leaned forward and peered beyond his plate at the name card. Her worst expectations were fulfilled. Sitting back, she took a deep breath. 'Look, I'm dreadfully sorry. I didn't mean to be rude. If I'd known it was you I never would have— Oh, dear, how embarrassing.'

'*Signorina*,' he said, slipping his hand over hers, 'please don't be upset. I assure you there is no need to be distressed. I've never been described as a potentate before, but it has a certain ring to it. I must remember to tell my PR people to slip it into the next brochure we do for Malvarina. In fact, the only bit I objected to was your certainty that I am trying to create a theme park.'

His hand was still laid over hers, warm and reassuring, and Victoria felt a delicious shiver run up her arm. She looked up at him. Their eyes met and she smiled apologetically. 'I'm always putting my foot in it. I'm truly sorry.'

He gave her fingers a light squeeze. 'The only way

I shall forgive you is if you personally visit Malvarina and allow me to dispel what I truly believe to be your false image of the island. I certainly intend for it to be very different from what you describe.'

'That's very kind of you,' she said, drawing her hand away. 'I suppose I should be fair and give the place a chance before judging it so arbitrarily. I'm sure it's lovely. I just don't want to move anywhere.'

'I understand. But if you have to move, Malvarina may not be such a bad spot as you think. But then I'm prejudiced.'

AN HOUR LATER, VICTORIA was surprised at how quickly the dinner had gone by. Before she knew it, the guests were being ushered into the ballroom where an orchestra was striking up. The Prince was still at her side, and Victoria realised that she was far more at ease in his presence than she had been while meeting Hollywood moguls and stars. There was something easy and natural about him. Amazingly, he felt like the only real person she'd met here.

'Would you like to dance?' Rodolfo smiled down into her eyes, and for a moment Victoria's pulse missed a beat. There was something very charming about this handsome man, she acknowledged.

She accepted the offer and accompanied him onto the floor. As his arms encircled her she felt a thrill course up her spine. She told herself to stop it immediately. He was just being polite, just trying to get people to go and live on his island—that was why he was being so nice to her. She must not lose sight of that. But it was hard not to feel light-headed as they twirled about the room and the musky scent of his aftershave reached her.

She could see Anne watching approvingly from the sidelines and groaned inwardly. She could imagine all the directives the woman would be giving her shortly. As the music subsided and they walked off the dance floor a flash went off in their faces and Victoria cringed involuntarily. At the same moment Rodolfo's arm slipped protectively about her and she felt herself being guided quickly out of the ballroom and through the French doors that led onto the terrace.

'Damn photographers,' he exclaimed as they stepped outside. 'They never give one any peace.'

'No, they don't,' she murmured, shuddering.

'I would have thought you would be used to that by now? Don't all movie stars crave the limelight?' He regarded her critically from under dark brows.

'Not me,' she replied with a half-smile, crossing her arms and staring out across the Croisette and the twinkling lights of the yachts beyond.

'Victoria?' Anne's voice at the French window made her turn around. 'I'm sorry to interrupt,' she said apologetically, smiling at the Prince, 'but that top Paris magazine I told you about wants to interview you.'

'Now?' Victoria grimaced.

'Right away, I'm afraid. It was the only available time.' Anne flashed a quick smile at Rodolfo.

'Okay. I guess I don't have a choice. Goodnight,' Victoria said, stretching her hand out towards the Prince.

'Goodnight.' He raised her fingers to his lips. 'And,

please, don't forget your promise.' Their eyes met, his full of laughter and challenge, hers tentative.

'Right,' Victoria mumbled, aware of Anne's interested eyes upon her.

Seconds later the actress and the agent were hurrying down the corridor back to Victoria's suite for the interview.

'What was that all about?' Anne enquired. 'What did you promise? I hope it wasn't a press interview, because I gave exclusive rights to the *Parisian Magazine*. You can't negotiate these things on your own, you know, and—'

'Oh, do stop it, Anne. Don't you ever think of anything but business?' Victoria complained, exasperated. 'He only asked me to get in touch with him if I ever went to that wretched island of his. And, since you're so keen for me to move there, I should have thought you'd be pleased.'

'Oh. Okay,' Anne muttered, taken aback. The Prince wanted to see Vic again. That could be great PR. Better not discourage her. On the contrary, the more she thought about it the more the idea appealed. By the time they'd reached the suite door she was forming a plan. 'Right, you go ahead, and I'll tell them you're ready.'

'Just a sec,' Victoria said, feeling the capsule in her pocket. 'I need to go to the loo.'

'Okay, but don't be long. They're waiting, and we're running late.'

Feeling like a prisoner, Victoria slipped into the marble bathroom. It was empty, and she leaned a moment against the sink and took a deep breath. How long would all this socialising go on? Why couldn't she just get on with the next film instead of having to go through all this agony?

But there was no way out.

Taking out the pill, she popped it in her mouth and drank a glass of water, then closed her eyes and waited for it to take effect. Ah! There. A minute or two later she raised her head, dragged her fingers through her hair, checked her lipgloss and braced herself. It was show-time once more. Still, as she stepped out of the bathroom and headed for the salon where the interview was to take place, a vision of the Prince flashed before her. She'd felt strangely reassured in his company.

AFTER VICTORIA HAD DEPARTED, Rodolfo stood for a few more minutes on the terrace, contemplating the night. In the background he heard the buzz of the party, the music, the laughter, the exaggerated exclamations and the smooth conversation. He had no desire to return inside. Something about Victoria had left him thought-ful, intrigued. Not just her ethereal beauty, which was without a doubt staggering, but the natural way in which she responded. There was no artifice in her manner, no guile. It was deliciously refreshing.

He must make a point of seeing her movie. Was she as good as was being made out? Perhaps. There was def-initely something special about her. He thought of her now, upstairs, answering a battery of questions from journalists, and wished he could have helped prevent it, detained her longer.

Then, all at once, he caught his breath as finally his memory jolted and he remembered who she reminded him of. How could he have forgotten or even hesitated? How had he not caught the likeness at once?

As Giada's face materialised before him he closed his eyes. When would it ever fade? Seven years had passed, and he'd had so many women since. But Giada's image and all she'd represented in his life remained firmly imprinted in his mind. And tonight, for the first time, he'd met someone who reminded him of her as never before.

Banishing the memory and turning on his heel, the Prince quickly reminded himself why he was there and returned to the ballroom, where he was immediately accosted by a fat lady who glittered with jewels and who owned a huge fortune in oil. She was interested in learning more about Malvarina.

Rodolfo replied politely, but recalled Victoria's words. Was he turning the principality into a theme park for the *nouveau riche*? He had wanted to preserve it as naturally and beautifully as possible. He needed to think about this initiative further.

After being buttonholed for twenty minutes he managed to make his escape and make his way upstairs. For a moment he hesitated, thought of phoning Victoria and seeing if she would like to have a drink with him. Then, realising she was probably exhausted, with a gruelling day ahead of her tomorrow, he decided against it and went to his suite.

CHAPTER THREE

SHE'D WON. BEST ACTRESS.

As she stood on the stage the following evening, receiving the trophy, Victoria was overwhelmed. She had made it, was being given one of the most prestigious prizes in film. Everyone was clapping, encouraging her, and tonight she felt good. This was recognition of her acting skills, not her beauty or her charisma, just her work. And for that she was grateful.

After a short speech she sat down next to Ed, who hugged her, while Anne glowed with pride on her other side. She knew she owed them a lot—everything, in a way. Had it not been for them, their patience and knowing how to get the best out of her as an actress, this would never have happened. But there was still all the press to face—more interviews, more emotion, another exhausting evening of being on show. And tonight she'd left her pills behind in the bathroom, hadn't slipped one into her pocket as she normally did.

Never mind, she assured herself. Tonight was different. She would make it through the evening without mishap.

As they filed out of the theatre where the award ceremony was taking place, Victoria caught sight of Rodolfo in the distance. Across the crowd their eyes met and he smiled. For a moment she wished she could go to him, spend the rest of the evening in some quiet spot chatting. All at once she remembered his mention that he liked to cook. A vision of him tossing pasta in the kitchen of his own castle surfaced and made her want to laugh. But as she smiled back at him a flash went off in her face, reminding her of exactly where she was.

SHE CERTAINLY HAD tremendous talent, Rodolfo realised, watching Victoria move through the hall surrounded by paparazzi and moguls. He had seen her movie earlier that day and had come out impressed. There was something magical in her performance, something that reminded him of a young Audrey Hepburn in the way she floated across the screen—an ethereal quality coupled with a shining talent. Yet there was a vital and deeply emotional side to her that became apparent in her performance, and that had gripped him, stirred something deep within.

He glanced at his watch. The party would go on for a while yet. He was planning to leave tomorrow and return to Malvarina, but something made him hesitate. Perhaps he would wait and see if an opportunity to lunch with Victoria presented itself. He would really like to see her again before he departed.

SHE KNEW THAT if she was going to make it through the rest of the evening she simply had to disappear upstairs and take another capsule. She seemed to have increased the amount over the last few days. But that was okay. It was just for now. When she got home she would stop taking them completely. She glanced about her. She had to go, even if that meant displeasing Anne and the others.

Slipping away unseen, she dashed to the lift and rode it up to her floor. Then she hastened down the corridor and inserted the key in the lock of her suite. To her amazement the door was open. Had one of the hotel staff been in her room? She shrugged, threw her evening purse on the sofa and headed for the bathroom. The meds were where she'd left them, on the shelf in the bathroom cupboard in a little brown pharmaceutical plastic vial. Reaching thankfully for the bottle, she tipped one out.

She was holding it in her hand when suddenly a figure jumped from behind the curtains. A flash went off, then another, and another. Victoria stood in silent mesmerised horror, like a rabbit caught in headlights, unable to react. It took several minutes for her to take stock of the situation, for the full reality of it to grip her. She had seen the woman quite clearly—a photographer who had dressed up as one of the hotel maids and invaded her privacy.

She'd been caught in the act.

What was she to do? In panic she rushed to the phone and got Reception to page Anne. Minutes later she was pouring out the truth to her agent in person.

'How could you, Vic? Why didn't you tell me? It's all gonna hit the fan.'

'Can't you do anything? Try and stop it? Not that there is any harm in me taking these pills—I mean they must be all right since the doctor gave them to me.'

'Oh, Victoria. Are you really that innocent? Good-ness only knows what your Dr Browne has put in this cocktail.'

'But how did anyone know that I was taking anything at all?'

'I don't know. These paparazzi nose out everything. Maybe you were seen visiting the doctor's office and that tipped one of them off. We'll never know.'

'Can't you stop them publishing the pictures?'

'I don't know. This is France, not the US. They have different laws. I'll have to tell Ed. He'll be furious, and it'll be my ass on the line. Oh, Vic. Why did you do it, for heaven's sake? And if you were going to, why didn't you tell me? I could've helped you out.' Anne paced the room agitatedly.

'I'm sorry,' Victoria whispered, slouched on the sofa, her head thrown back against the velvet cushions. Right now she couldn't think, couldn't register. Had she mucked up her career? Was this the end? What had she done?

Next morning the answer came loud and clear, as Anne slapped the French newspapers down on the table.

'Just look at what you've achieved,' she threw. 'Front-page headlines! *Bravo!* "Best Actress High On Drugs." All the details of how you frequented the offices of that sleazy doctor in L.A. They've dug up the whole damn story. Wonderful. Ed is so mad, I can't begin to tell you. He's talking about dropping you from his next movie. And if you thought the press were on top of you before, babe, you ain't seen nothing yet. They're swarm-ing all over the goddamn lobby. I don't know how we're going to get you out of here.'

'Look, I've said I'm sorry, okay? What else do you expect me to do? I can't make it un-happen.' Victoria placed her cup back in the saucer with a snap, all desire for coffee disappearing.

'I don't know. I really don't know,' Anne said, dragging her fingers through her short spiky hair. 'But we'll have to come up with something mighty quick if we're gonna scotch this thing. Nip it in the bud. That's the only way. Maybe putting you into rehab is the answer...' She shook her head and kept on muttering.

'I am not a drug addict,' Victoria protested, 'I just took a few pills to help me through all this hype. I never would have touched them otherwise. I didn't even know they were drugs in the real sense of the word.'

'Well, guess what? It's too late for that now. We'll just have to see how to repair the damage and hope it isn't too late.'

Victoria got up and left the room, her eyes filled with unshed tears.

She could bear it no longer.

RODOLFO SAW THE HEADLINES at breakfast and, putting down his glass of orange juice, read them, horrified. Was it possible? He read the details, then stared, eyes narrowed, at the picture of Victoria, one hand in mid-air, a bottle of pills in the other, her face a mask of terrified horror.

He experienced a rush of anger. At Victoria for indulging in this deplorable habit. At those around her who hadn't given her a break and had probably driven her to it. And at the photographers who had hounded her night and day, giving her no privacy. It was scandalous.

Rodolfo rose and paced the salon of his suite, agitated. He knew he must do something for the girl—must help her if he could. Who knew what kind of a time Ed Banes and the others were giving her? Not that that was an excuse for her behaviour, he realised. But still…

Picking up his mobile, he dialled his assistant and told him to find out the number of Victoria's suite. Minutes later the man called back to tell him she wasn't taking any calls. He wasn't surprised. Minutes later, as he entered the lobby, he got a good idea why. The place was abuzz with reporters, vultures agog with curiosity, avid to get a glimpse of their prey. Rodolfo watched them, disgusted. He was certain Victoria was hiding up in her suite.

Suddenly he took a decision. Heading up the stairs, he went to Ed Banes's suite and knocked. A bodyguard answered.

'Tell Mr Banes, His Majesty Prince Rodolfo of Malvarina wants to speak to him,' he announced haughtily.

'He can't see you right now,' the burly shaven-headed man answered in a Southern drawl.

'He will. Tell him I'm here to help out Victoria.'

The man shrugged and continued chewing gum. 'Okay. Wait here, sir.'

Rodolfo stepped inside. He could hear raised voices beyond the closed door. His determination to remove her from this place and these people's company increased tenfold.

When the door opened and Ed Banes appeared he seemed choleric. His shirt was unbuttoned at the neck and he looked like a man who hadn't slept in a while.

'Hi,' he said curtly. 'What can I do for you?'

'Actually, it's what I can do for you,' Rodolfo replied coldly. 'I came here to see how I can help you in this tricky situation Victoria's got herself entangled in,' he said calmly.

'Nothing you can do, I'm afraid. The kid's blown it. Come on in. Might as well, since you're here.' He showed Rodolfo into the salon, where Anne was pacing the floor and two other women stood by the window busily talking on cellphones. 'Trying to do some damage control,' he said, jerking his head at the two. 'What a stupid little fool. I can't believe she didn't even tell Anne what she was taking. We could've kept it all under wraps, gotten her the stuff ourselves, dealt with business.'

Rodolfo sent the man a withering glance.

'Personally, I think Victoria's health should be of primary concern,' he replied coldly. 'What I propose is that you create a diversion in the lobby—give a press conference or something. In the meantime I'll spirit her out the back way. Nobody is going to imagine that she would be with me. Perhaps you could provide a disguise?' he added, turning to Anne. 'I shall take her on my private jet to Malvarina, where I can assure you she will be looked after. And not badgered by any members of the press, or given any more drugs,' he added curtly.

Ed hesitated, rubbed his bald head and turned to Anne. 'What d'ya think?' he growled.

'I think it's a great idea. We were thinking of rehab, but this is a better option. What time do you want to do this, uh, Prince?'

'Right away,' Rodolfo snapped, taking the decision. 'The sooner we get her out of here, the better.'

'Hey, wait,' Ed said, eyeing him curiously. 'What happens if the press get hold of your ass?'

'I am very well able to cope, Mr Banes. Right now I would advise you to concern yourself with Victoria and containing this awkward set of circumstances. I'm well able to take care of myself—and Victoria, too, for that matter.'

'Fine by me.' Ed shrugged and flopped into an over-sized armchair. 'Let's get through this and move on. I have a movie starting in six weeks' time. The kid's under contract. I need her. But I can't have this kind of crap flying around my set.'

'Uh, right. Ed, let me deal with this,' Anne said quickly, taking Rodolfo's arm and guiding him to the door. 'I'll go up to Victoria with you. She's pretty upset, as you can imagine. This is really nice of you to help out.'

'Any time,' Rodolfo murmured, casting a final withering glance at Ed, disgusted at his attitude and his lack of concern for Victoria's wellbeing. Only dollars and cents seemed to count for Ed Banes.

Slipping into a service lift, Anne and Rodolfo managed to slip into the suite unnoticed.

'Vic, there's someone here to see you,' Anne said, opening the door of the salon, where Victoria sat huddled in the corner of the large sofa, her feet tucked under her.

She looked like a waif, wearing jeans and a tiny white T-shirt, her hair falling straight over her shoulders and her eyes red from crying. Rodolfo's words of censure died on his lips. There was a reason why she'd resorted to pills to help her through all this. For a moment he wanted to reach out, take her in his arms and offer comfort. But he knew that was impossible. Instead he looked at her hard.

'I'm very sorry that you are having problems, signorina,' he said curtly, stepping towards her.

'What are you doing here?' Victoria said in a shaky voice. 'Why did you come? To criticise me? Well, let me tell you something—' her voice trembled and she balled her fists '—I don't care if it was wrong, and I didn't know those pills were considered bad. The truth is that at least they helped me get through all those awful interviews and all that hype.'

'Maybe. That is still no excuse for your behaviour,' he said, sitting down next to her.

'And what right do *you* have to come barging in here, judging me?' she threw angrily.

'None,' he replied, taking one of her hands in his. 'Except that I realise how hard it has been for you, that you aren't cut out for this; you aren't the kind of person who enjoys the sort of publicity you've been exposed to. I have come to help you, that's all.'

His calm, low voice and his caressing hand soothed her. Victoria swallowed. She felt confused by his presence. For a moment she wondered if he'd come with some ulterior motive. Most people around her lately seemed to have one. But his mere presence was so comforting that she just accepted it. 'What do you think I should do?' she whispered shakily.

'If you agree to come back with me to Malvarina for a while, there you can get proper medical assistance, relax, and get away from all this. I think that would be the best. I guarantee complete privacy.' He squeezed her fingers reassuringly.

'Ed'll give a press conference in the lobby, and you and the Prince can escape the back way,' Anne urged. 'Here, put on this dark wig and these sunglasses. That should help. And go as you are. You look much younger, and no one will recognise you like that. Anyway, they'll never think that you and the Prince would be together.'

Victoria took a deep breath and looked from one to the other. It seemed like a good plan, and there really wasn't any other option. The thought of being able to escape the paparazzi seemed heavenly. She nodded. 'Thank you,' she murmured, smiling waveringly at Rodolfo.

'It's nothing.' He gave a dismissive wave of a hand. 'Leave your luggage. Anne can have it sent on to you. Take only your handbag and passport.'

Silently Victoria rose and obeyed. She wished for a moment she could take her pills with her. But then she realised that she must put a stop to her habit immediately. It would be hard, but she couldn't abuse Rodolfo's trust when he was being so generous and saving her from herself.

Minutes later Rodolfo had grabbed her hand and they were heading down in the service lift to the garage level of the hotel, then slipping through the work stations and kitchens and out into a back street, where a Bentley stood waiting. Hastily they jumped in and the driver accelerated swiftly away.

'Thanks,' Victoria muttered, letting out a long sigh of relief as she leaned back in the soft plush leather.

And for the first time in months she felt safe.

TWO AND A HALF HOURS LATER she was staring out of the window of Rodolfo's Gulfstream jet as it circled over the Mediterranean. Down below she could see the contours of Malvarina, its rich vegetation encircled by cerulean blue sea, rocky cliffs giving way to smooth, white, sandy beaches. She could distinguish what looked like large properties up in the hills and down by the water. Then a small town appeared and to the left, up on high overlooking the sea, stood a medieval fortress.

'That is the Castello Constanza,' Rodolfo said pointing down. 'The fortress and the island have belonged to my family since they conquered it in the tenth century. It has been through many wars and difficulties. We fought the Saracens, and the Ottomans. But in the end we prevailed, and today I hope to make Malvarina into a modern, well-run, financially solvent society.'

Victoria looked over at him, surprised at the passion and intensity she detected in his tone. She'd thought of him as a sophisticated playboy, simply trying to extract as much as possible from his inheritance. Yet now she sensed there was far more at stake for Rodolfo than mere money. This was about honour, about the wellbeing of his people. She smiled, glad that she'd taken the decision to flee Cannes and join him here in what looked like an enclave of peace.

Soon they had landed at the island's small airport and were swooped off in the Rolls Royce that awaited them on the tarmac. The car swerved through the sleepy little town of Malvaritza, and on and up towards the fortress. Peasants with well-loaded donkeys stopped by the roadside and waved. Victoria noted that Rodolfo always returned the waves, smiled and acknowledged them. She had the feeling he would always do this, however tired or absorbed by other worries he might be.

Then the vehicle slowed as they approached the castle and its portcullis entrance that stood just over an ancient bridge. The castle walls stood high, and Victoria experienced a moment's doubt: what had she got herself into? After all, she had no way of knowing what this man was really like. Once she was inside those walls she would be virtually at his mercy.

As though sensing her unease, Rodolfo turned and smiled at her. 'A bit daunting, isn't it? But don't worry. Inside we have all the mod cons. My grandfather, although quite antiquated in many respects, was determined to have the place modernised. I'm very thankful he did. It was quite a job to get everything shipshape.'

'I'm sure it must have been,' Victoria agreed as the car purred into a cobbled courtyard and immediately several members of the Prince's staff, dressed in traditional costume, moved to open the doors.

'Welcome to Malvarina and the Castello Constanza,' Rodolfo said, slipping her hand through his arm and moving forward. 'Let me show you around.'

'I'd love to see the castle,' she said. Though she still felt a little shaky, the dreadful episode of the night before began to fade from her mind as she looked around at her magical surroundings—at the worn stone walls topped with small turrets, the crooked windows and gables.

As they walked, she took a deep breath and exclaimed, 'What a lovely scent.'

'That's jasmine. It blooms most of the year here. We have quite a few tropical plants as well. This is bougain-villea,' he remarked, pointing to the lovely purple and white flowers creeping up the southern wall of the fa-çade. 'My mother planted most of it.'

'Does she live here?' Victoria enquired, as they headed into what appeared to be a great hall.

'Both my parents died in an accident when I was twelve,' he replied briefly, moving towards the window. 'Please, come over here and take a look at the view. It is magnificent from this vantage point.'

How sad that he'd been orphaned, Victoria reflected, as she stepped over and joined him by huge French win-dows that gave onto a vine-trellised terrace overlooking the tranquil sea. A yacht glided across the clear blue stretch of water, leaving a pristine white trail rippling in its wake.

'Where is that yacht headed?' she asked.

'Greece, probably. If you sail on you'll hit the Adri-atic coast. Would you like to sail?' he asked, lifting her fingers to his lips and letting them trail over the inner part of her wrist.

'Uh, well, I—yes... I suppose it would be very nice. I've never actually been on a yacht.'

All at once her pulse beat faster and her heart flur-ried. She had little or no experience with men. Nicky, her one boyfriend, had been just that—a boyfriend. She'd never felt attracted enough to contemplate going to bed with him. Now, as Rodolfo's lips grazed her skin she shuddered. There was no doubt that she was expe-riencing an unadulterated new and intense draw to this man. And she wasn't sure how to handle it.

'Perhaps I should show you to your room before we make any further plans,' the Prince remarked, letting go her fingers. 'We need to have a doctor take a look at you, and I am hoping that your luggage will arrive later today. But, anyway, we can get you some stuff in town. Malvaritza looks like a sleepy little village but it has some very fashionable boutiques with all the top brands. I'm sure you'll be able to find some suitable outfits and toiletries,' he said, smiling.

'Thanks. I'm certain Anne will have dealt with forwarding the luggage,' she replied, aware that she didn't even have a toothbrush with her. But that was a concern that was fast put to rest when she entered the ravishing suite of rooms allotted her.

Victoria gasped. Nothing in her short stay in Hollywood had prepared for the elegant refinement of the Castello Constanza. The reception rooms she'd spied were formally elegant and refined. But this! There was a four-poster bed decked with white voile curtains, and tapestries hung on the ancient stone walls, as well as an eighteenth-century Venetian mirror placed between crystal Murano wall sconces. Vases filled with freshly cut flowers graced the dressing table. A small plumped-up sofa had been strategically placed next to the window, through which the now familiar scent of jasmine invaded the apartments.

'It's lovely,' she murmured, letting her fingers trail over the lace coverlet of the bed, her eyes resting on the flounced brocade of the skirt of the dressing table, where antique silver brushes lay. It was old-world and beautiful. Yet, as her eyes roamed, she noted a phone and a fax machine. In the corner an almost invisible panel hid a flatscreen TV.

'I hope you will be comfortable,' he replied with a formal bow. 'Please feel free to stay for as long as you wish.'

'Oh, gosh, that's terribly generous. I don't want to be a nuisance,' she exclaimed, suddenly realising how unexpected her visit was—and perhaps inconvenient.

'Such a beautiful woman as you could never be an inconvenience to anyone,' he murmured, his eyes fleeting over her. 'Why don't you freshen up and join me downstairs for a drink?'

'Great. Thanks.' Victoria smiled nervously, brushed her golden hair back, and watched as he retreated and closed the door behind him.

She let out the breath she'd been holding. It was like a dream. Only this morning she'd been going through hell and now here she was, in a magical setting with the best looking, most sophisticated man she'd ever met.

To her surprise, when she opened the old rosewood armoire, a shimmering white and silver full-length sheath-style gown hung on one of the hangers. She lifted it out on the hanger and stared down at the high heeled silk sandals accompanying it. Was this for her? Then her eyes fell on a note, and she drew in her breath and opened it.

I hope this may serve its purpose until your luggage arrives.

She held the note, biting her lip, gazing at the bold black writing on the thick crest-emblazoned stationery.

How had he managed to have this dress conveyed here so swiftly? And how did he know her size? A less agreeable thought crossed her mind. He probably dated so many women that judging their dress size was child's play. Well, whatever. She would slip into the shower and then don the beautiful gown. At least she'd feel in tune with the setting.

An hour later dusk had settled over the island. The clear inky sky was dotted with bright flickering stars. Crickets chirrupped in a friendly fashion as she made her way down the wide stone staircase, hoping she wouldn't slip in her finely tied silk sandals. Victoria had worn many gorgeous gowns since hitting Hollywood, but none compared to the ethereal beauty of this one, chosen for her by a man she barely knew.

When she reached the terrace she saw him, dressed in a dinner jacket, leaning against the stone parapet and gazing thoughtfully out to sea, a glass held loosely between his fingers. She stood a moment and watched him, etched against the horizon. How incredibly good-looking he was.

And how totally out of reach.

All at once reality sank in and she realised how poles apart their lives were: she, the unknown girl from a small English village who by a miracle had been chosen to star in a Hollywood success story; he, the noble Prince, whose lineage dated back a thousand years. She swallowed. Oh, well. Might as well enjoy it while it lasted, she reflected moving towards him. Perhaps it was just a ploy to get her to invest on his island, she reminded herself. In a way she wished it was. It would make it easier, and perhaps temper the irregularity of her heartbeat whenever he appeared.

'Good evening,' she said, trying to sound nonchalant and sophisticated. 'Thank you for having this dress put in my cupboard. It was most thoughtful of you. The luggage still hasn't arrived, so it came in very handy.'

'I'm glad you like it. If I may say so it suits you very well.' His gaze roamed critically over her.

A flush rushed to her cheeks. There was nothing bold in his look, but still she felt as though his eyes saw far more—as though they were divesting her of the flimsy fabric, and caressing her skin. A tiny shiver coursed up her spine and she felt her stomach tighten.

'Would you like a drink?' he asked turning to a tray of ice that hosted an array of soft drinks. He poured her choice into a crystal tumbler and handed it to her.

'Thanks.' Victoria took a quick gulp and then another. Suddenly she remembered the pills. Until last night she would have relied on them to help her through the evening, yet tonight she had no sudden urge to rush and pop one. Not that she felt terribly bad or ill at ease with Rodolfo, but he did seem so terribly suave and elegant in this magnificent setting, so terribly out of her league...

'Come,' Rodolfo said, as if sensing her discomfort, reaching for her hand. 'Let me show you the rest of the terrace.'

Together they walked around and he showed her another view. In the distance she could see lights. 'Is that Malvaritza?' she asked.

'Yes, that is the town. I'll take you there when you're

feeling up to it. And we'll also go for a spin on my yacht, the *Mona Lisa*, so that you can see the island from the sea. It will give you a better notion of the place.'

'Thanks,' she murmured, leaving her hand in his, relishing the feel of his fingers lightly caressing the inside of her palm. Then, when she least expected it, he was facing her, looking down into her eyes through the moonlight.

'You are a beautiful woman, Victoria. Too tempting by far.'

She caught her breath as he drew closer, didn't draw away when he reached out and pulled her close, his expression almost harsh.

Their eyes held and she fell under his spell. In one swift movement his lips came down on hers, hot and demanding. She gasped, held back, then gave way. She had never been kissed like this before. It was as though suddenly Rodolfo dominated her being. He plied open her lips, his tongue delved, and his hands pressed the small of her back, bringing her close up against him. She could feel the hardness of his desire, and experienced a rush of torrid heat flash like hot lightning from her head to her core, felt the peaks of her breasts go taut.

There was little she could do now but submit, her body supple and pliable in his arms. She could feel his hands roam over the curves of her rounded bottom, up her ribcage, then stop tantalisingly at the side of her breast. Half of her knew she should draw back, the other wanted to beg him to continue, to assuage the delicious yet agonising frustration mounting within her.

'Victoria,' he muttered, his thumb reaching to graze the tip of her breast.

'Rodolfo,' she whispered hoarsely. 'We shouldn't… we mustn't. I barely know you. I—'

Reluctantly he drew back, eyes gleaming into hers. 'I know it has all happened very fast, but I find you very hard to resist, *cara.*'

She returned the look, then glanced away, straightened her dress and moved towards the parapet picking up her glass as she went.

Rodolfo watched her, then followed suit, eyeing her closely, noting the hot flush on her cheeks. There was a definite chemistry between them. Her reaction had been timid at first, then as passionate and full of pent-up desire as his own. Yet there was something naïve and spontaneous in her reaction, something that spelled inexperience.

He must be dreaming, he reflected, as they sipped their drinks. A Hollywood actress, one who had taken drugs and was a big star, could hardly be an innocent.

'Dinner will be served shortly,' he said in a neutral tone. 'I thought we should dine al fresco in the moonlight. Would that suit you?'

'That would be lovely. Are you not cooking tonight?' she added with a spark of humour.

'Not tonight,' he responded, with a laugh and a flash of white teeth, 'But I promise to introduce you to my special *Pasta Principesco* in the very near future. Do you know that they have it on the menu in one of the restaurants in town? I was very flattered as the owner is an exceptionally good cook. But tonight we will have special Malvarinian dishes. I hope you will enjoy our local cuisine.'

'I'm sure I will,' Victoria answered, wondering if there was anything she wouldn't like about this man and this amazingly enchanting fantasy world he lived in. But, she reminded herself, it was important to remember that it was just that: a fantasy, nothing more.

Dinner was as special as she had anticipated. Rodolfo made witty conversation throughout, and the servants served an array of delectable dishes, all of which were Malvarinian specialities. By the end, Victoria knew she couldn't eat another thing.

'That was simply delicious,' she said smiling and laying down her white linen napkin. 'You've spoiled me rotten.'

'A woman as beautiful as you should be spoiled,' he murmured, rising and coming behind her chair to draw it back.

'That's all very well,' she admonished breathlessly. For, although she was far more at ease with him than she had been earlier, his presence so close sent frissons running through her. 'One could get used to this sort of living,' she said trying to sound light, 'but, after all, it's really just a dream.'

'Not entirely. I like to believe that I'm very real,' he responded with an amused smile.

'Do you?' She cast him a sceptical look and let out a sigh. 'This is all so magical, so unreal. I think it's heavenly, but then I remember that soon I'll have to return to reality, to Hollywood and Ed and the next movie. And I don't know how I'm going to manage it.'

'Without the medication to help you, you mean?' he enquired, his tone challenging.

Victoria's face flushed. 'I know it was wrong, but there's no need to rub my face in it. I really had no idea what they were,' she muttered, tossing her hair back.

'I know you didn't. It was very wrong of that doctor not to inform you of what was in them. But I am merely wondering if you think you can kick the habit or if you plan to continue on the same course? If you were my—' He cut off, realising what he was about to say and the impropriety of it.

'If I was what? I belong to nobody, and what I do is nobody's business, either,' she responded belligerently.

'That is true. I'm sorry.'

'Plus, you don't know how difficult it was, there on my own. I knew nobody. Everyone expected me to fit in as if I'd been there all my life. When I met that girl and she gave me the doctor's name I felt better, realising I wasn't the only one who found it difficult to keep up the pace and—'

'You don't need to explain,' he interrupted, placing his hands firmly on her shoulders. 'I understand. I just hope that from now on you won't feel the need to ruin your health, your youth and your beauty, that's all.' She looked up at him, read the sincerity in his gaze and swallowed. 'If you hate Hollywood so much, why go back?'

'I have a contract with Ed.'

'But what about the actual work? I thought you enjoyed acting,' he said, signalling to a servant to lay the coffee tray on a low Ottoman by the parapet.

'I do. That's why I have to overcome this stupid fear, these silly inhibitions I have. It's absurd when I've been offered the chance of a lifetime. I've always wanted to act. Being taken to Hollywood and given this opportunity was all I'd ever dreamed of. It's just that now I—' She shrugged, looked out over the sea. 'It's all so superficial, so fake. Not at all as I imagined it. Again, just a sort of fantasy.'

'That's just how you described this place.'

'Well, I didn't mean it quite like that. It's a different kind of fantasy.'

'I'm glad you think so. I would hate to think that I live in a Hollywood dream world. I happen to have very real projects for this island.'

'I'm sure you do,' she said, seeing a gleam in his eye. 'Very different to where I come from. That's just pretty and old fashioned and comfortable.'

'But you love it?'

'Yes, I do. It's home.'

'And you regret the necessity of having to leave it?'

'I—' All of a sudden Victoria remembered Anne's comments, her financial advisors' insistence that she change her domicile, and all the reasons she hadn't wanted to come to Malvarina surfaced. Was this man just trying to seduce her into investing in his island?

'I'm sorry. That was a personal question and none of my business,' he murmured. 'But if, while you're here, you would like to visit some property I can arrange it.'

'Thanks,' she answered, a cold chill rushing through her. 'Would you mind awfully if I went to bed now? I'm really rather tired after everything that's happened.'

'Of course. You must be. I will accompany you upstairs and see that all is in order.'

'Oh, please—don't bother,' she said hastily, getting up and taking a step back. 'I'm sure I'll find my way. Goodnight.' She waved her hand abstractedly, then turned, quickly entered the large living room and headed towards the hall and the stairs.

WHAT HAD HE SAID to upset her? Rodolfo asked himself as he watched Victoria disappear into the shadows like a white and silver ghost. Had it been the mention of visiting property on the island? He had merely wanted to be of help. But he was fast realising that there was much more to this sensitive young woman than met the eye. Their kiss remained imprinted on his lips and the desire to possess her made him take a deep breath.

He stood pensive for a moment, then decided that he too would turn in early. He would have to take it slowly with Victoria. But he knew now that he definitely wanted to take her to his bed. But she was still fragile, and she was also his guest, and therefore he owed her every courtesy.

After a quick snifter of brandy he walked up the *castello*'s wide, ancient staircase, glanced at Victoria's door, then with a veiled smile headed on towards his own suite of apartments and his lonely bed.

CHAPTER FOUR

A SHAFT OF BRIGHT SUNLIGHT piercing the heavy blue brocade curtains woke her.

At first she had no idea where she was, wondered for a moment if she was on a film set. Then she saw her luggage in the far corner of the room. Little by little the events of the previous day played out and she remembered everything—from the terrible morning to the flight to the airport and, later, the kiss on the terrace yesterday evening.

At the thought of the latter, a delicious shiver coursed through her. She had never been kissed like that before. The thought that it could reoccur left her anxious, yet filled with a new and exciting anticipation. Of course Rodolfo wanted nothing but a fleeting sexual affair, an amusing interlude to pass the time. Maybe that was why he'd asked her here? But, whatever the reason, she surely could handle it? Surely she was mature enough to indulge in an affair without getting hurt? It was time she got some experience of life and love. Perhaps he was exactly the kind of man to gain that experience with. After all, there were no strings attached, plus he was a gentleman, and she'd never found any man so devastatingly attractive.

An hour later she was downstairs, dressed in a short white flared cotton designer skirt, small pink T-shirt and matching flat fifties-style shoes.

'I hope you slept well?' the Prince said when she joined him at the breakfast table.

Victoria smiled, noted how attractive he looked, dressed in jeans and a white polo shirt.

'Great, thanks.'

'Please sit down.' He'd risen to greet her and now they both sat at the glass table laid with attractive ceramic crockery. Not at all palatial, she thought with a tiny smile, feeling at ease as she sipped a delicious glass of chilled orange juice.

'I have taken the liberty of asking my doctor to come after breakfast and check you over. Then, I thought I would take you around the island, and we can lunch on board my yacht, the *Mona Lisa*.'

'Well, that's very kind. But I feel fine, and am sure I don't need medical assistance.'

'Perhaps. But indulge me and see Dottore Manfreddo. He is the Royal Physician and a delightful character. That way we'll both be assured that you are all right and we can forget that whole incident—okay?'

'All right,' she agreed with a reluctant smile.

'As soon as you're finished with him we'll set sail.'

'I'd love to. By the way, you suggested that I look at some property while I'm here. I think that's a good idea. I might as well make good use of my time,' she said, breathing in the gorgeous day, looking out over the cliff at the superb view, clearer now that the heat haze had subsided.

'Perfect. I can arrange for someone to show us something tomorrow.'

'Great.' Victoria realised that she hadn't felt so good in a long time. There was something so agreeable and easy about Rodolfo that she'd never encountered in any man before. Not that she knew that many men, she realised ruefully. But Rodolfo seemed interested in her, and her life, and she was able to forget that he was a prince, that his reality was so different from hers.

Together they enjoyed a pleasant and interesting conversation over the delicious array of fruit and pastries set before her. 'Gosh, I'll have to be careful not to get fat here,' she remarked, laughing.

'I don't see any danger of that happening,' he answered, his eyes fleeting over her in that same scrutinizing, yet admiring manner they had yesterday. 'Now, come. The doctor will be here any moment.'

'So, SIGNORINA, how are you feeling?'

'I'm fine. Better than I've felt in a while.'

'Good.' The elderly doctor smiled a wrinkled but reassuring smile and placed his index finger on her pulse. 'Your heart-rate seems perfect. No palpitations or shakiness since you have stopped taking the medication?'

'No. I don't even feel that I need it.'

'Excellent,' he approved. 'I think you have been lucky, young lady. In fact you haven't taken enough for it to harm you in the long run. But what will you do when you have to face a similar situation again?'

'I don't know,' she said with a sigh. 'I'll just have to cross that river when I come to it?'

'If you permit, I have another suggestion. Here in Malvarina we are very knowledgeable regarding herbal rem-
edies and teas. There is a special tea, made of a local herb,
that soothes the nerves without causing any harm to your
system. I would recommend you take some with you
when you leave. Sometimes, if you are feeling tense, you
can have a nice cup of this brew and you will feel more
relaxed without doing yourself any harm whatsoever. It
is well known on the island. I drink it myself sometimes.'

'Thank you, Doctor. That would be wonderful.'

'Now, I want you to relax and take it easy for a few
days—forget all this nonsense and enjoy yourself. That
is the best way to recover.'

They both rose and shook hands.

'Thank you again, Doctor. It was very nice of you
to come.'

'Not at all. Any request of the Prince's is a pleasure.'

They walked out into the drawing room, where Rodolfo was waiting. 'Everything okay, Doctor?' he said
frowning slightly.

'Absolutely fine. Victoria is a healthy young woman
and has not suffered any side-effects from the pills. I believe she did not take them long enough for them to
harm her.'

'Good.' He let out a sigh of relief and smiled.
'Thanks, Dottore.'

'I recommended some of our special island tea. I'll
have some sent over later.'

'Good idea.'

They all shook hands, then the doctor departed, leaving them alone.

'Let's go and enjoy the day.' Rodolfo took her hand and together they walked towards the courtyard, where they'd arrived. A silver Porsche convertible stood gleaming in the sun. 'Jump in,' he said, opening the door for her, 'and let's go for a spin.'

Victoria sat in the car, hair blowing in the breeze. She loved the island immediately, the scent of the orange and lemon trees, the lovely faded terracotta houses peering lazily from behind olive groves overlooking the sea. There was a gentle sense of peace in this place, and a pace of life that she identified with.

With time to explore Malvaritza, she could see that all its charm had been preserved: there was a small crooked church in the main square, which was bordered by little cafés where some old men played backgammon and others drank coffee and passed the time of day. As Rodolfo had promised, the town also housed some lovely shops, filled with exclusive designer brands and jewellery and also quaint boutiques. But all this was incorporated into the architecture and atmosphere with such extreme good taste and grace that it didn't spoil the overall feel of the place.

The town, she realised as they drove on down towards the sea—in fact the whole island—was like Rodolfo: tranquil, elegant and charming.

Soon they were entering a little fishing port below, and she could see a large yacht at anchor and wondered if that was the *Mona Lisa*.

Just as she was about to ask, Rodolfo pointed out to sea. 'There she is,' he said, a touch of pride in his voice. 'I had her built three years ago.'

'She's beautiful,' Victoria exclaimed, shading her eyes to take a better look at the vessel. She could see a small motor boat steered by a uniformed sailor approaching the shoreline as they parked the Porsche.

Minutes later they were on board the yacht. Leaning against the deck rail, Victoria sighed as the craft raised anchor and the vessel glided out to sea. Rodolfo stood next to her in the stern and together they watched the island recede.

'You're right about Malvarina, and I take back all the nasty things I said the other night in Cannes. It truly is a beautiful spot.' Victoria smiled, relaxed now, the soft wind mussing her hair as she gazed over the side at the white ripples of the wake.

'But not as beautiful as you,' Rodolfo said softly, slipping a hand over hers.

Victoria swallowed. There was a choice to be made: she could pull her fingers away and pretend that none of this was happening, then get in touch with Anne and tell her she was heading back to England. *Or,* she could court adventure, live an exciting experience and be none the worse for wear.

Part of her wanted to run; another part knew she was mesmerised and that her whole being wanted Rodolfo as she'd never wanted a man before. His fingers still covered hers. By not removing them she was tacitly sending him a signal. And all at once Victoria realised that she needed to know what it felt like to be held in a man's arms—a man whom she found devastatingly attractive and who knew the rules of a game she was far from proficient in. When his arm slipped about her shoulders she didn't flinch or move away but allowed him to pull her close.

'Ah, Victoria, you are so young and so lovely, *cara*,' he murmured above the purr of the yacht's engine. He wanted her, wanted to ravish her, take her to his bed and love her. But instinct told him not to rush it. After all, she'd just lived through an extraordinarily painful set of circumstances that had not yet been fully resolved. He must take care not to make things worse. He smiled down at her. 'We'll drop anchor by the Malva Caves. Have you ever snorkelled?'

'Actually, no, but I'd like to try.'

'Then you shall. We shall discover the caves together. You will enjoy that.'

'I would love it,' she agreed.

'Then come on, and let's look at the gear. Gino,' he called to one of the smiling bronzed crew, 'we need some snorkelling gear for Miss Woodward. Can you see to it?'

'Of course, Your Royal Highness. Immediately.' The man disappeared and returned minutes later with a mask and flippers. 'I think these should fit the *signorina* perfectly,' he said.

And he was right. Soon Victoria was wearing only the tiny white bikini that she'd slipped on under her clothes. She pulled on the flippers as the yacht slowed and dropped anchor near the entrance of a large cave, excited at the thought of snorkelling. Rodolfo helped her to the side of the boat and, laughing at their comic appearance, they dropped into the water.

Victoria had no fear of the sea, as she was a good

swimmer, so she followed Rodolfo towards the cave without hesitation. Through her mask she could see deep down onto the sea bed. Multicoloured fish glided below her, sea plants and shells shimmered as the sunlight illuminated the water. Then they arrived at the entrance of the cave and the sun gave way to dark shadows. Shortly afterwards Rodolfo stopped by a ledge and they rested, their arms reposing upon it.

'It's an amazing place,' Victoria exclaimed, pulling up her mask and peering around at the beautiful glistening blues and greens shimmering on the walls.

'It's the phosphorescent stone that gives it this effect,' he answered. 'Are you feeling okay? Shall we continue?'

'Great, thanks. Let's explore further.'

They lowered their masks once more and headed into the winding passages of the cave, which Rodolfo obviously knew well.

It was as they were heading back to the entrance of the main cave that Victoria felt a sudden suction dragging her down. She swam harder, fighting against the spiralling current, her legs and arms beating frantically. But instead of abating the suction grew stronger, as though an underwater cyclone was drawing her down into the dark depths below. Rodolfo was up ahead. Soon he would be out of reach.

Victoria panicked. Naturally he thought she was following close behind—had no idea she was desperately struggling to keep her head above water. In a fraught movement Victoria struggled with her mask and air pipe and finally managed to remove them.

'Rodolfo!' she yelled between gulps of water, as loud as her breathless voice would carry. But he simply went on swimming. 'Please, Rodolfo, help!' she cried again, her strength giving out.

Just as she thought she could not go on, that the water would win this battle and suck her under, she saw him turn.

Horrified, Rodolfo swam back as fast as he could. Something was happening under the water! He'd heard of this once before, many years ago. But the phenomena had never been known to occur again, and he hadn't thought of the caves as in any way dangerous. Diving under the gloomy water, he scooped Victoria in his arms and pulled her to the surface. She spluttered, could barely breathe, and clung to him for dear life.

'Victoria, *cara mia*!' he cried, securing her in a life-saving position and swimming with her back out into the open as fast as he could. The crew, who were watching attentively from the yacht, immediately realised that something was amiss. Within seconds Victoria was being lifted into a dinghy, where she lay in Rodolfo's arms still fighting for breath.

'What happened, *cara*? What did you feel?' he asked anxiously, as little by little her breathing normalised and she was able to speak.

'It was as if something was sucking me down below the surface. It was a pretty strong current that was impossible to resist... I thought I—'

'Shush—just relax and don't talk, *cara*. You'll be all right. I feel terrible that I unwittingly subjected you to such an experience. I shall have the caves roped off against swimming. It is too dangerous. *Dio,* anything could have happened!'

'Such a thing has not occurred for over fifty years, Your Royal Highness,' one of the older crew members said as they reached the yacht.

'I know. But I should have remembered,' Rodolfo said, in self-reproach as he carried Victoria up the steps and on board. There he laid her carefully onto the cushions in the stateroom. At once one of the sailors brought water and cognac and Rodolfo made her drink.

'Have some of this. It will make you feel much better,' he said, tilting the glass towards her lips.

'I'm fine, really,' she whispered, trying to sit up on her elbows. 'Just a little shocked, that's all.'

'I know. But now you'll be okay.' He brushed the hair from her face and looked into her eyes. 'I would never have forgiven myself if something had happened to you.'

Their eyes held and Victoria felt her heart racing once more. Was he about to kiss her again? she wondered, a thrill jolting her. Even in her weakened state she longed for his touch. The answer came as his lips met hers. Not hard and hot, like the day before, but tenderly, languorously, as though seeking to know her every secret. His arms came about her and he held her close. It felt wonderful, warm and secure, and for a moment Victoria floated, forgot her troubles and luxuriated in the feel of his mouth, which moved more urgently now, plundering as she responded. Her arms slipped up around his neck and she held him, her body racked with delicious new sensations and a longing for all that she had yet to learn.

'Victoria, I want you,' he whispered, gazing into her eyes. 'I want you as I have only wanted once before in my life,' he murmured, his voice was low and husky, filled with patent desire.

The truth was she wanted him too. As she'd never wanted any man before. She had never known such want existed until now. But what would be the consequences of such an act? What would it lead to? And did she care?

As though realising that what he had just said was inappropriate in the present circumstances, Rodolfo rose and stepped away. 'We are nearing the shore,' he said, clearing his throat. 'I will bring your clothes.'

Half an hour later they approached the castle. Even as Victoria tried to step shakily out of the Porsche, Rodolfo picked her up and, despite her protests, carried her into the castle and up the wide staircase to her room, where he laid her down on the lace coverlet covering the huge bed.

'You must rest now,' he said, pulling the sheet over her. 'Later, when you are feeling better, we can talk.'

She smiled, feeling suddenly drowsy, the brandy and the shock of what had occurred taking effect. A few minutes later she was asleep.

DOWNSTAIRS ON THE TERRACE, Rodolfo gazed thoughtfully out to sea. Today something unexpected had occurred, something he would never have imagined. He had experienced the fear of losing not just a guest, or a woman he was attracted to, but something more—something that reminded him so poignantly of Giada. The more he thought about it, the more he wondered if his attraction for Victoria wasn't just the usual passing shaft of desire that needed to be satisfied, but something deeper—something that spoke of emotion, of a need to share?

Ridiculous! he chided himself. He barely knew the girl, and what he did know wasn't a particularly good recommendation. What if she began taking narcotics again? How would he feel about that? But deep down he'd already realised that the reason she'd fallen into that trap was because of her desperate need to overcome an inner shyness, a sort of claustrophobia that she couldn't handle and a lack of experience. If the circumstances were removed, and now she was aware of the true dangers, the problem would probably be resolved. For she was a sensitive, vulnerable woman, not used to the hard, tough atmosphere of the movie business. It wasn't surprising she'd resorted to alternative measures to help her through the ordeal.

But what about the future? Victoria was scheduled to star in Ed Banes's next movie, which was due to begin filming in six weeks. If some measure was not taken she could just fall back into the old routine.

He clenched his fist. Not if he had anything to do with it! Whatever happened between him and Victoria had nothing to do with his determination to make certain that she be shielded from the more disagreeable aspects of the movie business. How, he didn't know yet. But he'd find a way.

CHAPTER FIVE

VICTORIA SLEPT FOR SOME hours, but awoke feeling revived and ready to join Rodolfo for dinner.

To her surprise, nothing was ready when first she entered the huge drawing room, with its eighteenth-century Italian elegance, and glanced into the formal dining room. She walked out onto the terrace. Evening had fallen and she saw Rodolfo, tall and slim, etched in moonlight, one foot raised on the low stone parapet, looking out over the cliffs to the midnight sea beyond.

'Good evening,' she said, moving onto the terrace to join him, a rush of heat surging through her as she watched him—so dark, handsome, sexy and attractive.

'Ah, Victoria, you are better, *cara*?' He moved quickly to her side and took her arm solicitously. 'Come and sit down over here,' he said, indicating one of the wrought-iron chairs to his right.

'I'm fine, really. I feel no after-effects whatsoever.'

'Good. Then why don't we go directly to my apartment? I have a surprise for you.' Looping his arm through hers, he drew her inside. Together they walked through the Great Hall and on towards one of the wings of the castle where Rodolfo had an apartment of his own.

'It's lovely,' Victoria exclaimed as they walked inside the high-ceilinged living room. She was amazed to see how modern the decoration was compared to the rest of the *castello*, which retained its classical style. In contrast this apartment was dotted with exquisitely designed Italian leather furniture and medieval antiques. Halogen lights played on brightly coloured abstract canvases hanging on the centuries-old walls. Opening straight onto the vast living space was an ultra-modern kitchen.

'So this is where you make your culinary delights?' Victoria teased, sitting down on one of the steel bar stools topped with velvet cushions and leaning on the granite counter as Rodolfo moved towards the stove.

'Here it is,' he said, raising his hands. 'I hope you'll like my pasta. That's what's on the menu tonight. We'll have a drink on the balcony, and then you can lay the table while I prepare the food.' He leaned over and pulled a bottle of virgin olive oil off the shelf in readiness.

'What? No servants, no pomp and ceremony?' she queried mischievously.

'No. Tonight it's just you and me, *cara*, and that full moon out there. A drink?' Without waiting for her to answer he selected a glass for her and poured from a wine bottle already uncorked on the counter.

'Thanks.' Victoria glanced at the glass he handed her, eyeing the rich dark red liquid.

'To your quick recovery,' he said, raising his own glass.

'To a successful dinner,' she returned, raising her glass.

'With such a guest, dinner can only be successful,' he replied gallantly.

'Your Royal Highness is too kind,' she murmured, fluttering her eyelashes and bowing her head comically before taking a sip of wine.

'Come, come, Victoria.' He laughed. 'No formal titles, I beg you. I am Rodolfo to you, and that is all. Let's step out and drink this on the balcony, shall we? The evening is quite fresh. Do you think you'll be warm enough?' He came around the counter and, slipping an arm around her, escorted her out onto the wide balcony which overlooked the floodlit gardens of the *castello*.

'The garden is divine,' she murmured, staring down at the manicured *parterres*, the flowerbeds and trimmed hedges, and listening to the soft sound of water pouring from a fountain. She breathed in the familiar scent that seemed to permeate the whole island, giving it an aura all of its own.

'No, *bella*, the garden is pleasant—*you* are exquisite,' he said, stopping himself from kissing her, knowing that if he allowed things to get out of hand right now there would be no pasta, no dinner, merely an immediate move into the bedroom.

If she was willing.

The question was an intriguing one: few women had ever refused him. He did not consider himself arrogant, merely self-confident, sure of his own charm and ability to seduce. He'd never been unfair or unjust, and had always acted the gentleman. Simply, he hadn't allowed his heart to get involved. Victoria was beguiling and lovely, and she reminded him of Giada—but was he really going to stop playing by his rules?

Together they stood leaning against the balustrade of

the wide balcony. The moon shone, full and bright, like a huge floodlight, illuminating the sky, the sea and the castle. The water below shimmered, as did the sparkling lights of the large yachts at anchor in the bay. It was magical, enchanting, unreal. And as Victoria sipped her wine she wondered if all this was nothing but a dream.

After a little while they went inside. Rodolfo directed her to a large antique sideboard, where the plates and cutlery were kept, while he busied himself tossing chopped onions and garlic in olive oil, selecting herbs and popping them into a large frying pan while next to it a huge pot of water simmered, awaiting the pasta. Then he switched on some music: a Baroque instrumental. It was soft and soothing, the quality of the sound perfect.

As she laid the table Victoria let out a sigh. How wonderful it must be to live with a man like this, in such an atmosphere, she reflected, to share such joyful and intimate moments. She barely remembered that he was a prince, simply looked at him as a man on whose company she was fast learning to depend.

And what a man.

Out of the corner of her eye she observed him, watched him, his shirtsleeves rolled up to reveal the taut tanned muscles of his forearms, his hair flicked back as he concentrated on his task. He wore an old pair of tight jeans and espadrilles. She swallowed. What, she wondered, would follow the pasta?

Nothing that she didn't want, she realised ruefully.

For it had become abundantly clear that, however

much Rodolfo might want her, he was too much of gentleman to do anything that she might regret or deplore.
The thought left her limp with longing. To know that he
respected her, that he wanted her yet would be willing
to abstain from demonstrating his desire in any way
that she might find offensive made him all the more
attractive, and left her feeling more vulnerable and tender than she ever had before.

Unconsciously she moved towards the kitchen, came
and stood next to him and watched as he stirred the
pasta, threw herbs deftly into the pan, added a touch of
salt and pepper, then turned and smiled into her eyes.

'It smells delicious,' she murmured, taking a deep
breath.

'Wait until you taste it,' he replied, concentrating again
on his undertaking. 'Here.' He lifted the wooden spoon
and dropped some of the sauce on her hand. 'Try it.'

'Mmm. It's scrumptious.'

'Good. Now, this is the important moment,' he said
as the water boiled and he tipped the pasta in. 'The
pasta must only stay in for three minutes, so that it is *al
dente*.'

'Can I do anything?' she asked, enjoying the sight of
him intensely focused on his cooking.

'Yes. Why not pour us some more wine?' He flashed
her a devilish grin, his teeth gleaming white against his
tan. 'I assure you this will be the best pasta you have
ever tasted, *cara mia*. I am an expert.'

'And modest to boot,' she giggled, as she busied herself pouring from the bottle of red wine that sat on the
counter.

'I see little point in being modest when one knows one is the best,' he said, dropping fettuccine into the pot with a flourish.

'I promise to give you an honest opinion,' she said, eyes flashing with humour as she handed him his glass.

'Thanks. Now, join me here and watch the maestro at work.'

Rolling her eyes in amusement, Victoria poured the other glass then stood next to Rodolfo. The sauce smelled delicious. She could detect several fragrances, including basil. But the rest she could not identify. 'What is that?' she asked, sniffing.

'None of your business,' he responded, tweaking a strand of her hair. 'It's a secret recipe.'

Victoria made a *moue* with her mouth as he circled his arm around her and stirred the pan with a wooden spoon with his free hand. Then he dropped a light kiss on the top of her head. She looked up and their eyes met.

'Not now,' he said, shaking his head wryly. 'I'm afraid this is the critical moment.' Taking his arm away, he grabbed the pot, tipped the pasta out into a large sieve, then replaced it on the stove and stirred in some olive oil.

Victoria looked on, amazed at how professionally he handled things. Next he was tossing the pasta back in the pot and adding the savoury sauce.

'There,' he said, mixing with two large spoons, 'ready to serve, *signorina*.'

Removing the large pot from the stove, he took it over to the table and placed it on a mat, serving large portions onto ceramic plates.

'Here you go,' he said, placing it before her. 'Now,

eat while it's hot, or it'll be no good.' Then he served himself and, sitting down opposite, raised his glass.

'*Salute.*'

'*Salute,*' she responded, raising hers.

'*Buon apetito.*'

Carefully Victoria twiddled some pasta onto her fork, thankful that she'd learned to eat it properly. As she dropped it into her mouth she let out a tiny groan of appreciation. 'It's simply delicious,' she murmured once she could speak. 'I was hoping I could find something wrong with it, but frankly I would be lying. It's perfect.'

'*Grazie.*' He smiled, inclined his head, and began eating.

For a few moments they ate in silence, enjoying the scrumptious dish. Victoria thought suddenly that she could go on doing this for ever and never be bored. He was so charming, so amusing, so easy to be around. Then she pulled herself up with a jolt. This was a ridiculous way of thinking. Here she was, spending a few days in this man's company. She mustn't allow her imagination to run away with her.

Rodolfo watched her across the table, thinking that he had rarely spent such a pleasant, easy-going evening. Victoria was unpretentious, lovely and natural. It was a big change from the sophisticated models he usually shared his time with.

By the time they'd finished dessert both were extremely relaxed with one another.

Coffee was taken out on the balcony, followed by a

small glass of *limoncello*, an after-dinner drink. It was past ten o'clock when suddenly Victoria's mobile phone rang.

Rodolfo passed her handset to her.

'That's weird. Anne already called me. Hello?'

'Hi, babe.'

'Who is this?' she asked blankly.

'Why, baby-pie, it's Bill—from Hollywood. I'm Janie's boyfriend. Remember her? She told you about Dr Browne when you were feeling stressed. I heard you were hanging out there on an island, with some prince or other. Guess you won't be using Dr Browne's services any more, but I could get you some special candy and deliver it personally to you, if you like.'

A chill gripped Victoria and she stared out to sea, swallowing. 'I don't want anything. And how did you get my number?'

'Wouldn't you just like to know? Thought you might like to make me a little gift. After all, the newspapers worldwide are lining up looking for folks to give 'em a good story about you. You're a hot item right now, babe. Thought you might like to do a deal, honey.'

Victoria froze. She glanced at Rodolfo moving around the kitchen area, discreetly staying away while she took the call. This couldn't be happening. What would he say if he found out who was ringing her?

'Well?'

'Look, I can't talk right now,' she muttered nervously, playing for time. She had to think, had to decide what to do—maybe talk to Anne and see if she had a solution to the dilemma.

Blackmail.

She never would have believed it was happening.

'Okay. You've twenty-four hours to make up your mind, honey-bunch. After that all bets are off.' He hung up.

Victoria sat motionless, her hand trembling. What was she to do?

Once he realised she'd hung up, Rodolfo came back outside. 'Nothing important, I hope?' he said, and raised a questioning brow.

'Uh, no. Nothing, really. Just—' She cut off, unable to lie, yet unable to tell him the truth. How could she explain that she was being blackmailed by a drug dealer who, by some mysterious means, had found out her whereabouts? She wanted to scream with frustration— would have done anything to be able to pour out her troubles to Rodolfo, to tell him the truth and be done with it.

But that was impossible.

He must never know how far she'd got into trouble. He'd been so kind and tolerant. But what if he knew this? He would be disgusted by her. The thought made her shiver.

'Are you cold?' he enquired, coming to sit next to her and slipping his arm about her.

'No, no, I'm fine,' she lied, swallowing.

'Victoria, I think you know that I want you very much,' Rodolfo said, letting his fingers thread through her golden mane of hair.

'I—'

'There's no need to say anything. Just let me lead the way.'

She hesitated. Then he rose. Unable to resist, she did too. She wanted this man more than anything, even though she knew that there was no future with him. But somehow it didn't matter. What she needed now was to be in his arms, to feel him hold her, forget the nightmare taking place in her public life and give way to her inner desires.

Slowly they moved through the living room and into the bedroom of the extensive apartment. Rodolfo closed the door, then turned her towards him.

'*Cara mia*, you are so lovely,' he whispered, his lips leaving a trail of kisses on her temple, her neck, and down to her breast. Her heart was beating so fast she didn't think she could breathe. Then his hands began slipping off her top. In one quick movement he loosened her bra. It fell to the floor and she stood before him, her golden hair falling over her naked breasts.

'*Bellissima*,' he murmured, leading her to the bed and laying her down among the pillows.

Soon they were lying naked next to one another. Victoria's pulse raced as she thought of what she was about to do. This was the first time she'd been to bed with a man. Would Rodolfo be disappointed at her lack of experience? But it was too late to turn back—too late to have regrets. All at once she knew that this man would always be special in her life, even though they would probably only spend a few days with each other.

He would be the first to love her.

'Victoria, you are so lovely, so beautiful.' He touched her cheek, then his fingers trailed down her neck to the tip of her breast. Lightly he caressed her, taunting.

And Victoria did not resist. It was too delicious, too wonderful to be here, lying in his arms, prey to new and wonderful sensations. When his lips sought the tip of her breast and his fingers coursed between her thighs she gasped at the novel awareness. Pulling her to him, Rodolfo pressed her against him, making her feel his desire.

'I want you, *cara*,' he repeated hoarsely, eyes holding hers.

Victoria couldn't reply, simply allowed him to continue this wonderful magic he was performing on her body, which left her pliant and limp with a need so strong she could not do anything but let out a sigh of longing. As though sensing her need, Rodolfo let his fingers venture further, seeking her core, caressing now in new ways, seeking the deepest secrets of her being. And Victoria gave way, let out a little cry when at last he brought her to completion, and she arched before falling back in his arms.

'You must tell what you like, what you want,' he whispered, still unaware that she had never shared an adventure like this before. Then, before she could answer, he straddled her, and lowered himself on top of her. How he wanted to reach inside her, feel the wet honeyed heat he'd already touched. But as he eased himself inside her a surprise awaited him. All at once he stopped, and his eyes sought hers.

'*Cara*, is this possible?' he said in a low husky voice. 'Are you a virgin?'

'Yes,' Victoria whispered, flushed with excitement and embarrassment. Perhaps Rodolfo would despise her for being such an innocent.

'But, my darling, you should have told me,' he murmured, drawing back. 'This puts a completely different light on the situation.'

He was about to withdraw completely when her arms came up about his neck and her eyes met his.

'No. It doesn't. I want you, Rodolfo. I want the first time to be with you,' she whispered, drawing him back towards her.

'Are you absolutely certain?' he muttered, finding it hard to exercise self-control when her body was arching towards him, her eyes filled with such passion and longing.

'Absolutely sure.'

For a moment he hesitated. Then slowly he entered her once more. 'I promise I'll do my best not to hurt you, *cara*,' he whispered.

Victoria knew a moment's pain as he penetrated her. Then it faded and her body relaxed. Heat rushed to her breasts, to her abdomen. She felt herself melting, needed to feel him deeper inside her. Her hips arched, following the rhythm of this new and exciting dance, until they moved together in a primal ritual. She threw her head back and let out a low gasp of delight when together they came, falling over the edge of a high precipice and collapsing in each other's arms onto the rumpled sheets.

As he lay holding her in his arms Rodolfo let out a sigh of satisfaction. It was ages since he'd experienced anything so intense as their lovemaking. In fact, if truth be told, he'd only known it once before—with Giada. Now, as he stroked Victoria's hair and kissed her temple tenderly, he felt a new and heightened responsibility towards this girl who had entrusted him with her womanhood.

'Are you all right?' he said, slipping away from her to lie next to her, his hand moving to her abdomen in a protective gesture that did not go unnoticed.

Victoria nodded. Her throat was knotted and she couldn't speak. So many emotions were going through her. It was wonderful, thrilling. Yet it was difficult to face the fact that the situation was nothing but a transient affair which would end in a few days when life went back to normal.

'I'm fine,' she whispered, when at last she was able to speak.

'Are you sure?' He looked down at her tenderly, his dark eyes filled with concern. She could read the doubt. Yet there was also a look of pride in his expression. And she realised that he was taking her initiation into the world of love much more seriously than she had expected. It touched her, and tears filled her eyes. '*Cara*, what is the matter?' he said, frowning, 'did I hurt you?'

'No, Rodolfo, it's nothing. I'm just a bit mixed up, that's all. So much has happened in the past few days, and now this. Don't get me wrong. It's wonderful. I'm glad it happened. I wanted it as much as you. It's just a lot to handle, that's all.'

'I understand, *cara*.' He held her close, kissed her hair and let his arms enfold her.

Victoria gloried in the embrace, wished it could go on for ever, and heaved a sigh of regret that soon she would be on her way and life as she'd known it for the past couple of days would be nothing but a distant memory.

CHAPTER SIX

'YOU CAN'T STAY HIDDEN there for ever,' Anne insisted next day, when Victoria phoned her, sitting perched on the balustrade of the terrace looking down past the olive groves at the sea.

'Anne, I—' Victoria wanted to tell her about Bill, about the awful phone call and how scared she was. But something stopped her.

'What is it, Vic?'

'Nothing.'

Anne hesitated. 'Vic, is something the matter?'

'No, not at all. In fact very much the opposite. The Prince has been a wonderful host.'

'Look, they want to shoot those pictures in London in four days.'

'Four days?'

'Exactly. I've made arrangements for a jet to pick you up on the island and fly you to London. I'll be there to pick you up.'

So she'd been right. It was all a dream that would come to an end as fast as it had begun. Victoria stared at the sea, at a woman leading a loaded donkey on the path below, and sighed.

'Vic? Are you still there? Tell me, how did you like

the island? See any property that you might want to invest in?'

'It's very nice. But frankly I'm not sure about it.' The thought of being on the island, so close to Rodolfo and having to perhaps see him with another woman, would be unbearable, she realised suddenly. The last thing she wanted was to live here if she couldn't be with him. 'We'll talk about it when I see you.'

'Okay. Fine. Have a good time. I'll call you again with the departure time. By the way, I think things are beginning to die down on the press front. Ed's cooled down.'

'Good. Bye then.'

Victoria swallowed as she laid down the receiver. She thought of Bill and the twenty-four-hour deadline he'd given her to come up with some cash. Should she pay him off and be left in peace for a while? Or would he simply become an ongoing threat, always there, ready to blackmail her whenever he wanted more money?

Her thoughts were interrupted by a movement from inside the *castello*. She looked up. A tall, slim blonde woman in well-cut white trousers and a black linen top, with a large leather handbag flung over her shoulder and a haughty expression, stepped onto the terrace.

'And who,' she demanded peremptorily, 'are you?' She tipped up her designer sunglasses to take better stock of Victoria.

'I'm staying here,' Victoria replied, bristling. Who was this creature, and what right did she have to question her?

'Oh. How strange,' she said. She had a foreign accent. 'Where is he—do you know?'

'Who?'

'Why, the Prince, of course. Who else?' The woman cast Victoria a withering look.

'I have no idea. Perhaps in his office,' Victoria replied coldly. 'He said he had business to attend to.'

'I see. Are you the new secretary?' the woman enquired, looking her up and down. 'Why aren't you inside working?'

'Look, I really don't see what business it is of yours who I am or what I do,' Victoria muttered icily.

At that moment Rodolfo stepped out onto the terrace. He took in the scene and cleared his throat. 'Alexandra. What an unexpected surprise. I didn't know you were on the island.'

'My yacht anchored this morning. You look in good form, *mein lieber*.' The woman sidled up to him, slipped an arm around his neck and deposited a kiss on his lips.

'Uh, yes, I'm fine. I see you've met Victoria,' Rodolfo added hastily, amazed at Countess Alexandra's extraordinary behaviour.

She was one of the women the council had suggested he marry. Seeing her now, next to Victoria, he realised how impossible that would be. Alexandra was domineering and cold, even though her beauty and chic were undeniable. He glanced at Victoria, saw the tempestuous pain in her eyes, and felt his heart sink. The way Alexandra was behaving, Victoria would naturally believe there was something between them.

'I haven't been introduced. I didn't know you allowed your staff to dawdle about,' Alexandra pronounced in a low sultry voice.

'Staff?'

'Well, isn't she your new secretary?' Alexandra said, as though Victoria weren't there.

'Whatever gave you that idea?' Rodolfo returned, annoyed, and stepped pointedly away from her. 'Victoria, may I introduce Countess Alexandra von Bellinghof? This is Victoria Woodward. You have perhaps seen her in the movie which won so much acclaim at the Cannes Film Festival.'

Alexandra looked taken aback, but she quickly came about. 'Ah, yes, of course. I should have recognised you immediately. After all, you've been front-page news for the past few days, haven't you?' The Countess's tone was patronising and laced with venom.

Victoria seethed inwardly, but held her temper in check. She could tell the woman was determined to provoke her but she wouldn't rise to the bait.

'Part of the trials of fame,' she answered languidly. 'One keeps on having to deal with the paparazzi and the gutter press.'

'Victoria is here *incognito*,' Rodolfo said hastily. 'I shall expect your complete discretion,' he insisted.

'Oh, goodness. Well, of course.' Alexandra waved a dismissive hand. 'I'm sure you have enough troubles without being hounded by the curious. Though, of course, if one has the unwholesome habits you're reputed to indulge in, then...' She let the rest of the sentence trail, turned from Victoria and shrugged. 'I suppose it's the best one can expect.'

Rodolfo's blood boiled, and he replied icily, 'Alexandra, you should have called before coming here. I'm

afraid this isn't a very convenient time. Why don't I give
you a buzz when I'm able to make some arrangement
to see you socially?' he said, slipping his hand under her
elbow and guiding her firmly back towards the living
room.

Victoria was pleased to see the woman's features
stiffen. Then Alexandra drew herself up and sniffed.
'Of course—I'm sorry if I'm in the way. I shall leave
immediately. You are obviously very busy. I imagine
you must be amusing yourself quite nicely,' she added,
in a low conspiratorial voice that was calculated to reach
Victoria.

Despite her anger, Victoria's cheeks turned red. Was
it written all over her that she'd slept with Rodolfo? Or
was the woman just a bitch? Whichever the case, she felt
diminished and offended.

'I'm sorry about that,' Rodolfo said a couple of minutes later. 'Alexandra was being particularly obnoxious
today.' He laughed, making light of the situation, but
Victoria could see that he was ruffled.

'Who is she anyway?'

'A German countess whose parents have a property
on the island.'

'She seemed to be quite intimate with you.'

'Hmmm.' He smiled ruefully. 'I have a feeling that
was for your benefit.'

'Why?'

'I think Alexandra sensed something between us.
She knows that the council of the island are urging me
to find a suitable wife and get married. They are concerned with the succession. Obviously Alexandra has

her own agenda.' He approached, lifted Victoria's chin and peered into her clear grey eyes. 'Don't tell me you're jealous, *cara*?'

Victoria caught the glint of male satisfaction in his eyes. 'Not in the least,' she answered, sending him a bright smile. She would not let him know the devastating effect of Alexandra's gestures. She would not give him that satisfaction.

Swooping an arm possessively around her, Rodolfo brought her up close. 'How about a drive around the island? We could picnic somewhere, if you like, or I could take you to lunch at my favourite restaurant in Lamara—a village at the end of the island. I promise you Alexandra won't bother us again. I sent her away with a flea in her ear.'

A slow smile hovered about Victoria's lips. His words mollified her defiant mood. 'Okay, that sounds very nice,' she said, lifting her face for his kiss.

THE RIDE TO THE OTHER SIDE of the island was delightful. Together they wandered hand in hand up a hill to the little rustic fish restaurant, all crooked whitewashed walls and bright blue shutters, perched on the edge of a cliff overlooking the pristine sandy beach below. Immediately a large grey-haired lady in a bright flowered apron, wreathed in smiles, came to greet them.

'Your Highness, what a pleasure to see you. And so well accompanied,' the woman said with a broad smile.

She showed them to a secluded table with a wonderful view, and soon the red and white checkered tablecloth was covered with all sorts of dishes, ranging from fried fish to squid salad, lobster and a local specialty of meatballs in a delicious sauce that Victoria had grown particularly fond of in the past few days.

Now that they were away from the palace, and Alexandra's oppressive presence, she'd recovered her mood of the night before. It was difficult to think of anything disagreeable like Bill's ultimatum when she was being treated to so much solicitude. Determined to enjoy herself, she pushed the impending threat to the back of her mind. What could he do that hadn't already been done? The scandal was fading, according to Anne—a seven-day wonder. Soon she would just be another item of old news.

Rodolfo was charming, as always, and she found herself melting inside when she looked at him, remembering all that had taken place the previous night. There was a new tenderness and intimacy between them that she had never known with a man before. What would it be like to leave? she wondered as she sipped a glass of chilled water. What would Hollywood and all the hype be like after this? That, and knowing that she probably wouldn't ever see him again? Her heart sank at the thought.

Just as she was about to take another sip of water a shadow fell on the table and she looked up. A scruffy young man stood there, a smirk on his face.

'Hi, gorgeous,' he drawled in an American accent. 'Having a nice day? Knew I'd find you if I looked hard enough.'

Rodolfo was looking at her, then at the young man.

'Who are you?' Victoria demanded, feeling her pulse

race and her stomach lurch. This had to be Bill. How on earth had he found her?

'You know what they say. You can run but you can't hide.' Bill wagged a finger at her and smirked again.

'What do you want?' she muttered, swallowing.

'I told you what I wanted when I called you last night. But I guess it's too late for that, honeybunch. You had your chance and you didn't take it. Tough.' With that he pulled a small camera from his pocket and snapped several quick shots.

'Who the hell is this?' Rodolfo rose quickly to his feet as Bill stepped niftily away from the table and made for the door.

'He's someone from LA. He—well—' Oh, how could she tell Rodolfo?

'What, Victoria? Tell me at once,' Rodolfo commanded, leaning towards her and taking her hand in his. 'You must tell me. He's taken pictures. I need to know.'

'He's the boyfriend of the girl who introduced me to the doctor who gave me the pills,' she said in a half-whisper. 'He's already tried to blackmail me. He—'

But before she could finish Rodolfo had spun on his heel and was marching across the restaurant. He caught up with Bill as he was about to get into his Jeep.

'Hey—you!' Rodolfo threw at the coarse-looking unshaven creature. 'Give me that camera at once.'

'You have to be kidding. This is tomorrow's headlines.' Bill patted the camera smugly. 'You may run your own little show here on your fantasy island, Your Royal Highness, but where I come from money talks. Sorry.' He made to switch on the engine.

But before he could do so Rodolfo lunged forward and caught him by the scruff of his neck. 'I'm asking you nicely,' he said, his voice low and filled with menace.

'Hey, leave me be,' the man said, trying pull away, his expression ugly. 'I have every right to take pictures of who the hell I want.'

'Not on my island, you don't. As you just pointed out, I run the show around here. If you don't give me that camera immediately I shall have you arrested for harassment. That, I believe, is a term that you should be familiar with where you come from?'

'Hey, you can't do that,' Bill protested. Then, after pushing Rodolfo away, he revved the engine and skidded off down the earth road, leaving a trail of dust in his wake.

Without hesitation Rodolfo pulled out his mobile and called the local police. They would stop Bill at the port. No way would he allow Victoria to be blackmailed or harassed by the press or by some unscrupulous drug dealer.

As he slipped his phone back in his shirt pocket and stepped back into the restaurant, it occurred to Rodolfo that his reaction had been somewhat out of proportion. It had been that of a man protecting the woman he cared for, he thought suddenly. He looked across at Victoria, standing uneasily by their table, not knowing what to do, and smiled at her reassuringly. He did care for her, he realised, more than he would have imagined—certainly more than he ever would have deemed possible. Last night, spent together in each other's arms, had been so special, so filled with extraordinary sensations and tenderness, that he would find it hard to forget.

Banishing his thoughts, Rodolfo went over to her. 'The police will cut him off further down the road or at the ferry, so don't worry. He won't leave the island with those pictures. And if he doesn't give the camera up voluntarily he'll go to jail for a few hours. That should do the trick.' He smiled down at her, his fingers touching her hair, and he made her sit down again. 'There is no need to worry, Victoria. All that is behind you now, *cara mia*. But you must swear something to me.'

'What is that?' she asked sinking back onto the chair, her hand still held in his.

'That if anybody should come bothering you or threatening you again, you will tell me at once. Trust me, Victoria. Above all, I'm your friend.'

She swallowed, then nodded silently, allowed him to pour her some more mineral water and sat with her hand covered by his.

'Promise?' He raised his glass to hers.

'I promise,' she said, smiling into his eyes. It felt strangely reassuring to know that he cared for her enough to worry about her well-being. 'I wish I didn't have to go back to Hollywood and that whole scene,' she said suddenly.

'Then why not drop the whole thing?'

'Because I love acting—and the script of this new movie. It's what I've always wanted. I can't just run away. I would never forgive myself. I just wish—' She cut off abruptly, looked down into her glass and sighed.

'What do you wish?' he asked softly.

'That I was made of sterner stuff,' she replied with a smile.

'You are strong. But that world is full of traps. I know—I've seen it close-up. Are you sure you have to go?'

'I have to. Apart from the fact that I'd never be able to face myself if I failed, I'm under contract. Ed would have a fit. No,' she said, shaking her head and sipping more water, 'I'm just going to have to face it.'

'And fall back into old habits?' he said, raising a harsh dark brow and withdrawing his hand from hers.

'No. I'm determined not to.'

'Easily said, when sitting here away from it all,' he remarked dryly. 'You don't *want* to go back to popping pills, but you can't guarantee that you won't when the going gets tough.'

'I will do my very best, I promise. And I'll have Dottore Manfreddo's tea.'

'That's not good enough,' he said harshly, his eyes meeting hers. 'I want you to swear to me that you won't ever take those things again. Don't you realise the danger? You have no idea what you're taking. They could kill you, Victoria.'

Her eyes met his full-on, and she read the concern and anger in them and felt sudden resentment at his attitude. 'Rodolfo, it's easy enough for you to judge. You live here, in this magical kingdom, protected from everything. It's different out there in the real world. I don't want to fall back into anything, and I don't believe I will now that I know the full truth, but I can't promise you that in a crisis I won't, because I don't honestly know. I'd be lying. Sometimes the stress is overwhelming and, as we both know, I'm not good at too much pressure.'

'You're right,' he conceded reluctantly. 'Will you at least promise me that if you're feeling down, over-whelmed or whatever, you will call me before doing anything rash, and that together we'll find a solution? As I said before, *cara mia*, I'm above all your friend.'

She nodded. 'I promise.'

Her friend. That was all. She supposed it was a lot but she wished he had said, *I'm the man who loves you.* But that wasn't to be, she argued reasonably. And she was foolish even to think of such a thing.

Several minutes later Rodolfo rang the police and was advised that Bill had been stopped on the road and his camera confiscated. He had left the island furious, threatening lawsuits. But that, as Rodolfo knew, was just hot air.

'He can threaten as much as he likes. The laws here do not permit harassment of my residents,' he said au-tocratically. 'Victoria, I suggest we go back to the *cas-tello* and take a long afternoon siesta?'

He sent her an intimate smile filled with promise. His tender eyes and fingers, caressing the inside of her wrist, sent shivers jolting through her. Was it foolish to allow him to make love to her again? Was it court-ing trouble? Perhaps. But how could she resist? She had only a few days left before the dream came to an end and she returned to reality. She knew that, whatever the consequences for her own heart, she must live it to the full or regret it for the rest of her life.

A HEAT HAZE SHIMMERED outside, but in the shuttered bedroom of Rodolfo's apartment the atmosphere was cool. Drawing Victoria towards him, Rodolfo slipped her top off, then her skirt and lacy undergarments. There was no pretence, no lingering over niceties, just a deep-rooted need to be in each other's arms, skin to skin, throbbing heart to throbbing heart.

As her bra fell to the floor and his eyes fell upon her upturned breasts he sighed. 'Ah, *bellissima* Victoria, how shall I be able to let you go?' he whispered, letting his fingers trail down her throat, then down to caress the tips of her taut nipples.

She swallowed, eyes closed, then let out a tiny gasp of delight when his thumb grazed the aching tips and his other hand reached between her thighs for that special secret spot inside that she had never known existed until yesterday.

Next they were lying on the bed. Rodolfo caressed her, relishing the warmth, her honeyed response as his fingers reached inside her, making her writhe with delight as expertly he stroked while he took the tip of her nipple between his teeth, taunted and laved, driving her to distraction.

Only when he knew she could bear it no longer, that he had brought her to a peak several times, did he allow himself the ultimate pleasure. In one quick thrust he penetrated her, making her gasp. This was not the tender lovemaking of yesterday, but a hot, harsh need for completion in which she joined him. Braced on his hands above her, Rodolfo took her in long deep thrusts that left her on the verge of madness. Then she curled her legs around his waist and brought him down upon her, and together they spiralled once more, reaching new heights of unexpected pleasure, spinning into a whirlwind of delight that knew no boundaries.

CHAPTER SEVEN

HER BAGS WERE PACKED and she was ready to go.

Gazing out over the cliff and down to the sea, Victoria could barely believe that her time on Malvarina had gone by so fast. The past days had been spent making love, dining in Rodolfo's apartment, living as if they were a couple, not two strangers who had come together by chance and whose lives were about to take different routes.

'The car is ready.' Rodolfo came up behind her and slipped his hands around her shoulders. 'I shall miss you, *cara*, more than you can ever imagine.'

Victoria swallowed. She had promised herself to be brave, not to let her feelings get involved. But that was impossible. Rodolfo was all she'd ever dreamed of in a man. Now she was about to lose him for ever. Silent tears coursed down her cheeks and she swallowed hard, determined to try and put up a good front.

'*Cara*, what is the matter?' he asked, seeing her tears. He raised his thumb to her cheek and brushed them away. 'You must not cry, darling. We have spent the most wonderful time together—a time that neither of us will ever forget.'

She nodded, forced herself to smile and pretend that all was well. 'I'm fine. Just a little emotionally upset at the thought of having to go back, that's all.'

He frowned. 'Victoria, remember your promise.'

She nodded, and he took her hand. With one last look at the sea she turned and followed him. This interlude would remain etched in her mind for ever, she realised.

Soon they were reaching the island's small airport, where the jet Anne had sent for Victoria was already on the tarmac. As she and Rodolfo alighted from the car and someone from the plane took her luggage, a familiar voice reached them.

'Rodolfo, darling.' Alexandra marched over towards them and, ignoring Victoria, slipped a hand onto Rodolfo's shoulder. She dropped a kiss on his cheek. 'It's been awfully lonely without you, *mein lieber*. Where on earth have you been hiding?' she asked, an insinuating smile touching her lips.

'I've been busy. You remember Victoria?' he said pointedly, removing her hand from his shoulder.

Alexandra turned with a raised brow and looked Victoria over from head to foot. 'Ah, yes, the Hollywood headline. I'd forgotten.'

Victoria stood her ground and gave her a similar look back, but didn't bother to answer. Instead she turned to Rodolfo. 'I'd better be going,' she murmured.

'Of course. Goodbye, Alexandra.'

'Bye-bye, *caro*,' the Countess schmoozed. 'I hope I'll be seeing more of you now that you'll be less occupied,' she added with a significant look.

Rodolfo simply picked up Victoria's tote bag, which she was taking with her on the plane, and slipped his hand under her elbow.

They walked in silence, accompanied by two airport staff. Victoria felt the pressure of his hand on her elbow and closed her eyes tight, as though trying to engrave the memory—the feel of him—inside her for ever.

Then they were at the plane. Rodolfo handed her bag to the crew and followed her on board into the sleek yet impersonal cabin, with its beige leather seats and glistening chrome tables.

'Well, I guess this is it,' he said, looking into her eyes.

'I guess so,' she answered as they stood uncomfortably aware of one another. Then suddenly she was in his arms and he was holding her tight. 'Take care of yourself, *cara*. And remember. I'm here if you need me. Stay in touch, won't you?'

She nodded into his shoulder, swallowing the flood of tears so near to the surface. Then she raised her face and his lips came down on hers, firm, warm and possessive. His arms caressed her back and they embraced. It was a kiss she'd hoped would last for ever, but inevitably it came to an end.

Rodolfo raised his head, smiled down into her eyes. 'I think I'd better go now,' he said. And, raising her fingers to his lips one last time, he kissed them. '*Bon voyage, cara.* Thank you for some of the most beautiful moments of my life. I will remember our time together for as long as I live.'

Then, before she could answer, he had disembarked and moved away from the aircraft.

Victoria flopped sadly into one of the wide seats and fastened her seat belt. Already the plane was preparing for take off. As it taxied on the tarmac she peered out of the window. She could see Rodolfo standing there, his hands shoved into the pockets of his jeans. Then, to her horror, she saw Alexandra walk up to him. He turned and talked to her. As the plane picked up speed she saw him turn and wave. She waved back. Then, as the plane lifted into the air, she leaned back and closed her eyes, and the tears she'd been holding back finally flowed freely.

She had never felt so alone.

THE LAST THING that Rodolfo wanted was Alexandra bothering him right now. He needed time to think, to take his bearings. And how he could ever have contemplated the council's suggestion that he marry this creature was beyond him.

'Look, I'm afraid I'm very busy at the moment, Alexandra. I'll call you when I have a moment.'

With a brief smile he headed back to the car, got in and switched on the engine. He did not feel like going straight back to the *castello*. Instead he drove slowly along the coastline, up the cliff and on to the places where he and Victoria had shared such delicious moments together. He felt worried about her, about her future, about what might happen if she got back into that same crowd and couldn't handle it.

But he had no right to try and retain her as he would

have liked. They both had their lives to lead. He must think of the future of the island—his ambition of making it into what he believed it could become, of a marriage of convenience, of an heir. Victoria, on the other hand, had a successful career in front of her that she must pursue.

Rodolfo stopped the car and looked out over the clear blue sea, remembering the moments spent with Victoria, the unimaginable pleasure he'd experienced in her arms—pleasure such as he had only felt with Giada, all those years ago.

Enough.

Switching the engine back on, he drove his car back towards the *castello*, determined to get on with his many duties. He would remember the last few days as an agreeable memory, nothing more. Real life stood between him and Victoria. And the sooner he realised it, the better.

CHAPTER EIGHT

VICTORIA HAD ONLY three days to spend in Hetherington before flying back to LA, and she planned to enjoy every minute of them. Ensconced in her favourite nook in her mother's home—the chintz-cushioned bay window looking out onto the lawn—Victoria watched as rain pattered down the window panes then landed in the flowerbeds below. She loved the manor house and everything about it—the tranquillity, the peace it afforded her, the safety and privacy, the authenticity and lack of glitz. It was about as different from her life in Hollywood as it could be.

Her mother had gone to London for the day, and Victoria was content to stay lounging about the house in a pair of old jeans and an oversized jersey that had once belonged to her father. Timmy, a black Labrador, sat adoringly at her feet, thrilled to have his mistress back. But, although she tried to focus on the film script she was holding, Victoria found her mind constantly wandering back to Malvarina and the wonderful hours spent in Rodolfo's arms.

What was he doing right now? she wondered, as her eyes strayed from the text and stared into the distance.

Was he at the *castello*, or with that dreadful Alexandra? Surely not. She couldn't believe that he would be capable of dating a woman like that. The mere thought of Alexandra lying in the Prince's arms made her clench her fingers into a tight ball. At the same time she quickly reminded herself that she had no right to judge him— no right to anything except the memories of those wonderful days they'd spent together. She had made a conscious choice, the choice of becoming a woman in his arms. And she didn't regret it. Well, not exactly, she argued. It was just hard to know that it had all been nothing but an adventure, a magical fairy story from which she must now wake up.

Or *should* wake from, she reminded herself.

This last preyed on her mind. It was all fine and dandy to think you could plan things as you wanted, live experiences and then walk away from them without consequences. But Victoria was fast discovering that it was far harder than she had imagined, and that Rodolfo was engraved on her mind as no man had ever been before. Wherever she looked she saw him, his smile, his piercing black eyes gleaming into hers, remembered his possessive gaze and soft words as he'd entered her, and the indescribable passion she'd experienced in his arms.

Would any man ever be able to offer her that same experience again? she wondered suddenly as the script fell to the carpet and she leaned back among the cushions. The mere thought of being held in anyone else's arms struck her as repugnant right now. She swallowed. Maybe with time she would learn to forget him, be able to move on. But for now she knew that to be impossible. Her whole being was enthralled by him, lived for him, dreamed and breathed him.

Idiot, she reprimanded herself. *He probably barely remembers that you exist. You were was just an adventure, another short-lived affair amongst many.*

The thought was so daunting that it brought tears to her eyes. She wiped them angrily away and sniffed. There was little use in feeling sorry for herself. After all, she'd made her own choice. No one had forced her into anything.

Remembering that she needed to phone Anne, Victoria dragged herself up and with a sigh reached for the phone. In a few days it would all begin again—the hype, the rushing from set to set, the make-up artists, and Ed Banes. She shuddered, dialled and held the receiver to her ear. She might as well get used to it. Nothing was going to change. Except that this time around she was determined to overcome her weaknesses and not allow herself to be tempted by an easy way out.

A MONTH LATER Victoria was not so sure.

She'd been back in Hollywood for over three weeks now. The movie was beginning. She spent hours being fitted into period costumes, and the more time she spent on the set the more tired and disgruntled she became.

'Cheer up, honey. It's not so bad. The scandal has all died down, and nobody even remembers the Cannes thing. Plus, we managed to scotch most of the bad news here in the US. So who cares what a bunch of Euros think, anyway?' Anne commented, as she struck another item from the list on her Palm Pilot. 'By the way, you've got to do the palace scene this afternoon.'

'I don't know if I can,' Victoria replied. 'I don't feel too well. Must be something I ate.'

'Oh, cripes, Victoria, this is not the time to get sick. Ed will have a fit. Don't do this to me,' Anne wailed, sitting down abruptly in the canvas chair opposite Victoria.

'Sorry. I just feel sick the whole time.'

Anne rolled her eyes. 'Take antacid medication, or something. Eat different. I don't know.'

As she did in most of her free moments, Victoria glanced surreptitiously at her phone. She had received only two messages from Rodolfo since her departure from Malvarina. One had been a brief text message, saying he hoped she'd returned safely, the other a reminder that she'd left a bikini and a skirt at the *castello*, and where could his staff forward them to?

But there had been no word, no sign, no mention of what had passed between them. And as the days had gone by his silence had engulfed her. She'd felt abandoned and alone. Then, one morning, she'd begun to feel sick. At first she'd imagined she must have picked up a tummy bug. But when she had also realised that her monthly period was a fortnight late, the penny had dropped. Filled with anxiety, she'd done a pregnancy test that had come up positive. Confused and unhappy, this morning she had gone to see a doctor.

All her fears had been confirmed.

She was pregnant.

She glanced at Anne, thought of the horror her agent would express were she to know the truth. Victoria herself had been flummoxed by the news. What was she to do? Who could she turn to in this moment of need? Her mother? No. Mummy would make her go home, abandon everything, and probably insist she get in touch with the father. And she had no intention of doing anything of the sort. It was her fault this had happened. She'd allowed things to go too far before letting Rodolfo know that she was a virgin. He couldn't be held responsible.

Yet, like it or not, she had to recognise that he was the father of the child now growing inside her. He had a right to know. And she had an obligation to decide what she would do.

'Helloooo?' Anne waved a hand at her. 'I'm talking to you. Could you concentrate on this conversation for just a couple of minutes?'

'Sorry. I was distracted.'

'So what's new?' Anne muttered. 'Look, if you're sick I'll call in a doctor. Just don't fail me this afternoon. The palace scene is a big deal. It needs to be perfect. I'll get Ed to give you tomorrow off, okay?'

Victoria shrugged. 'Okay.'

Two hours later she was parading in front of a set re-creating Versailles. Ed was with the cameraman studying angles. Victoria was feeling increasingly dizzy, as the air-conditioning wasn't working properly and the place was sweltering.

'Is this going to take much longer?' she asked, feeling a rush of nausea grip her.

'Just a few more takes, hon, and then we'll have all we need for today.'

Forcing herself to stand upright, Victoria took a deep breath, willed her wilting body to remain vertical. Just a few more minutes, she reminded herself. She simply must hold out.

The next thing she knew Victoria was waking up in the austere surroundings of a hospital room. She blinked. What on earth had happened? One minute she'd been taking a few dainty steps towards the fountains, and then everything had blacked out. She was alone in the room, but could hear voices in the corridor. Suddenly she remembered her pregnancy. Had they found out her secret? And if so what was she going to do?

As HE SAT DOWN to breakfast on the terrace of the *castello*, Rodolfo sighed. He could not help but remember the charming breakfasts shared in this very spot with Victoria. What was she up to? he wondered for the umpteenth time as absently he picked up the newspaper. Then he read the headline and an oath escaped him.

Hollywood Actress Victoria Woodward Hospitalised.

His pulse missed a beat as anxiously his eyes sought out the article, avid to find out what was wrong with her. Had she resorted to drugs again? But the article gave little real information, and he flung the paper down, irritated, his coffee and croissants forgotten as he paced the terrace, his expression set in a worried frown.

What should he do? He'd tried so hard over the past few weeks to forget her, to pretend that what had occurred between them was nothing but a passing fling. But to his irritation and frustration he had not been able to banish her memory as he had the other women in his life. Usually he was able to compartmentalise. But not this time. For some reason he couldn't explain, Victoria had seeped beneath his skin—her face ever-present in his mind, the memory of her writhing beneath him, her delicious mixture of innocence and primal female passion haunting him at every step. He was unable to escape her. Unable to flee her ghost. Everywhere he went he saw her. On the yacht, at table, laughing next to him in the car.

And in his bed.

Uttering another oath under his breath, Rodolfo pulled out his mobile phone and dialled. He would try and reach her. He must find out what was going on. He would seek information through Anne, and if that wasn't forthcoming then he had his own ways of finding out.

But two hours later he was no better off. Anne had been friendly, but unable to furnish him with any concrete information. And his other sources seemed to be having difficulty in finding out anything at all. By lunchtime he was so frustrated that, despite his better judgement telling him he was crazy, he decided he would go to Hollywood himself and seek her out. It made no sense. She probably wouldn't even want to see him. But Rodolfo knew that he couldn't bear the waiting, the not knowing. Would not rest until he knew she was all right.

Calling his private secretary, he announced his departure and ordered his jet ready to fly within the hour.

Several hours later he was crossing the Atlantic, determined to find out what was ailing Victoria—even if he had to bribe his way into the hospital.

BACK AT HER APARTMENT in Los Angeles, Victoria was being cosseted by an anxious Anne and her Mexican maid, Lupita. Thank goodness the doctor had agreed to keep her secret confidential. He was a nice, middle-aged man, who obviously had little time for all the excitement his patient elicited. But when she'd insisted on seeing him alone and had shared the truth with him he'd been surprisingly kind and understanding.

'Of course I'll respect your wishes, Miss Woodward. I realise that it's a hard decision to take. And if you need me, please call me at once. Does the baby's father know yet?'

'Uh, no.' She blushed. 'I—I haven't decided what to do yet. It's a rather complicated situation, you see—'

'No need to tell me anything,' the doctor had cut in, raising a hand. 'But I'm here if you need me.'

'Thanks. I appreciate it.' She'd smiled and thanked him, and felt that at least in him she had a friend. No one else, she'd decided, could know the truth. Not until she'd taken her own final decision regarding the future. She was still debating whether or not she should advise Rodolfo. What if he thought it was some sort of trick? Or—? Oh, dear. There were so many *ifs*.

Closing her eyes, Victoria allowed her head to fall back against the white cotton pillow and thought about Rodolfo, imagining him just as she'd seen him in Malvarina, with his dark hair and handsome features etched against the clear blue horizon, his laughing eyes shining into hers.

And suddenly she knew she wanted this child.

His child.

Could not, would not, do anything to harm it—whatever anyone said or did to try and influence her to the contrary.

'BUT I NEED TO KNOW where I can find her,' Rodolfo insisted to the austere secretary, eyeing him askance from behind her desk.

'I'm sorry, sir, but I'm afraid I can't furnish you with any information regarding Miss Woodward's whereabouts. I would advise you to call her agent.'

'I already have, damn it. Her phone isn't answering.'

'Then I'm afraid I can't help you.'

At that moment Dr Harper walked by, glancing at a file. At the sound of voices and the mention of Victoria's name he looked up and frowned. He was a sufficient judge of people to realise the man badgering his secretary was both powerful and truly concerned about his patient. It took him thirty seconds to conclude that he might just be looking at the father of Victoria's baby. When he'd mentioned the father she'd seemed so unsure and confused he'd wondered if perhaps it was just a silly mistake caused by a one-night stand. But this man was mature, no young Hollywood hopeful.

Now Dr Harper wondered whether it wasn't his duty to at least give the two people a chance to decide their future and not have public opinion do it for them. The man struck him as a familiar figure. Not an actor, he reflected, scanning his memory, but someone well known.

Then suddenly he recalled the face. It was no one less

than HRH the Prince of Malvarina. He remembered him from an international yachting event he'd been watching not long ago on TV. Could he be the father? the physician wondered.

'Sir, can I help you?' he said.

'Excuse me?' Rodolfo looked up and, seeing the doctor's querying gaze, straightened. 'Perhaps you can. I am looking for one of your patients. Victoria Woodward. But it seems impossible to get any information.'

'If you would step into my office, perhaps I can help you.'

Dr Harper's secretary watched with raised brows as the two men disappeared into her boss's office.

'Now, let me introduce myself. I'm Dr Harper. Victoria's physician.'

'And I am Rodolfo Fragottini.'

'I know. Prince of Malvarina,' he answered with a smile. 'I figured that if you've made the trip all the way from your island just to find out what's wrong with Victoria, you must have her interests at heart,' Dr Harper said, motioning to the chair opposite his desk while seating himself behind it.

'You are right, Doctor. I am very worried about Victoria.'

'The two of you are close?'

'Uh, we are friends, yes,' Rodolfo replied guardedly.

'Look, I know it's none of my business,' Dr Harper said slowly, 'but she seems a nice kid—a bit lost in all this Hollywood hype. I felt sorry for her. I'd like to think someone's looking out for her.'

'Then tell me where I can get in touch with her and you'll be doing us both a favour.'

'I'm afraid that is ethically impossible,' he said, shaking his head. 'I have no authority to give out any information regarding my patients.'

'At last tell me if she's okay.'

'She'll be fine.'

'Good.' Rodolfo let out a breath and the doctor watched him closely. 'For a minute I thought that perhaps she'd gone back to taking some medication she shouldn't.'

'Medication? Not at all. Victoria merely needs a rest. Look, if you like, maybe I could contact her and mention that you came by here and are trying to get in touch.'

'Would you, Doctor? I would be very much in your debt.'

'Then I will. Give me your number and I'll be in touch later today.'

VICTORIA COULD HARDLY believe it was true. After she ended her phone call with Dr Harper she lay in bed, her pulse racing nineteen to the dozen. Rodolfo here—in LA! Had he read the headlines and come to find out what was wrong with her? Or was it just a coincidence?

And now what was she going to do? She had dreamed of this moment, imagined that by some twist of fate or the waving of a magic wand he would somehow appear. And now here he was—downstairs. Lupita had just told her that he was on his way up.

Victoria dashed to the mirror and looked at herself.

She looked rather pale in her pale pink tracksuit. But never mind. She didn't care. What really mattered was what would happen now. Doubts and fears assailed her. Should she share her secret with him? Tell him she planned to have his child whether he wanted it or not?

At that moment the doorbell rang and she swallowed, sat down on the sofa and curled her legs under her. She didn't want to appear anxious. But it was hard not to when her heart was pounding so hard in her chest that she wondered it couldn't be heard out loud.

'Victoria.' Suddenly the room was filled with his presence. And as he stood on the threshold, tall and handsome in a well cut linen suit, Victoria found it hard to take her eyes off him. She longed to jump up and rush into his arms. Instead she exerted incredible self-control.

'Hello, Rodolfo,' she said casually, getting up as he crossed the room.

'Hello, *cara*,' he said, taking her hands in his and kissing her fingers tenderly. 'I came as soon as I heard the news. Are you all right?' He looked her over anxiously.

'I'm fine,' she murmured, basking in the joy of feeling him so close, the familiar whiff of his aftershave leaving her dizzy with delight.

'I insist on knowing exactly what is wrong with you,' he said in a masterful tone.

'Oh, nothing much,' she said, swallowing, ignoring the delicious shivers coursing through her body as their fingers touched, skin met skin and electricity sparked. 'Just a slight *malaise*, that's all. It's been pretty hard work on the set. Then the air-conditioning broke down, and it was unbelievably stuffy. I think that's what did it.'

'Are you sure?' he asked, his eyes piercing hers, as though seeking a truth he knew lay hidden there.

'Yes—well…yes, of course,' she muttered, pulling her hand away, finding it hard to look him straight in the eye. 'Uh, why don't you sit down, Rodolfo and tell me what brings you to LA?'

He thought of lying, of telling her he was here on business, but something inside stopped him. 'I came to find out exactly what's wrong with you, *cara*, and I don't intend to leave until I am satisfied that you are well again.'

'You mean you came all the way from Malvarina just to see if I was all right?' she murmured, her heart missing a beat.

'Yes, *cara*. I needed to know. Tell me, Victoria, it wasn't the pills again, was it?' His eyes bored into hers and she felt her cheeks flush.

'Of course not. I've never touched them again.'

'Good.' He let out a relieved sigh and sat on the plumped sofa next to her. 'That's one positive piece of news at least. But you look peaky—tired. You are overdoing it.'

'As I said, it's been quite tiring on the set,' she mumbled, trying to keep her thoughts straight, to decide what she should and shouldn't say. What would he think if she told him the truth—that she was expecting his baby? Would he be angry? Would he think her a scheming bitch? Would he—? The possibilities were endless, and for a moment she closed her eyes tight, trying to come to terms with his presence, the intensity of it, the need to feel his arms about her, to tell him what was going on in her life. But she was unable to say the words.

Rodolfo caught her off guard and his hand covered hers. 'Tell me, *carina*. I sense that something is wrong. Won't you confide in me?' He slipped an arm about her shoulders and drew her close. Victoria felt tears surface and swallowed. The scent of him, the nearness of the man she'd learned to care for so deeply left her dizzy. And all at once she realised the truth.

She loved him.

It was so plain to her that she almost gasped.

Why hadn't she realised it sooner?

Because she simply hadn't wanted to admit to herself that she'd fallen head over heels in love with a man who was nothing but a fantasy, a man who lived in a world so distant from hers, a man who was inaccessible. Reality hit—and hurt. So much so that she didn't think she could bear the pain. As his arm held her tighter and he turned her face up to his she found it hard to hold back the tears.

'What is it, *cara*?' he said, seeing the tears and frowning. 'What is the matter Victoria *mia*?'

Then, before she could answer, his lips sought hers, tantalising and warm, sending shafts of raw desire arrowing to her core. Unconsciously she slipped her arms around his neck, let out a sigh of longing and melted in his arms, succumbing to his touch as his fingers travelled up her ribcage, sought the tips of her taut breasts with an urgency that matched her need to be satisfied. When he reached them she let out a tiny cry of delight, gasped when he pulled down the zipper of the jacket of her tracksuit, heard his growl of satisfaction when he realised she wore no bra.

Soon she was lying back amongst the cushions, Rodolfo's mouth lowered to her breast. He flicked her with his tongue, then took the tip between his teeth, causing such delight, such agony and such need that she almost screamed with pent-up longing.

'How I've missed you, *cara*,' he murmured, pulling down the soft fabric of her sweatpants over her hips and letting his fingers linger on the inside of her thigh. Victoria gasped once more as his fingers wandered upwards, feeling her, sensing her needs, until he reached her, felt the soft warmth of her and slipped inside. 'Ah, you are so delicious, *carina mia*. How I have missed you. How can I be without you? I have thought of you day and night since you left, remembered each moment that you lay in my bed. Every night I lie there and think of you, see your hair upon my pillow and imagine your beautiful face looking up at me.'

'Oh, Rodolfo,' she whispered, as slowly his fingers played and teased until she writhed and, with a sudden intake of breath, swallowed the cry forcing its way from her lips and threw her head back as she came, arching towards him.

'That's right, *cara mia*, become my woman again,' he urged as she shuddered in response. 'We have to finish this, Victoria. I have to make love to you.'

'But we can't—not here, not now,' she murmured, still conscious enough to remember Lupita in the kitchen.

'Yes, we can. Come,' he said pulling her up.

She knew it was impossible to resist him. 'Lock the door,' she murmured.

Quickly Rodolfo marched across the room and turned the key in the lock. Then he returned and undressed her fully. *'Como sei bella,'* he murmured, allowing his hands to flow reverently over the gentle curves of her body. 'How wonderfully beautiful and womanly you are. You know, *cara*, your body has changed from a few weeks ago. Then you were a young girl. Now you have become a woman.'

Victoria shuddered. Surely he couldn't know? Surely it wasn't obvious?

But as she stood naked before him, feeling herself more his than ever before, it was hard to resist the temptation of telling him. Would it be the end of everything? she wondered, watching as quickly he undressed, revealing his sculpted body, and joined her on the couch. No, she decided. Even if she did tell him, first she would make love with him, experience those incredible sensations one more time. After that she would decide what was best.

But for now she would simply be his woman.

CHAPTER NINE

'HAVE SOME WINE,' RODOLFO said, leaning across the table, ready to pour into Victoria's glass as they sat having an early dinner served by Lupita.

'Uh—no, thanks. I don't think I will.'

He frowned. 'Why not? You are not taking any medication, and this bottle of Bordeaux is not to be sneezed at.' He smiled ruefully.

'Thanks, but I'm not in the mood. I have to work tomorrow.'

'Work? But that is impossible. You are too weak, too tired,' he exclaimed, reaching his hand and taking her fingers in his.

'Rodolfo, I was quite well enough to spend the whole afternoon in your arms,' she said, a smile curving her lips. 'I hardly think I can do that then make up excuses to Ed when the whole progress of the movie depends on my presence.'

'You are very responsible, *cara mia*,' he said with a shrug. 'I suppose, though I hate to admit it, you are acting correctly. But still, when I look at you, I get the feeling that you are somewhat fragile. I can't explain why.'

Victoria took a deep breath. This was the moment to

tell him the truth. The time had come, and she must face whatever consequences her words might bring. Nervously she fingered her napkin and prayed for courage.

'Rodolfo, there is something—something I have to tell you. I—' She cut off and swallowed, felt her heart racing and took a deep breath. 'It's not easy to tell you this. I didn't know what to think myself, except that now—'

'What are you saying, Victoria? Please be plain in your speech.'

'Sorry. I'm making a botch of it, I know, it's just that, well—'

'Victoria, I beg you,' he urged, frustrated. 'Is something wrong?'

'Not wrong, exactly.'

'Then what is it?' He leaned forward, his gaze pinning hers.

'I'm going to have a baby.'

'You're going to *what*?' Rodolfo sat motionless, watching her. His face turned pale.

'That's it. That's what I was trying to tell you. I'm pregnant. I'm going to have a baby.'

'So that is it.' He got up, threw down his napkin on the table and stared coldly at her. 'I should have guessed. Should have known when I didn't hear from you that as soon as you got back you would find another—' Rodolfo stopped abruptly, moved to the huge panoramic window and stared blindly out across the canyon.

He was an idiot, a fool. He should have known that once she was let loose in this town she would find herself a new lover. And now she was pregnant. No wonder she hadn't wanted to see him. He let out a harsh laugh and shook his head. It was typical. Probably some young actor. He had merely been feeding an illusion. She was not the innocent, lovely creature he'd been dreaming of all this time, but just another Hollywood star out to have fun and probably fit in a few marriages along the way.

Then he remembered their tryst of earlier this afternoon and he turned, looked across at her witheringly. 'You are despicable,' he said at last. 'At least you could have been honest and told me this before going to bed with me while carrying another man's child. Surely you must have some sense of loyalty?'

'Another man's child?' she whispered blankly. Then all at once she realised what he was implying. She sat frozen at the table, unable to react. This was worse, far worse than anything she had imagined. He seemed so angry, so disgusted with her. As though instead of bearing the seed of their love inside her she carried a monster—something to be ashamed of. Then all at once a rush of anger swept over her. Pride and pain came to her rescue.

'I see that you are truly the playboy you are portrayed to be,' she threw through clenched teeth. 'I was hesitating to tell you, and I was right. You are not worthy of my confidence and I would have done far better to have remained silent rather than told you. The thing is that I had some misguided idea that you should be told the truth.'

'What for? I think you are very well able to take care of yourself. Or maybe your new lover will. In fact I had better be going before he turns up. We wouldn't want any problems, would we?' he threw ironically. Then, picking up his jacket, he turned, and without another word slammed out of the room.

Victoria sank onto the sofa and buried her face in her hands. What had she done? How had she managed to give him the impression that the child was someone else's? And now it was too late.

She knew now that she had decided to keep the baby she had to tell Anne the truth. She was not about to give up her career, but she would have to be more careful, and the news would have to be carefully handled in the media. With that in mind she lifted the phone and dialled.

'YOU HAVE TO BE KIDDING?' Anne's eyes nearly popped out of her head. 'That's all I needed. And you're sure you want to keep it?'

'Of course I'm sure. If I wasn't I wouldn't even have told you about it.'

'But think of the publicity. Gee, everyone's going to want to know who the father is. Which reminds me— who is he?'

'It's nobody's business,' Victoria muttered.

'That's all very well, hon, but if you think the press are going to let you off the hook just like that, you've got another think coming. They'll hound you until they find out. So you'd be better to tell me now, and at least I can do some containment.'

Victoria thought about it and realised she was probably right. 'Okay. It's the Prince,' she said at last, her eyes filled with tears.

Anne listened carefully, a speculative gleam in her

eyes. 'The Prince, huh?' She'd heard he was in town and had visited Victoria. Lupita had informed her. This was all taking on a new dimension. 'Tell me, have you told him the good news?' she asked.

'As a matter of fact, I have,' she replied bitterly.

'Doesn't sound like he was too happy.' Anne pulled out her Palm Pilot and quickly checked something.

'Happy? He never gave me a chance to explain. He's convinced that I came back here to Hollywood, found myself a new lover and got pregnant.'

'What a mess. Why didn't you tell him he was wrong?'

'He never gave me the chance. He simply marched out of the door before I could even begin to explain.'

'Men.' Anne shook her head and sighed. 'Bunch of morons. Look, I guess if he isn't going to recognise the child we'd better keep things hush-hush for now. Anyway until I get a game plan together. I say we don't even tell Ed.'

'What happens if I feel awful on the set again?'

'I'll think of something. Don't worry. I'm just glad you told me, Vic.'

Victoria felt better now that she'd shared the news with Anne. In her own way the woman was trying to protect her. But her anger at Rodolfo was simmering. How she wished she could tell him straight out what she thought of him in a few pithy words.

But it was unlikely she would get that chance.

WHEN HER PHONE CALL with Victoria had ended, Anne took a decision that was not altogether ethical but which she justified in view of the circumstances. Getting in her car, she drove straight to the Los Angeles top hotel where she knew the Prince was staying. It might be hard to get access to him, but she had her contacts in Reception, knew a couple of people who could help her out. Plus she had the Prince's mobile number, which he'd given to her back in Cannes.

Pulling up at the hotel, Anne disembarked and made her way inside the lobby, which was unusually quiet. Several minutes later she was in possession of the number of the Prince's suite, thanks to the help of a diligent bellboy whose palm she'd greased generously.

Now, as she rode the lift, Anne wondered what exactly she was going to say to HRH Prince Rodolfo of Malvarina. After all, technically it wasn't her affair. Should she have made Victoria have a prenatal DNA test before confronting him? Would that have been better?

Well, it was too late now, and she might as well bite the bullet.

Walking down the corridor, she stopped in front of the suite and rang. To her surprise, the Prince himself answered the door.

'Hi. Remember me? I'm Anne Murphy—Victoria Woodward's agent. Could you spare me a moment?' Before he had time to refuse her Anne stepped inside the large living room of the suite, faced him and jumped in at the deep end. 'I heard the news. Vic just told me.'

'I see. And in what way does it concern me?' he asked coldly.

This man was too good-looking for words! Anne reflected, swallowing. No wonder Vic had fallen for him.

'I would say that it concerns you in every way possible,' she said. 'May I sit down?'

'Of course. What exactly do you mean? I fail to understand the connection, but go ahead.'

He sat stiffly opposite her, looking, she had to admit, extremely regal and daunting.

'Well, for one thing I think I'd want to know if a woman was carrying my baby,' she said with a sniff.

'Then address yourself to the baby's father,' he replied with a careless shrug.

'That's exactly what I'm doing.'

'What do you mean?' He frowned and his brows drew together in a thick line above his aquiline nose.

'That you are the father.'

'What?' Rodolfo rose so abruptly that he almost upset the chair.

'Yeah. Sorry to burst your bubble, Prince. But, hey—' Anne raised her hands and shrugged '—these things happen. It takes two to tango, as they say, and I guess you guys just should have been more careful.'

'How do you know this?' he queried, his voice deadly quiet.

'Because Victoria told me, and she's not in the habit of lying,' she replied with a touch of irony. 'You know, I don't know what kind of opinion you have of her—by the looks of it, not great—but she's a good kid, straight as an arrow. In fact I'd be surprised if she'd ever been to bed with anyone before you,' she threw, in a sudden moment of perception.

Rodolfo swallowed and his pulse raced. This couldn't be happening. Had he got it all wrong?

'Anne, I think we need to talk. If you are serious about Victoria being pregnant with my child, then that changes the whole face of the matter.'

'Thought it might.' She nodded wisely. 'But I wouldn't count on Vic being too cooperative any more. Looked as if she was ready to slaughter you, the last I heard from her. It'll take some ingenuity on your part to bring her around. She's on her high horse—says she doesn't need anyone to help her out, she'll bring the kid up by herself, thank you very much.'

'Bring my child, the heir to Malvarina, up by herself? Why, has she gone mad?' He stalked about the room. 'We shall have to talk at once. I will go over there and see her—put an end to this nonsense at once.'

'Oh, yeah? Got any plans in mind?' Anne asked casually.

'Plans? Why, of course. There is only one possible plan.'

'And that is?'

'Marry her.'

Anne stuck her tongue in her cheek and gave a satisfied nod. 'If she'll have you,' she said thoughtfully.

But she was already rubbing her hands with glee at the thought of what a publicity coup this would be. Wow, she'd never thought anything like this could take place ever again. Yet here it was—a sort of repeat of the Grace Kelly story. Why, the whole nation would be in an uproar.

'I DEMAND TO SEE HER,' Rodolfo told Lupita, whose short, wide form blocked his passage into the apartment.

'You no see Miss Vicky. She say no want see you. *Siento mucho.*' Lupita made as though to close the door in his face, but Rodolfo quickly leaned his hand against it.

'*Señora*, please,' he said, using all his royal charm. 'I must see the *señorita* Vicky immediately. It is terribly important.'

'But she no want see you,' Lupita insisted, shaking her wide-cheeked face decisively. '"No prince,' she say me. *No, no, y no.*' She waved a hand demonstratively.

Rodolfo was at a dead end. Should he try and bribe the woman? No. By the looks of it she was totally loyal to Victoria. Then another idea occurred. '*Señora*, Victoria is not well. I have a cure for her illness. That is why I am here.'

'You prince, not doctor,' Lupita said witheringly.

'But still, I know exactly how to cure her—to make her *feliz*—happy.' The woman relented slightly and he knew he'd scored a point. 'Look, please—*por favor*. Just a few minutes. *Cinco minutos.* If she really doesn't want me to stay I promise I'll leave.' He smiled once more, that irresistible smile that had melted so many hearts.

'*Bueno.*' Lupita rolled her eyes reluctantly and, stepping away from the door, let him in. 'But only *pocos minutos*—okay?'

'Of course,' he replied, stepping inside and straightening his jacket. Now it was up to him.

'WHAT THE HELL are you doing here?' Victoria demanded, rising from the sofa and looking him up and down from head to toe, eyes narrowed, her arms crossed firmly over her chest.

'I've come to apologise,' he said quietly. 'There has been a terrible misunderstanding. I am entirely to blame. I should have realised at once what you were trying to tell me.'

'Don't worry. I won't hold you responsible,' she said haughtily. 'I realise that this will be my baby and mine alone. I know you probably want me to get rid of it, but I'm afraid I can't do that. I love it already.'

'Get rid of it?' Rodolfo's brows came together as a wave of tenderness swept over him. He wished he could go to her, take her in his arms and make it all right. But he knew that right now that wasn't an option. He looked at Victoria, saw the flushed cheeks, the proud way in which she held herself. He would simply have to attack.

'Victoria,' he said firmly, 'I demand a proper explanation.'

'I just gave you one.'

'You told me you were pregnant,' he said coldly. 'You did not inform me as to the identity of the father.'

'The iden—' Victoria gasped and sat down, feeling suddenly dizzy.

'Rodolfo, I shouldn't have had to spell this out for you. *You* are the father. That should have been obvious to you from the start. Not that it matters, as you will not be expected to assume any responsibility now or ever for this baby. Mercifully, I can provide very well for it. What really hurts,' she said, looking up and meeting his gaze full-on, 'is that you believed me capable of betraying you with somebody else when—'

'*Ay Dio*, what have I done?' Rodolfo crossed the room in a few swift steps and grabbed her hands in his.

'*Carina*, forgive me, I beg you. I am a fool, an idiot. It's just that I could never imagine such a thing. I—you must forgive me.' He shook his head. 'I am stupid and proud, and used to women who would sleep with me and with others at the drop of a hat.'

'Women like Alexandra?' Victoria said, unable to hide the flash of jealousy.

'*Cara*, since you came into my life there has been no one, my love. But now we must think clearly. You say you are carrying my baby. But, *cara*, that is wonderful.'

'Are you sure you think it's wonderful?' she asked warily, amazed at his sudden *volte face*. 'A few minutes ago you didn't seem too happy with the news.'

'That is because I thought you were carrying another man's child. This is different.' He raised her fingers to his lips and kissed them one by one. 'You must leave the movie immediately and return with me to Malvarina. I have to have you where I can take care of you and my child.' His hand slipped to her belly and their eyes met.

'Ah, no, Rodolfo. Not so fast. An hour ago you were barely speaking to me; now you want me to turn my life upside down and follow you. I can't just up and leave in the middle of a movie. Plus, I don't know if I want to go to Malvarina.'

'Not want to go to Malvarina?' he exclaimed haughtily. 'What do you mean?'

'I have a career. I can't just give it all up.'

'Even to become Princess of Malvarina?' he said, holding her hand in his and gazing into her eyes. 'Victoria, I ask you formally. Will you do me the honour of becoming my wife?'

Her heart stopped. She couldn't speak. Was this real? Was Rodolfo, the man she loved and would love for ever, whom a few minutes ago she'd believed she was going to lose for ever, asking her to marry him, to become his princess? She hadn't even allowed herself to dream of anything like this, for it had seemed too impossible. But now he was here, begging her on bended knee.

'I—'

'Answer me plainly, Victoria. Will you be my wife and the mother of my children or not?' His gaze was stern and demanding now, and she caught her breath.

'Yes,' she whispered, overcome. 'I will. But first I must finish what I came to do.'

'We'll see about that,' he growled. Then, leaning down, he swept her into his arms. Their lips met in a kiss so passionate and so tender that Victoria felt dizzy once more.

But this time with emotion.

Now there was nothing left to worry about, nothing to yearn for. For all her most fantastic wishes had come true at last. All that remained was for them to ride off into the sunset of a magical enchanted future.

To Katrina, who made reseaching this book
in Cannes such fun!

MARRIAGE SCANDAL, SHOWBIZ BABY!

Sharon Kendrick

MATT & JEN IN RED CARPET SHOWDOWN!

Hollywood superstars Matt and Jen surprised fans when they both turned up to their film premiere in Cannes yesterday, despite their recent acrimonious breakup. The tension was fierce between them, but they put on brave smiles for the cameras and even sat next to each other throughout the steamy movie

CHAPTER ONE

A THOUSAND FLASHGUNS LIT the sky and the Mediterranean night was turned into garish day as the crowd surged forward.

'*Jennifer!*' they screamed. '*Jennifer!*'

Jennifer paused and smiled, the way the studio had taught her—"Don't show your teeth, honey—they're so English!"—but the irony of the situation didn't escape her. You could be adored from afar by so many—yet inside be as lonely as hell.

She placed one sparkle-shoed foot on the step of the red carpet—the famous red carpet which slithered down the steps of the Festival Theatre like a scarlet snake. Oh, yes. A snake. Lots of those around at the Cannes Film Festival.

At the back of the building lay the fabled promenade of La Croisette, where lines of palm trees waved gently in the soft breeze. Beyond foamed the sapphire-edged waters of the Mediterranean, into which the evening sun had just set in a firework display of pink and gold. But, despite the warmth of the May evening which caressed her bare shoulders, Jennifer couldn't stop the tiptoeing of regret which shivered over her skin.

Memories stayed stubbornly alive in your head, and

you couldn't stop them flooding back—no matter how hard you tried. She'd been in Cannes with Matteo during that first, blissful summer of their ill-fated romance, and she associated the whole dazzling coastline with him. Matteo had introduced her to the South of France and the heady world of films—just as he had introduced her to white wine and orgasm. Everything in life she thought worth knowing he had taught her.

'You okay, Jen?' came the gruff voice of her publicist, Hal, who—along with an assistant, had been shadowing her like a bodyguard all day, as if afraid that she wouldn't actually turn up for the screening of her film tonight. And, yes, she'd been tempted to hide away in the luxury of her hotel room—but you couldn't hide from the world for ever. Sooner or later you had to come out—and it was better to come out fighting!

Weighted by her elaborate blonde hairstyle, Jennifer dipped her head so that her low words could be neither lip-read nor heard by the crowds who were pushing towards her from behind the barrier ropes.

'What do you think?' she questioned softly. 'I'm being forced to parade in front of the world's media and pretend I don't care that my husband has been flaunting his new lover.'

'Hey, Jennifer,' said Hal softly. 'That sounds awfully like jealousy—and you were the one who walked out of the marriage, remember?'

And for good reasons. But she knew it was pointless trying to explain them. People like Hal thought she was mad. They had told her in not so many words that she couldn't *expect* a man like Matteo to be faithful. As if she should just be grateful that he had cared enough to put a shiny gold band on her finger. Well, maybe her expectations were higher than those of other people in the acting world, but she wasn't about to start lowering them now.

'It's just harder than I thought it would be,' she murmured.

They'd only split six months ago, and yet already the press had started describing her as 'lonely' and 'unlucky in love'—because, unlike Matteo, she had not fallen straight into the arms of a new lover. Maybe it was different for women. Didn't they say that men recovered more quickly from a break-up?

Her pride had been wounded and she wasn't sure she was ever going to be able to replace the man who had been her husband—though that was what the world seemed to want. She just wanted to get through this first public appearance at the world's most famous film festival—then surely anything else would be easy-peasy. Please God, it would.

'*Jennifer!*' screamed the crowd again.

'Don't even *attempt* to sign autographs,' warned Hal. 'Or there'll be a riot!'

'You mean there isn't already?' she joked.

'That's better,' Hal murmured approvingly. 'Just keep smiling.'

But as Jennifer began to slowly mount the staircase she heard different voices, which somehow managed to penetrate the clamour of her fans. The clipped, intrusive tones of professional broadcasters. Here we go, she thought.

'*Hey, Jennifer—have you met your husband's new lover yet?*'

'*Jennifer! GMRV news! Any plans for a divorce?*'

'Jen—are the rumours that Sophia is pregnant true?'

Pregnant? Surely that must be some kind of cruel joke? Jennifer gripped onto her sapphire silk clutch-bag so hard that her knuckles showed up white, but then she automatically relaxed them just in case a camera should pick up the tell-tale tension.

'Jennifer—how do you feel about seeing your husband here tonight?'

At first Jennifer thought that she must have misheard the last statement—her ears playing tricks with her and plucking a wrong note from out of the sea of sound. Matteo wasn't here tonight—he was miles away, in Italy, and she had agreed to attend the Festival because she had known that. They hadn't seen each other in months, and Jennifer was still emotionally wobbly. She wasn't naïve enough to think that their paths would never cross, but had just hoped that it would be without an audience. Especially so soon.

Like a child swimming in choppy waters and searching for a life-raft, she looked round at Hal—but the sudden frozen set of his shoulders made her tense with a terrible growing suspicion.

She tried to catch his eye, but he was steadfastly refusing to meet her gaze. And then the press pack were closing in again, and Jennifer's gaze was drawn upwards, as if compelled to do so by some irresistible force.

Until she saw him—and her ears began to roar as the world closed in on her.

It couldn't be. Please, God—it just couldn't be.

But it was. Oh, it was—for there was no mistaking the dynamic presence that was Matteo d'Arezzo.

Jennifer felt sick and faint—but somehow she sucked

in a slow breath of oxygen and managed to keep the meaningless smile on her face as she gazed in disbelief at the man who was standing at the top of the red carpet, surrounded by a small bunch of sychophants—as if he were king of all he surveyed.

His Italian looks were dark and brooding, and his body was lean and honed and shown off to perfection in the coal-black dinner suit. Legs slightly parted, his hands deep in the pockets of his elegant trousers, his casual stance stretched the material over his thighs— emphasising their hard, muscular shafts...leaving nothing about his virile physique to the imagination. Long-lashed jet eyes glittered in the olive-gold of his face, and they flicked over her now in a way which was achingly familiar yet heartbreakingly alien.

Jennifer's heart contracted in her chest. It had been so long since she'd seen him. Too long, and yet not long enough.

And women were screaming his name.

Screaming it as once she had screamed it, in his arms and in his bed.

Matteo.

She felt like a mannequin in a shop window—with the look of a real person about her, but a complete inability to move.

But she *had* to move. She had to.

The cameras would be trained on both faces. Looking for a reaction—any reaction, but preferably one which would provide the meat for a juicy story.

She willed some warmth into her frozen smile and began to walk up towards him, thanking her impossibly tight silk dress for the slowness of her steps.

It was a walk which seemed to go on for ever. The roar of the crowd retreated and the blur of their faces merged, and as she grew closer she could see the dark shadowing of his jaw and the cruel curve of his lips. Men like Matteo did not grow on trees, and his outrageous beauty and sex-appeal often made the casual observer completely awestruck. Well, he would not intimidate her as he had spent his life intimidating the studio. He was her cheating ex-husband—nothing more and nothing less—and she needed to take control of the situation.

She lifted her head as she reached him. 'Hello, Matteo,' she said coolly.

To see her was like being struck by lightning, and Matteo could feel the hot rods of desire as he saw the creamy thrust of her breasts edged by silk as deeply blue as the ocean. He tensed, his mind racing with questions as he stared down at his estranged wife.

Che cosa il hell stava accendo?

But his face stayed unmoving, even though his groin had begun to tighten, and he cursed his erection and despised the unfathomable desire which made him so unbearably hard. For there were women more beautiful than Jennifer Warren—but none who had ever made him feel quite so...so...

He swallowed down thoughts of what he would like to do, and how much he despised himself for wanting to do it. Weak was not a word he would ever use to describe himself—but something about the physical spell his wife had always cast over him was as debilitating as when Delilah had shorn off Samson's hair...

What the *hell* was she doing here? And why the *hell* had he not been told?

He knew that the cameras were trained on him—and on her—waiting for their reactions. A flicker of emotion here. A tell-tale sign there. Something—anything—to indicate what either was thinking. And if they couldn't find out, then they'd make something up!

Training took over from instinct and he kept the tightening of his mouth at bay. Only the sudden steeliness of his eyes hinted at his inner disquiet, and that was far too subtle to be seen. He would give them nothing!

The glance he gave Jennifer was cursory, almost dismissive—but visually it was encyclopaedic to a man who had grown up appreciating women, who could assess them in the blinking of an eye. He felt the quickening of his pulse and the silken throb of his blood, for the bright blue silk of her dress clung indecently to every curve of her magnificent body.

For a moment he ran his eyes proprietorially over the soft swell of her breasts and the narrow indentation of her waist, and he did so without guilt. Why the hell should he feel guilt? She was still his wife—*maledicala*—even though her greedy lawyers were picking over the carcass of their marriage.

Two of the Festival staff moved towards him to usher him inside, but he waved them away with a dismissive gesture.

Should he turn his back on her? That was what he *wished* he could do. But he decided against it—for would that not just excite more comment from the babbling idiots who would fill their gossip columns with it tomorrow?

Instead, he gave a bland and meaningless smile as she reached him, and looked down into her sapphire eyes, which were huge in a china-white face and blinking at him now in that way which always made him...

Don't do vulnerable, Jenny, he thought. Don't turn those big blue eyes on me like that or I may just forget all the anger and the rifts and do something unforgivable, like taking you in my arms in full view of the world and kissing you in a way that no man will ever come close to for the rest of your life.

'What the hell are you doing here?' she said weakly.

'Wondering if you're wearing any knickers,' he murmured.

'I'm surprised you haven't worked that out for yourself—women's underwear *is* your specialist subject, isn't it?'

How crisp and English she sounded! Just like when they'd met—and then he'd been blown away by it. That cool wit and ice-hot sexuality. But—like a rare, hothouse flower—she had not survived the move to the tougher climes of Hollywood. Her career had flourished, but their relationship had withered.

'Oh, *cara*, don't you know that when you're angry you're irresistible?'

She wanted to tell him that she didn't care. But it wasn't true. Because if she didn't keep a tight rein on her feelings then she might just let it all blurt out and tell him things that he must never know.

That the pain of seeing him was almost too much to bear, and that in the wee, small hours of the morning she still reached for the warmth of her husband in the cold, empty space beside her.

Then remember, she told herself fiercely. Remember just *why* you've haven't seen him in so long.

'I had no idea you were going to be here,' she said, gritting her teeth behind her smile.

'Snap!'

'You didn't know either?'

His black brows knitted together. 'You think I would have come here if I *had*?' he demanded softly. '*Cara*, you flatter yourself!'

Oddly enough, this hurt more than it had any right to and almost as an antidote to meaningless pain, Jennifer forced herself to ask the question which twisted her gut in two. 'Is your girlfriend with you?'

His mouth hardened. 'No.'

Jennifer expelled a low breath of relief. At least she had been spared *that*. Fine actress she might be, and pragmatic enough to accept that her marriage to Matteo was over, but she didn't think that even she could have borne to see the smug and smiling face of her husband's new lover. 'I'm going inside,' she said, in a low voice.

He gave a cold smile as he walked up the red carpet beside her and into the glittering foyer. 'Looks like we've got each other for company,' he drawled. 'Pity we're both on the guest-list, isn't it, Jenny? I guess that's one of the drawbacks of a couple making a film together and then separating soon afterwards!'

'Matteo!' It was Hal's voice. He had obviously judged it safe to talk to them.

Jennifer and Matteo both turned and—for all their differences—their expressions were united in a cold-eyed assessment of their publicist as he panted his way up the stairs and gave them both an uneasy smile.

Matteo spoke while barely moving his mouth. 'You're history—you know that, Hal,' he said easily.

'You tricked me to get me here, and you bring me face to face with my ex-wife in the most awkward of circumstances. I am appalled—*furious*—at my stupidity for not having realised that you would stoop to this level in order to publicise your damned film. But, believe me, I shall make you pay.'

'Now, let's not be hasty,' blustered Hal.

'Oh, let's,' vowed Jennifer, her bright smile defusing the bitter undertone in her voice. 'This is the most sneaky and underhand thing you've ever done.'

An official appeared by their side, a brief look of perplexity crossing his brow as he sensed the uncomfortable atmosphere. He made a slight bow. 'May I show you to your seats, *monsieur, madame*?'

Matteo raised his elegant dark brows. 'What do you want to do, Jenny? Go home?'

She wanted to tell him not to call her that, for only he had ever called her that. The soft-accented and caressing nickname no longer thrilled her or made her feel softly dizzy with desire. Now it mocked her—reminding her that everything between them had been an utter sham. And did he think she was going to hang her head and hide? Or run away? Was his ego so collossal that he thought she couldn't face sitting through a performance of a film she had poured everything into?

'Why should I want to do that?' she questioned with a half-smile. 'We might as well gain something from this meeting. And at least the publicity will benefit the box office.'

Matteo's mouth twisted. 'Ah, your career! Your precious career!'

Censure hardened his voice, and Jennifer thought

how unfair it was that ambition should be applauded in a man but despised in a woman. When she'd met him he had been the famous one—so well-known that she had felt in danger of losing herself in the razzle-dazzle which surrounded him.

It had been pride which had made her want a piece of the action herself—to show the world that she was more than just Matteo's wife—but in the end it had backfired on her. For her own rise to superstardom had taken her away from him and spelt the beginning of the end of their marriage.

She didn't let her smile slip, but her blue eyes glinted with anger. 'We're separated, Matteo,' she murmured. 'Which no longer gives you the right to pass judgement on me. So let's skip the character assassination and just get this evening over with, shall we?'

'It will be my pleasure, *cara*,' he said softly. 'But you will forgive me if I don't offer you my arm?'

'I wouldn't take it even if you did.'

'Precisely.'

Jennifer had been dreading the première, but it was doubly excruciating to have to walk into the crowded cinema with her estranged husband by her side. All eyes turned towards them with a mixture of expectancy and curiosity as they took their seats in a box. For a few seconds conversation hushed, and then broke out again in an excited babble, and Jennifer wished herself anywhere other than there.

But there was no comfort even when the lights were dimmed, because for a start she was sitting right next to him—next to the still-distracting and sexy body. And the giant image which now flashed up onto the screen made it worse. For it was Matteo. And Jennifer. Playing roles which they must have been crazy to even consider when their marriage had been showing the first signs of strain.

They'd been cast as a couple whose marriage was being dissected in an erotically charged screenplay. There were other characters who impacted on the relationship—but the main one was the other woman. The irresistible other woman, who threatened and ultimately helped destroy the happiness of the couple who'd thought they had everything.

Art imitating life—or was it life imitating art?

It wasn't real, Jennifer told herself fiercely. If she and Matteo had been strong together, then no woman—no matter how beautiful—could have come between them.

But it was still painful to watch. And even if she closed her eyes she couldn't escape, for she could still hear the sounds of their whispered lines, or—worse—the sounds of their faked cries of pleasure. Hers and Matteo's. His and the other woman's. How easy it was to imagine the other woman in his arms as Sophia, and how bitterly it hurt.

Jennifer watched as her own screen eyes fluttered to a close, her lips parting to utter a long, low moan as her back arched in a frozen moment of pure ecstasy.

'I'm *coming*!' she breathed.

All around her Jennifer could hear the massed intake of breath as the people watched her orgasm—watched her real-life husband follow her, his dark head sinking at last to shudder against her bare shoulder.

She closed her eyes to block out the sight and the sounds—but nothing could release her from the torment of wondering what the audience were thinking and feeling. Perhaps some of them were even turned on by the blatant sexuality of the act.

It was a ground-breaking film, but now Jennifer suppressed a shudder. It no longer looked clever and avant-garde, but slightly suspect. What kind of job had she been sucked in to doing—to have stooped so low as to replicate orgasm with her real-life husband while the cameras rolled?

And then—at last—the final line. The amplified sound of herself saying the words 'Now she's gone. And now we can begin all over again.' The screen went black, the credits began to roll and there was a moment of stunned silence as the cinema audience erupted into applause.

The lights went up and Jennifer stared down at her hands to see that they were trembling violently.

'Ah! Did the emotion of the film get to you?' mocked the silken tones of Matteo, and she looked up to see that his eyes were on her fingers. 'You've taken your wedding band off, I see?'

She nodded. 'Yes. I threw it away, actually.'

His black eyes narrowed. 'You're kidding?'

'Of course I'm not.' Jennifer wouldn't have been human if she hadn't experienced a thrill of triumph at the look of shock on his handsome face. But any triumph was swiftly followed by anger. Did he think it a comparable shock to seeing those snatched long-range photos of him kissing Sophia in a New York park?

She turned her blue eyes on him. 'What on earth *does* a woman do with a redundant wedding ring?' she questioned in a low voice. 'I don't have a daughter to leave it to, and I'm too rich to need to pawn it. So what would you suggest, Matteo? That I melt it down and have it made into earrings—or else keep it in a box to remind me of what a sham your vows were?'

He bent his head towards her ear, presumably so that the movement of his lips could not be seen, but Jennifer felt dizzy as his particular scent washed over her senses.

'How poisonous you can be, Jenny,' he commented softly.

'I learnt it at the hands of a grand master!' she returned, as he straightened up and she met his cold smile with one of her own. 'Oh, God,' she breathed, their slanging match momentarily forgotten. 'Here they come.'

Matteo shook himself back to reality, irritated to realise that he had been caught up with watching the movement of her lips and the way that the great sweep of her eyelashes cast feathery shadows over the pure porcelain of her skin. Insanely, he felt himself grow hard.

But he wouldn't beat himself up about it. You didn't have to be in love with a woman to want to...to...

Dignitaries were bearing down on them. He could see a cluster of executives and all the other acolytes that the film world spawned. His eyes narrowed and he turned to Jennifer.

'You're not going to the after-show party, I presume?' he demanded.

'Why not?'

'Perhaps it bothers you that I will be there?'

'Don't be silly, Matteo,' she chided. 'You aren't part of my life any more—why on earth should it bother me?'

His eyes hardened. 'Then we might as well go there together. *Si?*'

That hadn't been what she'd meant at all. Jennifer opened her mouth to protest, and then shut it again. Maybe this way was better. She would have Matteo by her side as they walked down the endless red carpet and into the waiting car. And while he might not have been faithful at least he had always protected her, and she missed that. Badly.

'People will talk.'

'Oh, Jenny.' His laugh was tinged with bitterness. 'People will talk anyway. Whatever we do.'

She met his eyes in a moment of shared understanding which was more painful than anything else he had said to her, for it hinted at a former intimacy so powerful that it had blown her away.

And suddenly Jennifer wanted to break down and weep for what they had lost. Or maybe for what they had never had.

'Come on,' said Matteo impatiently. 'Let's just go and get it over with.'

CHAPTER TWO

SOMEHOW THE LONG SCARLET flight of steps seemed
safer this time around—and so did the legion of press
waiting at the foot of them. As if Matteo had managed
to throw the mantle of his steely strength over Jennifer's
shoulders and was protecting her and propelling her
along by the sheer force of his formidable will.

Even the questions which were hurled at them about
their relationship had somehow lost their impact to
wound her. As if Matteo was deflecting them and bounc-
ing them back with one hard, glittering look and a con-
temptuous curl of his lip which made women go ga-ga
and photographers quake.

The party was in one of the glitziest hotels along the
Croisette itself, but Jennifer found herself wishing that it
was being held in one of the restaurants which lined the
narrow, winding backstreets where Matteo had once taken
her. The *real* Cannes—where such luminaries as Elizabeth Taylor and Richard Burton had eaten. But it didn't
really matter where the party was—she was going to stay
only for as long as necessary and then she was leaving.
That way she would save her face and save her pride.

They were in a room which was decorated entirely
in gold—to echo the colour of the Festival's most pres-

tigious award, the Palme d'Or. The walls were lined with heavy golden silk, like the inside of a Bedouin tent, and there were vases of gold-sprayed twigs laced with thousands of tiny glimmering lights. Beautiful young women dressed in belly-dancer outfits swayed around the room, carrying trayfuls of champagne.

But once she had accepted a drink Jennifer deliberately walked away from Matteo. She didn't need him, and she was here to show him *and* the rest of the world just that. She was an independent woman—why would she need anyone? That was what her mother had always told her, and it seemed that her words had been scarily prophetic.

The party might have had a budget to rival that of a small republic, but it was a crush—and less hospitable than some of the student get-togethers Jennifer had gone to in her youth.

An aging but legendary agent was holding court. A nubile starlet was not only falling out of her dress but also falling over from too much wine, by the look of her. A raddled-looking rock star was looking around the room with a stupid grin on his well-known face and suspiciously bright eyes. And from out of the corner of her eye she saw Matteo being surrounded by a gaggle of glamorous women.

Welcome to the world of showbiz, thought Jennifer wryly. But inside she was hurting more than she could have imagined it was possible to hurt.

She dodged passes, questions, and having her glass refilled—managing instead to find a very famous and very gay British actor who was standing in the corner surveying the goings-on with the bemused expression of a spectator at the zoo. Jennifer had played Regan to his King Lear, and she walked up to him with a sigh of relief.

'Thank heavens,' she breathed. 'A friendly face with no agenda!'

'Hiding from the vultures?' he questioned wryly.

'Sort of. Congratulations on your knighthood by the way. What are you doing *here*?'

'Same as you, I imagine. I may be an old queen— and a knight now, to boot—but I have to please my publicist like a good boy.'

'Don't we all?'

He surveyed her thoughtfully. 'I see you arrived with that adorable man you married—does that mean you're back together?'

In spite of the room's heat, Jennifer trembled—but she was a good enough actress to inject just the right amount of lightness into her voice. 'No. We're just playing games with the press. The marriage is over.'

'Sorry to hear that,' he said carelessly. 'Occupational hazard, I'm afraid. You'll get over it, duckie—you're young and you're beautiful.' He sighed, his eyes drifting to Matteo once more. 'Mind you—so is he!'

Jennifer grimaced a smile. 'Yes.'

'Go home and forget him,' he said gently. 'And stay away from actors—they're feckless and unfaithful and I should know! Marry a businessman next time.'

'I'm not even divorced yet,' she said solidly. 'And even if I were, this thing has scarred me for life—I'm through with marriage. Anyway—better run. Lovely to see you, Charles.'

They exchanged two butterfly air-kisses and then

Jennifer resolutely made her way towards the door and slipped away—not noticing that she was being followed by a Hollywood icon who had just gone through divorce number four.

Not until she was in a quiet corridor and he moved right up close behind her.

Jennifer jumped and turned round. 'Oh, it's *you*, Jack!' she exclaimed nervously. 'You startled me!'

He flashed his trademark smile. 'Well, well, well,' he drawled softly. 'Maybe my luck has changed for the better. You look damned gorgeous.' He crinkled his blue eyes and directed his gaze at her chest. 'So, how's life, Jennifer?'

Jennifer knew that his fame meant he got away with stuff that other men would be prosecuted for, and she should have been used to the predatory way that such men feasted their eyes on her breasts, but the truth was that she didn't think she'd *ever* get used to it. 'I'm fine, thanks,' she said blandly.

'Well, since we're in the same boat, maritally speaking...' His voice dipped suggestively and his swimming pool eyes gleamed. 'It can get a little lonely in bed at night—what say we keep each other company?' And then his eyes narrowed as a shadow fell over him and he looked up into a pair of black, glittering eyes. 'Well, well, well,' he blustered. 'If it isn't the Italian Stallion!'

Matteo wasn't bothered by the star's slurred insult, but he felt a shimmering of intense irritation as he saw the fraught expression on his wife's face. That and the blunt hit of jealousy.

'Are you okay, Jenny?' he demanded.

She wanted to tell him that it was none of his business, but instead she looked straight into his eyes. And, in one of those silent looks between two people who have lived together which speak volumes, her eyes told him that, no, she wasn't okay. 'I was just leaving.'

'What a coincidence,' Matteo murmured. 'So was I.'

The sex symbol frowned in confusion, looking from Matteo to Jennifer like a spectator at a tennis match. 'But I thought—'

'Well, don't,' Matteo interjected silkily. 'You're not paid to think—you're paid to act...pretty badly, as it happens, which is why your career is on the way down.'

And he took Jennifer's hand in a proprietary way which made her momentarily long for the past and loathe herself for doing so as he led her down a corridor.

'What do you think you're doing?' she demanded, shaking him off once they were out of sight.

'You wanted to get away from that *strisciamento*?'

'Well, yes. But not with *you*!'

'Are you certain?' His eyes glittered. 'I've discovered a service lift which bypasses all the press—if you're interested?' He arched his dark eyebrows as they came to a discreet-looking steel door at the end of the corridor which was light-years away from the luxury of the guest lift they'd ridden up in.

'Aren't you the clever one?' she questioned sarcastically.

'But of course I am—we both know that. Coming?'

Jennifer hesitated.

'Unless you're secretly hot for the *bastardo*?' he suggested silkily. 'And want to stick around?'

Jennifer glanced back along the corridor and then stepped into the lift beside Matteo, pointedly moving as far away from him as possible as the doors slid shut on them.

'You're going to have to watch your step, Jenny,' Matteo said softly as the lift began to whirr into action. 'Men like that eat women for breakfast.'

Jennifer stared at him in disbelief. 'How dare you?' she questioned. 'In view of what's happened how *dare* you take a holier-than-thou opinion on another man's behaviour? Have you tried looking at your own lately?' She clenched her hands into two tight fists, her breath coming hot and fast as the words came spilling out of her mouth. 'How's your *girlfriend*, Matteo?'

Matteo's eyes narrowed. 'Jenny, don't—'

'Don't you *dare* tell me "Jenny, don't"! Remind me of her name again.' Jennifer faked a frown. 'Oh, yes— Sophia! Not exactly a household name at the moment, but I guess that'll soon change with the magic of the d'Arezzo influence.'

'You didn't knock it when you used it yourself,' he challenged softly.

'You *bastard*! At least I was known for being a good actress *before* I met you—and not for pouting and lounging around half-naked in some over-hyped perfume advertisement! So, was she worth it?'

Matteo's black eyes flared. Had he meant so little to her that she could enquire after another woman as if she were asking the time? For, while he accepted that their marriage was over, Matteo knew that if he bumped into any lover of *hers* he would want to tear him limb from limb.

'I don't think that's any of your business, do you?' he drawled. 'You wanted a divorce—and you're damned well getting one! Technically, that makes me a free man, Jenny—and at liberty to date whom I please.'

'But you weren't *technically* free in New York, when you started your affair with her, were you, Matteo? When the cameras caught you kissing her?' The words were out before she could stop them and he stared at her, an odd expression in his eyes which Jennifer had never seen before.

'I hadn't slept with her then,' he said slowly.

The use of the word *then* cut through her like a knife. 'But now you have?' She swallowed. 'Slept with her?'

It was both a statement and a question, and there was a long and uneasy pause. For, no matter what the circumstances leading up to the act had been, Matteo knew he had broken his marital vows. 'Yes.'

Jennifer clamped her clenched fist against her mouth as the cold rip of jealous rage tore through her heart. But what had she expected? For him to carry on denying a physical relationship? To pretend that his undeniable attraction towards the stunning Italian starlet had remained unconsummated?

Matteo was a devastatingly attractive and *virile* man. He needed sex like most men needed water. Well, she had asked the question, and she had only herself to blame if he had given her the answer she had dreaded.

She had thought that the pain of their break-up couldn't possibly get any worse, but in that she had been completely wrong. He had said it now. He had slept with Sophia. His body had lain naked against hers, warm skin against warm skin. He had entered another woman, had pushed inside her and moved and then thrown his head back and groaned out his pleasure in the way she knew so well—the way he had done with her.

And spilled his seed inside her? Made this other woman pregnant, like the pressmen had suggested earlier?

Biting against her fingers, Jennifer fought hard to prevent herself from retching. The mind could be a wonderfully protective organ—allowing you to block things out because they were too painful to contemplate—but it could be capricious and cruel, too, and Matteo's words triggered an inner torment as images of his infidelity came rushing in, like some unwanted and explicit porn film.

Jennifer leaned against the steel wall of the lift, beads of sweat gathering above her upper lip as she pictured her husband naked with another woman.

Matteo frowned and made an instinctive move towards her. '*Cara*, you are faint?'

'Don't you *dare* call me that!' she spat, and shrank even farther against the metal, which felt cold against her bare back. She wiped the back of her hand over her clammy face. 'And don't you dare come *near* me!'

A wave of sadness washed over him and he wondered how something which had seemed so perfect could have deteriorated into a situation where Jennifer was staring at him as if he was her most dangerous and bitter enemy.

Maybe he was. Maybe that was what inevitably happened when a marriage broke down. Maybe the myth of an 'amicable' divorce was exactly that—a myth.

He stared at her as she moved a little restlessly, as if aware of how tiny the enclosed space was. Her proximity was distracting. Matteo's senses felt raw—as if someone had been nicking at them with a razor. Yet when he looked at her he felt nostalgic for times past, and that was always painful—for it had never been real.

Because memory played tricks with your emotions. It tampered with the past and rewrote it—so that everyone saw it differently. He knew that Jennifer's version of it would be different from his own, and there was nothing he could do about that.

But maybe that was only part of it. For the eyes didn't lie, did they? He studied her and thought how much time had changed her. Tonight she was all sleek Hollywood film star—her heavy blonde hair caught up in an elaborate topknot with a few artistic tendrils tumbling down around her face. Her gym-tight body was encased in clinging sapphire silk, and she was bedecked in priceless diamond and sapphire jewellery.

How little she resembled the rosy-cheeked girl with tousled hair and bohemian clothes he'd fallen in love with. Was it the same for her? Did she look at him and see a stranger in his face today?

And a floodgate was opened as the reflection triggered a reaction. Forbidden thoughts rushed into his head with disturbing clarity, and Matteo remembered the pure magic of meeting her. Of feeling something which had been completely alien to him.

CHAPTER THREE

MATTEO HAD BEEN FILMING in England. The 'Italian Heart-Throb'—as the newspapers had insisted on calling him—had agreed to play Shakespeare. It had been a gamble, but one Matteo had been prepared to take. He had been bored with the stereotypical roles which had brought him fame and riches, and eager to show his mettle. To prove to the world—and himself—that an Italian-American *could* play Hamlet. And why not? All kinds of actors were switching accents in a bid to show versatility in the competitive international film market. Some had even won awards for doing just that.

Jennifer had been playing Ophelia—but not in his film. She'd been what they called a 'serious' actress—stage-trained, relatively poor, and rather aloof. He had gone along one evening to watch her perform and had been unable to tear his eyes away from her.

They'd been introduced backstage, and he'd been both intrigued and infuriated when she'd given a slightly smug smile which seemed to say *I know your type*.

'I loved your performance,' he said, with genuine warmth, before realising that it made him sound like some kind of stage-door Johnny—*him*!

'Thank you. You're playing Hamlet yourself, I believe?' she questioned, in the tone of someone going through the motions of necessary conversation. Almost as if she was *bored*!

'You do not approve?' he challenged. 'Of someone like me playing one of your greatest roles?'

Jennifer blinked. 'What an extraordinary assumption to jump to! I hadn't given it a thought.'

And he knew that she spoke the truth. For a man who held the very real expectation that every actress in Stratford would be anticipating his visit as if it were the King of Denmark himself, Jennifer's uninterest inflamed him.

She was studying him, her head tilted slightly. 'But your reviews have been spectacular,' she conceded, in the interests of fairness. 'So well done.'

He knew that. Every theatre in the world wanted him, and Broadway was putting irresistible offers on his agent's table. But somehow Jenny's quiet compliment meant more to him than all those things. 'Have dinner with me tonight,' he said suddenly.

Jennifer put her head to one side, her tousled hair falling over her shoulders. 'Why should I do that?'

A stream of clever retorts could yield entirely the wrong result, Matteo realised. For the first time in his life he anticipated that she might do the unthinkable and *turn him down*!

'Because my life will be incomplete if you do not,' he said simply.

'You can't say things like that!' she protested, biting her lip with a mischievious kind of fascination.

'I just did,' he drawled unapologetically.

She stared at him for a long, considering moment. 'Okay,' she said, and smiled.

And there it had been—like all the old songs said—something about her smile.

Matteo had never really believed in love—considering it something which existed for the rest of the world, but which excluded him. He had seen glimpses of it, but never before had he felt the great rush of passion and protectiveness he experienced with Jennifer that day, which had been the beginning of their tempestuous and ultimately doomed union.

And now?

Now he believed that what had happened had been a cocktail of hormones which had combusted at a time in his life when he'd craved some kind of excitement. He had been right all along. Love was not real. It was a story they fed you which sold movies and books. That was all.

Jennifer rubbed distractedly at her forehead. 'This lift is taking for ever.'

He had been so lost in his thoughts that he hadn't noticed.

'Is it?' he questioned, as there was a sudden lurching kind of movement, followed by complete and deafening silence. Matteo looked from the disbelieving accusation in Jenny's eyes to the stationary arrow on the illuminated panel. 'Maybe you're right,' he mused. 'Seems like we've run into a little trouble.'

'Please tell me you're joking.'

'You think I'd joke about something like that? You think perhaps I've set this up?' he demanded. 'Lured you into this lift so that I can be alone with you?'

Jennifer turned glacial blue eyes on him. 'And have you?'

He gave a short laugh. 'Have I? Believe me when I tell you, *cara*, that I can think of a lot more agreeable companions to be stuck with than a woman who does not seem to know the reason of the word "trust"!'

'And I'd rather be with the devil himself than some arrogant and egotistical sex maniac who can't resist chasing anything in a skirt!'

His black eyes narrowed as he felt the bubble of rage begin to simmer up. 'You dishonour me with such a description!' he declared furiously.

'It's the truth!'

'Ah, but it is *not* the truth, and deep down you know that, Jenny! You saw the amount of women who threw themselves at me! It was never the other way round.'

Yes. Those women who would pass him their telephone numbers openly in restaurants, right in front of her face, as if she were just part of the furniture. Or those others, who would use more devious methods to get the attention of the devastatingly handsome actor.

The shop assistants and the flight attendants who would slyly slide him their details. The doctors and lawyers who would invent the need for a meeting with him. It seemed that none of them had any shame—any woman with a pulse wanted her husband.

'Did you ever stop to think what it was like for me, as your wife?' she demanded.

'Of course I did! You made it damned impossible for me to do otherwise!'

'Did you? I think you used to treat it as an amusing little game—batting those gorgeous eyes as if to say, *I'm not even doing anything, and still they bother me!*'

'Oh, Jenny—that was *your* insecurity talking, not

mine. I'd gone beyond the stage where I needed fans to bolster my ego.' His eyes darkened. 'But, beyond refusing to leave the house, the only way to stop women coming on to me was to increase our security—and that brought its own claustrophobia.' There was a pause. 'And anyway, you know damned well that I pushed those women away.'

'But you stopped pushing eventually, didn't you, Matteo?' she questioned, and she felt that familiar pain stabbing at her heart. And although part of her wondered why she was putting herself through yet more pain, she couldn't seem to stop herself. 'When you looked at Sophia. And you wanted her. Are you denying that?'

There was another kind of silence now—fraught and terrible in the already silent lift. Yes, he had been guilty of the sin of desiring another woman, but it should have remained just one of those unacted-upon desires which made up a human life. People were not immune to desiring other people even if they *were* married. Only the truly naïve believed otherwise. And it was the naïve who fell victim to mistaking that forbidden desire for love. Matteo had seen it, and known it for exactly what it was. Unfortunately, Jenny had not.

He had been filming with Sophia, and their on-screen chemistry had been so hot it had sparked off the set. Everyone in the industry had been talking about it. And eventually Jennifer had got to hear about it.

But even if she hadn't developed such an obsession with it their marriage had already been at crisis point. Their work schedules had kept them apart so much that all she'd been getting were reports from the newspapers and photos of him with Sophia. She had picked away at the rumours—like a teenager worrying at a blemish on her face—until eventually her jealousy and suspicions had blown up. Trust between them had already been destroyed by the time he had kissed Sophia.

'You can't deny it, can you, Matteo?' she persisted. 'That you wanted Sophia?'

'What do you want me to say?' he demanded. 'Because by then what I did or didn't do was irrelevant! We were no longer a real couple. We were so far apart from each other that we might as well have been existing on different planets.' He looked at her across the confined space and his dark eyes were sombre. 'You know we were.'

Jennifer bit her lip so that he wouldn't see it trembling, because now there was pain in *his* eyes, too, and somehow that made it worse. It was far easier to think that Matteo was immune to the hurt of their break-up. Because if he shared even a fraction of her heartbreak, then somehow that only emphasised the precious thing they had shared and now lost.

'Oh, what's the point in discussing it? There's nothing left to be said.'

Matteo stilled. 'Well, for the first time in a long time we are of one accord, *cara*,' he said softly.

Another barb. Yet more pain. But Jennifer silently thanked her ability to act as she kept her face from reacting and flicked him an impatient look instead. 'Look, just concentrate on getting us out of this mess, will you, Matt—since you're the one who got us into it.'

'Are you implying that I've trapped you?' he laughed softly.

'No implication,' she answered. 'You have.'

He narrowed his eyes and listened. 'Can you hear anything?'

'Unfortunately, no.'

'Got a phone?'

'No.'

'Me neither. The truly successful never carry phones to events like this, do they?' he mused. 'That would make us far too accessible to the big wide world—and there's always someone to take our messages for us.'

For a moment Jennifer was surprised by the unfamiliar note of cynicism which had crept into his voice. 'Surely Matteo d'Arezzo hasn't become disenchanted with the jet-set world which brought him riches and fame?'

'Isn't that inevitable?' he questioned drily. 'Doesn't it happen to everyone?'

'Not to you.' She shrugged. 'I thought that success was your very lifeblood.'

'Success on its own isn't enough,' he said tightly. 'I don't want to stay on this merry-go-round of a life until it chews me up and spits me out.'

Jennifer blinked. 'I can't believe you just said that.'

He looked at her and his eyes were like chips of jet. 'Was I really so ruthless, Jenny?'

She thought about the way they'd pored over their working schedules like two prospectors who'd just struck gold and now she recognised her own ruthlessness, too. Oh, how stupidly short-sighted you could be when fame came tapping at your door. She shrugged her shoulders. 'Maybe we both were.'

She felt the hot pricking of sweat on her forehead and ran her tongue over parched lips, noticing that his black gaze was trying not to be drawn to them. She hoped to

God that he didn't think she was giving him the come-on. Fractionally, she moved away from him. 'What are we going to do?'

'We don't have a lot of choice. We wait.'

'For how long?'

'How the hell should I know?' Did she think this was easy for *him*? Her standing so close and off-limits—her luscious body barely covered in some flimsy gown which made her look like...

'Do you want to sit down?' he suggested carefully. Because surely that way he wouldn't have to be confronted by the tantalising thrust of her breasts?

Jennifer didn't know if she dared move. She was aware that her panties were growing damp and that if she wasn't careful Matteo would guess. He had always been so perfectly attuned to her body and its needs that his senses would be instantly alerted to the physical manifestations of desire. Briefly, she shut her eyes, summoning thoughts which would kill that desire stone-dead. But it wasn't easy.

'You're okay?' he asked softly.

She opened them. *Think of his betrayal. Of his doing with another woman what he had stood up in church and declared was for her and her alone.* 'Oh, yes—I'm absolutely fine! Just wonderful! I'm trapped in a service lift in a foreign country with my cheating ex-husband. *Exactly* the way I would choose to spend my Saturday night!' She rubbed her fingertips against the necklace which was digging into her throat.

'Why don't you take that off?' he suggested, as he saw the red mark she'd left there. Her skin was moist and a damp tendril of hair was clinging to her neck.

She met his eyes. 'I beg your pardon?'

He gave a snort of savage laughter. '*Madre de Dio*—don't look at me like that!'

'I wasn't looking like anything!'

'Oh, yes, you were,' he contradicted softly. 'With shock and horror written all over your face. As if I were suggesting some kind of striptease when all I meant was that your necklace doesn't look very *comfortable*.' He ran a disparaging glance over the heavy, wide choker which gleamed around her slender neck. 'Studio told you to wear it, did they?'

'Yes.' But he was right. She was aware of the costly gems digging into her flesh, making her feel as if she was wearing some upmarket dog-collar. Blindly, her hand reached up behind her, tried to reach the clasp, but failed—and there was no mirror...

'You want me to do it for you?' he questioned.

Jennifer hesitated, because it seemed almost too intimate a thing to do. The putting on and the taking off of a necklace was the kind of thing a husband did for his wife in the seclusion of their bedroom when they were properly married—not about to enter one of the biggest divorce battles of the year. Yet what choice did she have?

'I guess so. Never has the word "choker" seemed so appropriate,' she added sardonically.

He gave a wry smile. 'Turn around, then.'

But, confronted with the sight of her bare back, Matteo found his mind slipping into forbidden places. He silently cursed as he felt his erection grow even harder, thankful that she couldn't see his face—for he was certain that it had contorted into a pained expression of exquisite sexual frustration.

'You see...ex-husbands do have *some* uses,' he observed evenly, and lifted his fingers to unclasp the necklace, letting it slide into the palm of his hand like a heavy and glittering snake. 'There. Better?'

'Much...thank you.' Jennifer composed her face and turned—noting the dull flush of colour which was accentuating his high cheekbones. She knew what it meant when he looked like that—or at least she thought she did. Was he just getting overheated, or...?

Did he still want her? Was he imagining what they would have been doing in here if they were still married? Him rucking up her dress and pushing at her panties, unzipping himself and thrusting deep inside her, with her back pushed against the steel wall?

Oh, Lord—what was the matter with her? How could the thought of sex with him be so unbearably exciting despite everything that had happened between them? Everything they'd said and thought and done and accused each other of.

'Do you want me to put it in my pocket?' he asked.

'What?' asked Jennifer blankly.

He held the gems up. 'This.'

'Sure.' She nodded her head and turned away, unwilling to watch him slide them into his trousers, some sixth sense telling her what her eyes did not want to see—that he was hard and aroused.

So why did that thought give her some kind of primitive satisfaction instead of shocking her to the core?

As the minutes ticked by she could feel beads of sweat trickling down her back and a faint dampness gathering beneath the heaviness of her breasts. Shifting her position in her high-heeled shoes, she could see the faint sheen on Matteo's olive skin, and she swallowed as their eyes met in an uncomfortable moment of awareness.

'It's hot,' he said huskily.

'Yes.' She looked into his face because there was nowhere else to look. Nowhere to run. The bare steel walls seemed to be shrinking in on them, and suddenly Jennifer was terrified of this false intimacy—frightened of the sensations which were beginning to creep over her skin and the thoughts which were flooding into her head.

She turned away from him and lifted up her fist, pounding it hard on the metal surface of the wall and wincing as she struck.

'Help! Let us *out*!' she called. But the silence was deafening. She raised her voice. 'Let us *out*!'

'Why do you shout when no one will hear us, Jenny?'

'Somebody's *got* to hear us! Because being in here with you is driving me mad!'

'I thought you liked that aspect of our relationship.'

'I wasn't talking sexual!'

His eyes drifted over the hard points of her nipples. 'Weren't you?'

'Oh, can't you keep your mind on something other than your bloody libido?'

Matteo almost smiled. She *was* angry. And she was aroused, too. He knew that with a certainty which only increased his own desire to an almost unbearable pitch. Would he ever again know a woman as intimately as he did this one?

She wished he would stop looking at her. She wished he was anywhere other than here. Because just his presence was making her have the kind of thoughts which were forbidden. Longing thoughts. Wishful thoughts.

'Help!' she screamed again, and this time she began to drum both fists against the wall. 'Please, somebody— *help* us!'

'Jenny, don't—'

But his words inflamed her even more—or maybe she was just in the mood to be inflamed. And seeing his insufferably enigmatic face as he calmly watched her losing it was like pouring paraffin on an already blazing fire. 'I'll do as I damn well please!' she retorted furiously. 'And you can't stop me!'

He wanted to marvel, because this raging woman was utterly magnificent, but he could see from the rapid movement of her breathing that she was in danger of hyperventilating. 'That's enough! Now, stop it,' he said flatly.

'No!' she yelled, and hot, angry tears began to spill from beneath her eyelids. 'No, I won't stop it!'

Swiftly he moved towards her, wrenching her away from the wall, and she whirled round, imprisoned in his arms, and began to beat against his chest instead.

'*Si,*' he urged her softly. 'Hit me. Hit me if it makes you feel better, cara!'

'Bastard!' She slapped him. 'You bloody, bloody cheating bastard!'

'*Si.* That, too.'

'*That's* for that bitch you slept with!'

He took her furious punch without flinching.

'And so is that!'

She made a little roar of rage as she drummed against his chest until her hands ached. And then suddenly her rage became frustration, and all the fight went out of her, to be replaced by a different kind of emotion. She shook her head, trying to deny it, her hands falling as she looked up and saw something change in his eyes, too.

The look of understanding, of empathy, and the fleeting look of sorrow had been replaced by something else. Something she knew all too well and had never thought to see again—even though she had longed for it in the sleepless nights which had followed his departure. And it was wrong. *Wrong.* Oh, so wrong. He had been to bed with another woman!

'Was she better than me?' she demanded.

'Jenny, stop it.'

'No, seriously—I want to know. Did you do it to her lots of times? Like you did to me when we first met?'

He winced as if she'd hit him, and then the need to destroy her foolish fantasy simply overwhelmed him. 'You want to know the truth?' he exploded. 'I did it to her *once*—just once—and it was the biggest non-event of my life. Do you know why that was? Because all I could see was *your* face, Jenny. All I could feel was *your* body.'

'Don't,' she croaked.

'But it's the truth,' he said bitterly. 'It's flawed, and it's not pretty—but it's the way it was.' His black eyes glittered at her bleakly. 'There—doesn't that make you feel better now?'

'Are you kidding?' she demanded. 'It still makes me wretched to think of you with another woman, no matter how much you hated it!'

But that was not the whole truth, for the stark admission had made her tremble with an unwelcome new emotion and her heart began to ache with sadness and regret. How the hell had it all come to this? How could love be so quickly transformed into all these other hateful negative emotions?

His eyes blazed black fire as they roved over her trembling lips. 'You want me,' he declared unsteadily.

'No.' Could he see the terrible need in her? 'No, I don't!'

'Yes. Yes, you do.' He reached out for her and pulled her into his arms in a movement which felt as natural as breathing.

'Stop it, Matteo,' she whispered.

'You want me to do this.' He began to massage the little hollow at the base of her spine, the way he'd always done when he wanted her to relax, and as if she was acting on auto-pilot she shut her eyes.

'Even if I do—we mustn't. We mustn't do this,' she whispered, half to herself. But, oh, the touch of his body made her feel as though great warm waves had washed over her.

'Why not?' he whispered.

'You know why.'

'No, I don't.'

'You do. We're separated.'

'What's that got to do with anything?'

Her eyes fluttered open. 'That...that...woman.'

'I just told you. It is over. Believe me, Jenny—it never even began.'

And Jennifer was so lost in the thrall of the soft black look in his eyes that his betrayal of the other woman thrilled her. Later she would be appalled at how easily she could be seduced. But not now.

Now her lips were parting with a greedy anticipation she could not seem to deny herself as he slowly lowered his head towards hers.

CHAPTER FOUR

IT FELT LIKE A LIFETIME since Matteo had last kissed her, and Jennifer's arms reached up to clutch onto his broad shoulders as if she was afraid that her knees might give way. But only her lips did that—parting in a soft sigh as he began to kiss her.

Because to her horror—but not to her surprise—Matt's touch was like lighting a touchpaper. Jennifer's skin was on fire, and her heart was skittering away with excitement and almost a touch of desperation—like a drowning woman who had kicked up to the surface of the water for one last gulp of sweet air.

I just want one last kiss, she told herself. One last kiss from the man I loved enough to marry. The man I thought I would have children with and grow old with. One kiss—is that so very wrong?

But adults didn't just 'kiss' and nothing more—particularly those who had been married and who were still in the throes of a powerful sexual attraction.

Jennifer tore her mouth away from his as he began to rove the flat of his hand over one swollen breast, circling it over and over again until the nipple felt so exquisitely hardened that she sobbed aloud with frustrated pleasure. 'Matteo!' she gasped.

'*Si.*' He ground the word out in between hot and shallow breaths, scarcely able to believe that this was happening. That he was doing this to her and that she was letting him—and, oh, it was good. Too good. *Madre de Dio*—it had been so long. And it was never as good with anyone as it was with Jenny. He teased her lips with his in a soft and provocative kiss.

With a disbelieving sob she moved her mouth fractionally from his, knowing that this was wrong—worse than wrong—it was a kind of *madness*!

'Matteo, we...we...*mustn't*. You know we mustn't!'

God forgive him, but he used his hands as ruthlessly then as he had ever done in his life. He had never wanted a woman more than he wanted Jenny at that moment. Not even on that first night when he had taken her to his bed. Nor the time when he had been a teenage virgin and the older woman who had seduced him had made him wait. *Because a woman likes a man to wait,* she had purred. Well, there was to be no waiting now—he didn't want it and, to judge by the frantic grinding of her hips, neither did Jenny.

For the first and only time in his life he wanted her so badly that he thought he was about to come in his trousers. But he reined his desire in with a rigid self-control not betrayed in his sensual movements. He drifted his fingers beneath the thin bodice of her dress and took her bare breast in his hand, cupping it experimentally and feeling her knees buckle as she relaxed against him.

'*Oh!*' she squealed.

All she knew was sensation. She felt the rush of pleasure overwhelm her—and somehow all thoughts of this being wrong just melted away. A hunger both sharp and irresistible bubbled inside her like darkest, sweetest honey, and carried her along in its heavy flow as he touched her nipple.

'Matteo!' she gasped again, only this time the word was spoken in wonder and not in half-hearted protest.

Desire was jack-knifing through him in a way that was barely tolerable. He felt the hot pumping of his blood, the frantic pounding of his heart. Could see the gleam of her eyes and the soft moistness of her lips. It was like entering another world—of love and intrigue and lust and betrayal. One where his powers were weakened. And she weakened him. Just as she always had done. Like no one else did.

Stop me, Jennifer, he begged silently as he touched his fingertips to the silken tumble of her hair.

Il Dio lo perdona! He lowered his head, brushing his lips against hers—a fleeting, butterfly graze—giving her time to realise. Time to stop.

But she did no such thing. Her hands moved from his shoulders to his neck, pressing his face closer, so that the kiss deepened almost before he had realised, and she was lacing her tongue with his.

He moved his hand to the fork between her legs and pressed there, hard. She almost jumped out of her skin.

Her words were slurred yet shaky with disbelief. 'Matteo...'

'*Si, cara mia?*'

'You...you shouldn't be doing that.'

He felt her wetness through the silk of her evening gown and closed his eyes. 'Oh, but I should. You know I should. You were born for just this, Jenny. Oh, God!'

She would stop him in a minute. Just a little more of this sweet pleasure and then she would push him away. Her head fell back against the metal wall of the lift as he began to ruck up her dress, and it was so close to her illicit fantasy of earlier that Jennifer almost fainted with pleasure.

His hand was on her bare thigh now.

Stop him.

And now it was moving up to her damp panties. Maybe she would let him bring her to orgasm first, and then she would call a halt to it.

Matteo felt her thighs parting and he could scarcely believe what was happening. *She wasn't going to stop him!*

He said something soft and very explicit in Italian, and Jennifer knew exactly what it meant for she had heard it many times before. It should have made her put the brakes on, halt this madness once and for all. And every ounce of reason in her body was screaming out at her to do just that. But she was so hot and hungry for him—hotter than she had ever been in her life—that she would have died right there and then sooner than not have him do this to her.

She whimpered as he slid her panties across and she heard the rasp of his zip. He rubbed his thumb across her swollen clitoris and Jennifer gave a tiny scream.

And then, to her utter horror—and his—the lift gave a slight lurch and they heard a distant mechanical thrumming.

They stilled as they listened—every nerve-ending straining for the sound that neither wanted to hear. The lift stayed unmoving.

Oh, thank God, thought Jennifer.

'You want me?' he demanded starkly.

Against his neck she nodded her heavy head mutely.

Matteo acted decisively. Ripping apart her delicate panties so that they fluttered redundantly to the floor, he plunged deep inside her and then effortlessly lifted her up so that she could wrap her legs around his back.

He began to move, slowly at first, wanting to prolong it—to make this heaven last until the end of time and then a little longer still. He made a broken little cry as he thrust in and out of her, knowing that he had never been this hard before, feeling her tremble uncontrollably in his arms. He felt the thrust of her hips towards him in unspoken plea, a gesture he knew of old. And Matteo cupped her buttocks and plunged deeper still, hearing her throaty moan of satisfaction.

And then the lights began to flicker, catching fragments of their movements like an old black and white movie. He moved faster still as the lift began to whirr into life.

Jennifer felt herself beginning to come. 'Matteo, no!' she gasped, but she knew in her heart that it was too late. Sensation caught her up and carried her away and she heard his oh-so-familiar groan as he went with her, felt the helpless shuddering of this big man in her arms.

Mixed in with intense relief and pleasure was confusion and anger as Matteo orgasmed inside her—aware that he had just put both their reputations on the line in a way which was scarcely believable. The flickering lights righted themselves just as he withdrew from her, and all he could see was her horrified face. 'Jenny—'

'What have we *done*?' she whispered.

His mouth twisted. Surely it was a little late in the day for regrets? 'You want a biology lesson?'

Her eyes were huge sapphire saucers. 'You seduced me!' she accused hoarsely.

He almost laughed out loud at her temerity. 'I *seduced* you?' he repeated incredulously. 'You may have always had a problem differentiating between truth and fiction, but that really is taking it a little far, Jenny!'

She wanted to hit him again. And she wanted him to make love to her again. Oh, what was she *thinking*? That hadn't even gone close to 'making love'. What had just happened had been a quick wham-bam-thank-you-ma'am.

All it had been about was swift gratification and intense pleasure. On a physical level it had been wonderful—on an emotional one completely empty. She turned her head away, not wanting him to see the shame and self-contempt in her eyes.

'Now what do we do?' she questioned shakily.

So she couldn't bear to look at him now? Was that it? She hadn't been so damned picky when she was grinding her hips against him! 'There's no time for an in-depth analysis,' he grated, as he heard an echoing shout in French from the bottom of the lift shaft and bent to pick up her discarded panties. 'I think we're about to be rescued.'

The blood was pounding at her temples and in her groin, and she closed her eyes in despair. Rescued? Dear God, no.

Despite his anger and misgivings, Matteo knew that he had to take charge—because otherwise this would develop from a regrettable one-off into a drama which could have lasting repercussions. Quickly he adjusted his clothing and raked his gaze over her, a nerve beginning to work at his temple as he saw that the front of her silk dress was dark with the stain of love-juice.

'Damn!' he exploded softly, as he stuffed her tattered panties into his jacket pocket.

She followed the direction of his gaze and blushed a deep scarlet. Oh, how *could* they have? But she saw the detached look on his face and took her lead from it. She would take it in her stride—as he was so obviously doing. Maybe he does this kind of thing all the time these days? she thought bitterly. 'So, now what do I do?'

'Here. Put my jacket on,' he instructed tersely. He helped her wriggle into it and buttoned it up for her as if she were a child.

Frantically she smoothed down what she could of her hair and wiped a finger under each eye, wondering if her mascara had smudged.

For a moment their eyes met, and Jennifer swallowed, wondering whether she would meet contempt or triumph in his. For what man could not be forgiven for feeling either or both those emotions when a wife who was supposed to hate him had just let him have frantic sex with her?

But there was nothing.

Not a clue, not a glimmer of what might be going on inside his head. He was as enigmatic as she had ever seen him—no, more so—and it was like looking into the eyes of a complete stranger.

Her own senses were clouded and confused, and she was having real problems telling fantasy apart from reality. Sex did funny things to you—it transported you back to another place and another time. It must have done. For why else would she have to stop herself from running her fingertips lovingly over the shadowed rasp of his jaw and following the movement with a series of tender little butterfly kisses? The way she'd used to.

Was that because women were made weak and vulnerable by the act of love in a way men never were? Women's bodies and minds were conditioned to mate with one partner—while men were programmed to spill their seed all over the place.

And at that thought Jennifer blanched. Had she remembered...?

Matteo's eyes narrowed. 'You aren't going to faint on me?'

'Faint?' She spoke with a brightness she was far from feeling. 'Don't be silly.'

He shook his dark head with dissatisfaction, because even though his jacket covered her to mid-thigh her cheeks were flushed and her eyes were wild. Her appearance gave away *exactly* what they had been doing. And this *was* a service lift, true, but that didn't guarantee that some sharp-eyed employee looking to make a quick buck wasn't waiting at the bottom armed with a camera or a mobile phone which could transmit an offending picture around the world in minutes. Was he prepared to take the risk? Did either of them dare?

No.

Without warning he bent and scooped her up into his arms, cradling her automatically against his chest so that she could feel the muffled thunder of his heart

'What the hell do you think you're doing?' she demanded.

He thought that was maybe a question she should have asked *before* they'd had that highly charged and erotic encounter, but he chose not to say it. Even thinking about it was making him grow hard again. He shifted position slightly, not wanting her to sense that he had another erection—because having sex with your soon-to-be ex-wife once could be classified as a mistake. But twice? No. That would defy description.

What was done, was done—they just had to deal with the immediate fall-out before they parted again for the last time.

'What do you think is going to happen now?' he demanded. 'That you are just going to stroll out of here with your messed-up hair and your smudged make-up and your rumpled dress? You don't think that will excite some sort of comment?'

She shrugged. 'Well, obviously—but—'

'But what, Jenny? You don't think that anyone with more than one brain cell will put two and two together and come up with exactly the right answer?'

'So what's your solution?'

'That you act! Just act, Jenny,' he urged, as he saw her perplexed frown. 'Act like you've passed out and you're leaning on me—act as if your life depended on it.'

And maybe it did, in a way—when she stopped to think what he'd just said. Certainly her reputation and her dignity demanded that she emerge from that lift not looking as though she had been ravaged by her unfaithful ex-husband.

The lift juddered to a halt, and it was worse than Matteo had anticipated. Outside was an excited crowd of four waiters, a couple of chefs, what looked like a maître d' and a cleaner.

But no one from the studio. Thank God. He knew that their giant protective machinery would have whirred into action to minimise the outcome, but then it would be out of his control. And he would not let that happen. Not in this case.

He saw one of the waiters surreptitiously slide a mobile phone from his jeans and spoke in furious and rapid French to him. The chastened man shrugged and replaced the phone.

Jennifer's ear lay against the strong pounding of his heart and she closed her eyes—Matteo's words seemed to come at her from a great distance. His French was as fluent as his English, and she didn't even attempt to understand what he was saying, only knew that there was an excited and jabbering response from the staff.

He bent his head and whispered in her ear. 'Don't worry,' he said softly in English. 'You're going to be okay.'

She wished he wouldn't talk in that masterful and protective way to her, even though he was being both those things. But it was going to make it harder, she just knew it was—so much harder to say their inevitable goodbyes.

She opened her eyes to find that they were following someone down a long and draughty corridor and then outside, through an ill-lit yard which was lined with bins and a large skip containing hundreds of empty bottles.

We must be at the back of the hotel, Jennifer thought, and pressed her head against him as an overwhelming fatigue began to wash over her. But then sex with Matteo always made her sleepy. What was that she had read once? That some hormone was released when you orgasmed, which made you want to curl up and snooze.

'You okay?' he asked.

'You bring me to the nicest places,' she mumbled, and gave a low laugh.

The sound was so delightfully inappropriate that Matteo couldn't prevent the memory which stole over his skin as he remembered the precious gift of laughter which they had brought to each other in the early days. Ruthlessly, he blocked it.

'It won't be much longer,' he said tightly. 'They're getting hold of a car for us.'

She had to stop herself from snuggling up to him, as if they were real lovers instead of estranged spouses who just happened to know the way to turn each other on.

'I ought to get back to the Hedoniste,' she said unenthusiastically.

'That's where you're staying?'

'Isn't everyone?'

Matteo's mouth twisted with scorn. The marble-built palace of a hotel was situated on the choicest part of the Croisette, and would be full to the brim with other actors, producers, directors, models and wannabes. 'No,' he said shortly. 'It's too much of a goldfish bowl—you can't risk going back there in that state. I'm taking you to where I'm staying.'

He wasn't asking her whether she'd like him to. He was *telling* her, in that autocratic manner which came naturally after a lifetime of having people run around after him. But Jennifer was too tired and too confused to argue—and, if the truth were known, she was glad that he had taken over.

Somehow he had managed to commandeer the use of a luxury car, and he settled her in the soft leather seat beside him, adjusting his jacket so that it modestly covered her and then barking out a terse instruction in French as the vehicle began to move away.

Dreamily, Jennifer turned her head to watch out of the window as the glittering crescent of coastline sped by in a blur of lights. They passed the cool marble splendour of the Hedoniste—and suddenly Jennifer was relieved that they weren't going near it, with its hordes of paparazzi and heaven only knew who else.

'Where's your hotel?' she questioned.

Matteo stared out of the opposite window—anything to avert his eyes from her, and from the knowledge that she was all rumpled, her dress all stained...by *him*... His fingertips were still sticky and warm from having been inside her, and if he drifted them close to his face her particular feminine scent pervaded his nostrils with a potency which made him hard all over again.

'It's not really a hotel.' He swallowed as the car swept through wrought-iron gates, past the dark shapes of lemon trees and cypress.

In the bright moonlight she could see that the hedges were fantastically shaped, and there was an odd-looking sculpture which was emphasised by soft lights pinned into a nearby tree. It looked old and very beautiful, and Jennifer blinked at it in astonished surprise.

'What is this place?' she asked quietly.

'It was once a villa belonging to one of Cannes's most famous residents—an English aristocrat who discovered the perfect climate here, and the stunning beaches. Now it is owned by an eccentric Frenchman—who will let rooms out, but only if the mood takes him.'

He turned his head and saw her looking down at her crumpled state of undress. 'He is very particular and very discreet,' he added. 'There will be no need to be seen by him, or by anyone else for that matter. One is able to bring guests to a place like this without the whole world knowing. For people in the public eye it is a godsend.'

She couldn't stop torturing herself with images of him bringing other women here in the future. Perhaps similarly unclad, and also recipients of his remarkable brand of lovemaking.

But Jennifer knew that she couldn't bring the subject up—certainly not now, when she was already feeling so vulnerable. The sex had been a mistake—but there was no need to compound that mistake by starting to quiz him about his future plans. That would only make her self-esteem tumble and put her in an even more vulnerable position.

Matteo had every right to do whatever he wished. Sex gave you no rights—not even if it was with the man to whom you were still legally married.

But then she remembered what he'd said about Sophia—and for the first time she was able to think about the actress without feeling sick. Had it been true what Matteo had said, about it only being the once and thinking about *her* all the while? Should the fine detail actually matter?

Of course it *mattered*. A one-off mistake—if that was really what it was—was completely different from a long-term affair which had been shrouded in secrecy and deceit.

But in a way that was worse—because it gave her a faint flicker of foolish hope that maybe the relationship wasn't doomed after all. But it was. Too much had been said and done to ever go back. A bout of wonderful sex wasn't a cure-all. Their marriage was in its death-throes, and that had just been one final, bewitching puff of life breathed into it.

She had to take responsibility for what had just happened between them back there, and then let it go.

But as he led her up a carved wooden staircase which was scented with sandalwood, Jennifer felt a very real shiver of fear ice her skin. *What if she wasn't able to just let it go?*

Well, you don't have the luxury of choice, she told herself. You'll have to.

At least the room was exquisite enough to distract her from her uncomfortable thoughts—with tall, shuttered windows which led out onto a moon-washed balcony. In the distance she could see the coloured glimmer of the town—like a muted version of the fireworks which would later explode in the night sky as part of the Festival celebrations.

'Oh, it's beautiful,' she said automatically, and turned round to find that he was watching her. She gave a nervous kind of laugh. 'What the hell am I doing talking about the view? Isn't this the kind of situation where you wish you could just wave a magic wand and suddenly it's different?'

'Don't you think I spend most of my life doing that?' he questioned bitterly.

'Matt—'

He shook his head. 'Let's not waste any time with re-criminations. There's no point.'

'No. But I have to say this. Thanks for...rescuing me and bringing me back here.'

'A while back you were angry with me for having had my wicked way with you.'

She didn't answer straight away, but she knew that she couldn't continue to act like an innocent little virgin who had been coerced into something against her will.

'Maybe I was angry with myself, for having allowed it to happen.'

'*Si*,' said Matteo slowly, in an odd kind of voice. 'I can understand that.' He gave the ghost of a smile. 'So, let's forget it ever happened, shall we?'

'Yes,' she said slowly, hoping her pain didn't show. 'Let's.'

He stared at her, washed pale by the moonlight. 'You can stay here—there's no way you can appear at the Hedoniste tonight—not looking like that.' His black eyes were hard and glittering as he saw her lips part in protest. 'Oh, don't worry, Jenny,' he drawled. 'We won't have to endure the temptation of sharing. I'll see if there are any more rooms available. Jean-Claude is bound to have something.'

'But I don't want to kick you out of your suite!' she protested.

His lips curved in a smile which was almost cruel. 'Then what else would you suggest?' he taunted softly. 'That I sleep on the sofa? Or perhaps we vow to share opposite sides of that huge bed?' He nodded his black head towards its satin-covered expanse. 'Want to try it, Jenny?'

And show him what a walk-over she was?

'Forgive me if I pass up your delightful offer,' she said tightly, and heard his bitter laugh as the door closed behind him.

But after he'd gone, reaction to all that had happened set in and a wave of lassitude washed over her. Her head was spinning and her limbs were aching, but really she ought to go and 'freshen up'. To remove all traces of Matteo from her body. If only you could take a bar of soap and scrub your heart clean at the same time.

Outside, she could hear the sound of circadas as she kicked off her shoes and wriggled out of her dress, letting it fall carelessly to the floor. She didn't care. The designer who had loaned it to her for free publicity would let her keep it. And given the state it was in she was going to *have* to keep it—but she knew she would never wear it again. How could she? She would never be able to look at it again without remembering...

Naked and shivering, she washed her hands and face and then poured herself a glass of wine from the heavy decanter which stood on the antique table by the window.

She meant to take only a sip, but the blood-red liquid filled her with a fleeting peace and contentment and she finished the glass and went over to the bed.

It was a typical Matteo bed, with a novel lying half-open on the pillow. She looked at it with interest until she saw that it was Italian and she didn't understand a word. But when was the last time she had read a book? She'd used to devour them in those days before the merry-go-round of publicity had filled her every spare hour.

On the bedside table was his mobile phone, and for a moment she was sorely tempted to flick through it and look at the messages. But she resisted. Dignity, Jennifer, she told herself sleepily. Try to retain just a little bit of dignity.

She sat down on the bed, moved the novel to one side and lay down, putting her head on the soft pillow. In a minute she would go and wipe off her make-up, but for now the room was spinning. She groaned and shut her eyes. Please make everything all right, she prayed. Let this all be over without any more pain—and please don't let me dream of him. Especially not tonight. Just let me have one night off from the tempting beauty of his dark face.

She hadn't been intending to sleep, nor to dream. But she did, and it seemed that her dreams were impervious to her pleas. One came to her which was frighteningly vivid. Through half-slitted eyes she could make out his lean, dark body bending over her. The raw, feral scent of him drifted upwards towards her nostrils.

She writhed against the mattress, holding her arms up, wanting him to stay with her. 'Matt,' she moaned softly. 'Oh, Matteo.'

When she awoke it was morning—with sunlight coming in bright horizontal shafts through the slats of the shutters. Jennifer sat up, blinking as she looked around the room. But the bed was empty, and so was the chaise-longue which lay underneath the window.

Her eyes strayed to the ornate wardrobe door, from which hung a floral sliver of a dress in layers of silk-chiffon in her favourite pink, and a pair of sandals which matched perfectly. Jennifer frowned. Where the hell had that come from? Had the good fairy flown into the room overnight and waved her wand?

Slowly, she got out of bed and went over to investigate. As well as the dress there was a matching bra and pants set, and Jennifer did not have to look at the size to know that they were exactly her measurements. And that somehow Matt had got hold of them at some god-forsaken hour and left them here for her.

And then she found the note.

Jenny. You looked too peaceful to wake and I found myself another room for the night. Don't worry about Hal—I will deal with him. In fact, try not to worry about anything. You should give yourself a break for a while—you look exhausted. Be kind to yourself and let's try to keep the divorce as amicable as possible. Matt.

It was a pleasant note, a reasonable note—the perfect note on which to end a marriage.

So why did she clutch it with white-knuckled fingers, tears beginning to stream down her face as if they were never going to stop?

CHAPTER FIVE

LONDON WAS RAINY and the flat felt cold and unwelcoming. Jennifer had been living there since the marriage split—she and Matteo had agreed that the luxury apartment would be 'hers', just as the ancient stone house on the island of Pantelleria would become 'his'.

The accountants had suggested that they sell their home in the Hollywood Hills, because apparently prices there had rocketed since they'd first bought it. Jennifer wasn't going to break her heart about *that*. It had never felt like a real home to her anyway. But then, where did?

Their schedules had been so frantic that they'd never seemed to have the time to do the things which other newly-weds revelled in. There had been no careful choosing of furniture or browsing over curtain material. Nor had there been any of the usual concerns about what they could or couldn't afford.

They'd been able to afford almost anything!

Matteo had made an almost obscene amount of money since leaving drama school, and his asking price now ran into millions of dollars.

That was one of the reasons why Jennifer had allowed herself to be tempted away from the stage and gone into films herself. Matteo had made hundreds of opportunities possible, and she had seized them with eager hands—for surely it would have been crazy to turn down such chances?

She'd wanted to be his equal in all ways—and yet when her own asking price had rocketed she had felt none of the expected joy or satisfaction. Just a kind of nagging feeling that somehow she'd sold out. And the price she'd paid for her glittering career had been frequent separations from her husband which had fed all her insecurities and doubts.

Sometimes she had found herself wondering what it would have been like if they had created a proper place together. Spent ages lovingly choosing items together, instead of suffering the incessant march of an army of interior designers who had transformed each one of their homes into dazzling displays which celebrity magazines had fallen over themselves to feature. Matteo had drawn the line at that. 'We have little enough privacy as it is,' he had told them angrily.

Maybe she should have done something to try and claw some of that privacy back—but Jennifer had been a brand-new player in the celebrity game, and she'd been too busy enjoying it to want to pull the plug on it. How easy it was, with the benefit of hindsight, to recognise the mistakes she'd made.

She glanced uninterestedly at the unopened post and the pile of film scripts waiting to be read. Then her mobile rang, and in spite of everything her heart leapt. Because she'd be lying if she denied fantasising about Matteo on her flight back from Cannes. She felt as if he had poured all her emotions into a mixing bowl and stirred them up. Maybe he was ringing her to ask if she'd got back safely? Or maybe just to say hello—because if the divorce truly *was* going to amicable then why *shouldn't* he say hello?

She picked up her phone and made her voice sound as cool as possible.

'Hello?'

'Jennifer?'

Jennifer's heart sank, and she immediately felt guilty that it had. 'Hello, Mum.'

'Where *are* you?'

Jennifer held the telephone away from her ear as the loud voice came booming down the line. Her mother always described herself as an actress too—though she had never progressed beyond the strictly amateur productions at their local village hall. The rest of the time she had spent living out her fantasies through her only child.

Quashing the terrible temptation to say that she was anywhere but England, Jennifer murmured, 'I'm at the London flat.'

'Why?'

'Well, why not?' questioned Jennifer. 'I *live* here.'

'No, I mean why aren't you doing the round of parties and interviews in Cannes? There's hardly been a *thing* about you in any of the papers!'

'That's because...because—'

'Because that bastard of an ex of yours was there, I suppose?' interrupted her mother viciously.

Jennifer bit her lip. 'Mum, I won't have you talking about Matteo that way.'

'Then you're an idiot, darling. He's made a complete and utter fool of you!'

'Look, I've just flown in—was there anything in particular you wanted?'

'Well, actually, yes! I was hoping to run an idea of mine past your agent! Or that rather nice publicist I met...what was his name? Hal? Yes, that was it! Hal! I think he took a slight shine to me!'

'Mum—'

'There are such *rubbishy* screenplays around at the moment that I thought to myself—well, why *shouldn't* I have a go?'

Jennifer counted to ten. And then on to twenty. Now was not the time to tell her mother that she'd sacked Hal. Or why.

Promising to visit very soon to talk about it, she managed to finish the call and went through to the kitchen while she listened to all the messages that had arrived while she'd been in France.

There were four calls from her agent. Two magazines wanted her on their cover, and a very famous photographer wanted to include her in his coffee-table book of the world's most beautiful women.

But Jennifer didn't feel in the least bit beautiful—she felt empty and aching, almost worse than she had when she and Matt had first split. At least then there had been endless, explosive rows, and she had felt that breaking up was the best thing to do. She had been carried along by the powerful storm of her anger and hurt.

But the episode in Cannes had been poignant and bittersweet. It had emphasised her vulnerability around him and reminded her of what they had once shared— but a pale imitation of the real thing. It had taunted her with what she was missing...that feeling of being properly alive. Because Matt was like the blazing sun in a summer sky, and when he wasn't around the world seemed dark and cold.

She spent the next few weeks lying low. She wore nondescript clothes and no make-up and kept her eyes down when she went out. As she had intended—no one recognised her. If you were a good actress, then no one should. It was more than just appearance. You could slope your shoulders and make your body language as low-key as possible.

She knew she ought to start trying to rebuild her life as a single woman, but her high-profile marriage had affected the way people saw her. She was famous now— and that had a knock-on effect on everything she did. She could no longer have normal friendships, because people wanted to know her for all kinds of different reasons. These days their motives had to be scrutinised, and Jennifer hated that. Fame separated you—left you lonely and isolated.

And going back wasn't easy. There were people she had been at drama school with, but she hadn't seen them for years. She'd just been so busy, with film after film, and she'd been living on the other side of the world. Fame and money changed your life—no matter how much you swore they weren't going to.

And then, before she could relaunch herself on the world, she began to feel peculiar. From being full of energy, she found that she could hardly drag herself out of bed in the mornings.

And her appetite increased. When she'd first met Matt she'd had the normal rounded body of a healthy young woman, but he'd taken her to Hollywood and she had realised that wasn't good enough. It was stick-thin or nothing. She had trained her appetite to be satisfied with sparrow-like portions, but suddenly they were no longer enough.

Now she found that she simply *couldn't* control her hunger, and it was scary to find herself wolfing down a bowl of porridge for breakfast every morning—and covering it with golden syrup!

She blamed the syrup for the nagging tightness of her jeans. But even when she cut out the syrup and dragged herself down to the exclusive gym in the basement of the apartment complex there was no marked improvement. In fact, quite the contrary.

When it hit her, she realized she'd been very stupid. She wasn't comfort-eating at all. But of course she had denied it—as she expected women who'd taken risks had done ever since the beginning of time.

Except she hadn't taken any risks!

Telling herself it was hysteria, she upped her sessions at the gym and began to wear more forgiving trousers.

But there came a day when her warped kind of logic refused to be heard any more. And that was the day she sent her cleaning lady out to buy a pregnancy testing kit.

She didn't really need to sit and wait to see whether a blue line would develop. She had known for weeks and weeks what the result would be.

Jennifer sat down on one of the sofas and buried her head in her hands. In that moment she had never felt more lost or more alone. But it wasn't as though she was going to waste time worrying about what she was going to do.

There was only one thing she *could* do.

She kept putting it off. And meanwhile time was

ticking away. Her shape was changing and the appetite which had consumed her had now deserted her. Maybe that was a blessing in disguise—because she didn't *dare* venture out to the local stores. Thank God for online shopping.

But she couldn't put off telling Matt for ever—and one morning, when the bright blue of the early-autumn sky seemed unbearably poignant, she hunted down her phone and found Matteo's programmed-in number. It rang for a while before he picked up, and his voice was wary in a way she had never heard it sound before. That in itself was a shock—the thought that Matteo was moving on, changing and growing and leaving her behind, while she remained stuck firmly in the groove of the past.

'Jennifer?' he said slowly. 'This is very unexpected.'

Was it really? Didn't it occur to him that she might want to discuss what had happened between them in France? Unless the caution in his voice was there for a more pragmatic reason—because she was disturbing him in the middle of...

Her words came out as if someone was strangling her. 'Can you...?' She swallowed. 'Is it all right for you to talk?'

He frowned. 'Sure.'

He wasn't giving her any kind of help—but then, why should he? *She* was the one who had instigated this conversation, and soon all his ties with her would be severed completely. She bit her lip. Except that they wouldn't. Not now.

'Matteo, I have to see you.'

His voice hardened. 'No, Jenny.'

The room swayed. *'No?'*

'There isn't any point.'

Jennifer felt the blood drain from her face as she realised that she had put herself in a position to be rejected. And that only increased her pain. 'Matt, you don't understand—'

'Oh, but I do—believe me, I do. I've been thinking about it a lot.' More than he'd wanted to. More than he could bear to. Matteo closed his eyes, wishing that he could blot out the memory of her legs laced tightly around his waist while he thrust deep inside her. Or—even more poignant—the memory of her blonde hair spread all over his pillow in Cannes. But their frantic coupling had been nothing but a mockery of a simple and tender intimacy which was gone for ever. Well, he would tolerate it—but he would *not* be used as some kind of stud to satisfy his ex-wife's sexual needs!

He kept his voice terse. 'What happened between us proved that we're still sexually compatible. That's all. Nothing more. That's not enough basis for a relationship—and it would destroy even the memory of what we once had.'

In her outrage and her shame Jennifer nearly dropped the phone. He thought she was ringing him in order to get him back! He thought she was begging him to come back into her life! Trying to resurrect a relationship that was dead!

She wanted to hurl the phone hard against the wall—to finish this conversation and all future conversations with the arrogant and egotistical *bastard* in the most satisfyingly violent way possible.

But not yet.

'Oh, don't worry,' she said coldly. 'Such an agenda couldn't be further from my mind.'

He felt a nerve flickering in his cheek. 'I'm glad we understand each other.'

'Perfectly.'

'So. Why are you ringing?'

She couldn't say it over the phone. She couldn't. It was the coward's way out and she wanted to see his face. *Needed* to see his face.

'There's some paperwork I need you to look at.'

And what? Look into those big sapphire eyes again and start seeing what he wanted to see instead of what was real? Letting himself confide in her and share his thoughts with her? Start wanting to tear her clothing off, with her letting him? Or would she? Maybe this time she would torment him by saying no, by flaunting her magnificent body and torturing him because it was hands-off.

'Can't you get someone else to deal with it?' he questioned impatiently.

'That's your answer to everything, isn't it, Matt? Why bother doing something when you can pay someone else to do it for you? No wonder you're becoming increasingly remote from reality!'

There was a short, angry pause. 'Do you really think I *want* to see you?' he demanded hotly. 'That I would voluntarily put myself in a position where I lay myself open to being insulted by you?'

'Matt, you *have* to see me.'

'*Have* to?' he repeated dangerously. '*Cara*, nobody, but nobody, tells me that I *have* to do something.'

She realised then that there was no way out of telling him over the phone. And maybe this way was best. At least it would be short—if not sweet. She would provide the information in the starkest way possible and leave him with the options. Maybe the best one was for him to leave her completely alone.

'I just thought you'd better know that I'm pregnant,' she said, and then she hung up.

For a moment Matteo listened blankly to the burr of the dial tone, his eyes staring unseeingly at the wall in front of him. And then her words slammed into the forefront of his mind with the impact of a sledgehammer.

'Jenny!' As if saying that would suddenly put her back on the line! He dialled her number, but predictably she let it go through to voicemail.

He shook his head as a floodgate of feelings swamped him. Disbelief and anger and frustration made his heart-rate soar, but the tiniest flicker of hope and joy dazed him.

A baby?

He didn't even know where she was!

Strega!

His mind worked around all the possibilities. She could be anywhere...but it was most likely that she was in their London flat. *Her* London flat, he reminded himself. He knew she wasn't crazy about staying in hotels—not if she was on her own. And then he remembered the night in Cannes, and his heart contracted.

He frowned as he rang the service number of the exclusive apartment block and spoke to the concierge, using blatant influence, charm and a hefty bribe to ensure that his enquiry was not passed on to Signora d'Arezzo. But, yes, she was there.

He allowed himself a brief, hard smile of satisfaction and then set about flying to England. Normally he might have cursed at a back-to-back flight from the States, but this wasn't normal. He didn't get told he was going to be a father every day of the week.

Beneath the knitted black brows his ebony eyes glittered with a hundred questions. But the one uppermost in his mind was the most important.

Was she telling him the truth?

CHAPTER SIX

THE KNOCKING ON THE DOOR wouldn't stop, and Jennifer knew that she could not lie there for ever, pretending that the outside world did not exist.

Slowly she made her way to the hallway and began to unslide the great bolts which had made their flat into a fortress. When she finally opened the door she was not surprised to see Matteo standing there, but it was a Matteo she scarcely recognised.

Uncharacteristically, he had not shaved. His dark hair was unruly—and his black eyes wild and angry. He walked straight in and shut the door behind him, and when he turned to face her his breathing was unsteady—as if he had been running in a long, long race.

'Now I see that your words are true,' he breathed, because for the first time in his life he felt out of his depth as he raked his eyes over her body.

She *was* pregnant! Rosily and unashamedly pregnant! Oh, the curve of her belly was not huge, but on a woman of Jennifer's slenderness it *looked* huge. Her breasts were swollen, and she had a look about her which made her appear quite different—but he couldn't pinpoint what it was. An experience which had changed her? The most profound experience a woman could have? Or just a kind of luminous fragility which almost took his breath away?

'You thought I would lie about something like this?' she questioned wearily.

He lifted his dazed eyes to her face to study that, slowly and properly, and there he could see changes, too. For her skin was whiter than milk and there were dark shadows beneath her eyes. He knew that pregnant women were supposed to glow from within, yet her eyes were dull, with none of their customary inner fire.

'*Dio!* What have you been doing to yourself, Jenny?' His eyes narrowed. 'Come through and sit down!' he commanded. 'At once.'

Jennifer laughed. After doing his utmost to wriggle out of coming to see her—how *dared* he? 'It's *my* home and I won't stand for being bossed around by you!'

He sucked in a low breath. 'I will forgive you your stubbornness because of your hormones. But I am telling you this—if you do not do as I say and go and lie down on the sofa, then I shall pick you up and carry you there myself!'

'Isn't that how we got ourselves into this whole mess to begin with?' she questioned bitterly.

Matteo opened his mouth to ask the question which was uppermost in his mind, but something told him to wait until she was comfortable.

He went through to the kitchen to make coffee while she settled herself, clicking his lips with disapproval as he looked inside the fridge. He carried the tray through and poured her a cup—just the way she liked it—and watched with approval as she slowly sipped it. His own lay cooling. Suddenly he could wait no longer.

'It is mine?'

She put the cup down quickly, before she dropped it. She had been expecting this, and had tried to tell herself that it was not an unreasonable question under the circumstances. But knowing something and feeling something were two entirely different things, and Jennifer felt as if he had driven a knife of accusation through her heart.

'Yes.'

'You are certain? There is no other candidate?'

Her mouth crumpled with hurt and scorn. *'Candidate?'* she echoed. 'You make it sound like a presidential election! No, there isn't another "candidate". I haven't slept with anyone else since the day I first set eyes on you.'

He looked up. 'You haven't?'

She heard the macho pleasure in his voice and felt as if she'd been scalded. 'No. Unlike you.'

His eyes narrowed. 'But...how can this be, Jenny? How can it?'

She looked at him. 'You're thirty-three years old, Matteo—do you really need me to tell you?'

'You took a chance like that when we were separated?' he demanded incredulously. 'You risked getting pregnant?'

Something inside her snapped. The weeks of waiting and wondering and worrying all came to a head. 'How dare you make it sound as if it was something I *planned*?' she exploded. 'It happened in a *lift*, for God's sake! A lift which *you* found! If anyone planned it, it must have been you!'

'Oh, don't be so ridiculous!' he countered, and he

saw her eyes darken in response. With a giant effort of will he drew a deep breath, trying to contain his emotions. But it wasn't easy. Yet he knew that he had to make allowances for her condition. He had to. For Jenny held all the cards, and if he was not careful...

'If you were unprotected then you should have told me, Jenny. And, yes, we were hot for each other—but there are other ways we could have pleasured each other without risking this type of consequence.'

Jennifer clapped her hand over her mouth as if she was going to be sick. 'I'm having a baby!' she choked. 'And all you can think about is mutual masturbation!'

'Jenny!' he protested. 'How can you say that? This is not like you!'

'What isn't? I don't know what *is* like me any more! And what do you expect me to say in the face of your monstrous accusation? If you must know—I *was* still on the Pill—'

'And why was that?' he shot back immediately. 'If, as you say, there was nobody else but me and we were divorcing?'

Jennifer's hand fell from her mouth to lie protectively on her belly as his suspicions reinforced how hopeless it all was. 'Because my periods are heavy—*remember*? My doctor thought it advisable. But it must have let me down.' She gave him a crooked kind of smile. 'Don't they say that the only surefire form of contraception is abstinence?'

'But you never got pregnant when we were married—when we were having sex every second of the day!'

'Maybe I wasn't taking it as fastidiously as I used to.' Jennifer shrugged listlessly. 'Blame it on me, if it makes you feel better.'

'I don't want to *blame* anyone!' he grated. 'Recriminations aren't going to help us.'

Matteo was silent for a moment as for the first time in his life he felt authority slip from his fingers. He could not get his way here by coercion or charm. Jennifer was in the process of divorcing him. She no longer loved him. What happened now was *her* decision. She was in the driver's seat, and suddenly he felt out of his depth. 'What do you want to do?' he questioned quietly.

'I'm having the baby,' she said flatly.

'Of course you are!' But a great warm wave of relief rolled over him and for the first time he smiled—a smile so wide that he felt it might split his face in two. 'And look at you, Jenny—you are so big...it must be...'

She could see him doing mental arithmetic and the expression on his face was almost comical. Jennifer smiled too—realising how long it had been since she'd done *that*. 'Nearly sixteen weeks.'

'That long?' he breathed. 'My God. Jenny...this is a miracle.'

'Yes,' she said simply. And in that moment the divorce and the anger and the bitterness and the tearing apart of a shared life all seemed inconsequential when compared to the beginning of a brand-new life.

But her emotions were volatile, and hot on the heels of her heady exhilaration came the despair of the situation into which their baby would be born.

A shuddering sob was torn from her throat and Matteo sprang to his feet, going over to her side and taking her hand between his. 'You are in pain?' he demanded.

She shook her head. 'No, I'm not in pain,' she sobbed. 'I'm just thinking how hopeless this all is.'

'Shh.' Now he lifted his hand to her wet cheeks and began to smooth the tears away, his heart contracting in genuine remorse as he saw the expression in her blurry eyes. 'It is not hopeless,' he said softly.

'Yes, it is! We're getting a divorce and you don't love me!'

'But, Jenny, I will always—'

'No!' She sat up, her face serious, the tears stopping as if by magic. 'Never say it, Matteo,' she urged. 'Don't say something to try and make it better, because if it isn't true then it will only make it worse. I'm not a little girl who needs to be given a lolly because she's hurt her knee. This isn't about me, or the way I feel, or the mess we've made of our relationship. This is about someone far more important than both of us now...our baby.'

Matteo stared at her, his fingertips lingering for one last moment on her face. 'You sound so strong,' he breathed, in open admiration.

'I have to be,' she said simply. 'I'm going to be a mother—maybe it comes with the job description.'

And he needed to be strong, too.

He needed to take control. But he must not do it in a high-handed way or she would rebel; he knew that. He must allow Jennifer to think that *she* was making all the decisions.

'Have you thought about what you want to do?'

'I've tried.' There had been a fantasy version, about taking a time machine and fast-rewinding so that the episode in the lift had never happened. Or back further still, to a time when they'd still been in love and they could have conceived their baby out of that love, instead of out of lust and anger and passion.

But she was dealing with reality, not fantasy—and that posed all kinds of problems.

'Oh, Matt—I just don't know *what* to do for the best. If I stay around here—or even if I go back to the States—it'll soon become obvious that I'm pregnant.' She glanced down at the swell of her belly. 'Though you can tell that even now, can't you?'

'Yes. Any eagle-eyed observer would spot it—and there are hundreds of those out there.'

'I know. And once word gets out everyone will want to know who the father is—and I won't know what to say.'

'But you *do* know who the father is!'

'And think of the questions if we tell them! Are we getting back together? And if we aren't then *why* am I pregnant by you? Or what about the worst-case scenario? Some sleazy journalist bribing someone at the hospital to get my due-date! Then they could work it back to the Cannes Festival—and I'll bet that at least *one* of the staff at the hotel could be bribed into giving them a story that we came out of the lift in a state of partial undress! Can you imagine the scoop *that* would provide?'

'Jenny—'

She shook her head. 'Or, if we *don't* tell them, then the questions and conjecture will be even worse! Every single man I've so much as said good morning to will come under intense scrutiny! There will be all kinds of tasteless headlines—*Who Is The Father Of Jennifer's Love-Child?*'

'Jenny, Jenny, aren't you getting a little carried away?'

'Am I?' Her blue eyes were clear and defiant. 'Think about it, Matt—is it really such an incredible idea?'

And that was the worst of it—he *could* see it, quite

plainly, as if someone was playing a film inside his head. In a way, fame robbed you of simple humanity. They had become *things*—to be dissected and picked over. He shook his head and his eyes were clouded with a bleak kind of sadness. 'And I brought you into this crazy world of showbiz,' he said huskily. 'What kind of a lover would do that?'

A few months ago she might have agreed with him, but so much had changed—and not just the baby. Though maybe *because* of the baby. And it was all to do with responsibility—acknowledging it and accepting it. It took two to do everything in a relationship— to fall in love and then to wreck it. You couldn't place the blame on one person's shoulders.

She shook her head. 'Oh, Matt—that's not what I'm saying! You didn't frogmarch me into the studios with a gun at my head, did you? I wanted fame, too. I saw what you had and I wanted it with a hunger which sometimes frightened me—but not enough to stop me! But none of that's important. Not now—we can't change the past. But I don't want any more pressure—because that will put pressure on the baby.' She looked at him with an appeal in her eyes. 'Just what kind of story *are* we going to give the press?'

He swore in Italian, getting up to pace up and down the polished oak floors of a flat in which he had slept for barely more than a dozen nights in the two years he'd owned it—he, a man who'd grown up in a cramped tenement building in New York? How crazy was that?

'Why should the press be our first consideration?' he exploded.

And, in spite of everything, Jennifer's lips curved

into a rueful smile. 'That's like asking why the grass is green!'

He let out a pent-up sigh and went to look out of the window. Below lay Hyde Park in all its glory. Joggers moved along the paths and mothers and nannies strolled with pushchairs beneath trees which were beginning to be touched with autumn gold. Soon winter would arrive. The London streets would be washed with rain or dusted with frost or even—if they were very lucky—heaped with snow.

And Jennifer might trip and fall!

He turned round. 'Have you told your mother?'

'Are you kidding?'

'Don't you think you should?'

'Why? The first thing she'll do is think that being a grandmother is going to make her sound old. And the second will be to give me a hard time over the damage this is going to do to my career.'

'She hates me,' he observed.

'She hates all men, Matt, not just you. Ever since my father walked out her view of the world has been distorted.'

It occurred to him that Mrs Warren had influenced her daughter more than Jennifer had perhaps ever acknowledged. Had she learned at her mother's knee that all men were inherently unfaithful? Was that why she had always been so suspicious of him? Only now could he see—too late—that maybe he should have sat down and talked about it with her instead of becoming increasingly frustrated at her lack of trust and her willingness to believe the rumours instead of listening to *him*.

'You're going to have to tell her some time.'

Jennifer briefly closed her eyes. 'I know I am. Just not yet. If we think outside interest would be intrusive, then just imagine...'

Matt shuddered. 'I would rather not.'

It occurred to him that the two of them had not spoken with such ease for a long time. And that was good, he told himself. Jenny was right—they could not change what had happened, and in the conventional sense their relationship was over. But civility between them must be maintained. He had wanted that before, but in view of the baby it had now became imperative.

'Shall we go to Pantelleria?' he asked softly. 'To the *dammuso*? We could both do with a little rest and recuperation.' His eyes narrowed as they took in her pinched face and pale skin. 'Particularly you,' he added.

Her mouth suddenly dried, but only her attitude of mind could save her from plunging into regret. For surely Matteo's suggestion made sense? A place which she knew offered refuge and peace. Possibly the only such place in the world—at least for them.

Pantelleria—the black pearl of the Mediterranean. The beautiful island where they had spent their honeymoon. Where wild flowers bloomed and rare birds visited.

There, Matteo owned a simple square white house built of volcanic stone, with shallow domes and thick white walls which stayed deliciously cool in summer. She remembered them lying together in bed on the last morning of their honeymoon and vowing to return as often as they could. But of course that had been one of many promises broken by a lack of that most precious commodity...time.

And nothing had changed there.

She stared at him blankly. 'How can we? I've got two films lined up.'

Matteo shrugged. 'Cancel them.'

'I can't do that!'

His black eyes glinted. 'Can't? Or won't?' he challenged softly. 'What's more important to you—your work or your marriage?'

'I notice you're not offering to do the same!'

'Oh, but that's where you're wrong, Jenny.' He gave a brief, hard smile and his eyes were as brittle as jet. 'If I have to cancel a couple of films to take this course of action, then so be it.'

It was like seeing a side of Matteo she'd never seen before—it was certainly the first time she'd ever seen a chink in the tough armour of his ambition, and Jennifer was momentarily taken aback. 'You'd risk your career?' she whispered. She nearly added *for me*, until she reminded herself that it wasn't for *her*—but for their baby. And what was wrong with that?

'My career will always pick up,' he said arrogantly. 'But films can wait. This can't,' he finished, with another shrug of his broad shoulders.

Jennifer knew that despite his almost careless air this was a supreme sacrifice for Matteo. He had made films almost back to back ever since she'd known him—and way before that. As if he was frightened of stepping off the merry-go-round of successful work which bred still more work.

And now that it had become a real possibility—instead of a throwaway remark—Jennifer could see the sense in Matteo's suggestion that they escape together, to a place which she could see might act like a balm on their troubled spirits.

The island lay halfway between Africa and Sicily—where Matteo's ancestors had come from and where secret-keeping was legendary, taught from the cradle. On Pantelleria Matteo wielded the influence of his birthright, not that of the fickle fame brought about by celluloid.

They had been happy there—and part of her wanted to hang on to those precious memories and leave them intact.

He saw her hesitation and suspected he knew its cause—for did he not have misgivings about returning there himself? Would it not unsettle him—reminding him of the dreams they had shared and never realised?

'You know you would be safe there.'

Safe? Alone with Matteo? That was a definition of *safe* she wasn't sure existed. Jennifer felt as if her life were a pack of cards which someone had thrown into the air to see where they would land. 'But how long would we stay there, Matt? I mean—I don't want to have the baby there.'

The brittleness had gone and now his eyes gleamed. 'You think that no child has ever been born on Pantelleria?'

'How long?' she persisted quietly.

'Long enough to bring the colour back to your cheeks and for you to rest and eat good food.' There was a pause. 'And long enough to decide what we are going to tell the world. To decide what our strategy will be.'

From a supposedly hot-headed and passionate Italian it was possibly the coldest and most matter-of-fact declaration Jennifer had ever heard.

CHAPTER SEVEN

MATTEO ORGANISED THEIR TRIP to Pantelleria with a degree of organisation to rival a military campaign. Despite the loyalty of his staff—who these days had to sign a watertight confidentiality agreement—he entrusted relatively few of them with the knowledge of their whereabouts.

As he said to Jennifer—this was just too big a story to risk.

And that was all this was, she reminded herself. A damage limitation exercise over a story which had the potential to explode in their faces.

Jennifer had forgotten how extraordinarily protected you could feel in the exclusive coterie of Matt's inner circle—but this time there was a subtle difference.

'Your staff are being unbelievably nice to me,' she said, as they waited for their baggage to be loaded onto the private jet which would fly them to the island.

Matteo snapped shut his briefcase and frowned as he looked up at her. 'Aren't they always?'

Jennifer switched her phone off. 'Oh, forget I said anything,' she said airily. She certainly wasn't going to blow the whistle on anyone.

But Matteo laid his hand on her arm, and the unexpected contact caught her by enough surprise to lower her defences. 'Jenny? Tell me. Because if you don't then how the hell will I know?'

And maybe it was her duty to tell him. Nobody dared tell Matteo anything. And even when they did they told him what they thought he wanted to hear. 'They normally put a barrier between you and the rest of the world.'

He narrowed his eyes. 'Well, yes, I suppose they do—but surely you can understand why?'

'From the world, yes—from your family, no.' She hesitated. 'Once, I remember trying to get through to you on the phone, and being completely stonewalled and unable to reach you. They dismissed me as if I was some kind of disgruntled ex-employee! It made me feel so...'

'So what?' he prompted.

Jennifer hesitated—but what did she have to lose by telling him? 'So isolated, I guess.' Jennifer shrugged. 'Mind you, that was after we had separated. Maybe they were acting on your instructions.'

His face darkened. 'I gave no such instructions.'

In fact he remembered feeling pretty isolated himself. The rupture of their relationship had given him a sense of being cut adrift from all that was familiar. Because even when their marriage had been in an appalling state they had still been in contact. She had still been his anchor, the person he turned to to confide in. He'd telephoned her from locations around the world, or she him. But once she had left—that had been it. Nothing. As though he had never even occupied a tiny part of her life. She had cut contact completely—or so he had thought.

Now it seemed that his staff had been instrumental in that sudden severing of all ties, and his eyes narrowed thoughtfully as he stared at her. He employed people to act on his decisions, not to make them for him.

'So, how many of the famous d'Arezzo workforce will be accompanying us to Pantelleria?' asked Jennifer.

'None.' He savoured the moment. '*Nessuno.* Just us.'

Jennifer blinked in surprise. 'No chef?' she echoed. 'But you always take Gerard with you!'

A sense of regret washed over him. Was this what he'd intended when he had started chasing his dreams? To employ so many staff that he seemed to have lost control of his own life? 'I'll do the cooking,' he drawled.

Jennifer's surprise increased. '*You?*'

'Do you really consider me incapable of living my life without any staff to help me, Jenny?' he demanded exasperatedly. 'That I never knew what it was to be cold or go hungry? Or to take jobs that I hated in order to survive before I got my big break?'

'Well, in theory, no—of course I don't. But when I met you you were so successful that it was hard to imagine you being anything else. Like a slim person telling you they once had a weight problem. You can't quite believe it.'

'Well, believe it,' he said quietly, and smiled. 'And come and meet our pilot.'

He had given her a lot to think about on the flight, but the reality of what they were doing hit her when the luxury private jet touched down, and she turned to him with wide eyes. 'Are we completely mad, do you think?'

He gave a lazy smile. 'Very probably.'

And the easy intimacy of that smile spelt danger, reminding Jennifer to be on her guard. To be careful to protect her feelings. Because nothing had changed between them. This trip didn't mean that they were compatible, or that they weren't in the process of getting a divorce. She was having a baby. That was all.

Pantelleria's October air was still deliciously warm, and coastal flora bloomed in a profusion of pinks and reds and yellows. The crystal blue waters which surrounded it were rich in lobsters, and in the fertile valleys of the interior grapes grew as large as plums. It was like paradise.

Matteo felt the weight of expectation lift from his shoulders as he drove along the familiar unchanged roads to the Valle della Ghirlanda and his *dammuso*.

These days, superstars visited the island, but Matteo had fallen in love with Pantelleria as a child—when his parents had saved up enough money to send him to stay with one of his aunts during one long, dry summer. His family had laughed when he said he'd own a house there one day, but sure enough he'd done it—buying the *dammuso* with his very first film cheque. He had set about completely modernising the old building, whilst making sure it retained its natural charm.

It offered two terraces—one by a vast swimming pool which had a backdrop of the distant sea. The high walls hid a secret pleasure garden, with an irrigation system which had been built by the Arabs during their four-hundred-year occupation.

But it was the cool, domed main bedroom which Jennifer longed and yet dreaded to see—with its huge bed and restful simplicity. If only she could close her eyes and take herself back to the person she'd been then...would she have done anything differently? Would he?

'I guess you'd better sleep in here,' said Matteo, as they both stood in silence looking into the room.

'And you?'

He shrugged. 'The guest room is prepared.' He wondered if she would heed the unspoken question in his voice. Was she thinking of inviting him into her bed—to maybe build some kind of way back through the physical intimacy of being close once more?

But Jennifer didn't hear; she was struck dumb by the chain reaction of feelings which had been sparked by being in this room, this house. Delight, sadness, regret and sorrow—all those emotions and a hundred more besides flowed over her in a bittersweet tide.

She stared at the bed as if it was a ghost—and in a way it was. And imagine if the ghost of her honeymoon self were to look up and see what had become of her and Matteo. Separated—with only an unplanned baby holding them together. How heartbroken that madly-in-love Jennifer would have been.

'Our baby should have been conceived in a bed like this,' she whispered—as much to that ghost of her former self as to the man by her side. 'Not in some seedy lift.'

'So many *should haves*, Jenny,' he said, and his deep voice was etched with pain, too. 'We should have listened more. Trusted more. Talked more. We should not have been too proud to say what was on our minds.'

'We should not have been parted so much,' she ventured—because this was a game it was frighteningly easy to play. There was a whole list of things they had done wrong without meaning to. Had she and Matteo just got unlucky? Or had they simply been too bound up in selfish interests to cherish their marriage properly?

'Do you think those problems happen with all couples—only some work out how to deal with them?' she questioned.

'I think we both struggled so hard to make it in our own careers that we forgot to put any work into the relationship,' he said slowly. 'And I think that once success arrived we felt that our lives were charmed and nothing bad could touch us.'

'But we were wrong,' she breathed.

'Oh, yes.'

'Oh, Matt,' she said brokenly.

He wanted to take her in his arms and hold her tight against him, kiss away her cares, but she looked so tense—as if one touch would shatter her into a thousand pieces. In the dim light of the shuttered room he thought how pale her face looked.

'And now?' he questioned. 'What must I do to ensure that there will be no regrets in the future?'

Be in love with me again, she thought. But you couldn't ask for that. A precious gift like love could only be given, never demanded. 'You think I have a magic formula?'

Now he noticed the shadows which darkened her eyes and he wanted to kiss them away—but he had forfeited the right to tenderness a long time ago. 'I am burdening you with too many questions. So sleep,' he instructed grittily. 'I will leave you in the peace and the silence and you will sleep.'

And, miraculously, she did. For the first time since she had left Cannes—and maybe even before that— Jennifer slept as if someone had drugged her.

SLIDING ON A filmy white kaftan over her swimsuit, she left her hair loose beneath a wide-brimmed hat and went out into the bright sunshine to find Matteo.

He was lying on a lounger by the pool, wearing wrap-around shades and reading a film script. He had on nothing but a pair of swim-shorts, and Jennifer's feet faltered as she grew closer, for the sight of his near-bare body was utterly spectacular. And, let's face it, she thought, you haven't seen it for a long time.

His skin gleamed like olive satin, each muscle so carefully defined that he could quite easily have featured as an illustration in a medical student's anatomy book. Dark hair curled crisply over his chest and arrowed down to a V over his hard, flat belly, darkening over the powerful shafts of his legs.

She blamed the heat for the sudden drying of her mouth as Matteo slowly lifted his head. His eyes were unseen behind the shades, but Jennifer knew that he'd been aware of her watching him.

'Enjoying the view?' he questioned softly.

She jerked her head to stare out at the sapphire stripe of distant sea. 'It's...exquisite.'

He smiled. 'Come and sit down over here. I'll fetch you something to drink.'

Her legs felt like cotton-wool, and inwardly she despaired. Wasn't the whole point of being here to get herself fit and rested? If she started living on her nerves and constructing fantasies about her ex then she might as well have stayed in England and faced the press.

He brought her something cool and fizzing which tasted of lemons, and she gulped it down.

'Hungry?'

'Not really.'

'Am I going to have to force-feed you, Jenny?'

'No. Just give me a little time to acclimatise. Anyway, I ate on the plane—and I'm not stupid.' She sank into a lounger. 'Ooh, that's nice!'

'Isn't it?' He gave her a hard smile as his eyes flickered over her kaftan. 'Aren't you going to get a little sun on your body?'

What could she say? An excuse would sound feeble but the truth would sound far worse. That she felt suddenly and inexplicably shy about disrobing in front of him.

But you're having his baby, for God's sake! And you were married to him!

'Of course,' she said lightly, and turned her back.

Behind his dark glasses, a thoughtful look came into Matteo's eyes. Shyness indicated that she was uncomfortable. Or was it something else? He leaned back against his lounger, affecting rest—but his body was tense as she turned around again and a sigh of something approaching wonder escaped from his lips.

In the bikini, her pregnant shape was like a visual feast—with its brand-new curves and soft shadows. He saw the swell of her belly properly for the first time and was filled with a fierce and primitive pride. For—no matter what the circumstances of the conception—nothing changed the fact that beneath her heart, his child grew.

His own heart pounded, and he swallowed down the sudden lump in his throat. His child.

And Jenny was still his wife. By law they remained married, with all the rights that gave an individual—even in these days when marriages could be dissolved so easily. Was he really going to let that go so easily now, when there was a baby on the way?

True, she might grow strong and well here on Pantelleria, and true, they might fabricate such a wonderful explanation about why she was pregnant with his baby that no one would ever bother them again. But even if this latter and extremely unlikely scenario occurred—where did that leave him?

On the sidelines, that was where. While Jenny would go on to give birth and, sooner or later, another man would fall for her pale blonde beauty and her quirky character and her particular talents—and then what?

He would be relegated to weekends, and then to less and less contact with the child. And why not? He would never have lived properly with its mother—so why should he expect the child to love him?

An unbearable pain caught him unawares. It churned in his guts and twisted in his heart.

At that moment he saw Jenny slide her leg up to bend her knee, and he knew that he still held a powerful weapon. Could he not work on her desire for him and tie her to him with *that*, even if that was as far as it went?

He lifted the sunglasses from his eyes and put them on the ground as the sun glinted off the pale flesh of her thigh.

'You'll burn,' he said thickly.

She heard the note in his voice and knew what it meant. She knew that she had a choice. She could either thank him for his concern and go up to her room and cover herself from head to toe in Factor 20, or...

She shut her eyes. 'Do you want to cream me up?' she murmured.

Her words made him so aroused that for a moment

he wondered if he had dreamt them. But the languid pose she was holding told him that she had said them and meant them.

He noticed that she had her eyes closed, and that amused him as he moved slowly towards her. Was she trying to block out the sight of an erection which felt as hard as a rock against his belly?

He kneeled down beside her and squeezed a dollop of cream into the palm of his hand.

'Turn over,' he commanded.

She wriggled onto her stomach and, starting with her back, he loosened her inhibitions, unclipping her top and massaging the cool cream into her baking skin.

'Now lie on your back,' he instructed huskily.

Jennifer tensed as he peeled down her bikini top, and she nearly passed out with pleasure as he began to circle the palm of his hand over one hard globe, marvelling at the new and intricate tracing of blue veins there.

The cream felt deliciously cold, and Jennifer squirmed as her nipple peaked against his hand. 'Oh!'

But Matteo said nothing, for he sensed that words might shatter the highly charged atmosphere of erotic desire. He began to work on the other breast instead, hearing her gasp and seeing her squirm as he let his fingertips slowly glide down over the swell of her belly.

It was like being on familiar territory but discovering a whole new landscape. Like finding that a lush orchard had grown on a piece of previously barren land.

Wonder made him momentarily break his vow of silence. *'Madre de Dio!'* he whispered, and pulled down her bikini bottoms, sliding his finger to her wet, warm heat and hearing her gasp again, only sharper this time.

He began to kiss her until she moaned in an unspoken plea and he kicked off his shorts, carefully lowering himself on top of her so that they were properly naked at last. Her arms encircled his neck and Matteo buried his face in her soft neck and sighed. like a man who had come home.

They stayed like that until he lifted his head at last, tracing her mouth with his fingertip. 'I don't how I'm supposed to do it with a pregnant woman,' he murmured.

'You?' Her voice was slumberous as she smiled. 'Just do what you normally do.'

'But I don't want to hurt you. Or the baby.'

Matt could hurt her in a million different ways, but never like this. 'Just do it,' she urged. 'Let go.'

He reached down to find that she was soaking wet, and with a sigh of exquisite relief he thrust inside her. He began to move, slowly at first, teasing her and teasing her and teasing her. Enjoying the luxury of a long coupling—but it was never going to be long enough. He could barely wait for her to orgasm, but somehow he managed it—and then he let his own happen, in glorious golden waves which just kept on rocking him.

It seemed to take for ever to come back to earth, and when he did he lifted his head to look down at her, inordinately pleased at the dreamy smile of pleasure which curved her mouth.

'Jenny?' he whispered.

Her eyelids fluttered open and she looked up at him. *I love you,* she thought. *Is there any chance that one day you could love me, too?* 'What?' she mumbled drowsily.

'Can I sleep with you tonight?'

The wind made music out of the chimes which hung

in the trees, and the world seemed suspended as it waited for her answer.

Jennifer closed her eyes and touched her lips to his neck. It was not what she had wanted to hear, but it would do. 'Yes,' she breathed. 'Yes, you can.'

THE DAYS DRIFTED into one another, like a river running into the sea, and Jennifer grew brown and slow and contented. She slept and ate good food and swam like a fish—sometimes in the pool and sometimes Matteo took her out in his boat to splash in the clear waters— and her hair grew pale and he told her she looked like a mermaid.

And every night he slept with her, and made love to her in a hundred different ways, both in and out of bed.

In fact, it was almost like a second honeymoon—except that honeymoons were held together with the glue of shared love, not the unreliable adhesive of an unplanned pregnancy.

'What is it?' he questioned softly one afternoon, when they had gone upstairs to lie beneath the cool, curved dome of the bedroom ceiling for their customary siesta.

'I didn't say anything.'

'You didn't have to. You were frowning.' His fingers traced an imaginary line just above her nose.

Jennifer closed her eyes, because the subject playing on her mind was one that she would rather keep hidden away. It was so like paradise here that she didn't want to introduce the serpent of reality.

And yet hadn't their inability to communicate been one of the primary causes of their break-up? Geographical distance had been the reason for that—but you didn't need to be thousands of miles apart from someone to fail to interact with them on an adult level. And they couldn't keep pretending that there weren't a million unresolved issues simmering beneath the surface of this extended holiday.

'Well, we haven't discussed how long we're staying here, or what we're going to do when we get back—in fact, we haven't made any real plans at all. We've been burying our heads in the sand, and—whilst it has been lovely—I feel a bit as if I'm in limbo. As if the real world were a million miles away.'

'Well, that *was* the intention in coming here.'

'But it can't continue indefinitely,' observed Jennifer, smoothing her hand over her belly and watching as his black eyes followed the movement with fascination.

She remembered the very first time she had slept with him. In the morning she had woken first and lain there feeling slightly dazed, thinking, *I'm in bed with Matteo d'Arezzo!* 'Can it?'

'No.' The rumpled sheet lay tangled around his naked thighs as he moved over her, the powerful shafts straddling her, and for a moment Jennifer thought that he was going to drive his erection into her aching body. But his face was dark and full of tension. 'Tell me what it is you want, Jenny.'

She shook her head. 'That isn't fair. Are you too frightened to say what it is that *you* want?'

And at that moment he *did* know fear—he who had been fearless for most of his life. But it was time to take a gamble. To lay down the guidelines for the only situation he could see working for the two of them. He just hoped that he had softened his prickly ex-wife enough for her to be agreeable.

'I'm Italian—' he began.

'You were brought up in America,' she pointed out. 'And what's that got to do with it?'

'I *believe* in marriage,' he breathed. 'But especially a marriage which involves a family. I want us to try again, Jenny' he said, and Jennifer heard the unmistakable ring of determination in his voice. 'To be man and wife. To bring our baby up within a secure family unit. Don't you want that, too?'

She nodded, too choked for a moment to speak. Had she thought that he might threaten her with a legal battle if she did not accede to his will? Possibly. The very last thing she had expected was that heartfelt appeal, and it affected her more than was probably necessary. Or wise.

'Of course I do,' she said eventually. 'It's what every mother wants for her baby.'

Not for herself, Matteo noted coldly, but he nodded and kept his face impassive.

She wanted to say, *And if there were no baby, would you still want me, even then?* But she wasn't strong enough for that. Because she might still be in love with Matteo but not so much that she would let it blind her. Because if there was no baby, then there wouldn't be a relationship.

'We need to do it properly this time around.' He tilted her chin up and his black eyes were hard and glittering. 'We will not lead separate lives again, *cara*. I don't know how we'll work it out, but we will.'

'And I won't listen to rumours...won't allow jealousy to flourish.'

'I won't give you cause to feel jealous ever again,' he grated.

'You're going to give up being a film star?' she said, half joking.

He smiled, his mind already working out their schedule. 'Shall we fly to England and tell your mother together? And I'll tell my office to answer any enquires with a short statement announcing that the divorce is off.'

Jennifer recognised the light of triumph which burned at the back of his eyes as she nodded her head in agreement. This might be as good as it got, but she wasn't going to knock it. She had tried living without him, and that was much, much worse.

CHAPTER EIGHT

'I CAN'T BELIEVE IT!'

'Just say you're happy for us, Mum!' pleaded Jennifer.

She and Matteo had driven straight from the airfield to her mother's elegant cottage near Bath, knowing that as soon as they were back in England word would get out about the pregnancy, and wanting her to hear it from them first. But now, looking at her mother's expression, she began to wonder why they'd bothered.

Mrs Warren's heavily made-up eyes flicked over her daughter and came to rest on Matteo again. She shook her head in disbelief. 'But I'm too young to be a grandmother,' she declared.

Matteo's expression didn't flicker, and he did not risk glancing over at Jennifer. He squeezed her hand instead. 'Of course you are,' he said smoothly. 'Everyone will believe that you are the baby's aunt!'

'Do you really think so?' Mrs Warren looked slightly mollified as she automatically patted her faded blonde hair. 'Does this mean the marriage is back on?'

This time he *did* risk it, and he read the understanding in Jenny's eyes. *'Si,'* he said slowly. 'It is. We have settled our...*differences*.'

Mrs Warren nodded. 'Well, I suppose I'd better look on

the bright side—I always got much better service on air-lines when I mentioned that Matteo was my son-in-law!'

Matteo's mouth twitched. 'Then that is a good enough reason for the marriage to continue, surely?' he said gravely.

'Mum, Matteo's going up to London on business, and I thought that I might stay here with you for a day or two. We could have lunch, if you like.'

Mrs Warren brightened. 'In a restaurant, you mean?'

Jennifer nodded. Her mother loved eating out with her famous daughter, and all the attendant fuss. 'If you like.'

Matteo's eyes narrowed. 'You're sure?'

She shrugged. 'Why not? No good hiding away—we were spotted and snapped at the airport, after all.'

'I'm sending two minders with you,' he said grimly.

'Ooh, goody!' squealed Mrs Warren.

In a pale restaurant overlooking the beautiful old city of Bath, they ate exotic seafood and salad, and Mrs Warren drank copious amounts of champagne 'to cele-brate, darling!' while the minders sat a not-so-discreet distance away. Jennifer even posed for a photo with a little girl who was waiting outside the restaurant with her mother.

Maybe I'll have a little girl too, she thought as she crouched down and smiled. And she'll have dark eyes, just like Matt's, and gorgeous curly hair.

But when they got back to her mother's house there was a crowd of pressmen milling outside, and the mind-ers had to barge their way through.

'What the hell is going on?' asked Jennifer, frown-ing. 'How ridiculous! Surely one pregnant actress doesn't merit *this* kind of interest?'

The phone was ringing when they got inside, and Mrs Warren took the call, her face growing white as she listened. 'Yes, she's here—I'll see if she'll speak to you.' She held the phone towards Jennifer. 'It's a reporter. Wants to speak to you.'

Jennifer pulled a face and took the phone. 'Hello? Jennifer Warren speaking.'

'Jennifer—were you aware that Sophia Perotta has given an interview to a London evening paper about her affair with your husband?'

'I wasn't,' she said calmly.

'Did you know that he was cheating on you with her throughout your marriage?'

There was a pause. 'I'm not going to comment on that,' she said, still in that strange, small voice of calm. 'And now I'm really going to have to go. Goodbye.'

She put the phone down and ignored all her mother's questions, but inside she felt queasy, and the feeling of nausea just grew and grew inside her. She only just made it to the bathroom before she started vomiting— and the frightening thing was that she couldn't stop.

'I'm calling an ambulance!' her mother exclaimed dramatically. 'I knew you should never have got back with that cheating bastard!'

Feeling as if she was taking part in one of her own films, Jennifer was rushed to hospital with sirens and lights blazing, wishing that her mother would just go away. She rolled around in agony, clutching her abdomen—her stomach was empty but she was unable to stop the dry retching which was making her throat burn. 'Am I going to lose my baby?' she cried.

'Shh! Try to calm down,' soothed the nurse in the

emergency room. 'The doctor is on his way down now to see you.'

Which did not answer her question at all. And Jennifer closed her eyes as tears began to creep from behind her tightly shut lids.

All this for nothing. Now she would lose the child she had longed for, and along with that terrible heartache would come her final separation from Matt—for he would not want her without the baby. Why would he?

AROUND A LARGE TABLE, Matteo sat with his lawyers—his face chalk-white beneath the tanned skin. On the front page of London's biggest-selling evening newspaper was a huge photo of a pouting Sophia Perotta—her brown eyes as widely innocent as a baby deer's. And there was the splash:

Cheating Matteo Was A Stallion In The Bedroom!

'Can she say this?' he demanded hotly.

'She already has.'

Matteo's fists clenched and he banged one down hard onto the table, so that the lawyers jumped. 'Let's sue her. Let's take the bitch for every penny she's got!'

'Are you certain you want to, Matteo?'

'It's a pack of lies!'

The lawyer coughed delicately. 'Did you or did you not have sex with her?'

Matteo flinched. 'Once!' he gritted, a feeling of disgust creeping over his skin. 'And only when my wife was divorcing me.'

'That's your story,' said the lawyer stolidly.

Matt turned on him, his black eyes flashing with anger, and suddenly he understood. 'Oh, I see,' he said slowly, and nodded his dark head. 'It's her word against mine.'

'Precisely. She's deliberately vague about dates and times, but explicit enough about your er...skills...in the bedroom department to make it clear that you *did* have sex with her. The dispute is when. She says it was during your marriage. You say it was not. We can try fighting it, if you want, but the publicity...'

He let his voice tail off, and Matteo knew what he was saying. 'I've only just got back with my wife,' he said urgently.

And she's pregnant.

Oh, Jenny.

Jenny.

It was at precisely that moment that one of his aides came grim-faced into the room, with a message from the hospital.

The journey back to Bath was a like a trip to hell. The worst thing was the not knowing—but no one would tell him anything and he couldn't get hold of Jenny's mother. It was an exercise in powerlessness, and Matteo had never felt so frighteningly out of control.

He made silent pleas to God. He prayed for their baby, and he prayed for much more than that, too. But Jenny would never forgive him for this. How could she?

'I want to see my wife!' he said to the overwhelmed receptionist at the desk.

'Mr d'Arezzo?' she verified breathlessly.

'Let me see her,' he pleaded.

'The doctor wants to see you first, sir.'

'Jenny!' he cried.

'He looked like a broken man,' the receptionist was to tell her colleagues in the canteen later.

Fearing the worst, Matteo paced the room they'd placed him in, and his eyes were bleak when the doctor walked into the room.

'My wife? How is she?'

'Your wife is fine, sir—'

'And the baby.' Matteo swallowed. 'She has lost the baby?'

The doctor shook his head and smiled. 'No, the baby is fine.'

'It is?'

'Absolutely. The heartbeat is perfect—the scan is normal. We've put a drip up, of course, because your wife was dehydrated, and we'd like to keep her in for—'

'But why has this happened?' breathed Matteo, and dug his nails so hard into his clenched palms that he did not notice he had drawn blood. 'It is shock which has caused this?'

'Shock? Oh, no. Your wife has food-poisoning, Mr. d'Arezzo. You should tell her to keep clear of prawns in future—particularly during pregnancy.'

Hot on the heels of exquisite relief that his wife and his baby were going to be all right came the bleak realisation that Jenny would never want him now. How would he feel if the situation were reversed? Could he bear to think of her in the arms of another man? And then to read about it in graphic detail in a newspaper, even if the facts *had* been twisted?

He walked along the corridor, and when they showed him into her room she was asleep against a great bank of pillows. She looked so small and so fragile that his heart turned over, and seeing the curve of her belly made an indescribable pain hit him.

Feast your eyes on her now, he told himself. For this will be the last time you shall see her so defenceless and vulnerable. Your access to her and to the baby will be barred from now on, and she will look at you in the wary and watchful way in which divorced wives do. From now on your relationship with Jenny will consist of brief meetings and visitation rights—and a whole legal framework.

'Aren't you coming in?' she said softly, without opening her eyes.

He stilled. 'Jenny?' he whispered hoarsely, as if a ghost had spoken to him.

She opened her eyes. 'Hello.'

He started. 'Did you hear me come in?'

'Yes.' And she had felt his presence, too—her senses were so alerted to him.

He rubbed his hands over his face, suddenly weary. 'I'm sorry.'

'So am I.' She managed a smile, wanting to banish some of the bleakness in his black eyes. 'But that's what comes of eating seafood! I shall have to be more careful in future.' She gave him a wobbly smile. 'But the baby is safe, thank God.'

He felt as if she had driven a stake through his heart. 'Jenny, don't!' he said savagely. 'Rail at me and tell me you hate me, send me away, but don't do this to me! For when you are kind it makes it so much harder, and I cannot bear to see it crumble—not what I thought we were on the way to regaining—' He shrugged his big shoulders. 'I just don't think I can bear it,' he repeated brokenly.

Jennifer stared at him. 'Matt—you're not making any sense. Didn't you hear me properly? Don't torment yourself. Please. Your baby is safe. Isn't it wonderful?'

'Yes, it's wonderful,' he said heavily. 'But I deserve all the torment in the world.'

'Would you mind telling me what the hell is going on?'

He blanched, praying for the courage to give his wife the facts which would finally put closure on their marriage. 'You haven't been shown a newspaper?'

Jennifer stilled. 'No. They've been keeping me quiet.'

He nodded. 'Well, you're going to find out sooner or later.'

'Matt, just *tell* me!'

'Sophia Perotta has given an interview claiming that I cheated on you with her throughout our marriage.'

Jennifer stared at him, searching his black eyes, the sombre slash of his mouth. 'You told me that it was just once. Afterwards.'

He nodded.

'So she's lying.'

Matteo stared at her. 'Jenny?'

'You told me you did not stray in our marriage. I believe you.' She had to believe him, or else there was no future for them.

She had done a lot of thinking in that quiet white hospital room, and had come to the conclusion that she couldn't spend the rest of her life reacting like a spoiled teenager. She was a woman with a baby on the way— who needed to look at a bigger picture than pride and hurt feelings.

'I know what happened between you, and I have to

learn to live with that—but that doesn't mean I need to torture myself with badly written detail. We've both made mistakes, Matt, and one of those was my lack of trust, I don't intend repeating it. It's the way things were—but I'm more interested in the way things are *now*. And I'm going to work at our marriage—because I want it to survive.'

'Survival?' he asked, and his heart sank. 'That is all you hope for?'

'Isn't that enough? Trust and respect make a pretty good substitute for love. When we were apart I missed you more than words can say, and I want to be married to you. Just as you want to be married to me. B-because we're having a baby.'

'No!' he denied furiously. 'No!'

She started. 'You don't want to be married to me?'

He could have kicked himself. She was ill, and yet managing to be so understanding that she'd taken his breath away—while he was behaving with all the finesse of a bull. 'I don't want to be married to you *just* because of the baby,' he corrected. 'I want to be married to you because I love you.'

'Don't say that,' she said shakily. 'Please.'

And then he saw his own fears and uncertainties reflected in her sapphire eyes. 'Even if it's true?' he whispered. 'And you the great champion of the truth? Do you know something else, Jenny—I will carry on telling you that I love you even if it takes for ever for you to believe me and to learn to love me back again.'

Joy licked over her skin with warm fingers, and tears began to well up in her eyes and spill down her cheeks. 'I'm a quick learner,' she wept. 'I already do. I've never stopped—and if you don't come over here and hold me properly then I shall create a scene as only an actress can!'

He was smiling as he took her in his arms—as if she were a delicate parcel and any pressure might make her snap.

'Hold me tighter,' she protested.

'Later,' he promised, as he eyed the needle in her arm. 'I'm not risking the wrath of the doctors.'

And Jennifer laughed, because she had never seen her husband look intimidated over *anything*. 'Won't you at least kiss me?'

'Mmm.' His mouth curved. *'Posso controllare quello,'* he murmured, and touched his lips to hers. He kissed her until he felt her heart hammering like a little bird, and he rested his palm over it and sighed softly. 'Now you must rest,' he said firmly. 'And listen to what I have to tell you about our future.'

She leaned back against the pillows.

'After my next two films I'm taking a break from acting—because there are a thousand possibilities out there and I don't want to be at the opposite end of the world from you any more. Especially if you're on location with the baby.'

'But I won't be on location with the baby,' she said softly. 'Because I don't want to live that kind of life any more, Matt.' She edged her way a little farther up the bed. 'Acting works well for lots of people, but I want to look after my baby myself, and concentrate on you and me. At least for a while. After that we can reconsider— maybe take it in turns to film. Or maybe I'll just retire and have a big, old-fashioned, Italian-sized family!'

Matteo stared at her, his black eyes full of gratitude

and wonder. And excitement. Because for the first time in his life he could understand what it was all about. The houses didn't matter, nor did the awards and the fame and the riches. Jenny and the baby they would have— *they* were what mattered. His family. *Their* family.

They were still blinking at each other like two people who had emerged into the sunlight after a long time in the dark when there was a brisk rap on the door. In walked a nurse, with two minders close behind.

One of them came up to Matteo and spoke rapidly in his ear. When he'd finished, Matteo looked over at Jenny.

'Much as I'm grateful for your mother's spirited defence of my morals—I think I'd better go downstairs, *cara mia*,' he said, a smile playing around the corners of his mouth. 'I'm afraid that your mother has just started to hold a press conference!'

For Mark. Thank you for believing.

SEX, LIES AND A SECURITY TAPE
Jackie Braun

CANNES-DID CAMERA!

It's the steamiest movie at the Cannes Film Festival—and it's only available via the Internet—but it's causing the biggest scandal ever for Senate hopeful Colin McKinnon. Action movie star Colin and hotel-chain heiress Tempest Herriman were caught on a Cannes security camera when their elevator got stuck between floors—and

CHAPTER ONE

TEMPEST HERRIMAN HADN'T meant to flash her breasts at the paparazzi after leaving the Oscar night bash at Morton's. The incident had been more of a wardrobe malfunction than a willful act of public lewdness.

Three years later, however, that distinction remained immaterial. The revealing shot had graced a dozen tabloid covers and induced a slew of Internet downloads when it was first snapped, key body parts appropriately blurred or not, depending on the publication or Website. And the photo kept turning up at the most inopportune times.

Like now, she thought, as she stepped into the reception area outside producer Stan Dartman's office.

The middle-aged woman seated behind a horseshoe-shaped desk didn't spare a glance over the top of her hot pink bifocals when Tempest entered. All her attention was focused on the celebrity magazine in front of her. As Tempest's luck would have it, the page the woman was reading sported a large reproduction of what had become known as the "Are they or aren't they?" breast shot.

Tempest leaned a hip on the desk, flipped her trademark tumble of red hair over her shoulder and tilted her head for a better look. Even though the photo was digitally blurred, she had just enough vanity to wonder how anyone could question her bust's authenticity.

"You know, according to an Internet poll eighty-three

percent of respondents believe they're the real deal," she informed the woman.

"Give me a break. Those things are as fake as—" The receptionist glanced up then and her words broke off. Slapping the magazine shut, she asked frostily, "Can I help you?"

"Tempest Herriman in the flesh. So to speak." She offered the full wattage of her smile as she scooted off the edge of the desk and stood. "I'm here to read for a part in Mr. Dartman's new movie."

She said it with pride. This was a plum role, and Stan was one of the Hollywood elite—a hands-on producer known for the Midas touch when it came to backing pictures.

"A part?" The receptionist smirked and made a show of scanning the appointment book before picking up the telephone.

"Tempest Herriman is in the lobby. She claims to be here to read for a part."

Tempest narrowed her eyes, but managed to bite her tongue. *Claims, indeed.*

She had spent countless hours preparing for this moment. The role of Roxy Remington was going to be her big break, and some nasty, tabloid-reading secretary wasn't going to ruin it for her.

She could picture herself walking the red carpet at the première, her name in black lettering on the lighted marquee. Maybe she'd snag a Golden Globe nomination for Best Supporting Actress. Hell, an Oscar. The part was that good, and she knew she could do it justice. She'd prove to all of the naysayers, her ex-boyfriend chief among them, that Tempest Herriman was not just some bored hotel chain heiress trying to parlay the celebrity that came with her billion-dollar fortune into a film career.

"I'm sorry, Miss Herriman. Apparently there's been a mix-up. All of the parts for *Flights of Fancy* have been filled, or soon will be. Mr. Dartman apologizes for the inconvenience and says to tell you he appreciates you stopping by. He'll keep you in mind for another project."

And with that Tempest came crashing back to earth.

"He appreciates me stopping by? I flew in from New York for this."

The receptionist barely blinked, and Tempest knew what she was thinking. *You're worth billions. You can afford it.*

"I'd like to see Mr. Dartman, please."

"Sorry." The woman looked anything but. "He's going to lunch shortly, and his afternoon is booked. Maybe you could leave the number where you're staying and he can call you when he gets a free moment?" she suggested.

Don't call us. We'll call you. God, how embarrassingly cliché.

Tempest wanted to scream. More horrifying, she wanted to cry. But she pasted a smile on her face and, in her best finishing school voice, said, "I'm staying at the Beverly Hills Herriman. Of course. If Mr. Dartman wants to reach me, I'm sure he'll have you look up the number. Have a nice afternoon."

She made it all the way outside before her bravado fled and the first tears of frustration leaked over the lower lids of her heavily made-up face. Roxy *would* have to wear too much make-up, she thought, as she swiped away black streaks.

Tempest had been so sure she could land this part. At the very least she'd expected to leave the audition knowing that the director and producer had been impressed by what they saw.

You can't buy your way onto the big screen. Her very first agent had told her that—right after she had fired him. Nor could she earn her way there. She was so tired of being stereotyped as having more money than talent.

And that damned photograph! At this rate the body parts in question would be sagging past her navel before they'd lost their ability to sell papers and set tongues wagging.

It was midday in Los Angeles, and the traffic was as thick as the smog. She was in no hurry to get into her car and face it. Defeated, she slumped onto one of the benches that flanked the exit at the rear of the building. As she searched through her handbag for a tissue the doors swung open and her embarrassment turned to mortification. Stan and a man she recognized as a casting director walked out first. Behind them was none other than Colin McKinnon.

Her heart thudded painfully, and then for a moment it seemed to stop beating entirely.

"Hello, Tempest."

He *would* have to look as sinfully handsome as she remembered: square jaw and brooding dark eyes that contrasted nicely with the surfer-blond hair that he was wearing a little shorter these days. Even so, she found herself catapulted back three years to that blissful month they'd spent together in a bungalow on a secluded beach on Kauai. They'd been dating for five months, and Colin had surprised her with the invitation after his latest film project had wrapped. Tempest had already been half in love with him at the time. She'd thought, hoped, after that month in Hawaii the feeling was mutual. Colin had a reputation for running hard and fast from commitment, and her own track record in serious relationships had been less than stellar. But it had felt so different.

Then the photograph had appeared, and Colin had disappeared. She'd gone to a restaurant to meet him for dinner a week after the party at Morton's. She'd waited. He'd never showed. Since then, whenever an interviewer or reporter brought up her name, he'd dismissed their affair as a brief and casual fling.

Tempest was still bruised, not to mention confused by what had happened, although she'd long given up trying to talk to Colin about it. He hadn't returned any of her phone calls, and had managed to avoid all contact with her since then.

Now, standing before her, the bastard had the nerve to wink.

"Nice outfit."

She fumbled in her bag for her designer sunglasses and hastily put them on. The spiky black heels she wore added four inches to her five-foot-nine frame, and so she was eye-to-eye with him when she stood.

"I came to read for a part, but it seems there was a mix-up."

The casting director hastily excused himself, and Stan Dartman smiled nervously before pacing several steps away with an apparent fit of coughing. Colin held his ground.

"Yes, we're looking for *actors*."

She absorbed the low blow. The insult didn't surprise her as much as what his words implied. "We?"

"I'm directing *Flights of Fancy*."

The world seemed to fall out from below her feet, and what she had hoped would be her career-making role tumbled right along with it.

This couldn't be happening. It just couldn't be.

"I—I thought Bob Wyman was the director."

In fact, she'd read in *Variety* just the previous month

that Colin was going to be taking a break from movies after his current film, *Collusion,* was released. He needed to concentrate on his upcoming bid for the US Senate.

Rumors had been circulating for years that he planned to take a page out of Arnold Schwarzenegger's book and run for public office. He'd told her as much himself three years earlier. Now it appeared to be more than speculation. The race for one of California's US Senate seats would be wide open in the next election. The entrenched incumbent who held it had announced this would be his final six-year term. Colin still had to win the primary election, but he seemed a shoo-in to appear on the general election ticket the fall after next. Some of the folks on the Sunday morning talk shows already had him elected.

"Change of plan," he replied smoothly. "I came on the picture as a favor to Stan."

The producer finally finished clearing his throat and stepped closer. "I want to apologize for your wasted trip from New York, Tempest. I tried to reach you to cancel our meeting, but you'd already left. I'll be happy to reimburse you for expenses, if you'd like."

"What I'd like, Mr. Dartman, is the chance to read for the part of Roxy Remington. That is why I came."

The producer glanced at Colin and apparently noted the tight line of his lips. "I'm sorry."

"I see."

To Colin, Stan said, "Our lunch reservation is at one."

"Go on. I'll meet you there." Colin waited until the other man was out of earshot before saying, "Setting your sights a little high, aren't you, heiress? It's a hell of a leap to go from a cameo on a prime time sitcom to a supporting role in a Dartman-produced feature-length film."

How had she ever imagined that a kindred spirit lay beneath that handsome façade? He was just as cruel, just as assuming, as the worst of her enemies. And yet three years ago... She pushed away the memories before the wound could reopen.

She longed to give him a piece of her mind, but she would settle for proving him wrong about her acting. Unfortunately, as the director on this picture, he was her last hope. No way would Stan allow her to audition, let alone cast her as Roxy, without Colin's approval.

Tempest swallowed her pride.

"I'm perfect for the part of Roxy Remington."

"You do have some of her attributes," he agreed. His gaze took an insulting tour of Tempest's leather-clad figure. "But we're looking for someone a little better known."

"People know who I am." She regretted the words as soon as they'd left her lips.

"Exactly, Tempest. And I'll keep you in mind the next time I'm looking for someone with a talent for drinking Cristal out of her designer pumps while dancing on nightclub tables."

She didn't point out that it had been a long time since she'd engaged in such silly antics. Instead, she said quietly, "It's not *all* true. Everything they write about me isn't based on fact. You of all people should know that."

At thirty-eight, Colin was already a Hollywood legend. He'd made a name for himself in a number of big-budget action movies during his twenties, and then had shocked the entertainment establishment to its core by trading starring-role status for a director's chair at the height of his popularity. In the interim, his wild-oat-sowing had been well documented—and, he'd once confided in Tempest, somewhat embellished. These days, however, he rarely showed up on the tabloids' radar. Given his political aspirations, she thought she understood why.

"Do pictures lie?"

She closed her eyes briefly. "They don't tell the whole truth. For instance, outside Morton's—"

"You enjoy the attention," he interrupted, cutting off her attempt to explain. "You court it, crave it. In fact, I think you actually get a kick out of making a spectacle of yourself."

Tempest blinked. Was that really what he thought of her? Once upon a time he'd seemed to see much more. And that had been before she'd spent three years meticulously overhauling her personal life.

She raised her chin a notch. "Maybe at one time that was true, but people can change. You did—from Hollywood stud to respected director," she reminded him. "And now you're entering politics."

"That's right. And it's hard to garner respect if the public thinks you're a punchline."

He'd told her something similar in Hawaii, when they'd cuddled together in bed after making love, sharing their dreams for the future. When she'd told him about her acting ambitions and determination to be taken seriously he hadn't laughed. Then.

Now, even as she murmured, "I've changed," he was smirking.

"You'll understand, I'm sure, if I have a hard time believing you," he drawled.

"It's true."

She had the therapy bills, the stack of self-help books, and the hours of acting lessons to prove it.

"No longer a self-absorbed party girl?"

"No."

"So, you didn't spend seventy grand on a night out with friends last month?"

She closed her eyes, sighed. She supposed she should have been flattered that he apparently kept tabs on her, but it was clear he still didn't want to hear her version of events.

"They wanted to see Paris. I obliged. What's the harm? I can afford it. And before you ask, yes, the other story in that issue of *Inquiring Minds* was true as well. I did spend a quarter-million dollars on a pair of sapphire-studded shoes and a matching handbag while I was there."

In truth, the Paris escapade had included a young woman terminally ill with a brain tumor. She'd never seen Paris, she'd told a friend, who had then written to the Herriman Hotel in Paris to beg a favor. The manager had denied the request, but then Tempest had gotten wind of it. And Tempest had made sure the young woman had a trip to remember—as well as some highly impractical but lovely new shoes to wear afterward.

That part hadn't been reported, though. Only Tempest's seemingly frivolous escapades made headlines. She was used to that. Her parents might hold press conferences to announce their largesse, but Tempest preferred anonymity when doing charitable work or donating money. Too many people already assumed that everything she did was for her own gain.

"Blue your favorite color?" Colin asked.

She didn't know why it should rankle so much that he'd apparently forgotten it was yellow. With a casual lift of one hand, she replied, "Of course."

"Well, you can buy all the expensive shoes you want, but the part of Roxy isn't for sale."

"I don't want to buy it. I want to earn it," Tempest snapped, indignant.

"Right."

"I'm not asking for a favor or special treatment. I just want an audition. Give me the chance to read, Colin. Afterward, if you're unimpressed with my interpretation of the role, you can tell me so. Is that too much to ask?"

"Yes."

He started to walk away, but she stopped him with a hand on his arm. "Why do you hate me so?"

"You don't know?"

She raised her chin. "You stood *me* up, remember? You never even called, or returned my calls."

"Don't tell me you're still wondering why?"

She felt her face heat and she glanced away briefly before replying. "The picture?"

"The picture," he repeated bitterly.

"It was stupid—a mistake," she said, recalling how, when heckled by the paparazzi, she had foolishly tried to toss her hair—only to discover it caught in the clasp of her halter-style gown. She had tugged and the clasp had given way, and because the gown's straps were encrusted with gems, their weight had yanked the entire front of the dress to her waist in the click of a camera shutter.

"Will March must have told you what happened," she said. Colin had departed the party earlier, leaving Tempest in the care of his best friend and one-time agent.

"Will told me, all right," he replied, the words as sharp as shards of glass. They seemed out of proportion with the sin she had committed.

Still, she asked, "Haven't *you* ever done anything you regretted afterward?"

His dark gaze never wavered. "Yes."

And with that one word he managed a wound so deep Tempest marveled that she was still standing.

He regretted her.

"Look," he said impatiently, "I've got to leave. Stan will be waiting for me at the restaurant."

She swallowed, grateful for the sunglasses that hid the fresh tears gathering in her eyes.

"Then you'd better go. You don't want to keep Stan waiting."

COLIN SAT IN HIS CAR for a moment and waited for the urge to strike something to pass. Tempest had had the nerve to look surprised, wounded, even, when he knew she was far too shallow and calculating to have emotions like that.

No, pictures didn't lie. The bared breasts shot he could almost dismiss, even though just days prior to the photo being snapped she'd told him that she planned to tone down her outrageous ways.

But what he couldn't shrug off was the fact that she'd thrown herself at his best friend in the limousine after leaving Morton's. The following afternoon Will March had told Colin about Tempest's impromptu striptease for the photographers. And then Will had confessed that Tempest had propositioned him on the ride home.

"I thought you should know, since things seemed to be getting serious between you two," Will had said.

Serious? Colin had crazily imagined himself in love with Tempest, a fact that at the time had had him scared half out of his wits. But her actions had knocked him back to his senses. Maybe he should thank her for that.

He should have guessed she couldn't be faithful. It had been stupid to believe Tempest could be when few of the women who had mattered in his life had been in the past. His own mother had cheated on his father, with deadly consequences.

Love makes you weak. His father's words echoed in the car now. It was the last thing Michael McKinnon had said twenty-two years ago, before blowing out his brains.

Colin shifted his Mercedes coupe into drive and raced out of the parking lot with a squeal of tires. He was leaving for Cannes in the morning, glad to put an ocean between him and bitter memories. The hustle and hype of the eleven-day international film festival would be sure to take his mind off Tempest Herriman.

I've changed.

Only a fool would believe her.

CHAPTER TWO

"THE MAN'S A FOOL."

Audra Conlan Howard Stover gave Tempest's hand a sympathetic pat before picking up a double mocha latte for a delicate sip.

They were seated in a trendy coffee bar just off the main lobby of the Beverly Hills Herriman. Tempest had intended to pack her bags and jet back to the East Coast immediately after returning from the non-audition, but Audra had stopped her.

"You're already here. Come on, stay a couple of days. We rarely see one another any more now that you spend most of your time in New York," her friend had said.

Audra was one of the few people who knew that, in addition to having a small part in an off-off-Broadway production, two things kept Tempest in Manhattan. First, the Herriman Foundation offices were there. Tempest had a seat on the board, and she took her obligations very seriously. And more importantly, living there put an entire continent between her and the man who'd broken her heart.

"I really wanted the part of Roxy," Tempest murmured, stirring more sweetener into her French roast.

"You want me to pay a visit to Stan Dartman?" Audra asked. "I met him a few times. He won't remember me, but I'm pretty sure he'll remember my cleavage."

"You'd seduce him on my behalf?" Tempest said on a laugh.

"What are friends for?"

Although Tempest knew Audra was only joking, she was still a true friend. She was one of the few people Tempest knew she could count on in a pinch.

The two women had a lot in common, with notoriety topping the list. Net worth came next. While Tempest had inherited her vast wealth, Audra had married into it. They had met at a party several years earlier, and something had just clicked. Since then they'd kicked up their high heels together on plenty of occasions. Unlike Tempest, however, Audra showed no signs of slowing down.

At twenty-eight, she'd been married twice, divorced twice, and was now in the midst of a torrid affair with Trent Kane, an actor as well known for his talent in front of the camera as for his drug problem off screen. That fact made Tempest nervous on her friend's behalf, but she knew better than to confront Audra outright with her concerns. Nothing could sink a friendship faster than a man. Still, she had dropped several hints.

"What would Trent think about your seducing Stan for me?" she asked mildly.

"Hmm. Couldn't say." Her friend frowned.

"Away again?"

"Yes. In Cannes." Audra brightened then. "Let's go there."

"To Cannes? Now?"

"Why not? The film festival is about to start." Audra was grinning as she tucked a hunk of white-blonde hair behind one ear. "Besides, do we really need a good reason to spend time in the South of France?"

It sounded like more fun than moping around her New York apartment. Still, Tempest hedged. "I don't know."

"I hear Colin is going. His film *Collusion* is under consideration for the Palme d'Or. The movie has been creating a lot of buzz in the foreign press. Trent says Colin's got a good shot at taking top directing honors. That should put the man in a good mood and ready to listen to reason."

"I can't just go to Cannes."

"Why not? You told me the show in New York is about to close anyway, and I'm sure you can take a week or so off from your duties at the Foundation."

"We don't have Festival credentials," she said, groping for an excuse.

"Temp, you're an actress. You can get them. Even if you can't, do you think they're going to turn a Herriman away at the Bunker?" she asked, using the nickname for the Palais des Festivals.

"It makes me look desperate."

"Honey, you could never look desperate." Audra nibbled thoughtfully on her biscotti before adding, "But these are desperate times. If Colin won't let you read for him here, go there and do it, before he has a chance to say no."

"What? An ambush audition in some hotel lobby? You've got to be kidding."

Audra grinned. "Why not? Get him in a situation where he can't refuse, and then dazzle him with your talent. If that fails, strip off every last bit of clothing and take a stroll down La Croisette."

"It's been done," she observed dryly. "Besides, I don't need to dazzle Colin McKinnon. I wanted that part, but I do have other options for advancing my career."

She said it, and she almost convinced herself she meant it. But that was before the telephone conversation with her agent the following afternoon.

"A music video! You want me to do a music video?"

"More than a few actresses have moved on to bigger projects that way," Doris Benedict soothed.

"By starring in a music video?"

Doris coughed delicately. "It's really not starring. It's more like a walk-on part."

"No. Absolutely no more walk-ons. I'll never be regarded seriously if I keep taking such bit parts." Before her agent could respond, she added, "And if you give me that tripe about how there are no small parts, only small actors, I'm going to scream."

"I was just going to say that even small parts add up on a resumé."

"Well, then my resumé should be stellar by now, shouldn't it?" she snapped in frustration.

Ever the diplomat, Doris tried again.

"I'm really sorry the audition with Stan Dartman fell through, Tempest, but that's the business—and this video is work. Filming starts tomorrow morning in New York. I think you should hop on your private jet and do this."

Tempest did board her private jet later that day, but her ultimate destination wasn't New York. Seated in a comfy leather chair across from a dozing Audra, she sipped Chardonnay, enjoyed a small wedge of Gouda, and brushed up on her French.

CHAPTER THREE

COLIN DID A DOUBLE-TAKE when he saw Tempest get out of a limousine and glide up the red carpet outside the Palais des Festivals.

What in the hell was she doing here?

He couldn't ask her now, though. She was smiling and waving graciously to the photographers who were lined up six deep along the velvet ropes on La Croisette, screaming out her name. The last thing Colin wanted was to appear in a picture with her and have ancient history resurrected and then blown out of proportion by the tabloids. That, he assured himself, was the only reason he was eager to keep his distance.

"This way, Tempest! Look this way!" the photographers shouted.

"Over here, sweetheart. Give us a smile."

She complied like the professional celebrity she was. This was an expected part of the spectacle after all. Everyone from bona fide stars and starry-eyed wannabes stopped, primped and posed for the media hordes before making the long hike up the steep steps of the Palais.

She was still one of the most beautiful women he'd ever seen, he thought with reluctant admiration. The backless dove-gray gown scooped low in front and flowed over the curves of her full figure like a silk waterfall that ended with a two-foot train. The gown's clingy fabric left just enough to the imagination to be dangerous.

He swallowed thickly. He'd bet his SAG card she wasn't wearing anything underneath it.

Her hair, that wild tumble of auburn he'd once fisted in his hands, had been subdued into a sleek up-do and secured with a spray of diamonds.

The overall look was vintage Hollywood: plenty of glamour, with that blatant sexuality of hers banked and smoldering like the red hot coals of a fire.

She could make men burn. He knew that firsthand.

Gretchen Wangler, a reporter for the American television tabloid *Hot from Hollywood*, snagged Tempest by the arm as she attempted to walk up the steps.

"Here's a familiar face," the woman purred into her microphone. "Tempest, your gown is divine. Is that Dolce and Gabbana?"

"Actually, it's an original Danielle Salvatore."

Gretchen looked surprised. The woman prided herself on knowing fashion, and so she cast an anxious glance toward the camera.

"Danielle Salvatore, you say? I don't believe I'm familiar with her."

"That's because she hasn't been discovered yet," Tempest replied with a patient smile. "Danielle's a native New Yorker, working days right now at a coffee shop in SoHo and spending her nights in charge of wardrobe at a small theater I've done some work in. She designed this gown and a couple of others for me as a favor."

Colin frowned. Tempest was a legend when it came to starting fashion trends. If she carried a certain kind of handbag or wore a brooch, it became the must-have accessory of the season. This public announcement and the resulting exposure were sure to help jump-start the fledgling designer's career. It was a generous thing to do.

And calculating, he decided, when she glanced past the reporter and locked her sea-green gaze on him with all the precision of a sharpshooter.

"She's an incredible talent, just waiting to be discovered. She deserves a break."

Gretchen Wangler turned to see what had captured Tempest's attention and then smiled greedily.

"Colin McKinnon! A moment of your time, please?"

He was left with no choice but to comply. His efforts to avoid sharing a photo frame with Tempest now were moot. They would be paired on magazine covers and in entertainment show sound-bites for weeks, if not months, to come. He had little doubt his political opponents would use the photo when they harped on Colin's "Hollywood values."

Still, he smiled warmly and kissed the air near the reporter's left check.

"Gretchen. Good to see you."

It was a lie. The woman was vicious—a piranha ready to strip his bones clean with little provocation. He'd been on the receiving end of her brand of journalism before. In Hollywood circles they called it being "Wangled." So, Colin knew it paid to be nice to her, even when he felt like telling her to jump in the Mediterranean.

"You know Tempest, of course," Gretchen said, splitting a sly look between the two of them. Gretchen had been the one to break the news of their affair.

"Yes. How are you?"

The words came out stiff, despite his best efforts to appear relaxed and nonchalant.

"Fine, thanks." Tempest smiled, a quirking of full

ruby lips that he didn't trust—and for good reason. A moment later she baldly informed Gretchen, "Colin and I ran into one another just the other day outside Stan Dartman's office."

"Hmm, a producer and a director meeting with an actress? Anything you'd care to announce today?" Gretchen asked eagerly.

"No."

Colin was firm in his reply, but Tempest merely fiddled with the back of one chandelier earring. She looked like the proverbial cat that had swallowed the canary. Gretchen all but salivated.

"Come on, Tempest," the reporter cajoled, pushing the microphone closer. "Just between us girls—have you been cast in *Flights of Fancy*?"

"As you know, Gretchen, you-know-who's been tapped for the lead. It's been all over the papers—hasn't it, Colin?"

Tempest winked at him and he gritted his teeth.

"I know that," Gretchen said, sounding slightly put out. "But that still leaves a juicy supporting role open, my dear." She raised her eyebrows as high as the taut skin of her forehead would allow. "Well?"

"I'd love the role of Roxy Remington, of course. Any actor would. She could be a completely unlikable character, given the fact she's a prostitute, but she has spunk, nerve. She yearns to be something more than what she is. Don't get me wrong, this is not Julia Roberts's Vivian, in *Pretty Woman*. Roxy is too gritty for the hooker-with-a-heart-of-gold kind of portrayal. She's a diamond in the rough—emphasis on *rough*."

"Sounds like you know the character well," Gretchen remarked.

Tempest lifted her bare shoulders in a delicate shrug. "I've read the script."

"And?"

"And nothing. I haven't even had an audition," she replied.

The limousines were backed up on the street, and more stars converged on the carpet behind them. Colin caught a glimpse of an actor who had reportedly just been released from rehab, and found himself almost grateful for the man's struggle with addiction. Bigger fish to fry, as the saying went. And so he was saved, for the moment anyway, from having to answer any uncomfortable questions Gretchen might have about the movie he'd just signed on to direct.

Gretchen wrapped up the interview, but before nudging the pair of them along she said, "I'll expect an exclusive interview with you both later."

"I'm staying at the Herriman, of course," Tempest said. "Where are you, Colin?"

And he was forced to divulge that he had a suite of rooms at the Carlton.

The walk up the steps of the Bunker was long and tortuous, especially since Tempest had slipped her arm through his. The move was as practical as it was shrewd. Although the steps of the new Palais had been rebuilt several years earlier to correct their dangerously steep angle, they nonetheless had to be difficult to maneuver in a full-length gown and high heels. Still, he knew she was taking delight in his discomfort.

As expected, she stopped at the first landing and waved to the crowds of reporters, photographers and fans below. He kept his back to her as the flashes popped. At the very top she again posed for the cameras before gliding through the Palais doors, all the while still clutching his arm.

Unless he wanted to create a scene, Colin was forced

to stay by her side in the role of escort. He waited until they were inside the building, away from the prying eyes of the media, to haul her to a secluded corner and give her a piece of his mind.

"What do you think you're doing?" he demanded.

"What do you mean?"

"You know what I mean. You're playing with fire, feeding such a pack of lies to Gretchen Wangler of all people."

"I said no more than the truth," Tempest countered. When he scowled, she added, "Let me recap my response for you. I said that I saw you outside Stan Dartman's office. I said that the role of Roxy is a plum part any actor would covet. And I said that I haven't had an audition."

He blew out a breath in frustration. He hated that she was right. She hadn't lied. She'd just finessed the truth in a way that would have made the best political spinmeisters sit up in admiration. Maybe he should offer to put her on his campaign's payroll. God knew, he wouldn't want her working for an opponent.

"What are you doing here, Tempest?"

"I'm in Cannes for the Festival," she replied innocently. "I came with Audra, but she disappeared into Trent Kane's hotel room a few hours ago and hasn't come up for air yet. I decided to come to the official screening of your film by myself."

She stepped closer, bringing the scent of her perfume with her. She tucked her small clutch beneath one arm and raised her hands to brush nonexistent lint from the lapels of his tuxedo. Afterward, she rested her palms there, and he swore he felt the heat from her hands singeing his skin.

Unbidden came the memory of the desperate way

those slim fingers had once helped rid him of his clothing, undoing the buttons of his shirt one at a time before finally giving in to passion and rending the garment at the seams.

"I've seen the ads and read the articles in the trade publications. The film's enjoying a lot of buzz. All that talk has me worked up a bit, as I'm sure was the intent."

"Of course," he said, although he was certain of nothing at this point except that she smelled like sin and looked like heaven.

She stepped closer still, one silk-covered thigh sliding intimately along the inside of his. His hands came up before he could stop them and spanned her waist. Push her away, his mind ordered. He pulled her closer.

"I'm curious to see if it lives up to all the hype. Most things don't."

Lost in the memory, he murmured, "But some things do."

He leaned forward after he said it.

His mouth had barely brushed her lips when she stepped back, breaking all contact and smiling triumphantly. He blinked, tried to clear his head. It wasn't until she'd walked away that Colin realized Tempest had just quoted Roxy's lines from Scene Three.

TEMPEST RETREATED to the ladies' room, determined to revel in the success of her performance. The shock on Colin's face was worth the price she was paying now for that intimate contact. She'd forgotten how rock-solid his build was, how thrilling his touch could be. She'd ended the kiss almost before it started, but the barest brush of his lips had brought the bittersweet memories flooding back.

Perhaps Tempest understood Roxy so well because,

though the differences between them were many and vast, Tempest, too, knew what it was to yearn for something unobtainable.

Her hand shook as she reapplied her lipstick.

HER PLAN WAS TO LEAVE as soon as the screening of Colin's film was over. Tempest picked up her clutch and headed for the exits, discreetly wiping tears from her eyes.

She didn't like admitting it, but his film was incredible. She knew from reading the trades that he had both directed and produced this one. And he'd managed to come in under budget, using lesser known actors and obscure locations. The result was a moving piece that for all its direness still managed to leave one feeling upbeat, hopeful.

Around her, Tempest heard the murmurs of approval. Since she was fluent in French and Italian, she knew the praise came from more than one side of the Atlantic.

"I hear he's going into politics," someone said in English. The speaker was definitely American.

"Hollywood's loss will be Washington's gain," another replied. "The guy's young and talented, and good-looking to boot. Ten, fifteen years from now, we could be hearing *Hail to the Chief* when he enters a room."

She smiled, unable to stop the pride she felt on his behalf. She could picture an older Colin as the nation's Commander-in-Chief, giving the State of the Union address or kicking off the annual Easter Egg Hunt on the White House lawn. He'd need a first lady, of course. Someone with an impeccable reputation, who was attractive in a conservative way. She would wear pearls, neat two-piece suits in pastel hues, and keep her hair short and tamed.

Are they or aren't they? Such a question would never be asked.

Tempest spotted Colin in the director's box, shaking hands, accepting backslaps. He was a man on the move, his star rising as fast as a streaking comet. Their gazes locked for one electrifying moment. The part of her that wanted to celebrate his achievement trumped the urge to see him crash back to earth. She nodded once, and then slipped out of the huge auditorium.

Her getaway, however, was not clean. An acquaintance stood near the exit, chatting in her overly animated way with a couple of companions.

"Tempest!" Cleo Hathaway exclaimed. "Don't you look gorgeous this evening?"

The petite brunette excused herself from her friends and rushed over to send an air kiss in the direction of Tempest's left ear.

"Cleo. Nice to see you."

Cleo was a character actor who had worked with just about every hot property in Hollywood, although few people who saw the movies would ever remember her name. Still, her career had been lengthy and successful—a fact she liked to rub in Tempest's face, all while smiling innocently with her trademark overbite.

"I didn't realize you were going to be here," Cleo said. "When I ran into you a couple of weeks ago in New York you didn't say a word about coming to Cannes."

"Spur of the moment. I wasn't sure I could get away."

"So many pressing engagements, I'm sure," she said, offering a horse-faced grin that took none of the sting out of the intended insult.

"Yes—and, speaking of which, I'm on my way now to meet friends for drinks," Tempest lied.

Cleo didn't take the hint. In fact she laid a hand on Tempest's arm to keep her from leaving.

"Did you just come from the screening of Colin McKinnon's latest movie?"

"*Collusion.* Yes."

"What did you think of it? I hear he's a favorite for the Palme d'Or."

From the way she was eyeing Tempest, it seemed clear she was waiting for some good gossip to pass on. Tempest chose her words carefully, but spoke the truth.

"The film is very good—excellent, actually."

"I heard it's as depressing as they come. Did you think it was?"

"It's dark," Tempest said. "But it has a powerful message. The script is incredible, and so is the acting. If Colin weren't already a respected director, he would be after this film."

Cleo stepped closer, but didn't bother to lower her voice. "I heard he slept with the lead actress. No wonder he wrung such an Oscar-worthy performance out of a little nobody like that. The man can inspire me any time he'd like."

The thought of Colin being intimate with another woman left Tempest queasy, but she pushed from her mind the stark image Cleo's words conjured. Just because she hadn't done more than go on an occasional date in three years, it didn't mean he had been sitting home alone, pining.

"Of course you've slept with him, so you'd know," the other woman added.

Tempest squared her shoulders. Cleo fed on set gossip and loved to trash others in the business. Someone needed to put this nasty little busybody in her place.

"Inspired or not, I doubt *you* could have done that

part justice. As for Colin, he doesn't need to sleep with anyone to get them to do their job well. He's a gifted director who recognized a dream script when he saw it and was lucky enough to find the right *nobody* to interpret the role of Julia."

That said, she turned—and walked straight into the broad chest of the man under discussion.

Colin steadied her with a hand on her waist—a proprietary hand that he failed to remove.

"Defending my work ethic?"

He divided a look between the women, clearly enjoying the blush that stained Cleo's freckled cheeks. Tempest was pretty sure her color was high as well, but the reason seemed to have more to do with the placement of his hand and the delicious warmth radiating out from that point of contact than the fact he had overheard their conversation.

"I-I have to leave now," Cleo announced, looking flustered. "Excuse me."

Tempest took a step away as well, forcing Colin to drop his hand. He glanced briefly at his palm and frowned, as if just realizing he'd been touching her still.

Tempest moistened her lips. Her tone was sincere when she said, "My compliments to you on *Collusion*. It's extraordinary, Colin, really."

"High praise, indeed, coming from you," he replied with a cocky smile.

She sighed and shook her head. "I was paying you a compliment."

"As I was you."

"Oh."

"I've never doubted you know quality when you see it, Tempest. It's hard for you not to, since you were born with a silver spoon in your mouth."

"Is it so difficult to be nice to me?" she asked quietly.

Colin tilted his head to one side and regarded her for a long moment.

Finally, he said, "You might make one hell of an actress after all, heiress. You almost made me believe I hurt your feelings."

She swallowed and forced a smile to her lips. "Next time I'll be sure to add some tears."

"You do that."

CHAPTER FOUR

TEMPEST CHECKED HER WATCH again and sighed. She had been waiting for Audra outside one of the screening rooms in the vast Palais for the past twenty minutes, and her friend had yet to show.

She turned, planning to go back to her suite at the Herriman, and spotted Colin just down the hall. Will March and another man stood with him. From news reports she knew that these days Will was Colin's campaign adviser. She was vaguely surprised to see him in Cannes, although she supposed their close friendship warranted his attendance. This was a big festival for Colin, after all.

She heard Colin chuckle then, and the easygoing sound plucked at her memory. She'd always loved his laugh. It went nicely with his wicked sense of humor and his penchant for practical jokes.

Once Tempest had visited him on the set of a movie he was directing only to have Security clap her in handcuffs and allege she was trespassing. The guard had delivered her to a small, windowless room, where she'd sat sputtering in rage and fear for a good fifteen minutes before Colin had walked in. Grinning. Then he'd pushed the door closed, flipped the lock, and, oh, the uses they'd come up with for those cuffs.

The recollection had Tempest smiling now, and that

was when Colin saw her. For a long moment their gazes held, and the past seemed to usurp the present, bringing old needs bubbling back to the surface. Did he feel it, too? The smoldering look in his eyes seemed to suggest he did.

But then Will tapped Colin's arm and the moment was lost.

Tempest wanted to turn away and run, but she knew from experience that the memories would chase her. Instead, she decided to confront them—and the man who inspired them. Bracing for Colin's reaction, she walked to where he stood.

He didn't want to see her—or be seen with her—but she'd come to Cannes on a mission. She planned to carry it through. The quicker she was able to convince him she was perfect for Roxy, the better. It was like swallowing foul-tasting medicine: best to get it all down in one shot. Of course if she got the part she would have to spend months on location with him. But she would worry about that later, she decided, wondering if maybe that was just what she needed to finally exorcise the bittersweet memory of their happier times.

"Hello, gentlemen," she said when she reached them.

A muscle ticked in Colin's cheek, but he didn't speak.

"Tempest," Will said coolly, glancing in his friend's direction.

Only the third man looked pleased to see her, and that was because his gaze was locked on her cleavage. He was tall and rotund. Despite the designer cut of his tuxedo, and the advantage of height, he didn't wear it well. Its clean lines were obscured by his protruding midsection. Definitely not Hollywood—and yet something about him seemed vaguely familiar.

"I'm Benton Landry," he said to her breasts.

"Of Landry Industries," Tempest supplied, and the puzzle piece fell into place.

She'd never met Landry, but she knew him by name and net worth. He was a shrewd businessman, and a big financial supporter to several senatorial candidates in large states. He also donated lavishly to worthwhile causes, so he sometimes ran in the same circles as her parents. None of that changed the fact that his corporation had a lousy environmental record at its factories in the United States, and a reputation for unfair, even underhanded business practices in its operations abroad.

"Enjoying the Festival, Miss Herriman?" Landry asked as his gaze slid south again. Somehow she doubted he was admiring the simple gold chain looped around her neck, but the murderous look on Colin's face made it almost worth being subjected to the man's leer. Surely Colin couldn't be jealous?

"You can't have a bad time in Cannes," she replied lightly. "I think it might be against the law."

"We were just going over to the Carlton," Landry said. "Maybe you'd care to join us?"

"I'm sure Tempest has better things to do," Colin said, his expression just this side of frigid. "I doubt a conversation about international trade would appeal to someone more interested in Gucci than GATT."

The comment had Tempest seething. Three years ago she'd sworn he'd believed her capable of intelligent conversation and understanding current events. She offered a demure smile that she hoped was in direct contrast to her dress—a boldly cut yellow beaded chiffon number that ended mid-thigh.

"Oh, I don't know, Colin. In the company of three handsome men I just might find a discussion about the General Agreement on Tariffs and Trade quite exhilarating. Market access can affect fashion, as well as the kinds of goods Mr. Landry creates."

With a smug smile, she accepted the industrialist's arm.

LE BAR DES CÉLÉBRITÉS WAS full to bursting with various agents and actors, directors and producers, all huddled around tables talking excitedly and seemingly in the midst of cutting the deal of their lives. This was the place, Tempest knew, where the future was decided, or at least helped along, for many in the business.

She wanted to be one of them—which meant she had to stop rising to every scrap of bait Colin tossed in her direction. She needed him to if not like her at least tolerate her and respect her as an actress if she was going to get that part. She sucked in a deep breath and slid into the chair next to Will's. On the other side of the table, Colin glowered.

She smiled bravely.

The waiter came and Colin ordered a Scotch.

What was Tempest up to now? He almost didn't want to know. The woman was full of surprises. Like her intelligence. No, that wasn't quite a surprise. He'd merely forgotten how quick-witted she could be. Why, he wondered, had it been so much easier to remember her as vacuous?

Will took out a pack of clove cigarettes and offered Tempest one, which she refused.

"Do you mind?" his friend asked.

She smiled sweetly and laid a hand on Will's sleeve. "Actually, yes."

The contact was brief and polite, but it still had Colin's gut twisting. Did she still want his best friend?

It didn't matter, he told himself. Any feelings Colin had had for Tempest were long over. So what if his attraction for her lingered? She was a beautiful woman. What red-blooded man wouldn't find his blood pressure—among other things—rising when she was near? As for anything deeper than lust, even the possibility was past tense. Right now he had his future to consider. And part of that future was seated at their table.

Benton Landry was a huge contributor to the party. He donated personally as much as legally allowed, and through various political action committees representing Landry Industries and its subsidiaries he donated millions more in so-called soft money, which Colin personally believed made a mockery of the campaign finance laws.

Colin had been told to meet with Landry, who was in France on business, and treat him like visiting royalty. The edict, which had come from officials high in the party, didn't sit well. Landry had made it clear he didn't want to see an action-hero-turned-director on the ticket in the next election. Colin was no fan of Landry's either, and, now that the older man's gaze was riveted to Tempest's bust, he also felt a murderous urge to wring his neck.

"So, Mr. Landry—" Tempest began.

"Benton, please," he interrupted, taking the fat stump of an unlit cigar from the corner of his mouth.

"Benton. Did you get a chance to see Colin's film?"

"I saw it."

"Very powerful, wouldn't you agree?"

She winked at Colin, setting his teeth on edge. But then Landry took center stage, issuing a snort that apparently served as his opinion.

"I take it you didn't like it?" Colin said evenly.

Benton's face twisted in disgust, and though he hadn't lit the cigar he made a show of grinding the tip into the crystal ashtray on the table.

"I thought it was too violent and contained too much gratuitous sex." Squinting at Colin, he added, "For the past several years Congress has been making noise about taking measures to clean up the filth that comes out of Hollywood. Do you have an opinion on that, *Candidate* McKinnon?"

Colin willed the red to ebb from his vision. Temper your reply, he silently ordered himself. Temper your words. Temper... Tempest? She was now speaking.

"It's true, Benton, that some movies use violence, nudity and four-letter words as a crutch, because they lack substance. But other movies, such as *Collusion*, are made more powerful because of the inclusion of coarse language and stark images."

Colin didn't need or necessarily even want Tempest's support, and yet he found her succinct defense of his work oddly touching.

"I can understand why *you* would feel that way, Miss Herriman." Landry's tone was patronizing. It turned crisp when he addressed Colin. "But surely as a candidate hoping to court voters you don't agree that there's a place for obscenity in film?"

"You make it all sound black and white," Colin answered evenly.

"Forgive me. I know it's not. It's in full color, and being splashed across the big screen as well as the small one. Families can't get a break from it." Landry's calculating gaze swept to Tempest when he added, "They're tired of Hollywood's so-called values corrupting their children."

What a hypocrite, Colin thought. This man spouting off about values and morality had once been accused of using child labor in one of his overseas factories.

"Funny you should bring up children—"

Across the table from him, Will cleared his throat with a nervous cough. "Ah, here come our drinks."

With an effort Colin reined in the worst of his temper. It shouldn't surprise him that Landry was bent on twisting his words and turning what Will had billed as a friendly get-together over drinks into a take-no-prisoners debate. Benton made no bones about the fact he'd prefer to see Colin's main challenger on the ticket after next March's primary, but eleven months out the polls were already showing Colin slightly ahead.

He couldn't decide what bothered him more, though. The fact that Landry was trying to bait him or that Tempest wasn't and yet he still found himself eyeing the lure. Candlelight danced in her gaze and shot fire into the heavy mane of her hair. She raised the wine the waiter handed her to her mouth, resting the glass's lucky rim against her lush bottom lip.

Colin licked his own and then tossed back half of his Scotch in a single gulp.

Landry did the same, not bothering to stop at half, and then pushed his chair back from the table.

"I'm afraid I can't stay."

Will was on his feet in an instant.

"Let's get together again before you return to the States. I know you have concerns about the EU's allegations of unfair trade practices, and about what sanctions from the World Trade Organization could mean to your company, should they occur. Colin can give you his position on those issues."

Landry nodded, but addressed Colin. "I'd like a word with you in private."

Colin followed the older man to a quiet corner outside the lounge.

"I'm going to be blunt," Benton said, pulling a fresh

cigar from the breast pocket of his tuxedo and using it to point at Colin. "I don't like you."

"That's come to my attention," Colin replied evenly.

"You're in a horse race right now, son, neck-and-neck. And you and I both know the outcome will be decided in March. No matter which opponent winds up on the general election ballot, he'll be beatable. Our party's primary election is the real story. Now, I like Bill Stowman," he went on, referring to Colin's chief challenger, "but a lot of other folks in the party think *you're* going to win. Name recognition and charisma have their uses."

"I *am* going to win. In March and in November."

"That takes money and endorsements."

"With all due respect, sir, it takes more than money and endorsements, because neither one of those things guarantees the public a qualified senator."

Benton nodded, as if to concede the point. "True, but if I make sure both of them get tossed behind Stowman you'll face an uphill battle come March. You don't want me for an enemy."

"I'm not sure I want you for a friend," Colin replied.

Benton laughed harshly. "I almost admire your honesty. But you'd better learn how to go along to get along, or this campaign will be your last."

"Are you threatening me?"

The older man smiled cagily, but shook his head. "Of course not. I never make threats. I believe in action. Now for that advice—"

"I thought you'd already given it."

"Well, here's some more. And you'd be wise to heed it. Don't pick up where you left off with Tempest Herriman."

"Nothing is going on between me and Tempest," he said tightly.

Benton's nod was brisk. "Good. I don't think I need to tell you that as lovely as I find that young woman and as impeccable as her pedigree might be, she's poison when it comes to your political ambitions."

Other people, including Will, whom he respected a lot more than he did Benton Landry, had told Colin the same thing before he'd figured it out on his own. But he resented like hell the unsolicited advice now.

"There's more to Tempest Herriman than meets the eye," Colin said.

The words slipped out, surprising Colin. Before he could wonder about their origin, though, Benton was speaking again.

"God, that's hard to believe—given that half the free world has seen most of what's under her clothes."

The man's bawdy laughter had Colin's hand curling into a tight fist. "That's not what I meant."

"So she's deep as the ocean?" Benton laughed again, but he was as serious as the business end of a shotgun when he added, "Find yourself some boring little nobody who will stand by your side and smile adoringly at you while on the campaign trail. That's what plays well with the voters. A woman like Tempest is only good for one thing."

A woman like Tempest.

Colin walked back into the lounge with Benton's parting shot echoing in his head. Why on earth had his first instinct been to offer a rebuttal?

"What did he say?" Will asked eagerly when Colin reached the table.

His gaze slid to Tempest. *Find yourself some boring little nobody.* He didn't plan ever to get serious with a woman again, but if he did would that be what he wanted? Tempest was many things, but no one could accuse her of being boring.

"He offered me some advice."

"You don't look happy about it," Tempest said quietly. "Are you going to take it?"

Colin settled into the seat opposite hers. "I haven't decided—"

"I'll call Benton later and get things straightened out," Will interrupted. "I told the party leaders that your meeting with him during the Festival was a bad idea. He's so anti-Hollywood, I don't know why they expected him to change his views now."

"Wishful thinking," Colin muttered. There seemed to be a lot of that going around. He downed the rest of his Scotch.

"Another round of drinks, gentlemen?" Tempest asked. "I'll even buy."

"I think we'd better call it a night," Will replied. At the same time Colin said, "Why not?"

"Colin, I don't think—" Will began.

Colin's gaze never strayed from Tempest. "You don't have to stay, Will. I don't require a chaperone."

His friend got to his feet on an oath. "All right. Good night, Tempest."

"Will." She held out a hand to him. "It was good to see you again."

"Same here." He slid a knowing look toward Colin as he asked, "How about a kiss for old times' sake?"

Tempest laughed, but if she was embarrassed it didn't stop her from rising to her feet and giving Will a hug and a chaste peck on the cheek. Colin gritted his teeth throughout the brief exchange. He was angry with his friend for the blatant reminder of her fecklessness, angry with himself that he needed to be reminded.

Love makes you weak.

He pushed away the words, and the ugly mental

image that came with them. Colin had been the one to find his father. Nothing about that memory had improved with age. It was a good thing he'd never fallen all the way for Tempest.

He considered leaving the lounge. He could catch up with Will and spend the next couple of hours talking campaign strategy or meet with other friends and take in another movie screening. But, to prove to himself that the attraction he felt for Tempest didn't go beyond basic chemistry, he ordered another Scotch when the waiter came.

"And I'll have straight tonic with a twist of lemon, please," she said.

"No Cristal to pour in your shoes?" he asked.

She seemed to stiffen at the taunt, but then she shrugged.

"Actually, I haven't done that in years. In fact, these days I rarely indulge in more than a glass of wine when I'm out. Dulls the senses, you know."

At his snort of disbelief she pursed her lips, but her tone was flippant when she added, "Okay, you've got me. The real reason I'm not asking for Cristal is that my shoes are open-toed slingbacks. Since I can't drink champagne out of them, what would be the point of ordering it?"

One long, slim leg peeked out from the side of the table to show off her strappy excuse for a shoe, and Colin nearly groaned aloud. He'd forgotten all about the little rose tattoo just above her right ankle. She had another one, he knew, substantially higher on that same appendage.

This groan made it past his lips, but he disguised it as a cough. "I didn't realize you were so pragmatic."

"I've been working in that direction," she replied seriously as she fiddled with the edge of a cocktail napkin. "I've been working on a lot of things, actually."

Curious, he bit. "Such as?"

She shrugged. "I have a small part in an off-off-Broadway production. Actually, the play's folded—or will have by the time I return to New York. But it's been a wonderful experience."

"I did some of that myself when I was still bussing tables and waiting for my big break."

"I know. I remember you telling me that. It's where I got the idea."

"It's good training," Colin admitted grudgingly.

She chuckled softly. "That's what I comforted myself with after I read the scathing review that ran in the *Village Voice*. But I had the time of my life. The cast and crew were incredible."

"There's a sense of camaraderie in those small theaters that's hard to come by elsewhere in the business," he mused. "And you learn a lot if you're open to criticism—constructive or otherwise."

"I have been." She sipped the tonic water the waiter set in front of her, and waited for him to leave before adding, "A person I greatly admired once told me you only get out of something what you're willing to invest in it in the first place."

Colin glanced up sharply. *He'd* said that to her in Hawaii. True, he'd been talking about her acting ambitions at the time, but he'd also begun to think it might apply to their relationship. He'd actually been mulling over a permanent commitment. But fate had stepped in and saved him from making the monumental mistake his father had.

Yet here he sat, three years later, letting the same woman wind him up again with those big green eyes, that beguiling smile and the illusion of sincerity.

"I've been taking acting lessons, too. From Celia Church," she was saying.

Colin's bitter laughter startled Tempest, as did the cool speculation that had his gaze turning brittle. Even before he began speaking she knew those few minutes of camaraderie they'd just shared were over.

"And I thought Landry was tossing his money around. How much did you have to pay Celia to take *you* on as a student, heiress?" he asked.

Tempest swallowed the sudden lump in her throat, feeling blindsided by the slur. Retreat and regroup, she decided.

"Well, you know, money's no object."

To underscore the point, she opened her beaded evening bag and produced enough currency to cover their drinks. She laid it on the tabletop as she stood. "As promised, these are on me. Goodnight."

"Going away mad?"

"Not at all." But she stopped and turned. "As a former student of Celia's, you of all people should know that she only takes on actors who show potential—no matter what the size of their bank account."

"That used to be the case." He nodded. "Now you've got me seriously wondering."

She reeled in her temper as she wound the thin strap of her handbag around one hand. It didn't matter what he thought of her personally, she reminded herself, as long as she got that part.

"If you'd give me a chance to audition, you wouldn't have to tax yourself."

"No," he said flatly.

She raised one eyebrow in challenge. "Afraid I might be that good?"

He leaned back in his chair and crossed his arms. "Sorry, heiress, but I don't have time to indulge your fantasies."

Tempest was angry enough to spit nails. The man could be so maddening. Approachable and almost kind one minute, cruel and demeaning the next. She turned, ready to march away, but then thought better of it. She could use these emotions—channel them into something productive.

She settled back into her seat with the same ease with which she settled into the character she longed to make hers. Roxy's thick skin and clever way with words gave Tempest courage.

"Are you sure about that? You might enjoy yourself."

"Don't, Tempest," Colin warned, and ran a hand through his hair in irritation. "I'm in no mood for games right now."

That line wasn't in the script, but she'd decided to stay in character and ad lib. Leaning across the table, she loosened his black bow tie.

Pulling him forward slightly with the short ends of it, she asked huskily, "What are you in the mood for?"

"The check."

She might have given up then, had she not noticed that the fingers curling around his glass of Scotch were bone-white. Emboldened, she slowly slipped the tie free of his collar and let it drop onto the tabletop.

"Are you sure? Why don't you tell me what you really want?"

He seemed to study her for a moment as he sipped his drink, dark eyes burning hot enough to scorch the bare skin just above her low neckline where his gaze lingered. His voice was bitter, begrudging, when he replied, "I want what most men want when they see you, I'd imagine."

"Are you recalling how hot it was? How good it felt to break apart and burn?" It wasn't only Roxy who spoke, whose bold gaze flicked over Colin's handsome features. Her voice was an intimate whisper of remembrance when she added, "You still want me."

"Damn you, Tempest."

She took that as a yes, even though she wasn't sure if he was cursing her as a woman or as an actress. Roxy's imaginary life, however, was so much safer at the moment. And so Tempest stayed in character.

"Do you want to know what I want?"

"I think I know."

"Men always think they know," she mused with a slight shake of her head. Then Roxy's husky voice purred, "Let me tell you, so there will be no mistaking. I want a five-speed convertible, cherry-red because that's my favorite color. I want a big house on a hill in the country, with open land sprawling around it in all directions so I can see when trouble's coming."

She had his attention. He hadn't so much as blinked during Roxy's monologue. And so she liberated a clove cigarette from the slim pack Will March had left on the table, drew one out and lit it. Roxy was a chainsmoker, according to the script.

"Are you trouble?" she asked.

Then she took a deep drag on the cigarette, intending to blow out the smoke in a silky stream, but a fit of coughing interrupted her otherwise inspired interpretation.

Humiliation burned high on her cheeks even as the acrid smoke seared the inside of her throat and nasal passages. Colin put his hands together and clapped, drawing the attention of some of the other patrons. Where a moment ago he had looked interested, stirred, now his expression held bored amusement. Tempest wasn't sure what she wanted to do more: murder him or die herself.

"I'll recommend you for a spot in the anti-smoking campaign. Those public service announcements are always looking for a recognizable face. They don't pay anything, but then, as you said, money's no object."

She angled up her chin and ignored the jab. "If I want the part of Roxy, I suppose I'll have to develop a two-pack-a-day habit."

Colin rose to his feet and reached into the pocket of his trousers for his money clip. Peeling off a couple of bills, he said, "Keep your money, heiress. I'll pay for this round. And, before you rush out for a carton of smokes, let me tell you that lung cancer wouldn't make you any more convincing."

He was a liar, she decided. She could see the proof.

"So you say. But you look pretty convinced to me," she remarked dryly, her gaze darting to his pants and the unmistakable ridge of arousal pressing against the fly.

Colin buttoned his jacket, his expression colder than a blast of Arctic wind. When he spoke, his words had the same effect as a well-delivered slap.

"Porn turns me on, too, Tempest. Doesn't make it good acting."

CHAPTER FIVE

THE NOTE ARRIVED IN TEMPEST'S suite the next morning as she and Audra shared a late breakfast.

> *Meet me aboard the King's Ransom at five o'clock this afternoon. The boat is docked in the harbor just west of the Bunker. I owe you an apology for yesterday.*

He'd signed it simply "C".

"Are you going?" Audra asked.

In answer, Tempest tossed the invitation into the trash and walked back to the table. She still felt raw from their byplay in Bar des Célébrités.

"You've got to go!" Audra cried.

"I don't *have* to do anything. Besides, I prefer to be the one calling the shots."

"This isn't like sex, Temp. Being on top here doesn't improve your chances for satisfaction. You need to meet Colin McKinnon on his terms, and still blow him away with your acting."

"I'm not sure I want the part any longer," she mumbled, sipping her juice. "There will be other roles."

Maybe her tunnel vision where this part was concerned had been a mistake. After all, every time she thought she'd convinced Colin that she could act, not to

mention that she had changed immensely from that frivolous socialite he'd once dated, she'd wound up feeling
like a fool. Or, worse, shaken to the core. Obviously the
man could still get to her, and she didn't like knowing
that one bit.

What was the point of moving on in her life if with
a few careless words Colin could draw her back to a
time and place when she'd been so foolishly filled with
hope that he would see beyond the headlines and hoopla
to the flesh-and-blood woman who loved him?

"You were born to play Roxy. It's the role of a lifetime, Temp."

"I know it is," she replied, unable to quibble with the
description. She'd felt that way since she'd first read the
script three months ago, and had all but salivated in anticipation of an audition. Of course that was when she'd
thought Bob Wyman was directing. Now, she murmured, "Is it worth it?"

"You tell me."

"I want to be taken seriously, Audra. Everything I've
done with my life for the past three years—all the
changes I've made—will be for nothing if everyone
continues to think I'm just playing at a career in acting
until something else sparks my interest."

"You have something to prove," Audra agreed, and
pursed her lips knowingly. "That was why I came to
Hollywood eight years ago, too. I haven't proved much
of anything, except that the high school counselor who
told my mom I wouldn't amount to much was right."

"That's not true," Tempest disputed, surprised by her
friend's bald statement.

Audra seemed to shake off her sudden melancholy.
"No, no, of course it's not. For either of us. You have to
keep trying. You told me you had McKinnon eating out

of your hand last night." She giggled then. "Well, at least until you started to cough uncontrollably."

"You'll have to teach me how to smoke if I get this part."

"Actually, I've been thinking about quitting."

"Surgeon General's warnings about the health consequences finally penetrate that thick head of yours?" Tempest asked. She'd been nagging her friend for a couple of years now to kick the habit.

Audra merely shrugged. "It's hell on my skin, not to mention my clothes. I burned a small hole in my gown last night. It's not as if I would ever wear the same dress twice, but still."

"Well, as long as you've got your priorities straight," Tempest said dryly.

"And what's your top priority right now?"

"Roxy," she said.

But Tempest knew it went deeper than that. She wanted some of her pride back, too. Maybe she could accomplish both by facing Colin today.

Rising, she walked to the wastebasket and dug out the crumpled invitation, smoothing the wrinkles as she returned to the table. She would go. She would be the bigger of the two of them. She would show Colin McKinnon that she could forgive and forget, and she would prove to herself that she could move on.

THE WEATHER WAS GORGEOUS, the breeze just brisk enough to rustle the fronds of the palm trees as Tempest hurried along La Croisette to the harbor, one eye on the lookout for the paparazzi she'd managed to shake a block back. She had chosen simple attire for this meeting with Colin, although it could hardly be said that she was dressed down in a flirty thigh-skimming dress the color of warm rum. A pair of dark-rimmed glasses shaded her eyes from the sun, and she tipped them down to read the names on the boats anchored in the harbor.

A yacht as big as a city block snagged her attention. Then she spied the broad-shouldered man who stood on its richly stained deck, the wind tossing his sun-kissed hair. *King's Ransom*, she mused, wondering if she would wind up paying such a price to get back her sanity after the evening was through.

She waved at Colin and then took several deep, fortifying breaths as she waited for him to pilot a small dinghy to the dock to get her.

"I wasn't sure you would come," he said. Then he extended a hand to help Tempest into the rubber craft.

She stared at his strong fingers for a long moment, remembering. There was still time to back out, to retreat and run. Instead, she infused her smile with haughty confidence and accepted his assistance.

"I never pass up an opportunity to see someone grovel," she replied smoothly.

The boat swayed beneath her feet before she could take a seat, nearly upsetting her balance, and she was grateful she'd chosen the pointy-toed Kate Spade skimmers to go with the dress, rather than the impractical pair of heels she'd originally considered. As much as she admired the inviting water of the Côte d'Azur, she didn't want to humiliate herself by going swimming in it right now.

"Who says I intend to grovel?"

"You will," she replied knowingly.

"Want to bet?"

He started up the motor with a yank of his wrist and the dinghy shot away from the dock with enough speed to have Tempest gritting her teeth and holding on tightly. She didn't bother to reply until they reached their destination.

As Colin secured the dinghy to the yacht, she reminded him, "Your note said you wanted to make amends for your nasty behavior yesterday. From where I'm sitting that would require groveling. Lots of it."

He offered what Tempest considered his "cinema smile"—the dazzling display of teeth that had caused women in theaters across the country to sigh back in the days when Colin had filled the screen as an action hero and bankable box office draw. It wasn't the lazy grin that had once made her knees weak. For that, she was grateful.

"View's a bit different from where I'm sitting."

"Oh?"

He shrugged, nonchalant. "You and Landry have a way of bringing out my inner jerk. Will March suggested I find a way to get over that. I decided to practice on you first. Much less at stake."

"You do need to work on your people skills," she replied, irritated anew.

He stood and swept a hand toward the metal rungs of a small ladder dangling over the side of the yacht.

"And speaking of the view..."

Until that moment, Tempest hadn't considered that getting on board would require the suspension of all modesty, given the way she was dressed. Today of all days she would have to be wearing a thong.

"Anything the matter?" Colin asked. Wicked humor danced in his eyes and, damn him, there was that grin.

"I'll let you go ahead."

He declined with a shake of his head. "Oh, no. Ladies first. I insist. This way I can catch you if you slip. It's all about safety, heiress. We wouldn't want your billion-dollar butt bobbing around in the Mediterranean."

Safety, my thonged fanny, she thought. But she raised her chin and set one foot on the bottom rung of the ladder. If living life in the glare of the public spotlight had taught her one thing, it was to hold her head up high no matter how humiliating her current predicament.

So up she went, confident enough in the six hours a week she spent sweating on the Stairmaster to call over her shoulder, "Is your mind still on safety?"

Colin said nothing, but he was no longer grinning. In fact his jaw was clenched tight when he joined her on the deck. She took some satisfaction from that.

Even so, she moved away from him, eager for some distance until her equilibrium was restored. She walked to the rail on the other side of the deck, telling herself it was the gentle roll of the sea that made her legs so un-steady. The silence stretched as they regarded one another.

Finally, she asked, "Is this boat yours?"

Colin had once told her that he wanted to take an en-tire summer off from filming and sail the west coast of North America, from the Puget Sound to the southern tip of Mexico's Baja Peninsula, and then anchor off Los Cabos for some well-deserved R&R. At the time he'd offered to take Tempest with him.

"No. It belongs to a friend. I asked to borrow it for this evening. As you well know, the paparazzi are thick around the city during the Festival. I don't want any in-triguing shots of us together winding up on the front pages of the tabloids. 'Are they or aren't they' might take on a whole new meaning."

She ignored the jab.

"So, you never bought a boat?"

"No." He shrugged. "I've been too busy these past few years to get away. If I ever do buy one, though, I'll probably go a little smaller. This one requires a six-man crew. I like my privacy."

"My parents' yacht is about this size," she said con-versationally. "When I was growing up they used to spend a couple of months on it every summer, puttering about the Caribbean or the Greek Isles. Sometimes I joined them for a week or so."

He coughed, and seemed at war with himself for a moment before saying, "I ran into your folks at a party fundraiser in D.C. a few months ago."

"Oh?"

"Didn't they mention it to you?"

"Well, you know how it is. We don't really converse that often." Tempest shrugged. "Unless you count e-mails."

"It's a very convenient way to communicate."

"And very impersonal," she added.

"I'm sorry that things between you haven't improved on that score."

She glanced up sharply, half expecting to see a derisive smirk, but his gaze was sincere. Apparently he remembered how hurtful Tempest found her parents' aloofness.

Frances and Miles Herriman enjoyed a separate life from their only daughter, so separate Tempest sometimes wondered why they had bothered with offspring in the first place. It didn't sit well that she often felt she owed her existence to their need for an heir rather than their desire for a family.

Over the years, it had seemed to Tempest that the only time she heard from them was when she'd done something disappointing. For a while, in her late teens and early twenties, she had "disappointed" them nearly every week. Her therapist claimed that her subconscious need to spite her parents was behind much of her outrageous behavior.

Thinking of that now, she said, "It took more than a couple dozen years, but I've accepted that they will never be the most loving parents."

"No one's parents are," he murmured, intriguing Tempest. Even when they'd dated he'd never spoken of his family, other than once when he'd mentioned that his father was dead.

"Your mother must be proud of you," she said. "You've conquered Hollywood and it looks like Washington will be next."

His expression turned cold and brittle.

"Let's not go there."

"Sorry," she replied, although she had no idea why she was apologizing.

When he just continued to stare at her, she groped for something to say. "Maybe I should have brought my bathing suit. The sun feels wonderful. For every nice day we have back in New York, we pay for it the next."

"I didn't invite you here to talk about the weather, Tempest. And for what I have in mind you won't need a swimsuit."

His dark gaze singed her skin, but she raised her chin and asked, "Why am I here, then?"

Hell if I know, Colin thought. He'd planned out this scene perfectly, directing it in his head, but now he wasn't so sure it would play the way he had intended. What was it about this woman? He'd convinced himself she was shallow, and yet he still felt in over his head. Was this how his father had felt? he wondered. So blinded by a woman's beauty that he lost sight of the bigger picture?

Tempest could ruin his reputation, ruin his chances for election—or so he'd been reminded by one of the bigger donors to his political party just the evening before. Will March had reminded him of that, too. His friend knew from personal experience how devious Tempest could be. Colin knew from personal experience how devious women in general could be.

"Come inside?" he requested, turning away from her.

In the yacht's main salon a song from Norah Jones's latest CD played on the stereo. The singer's warm, clear voice filled the room, where the shade had been pulled to ensure maximum privacy. He'd lit a dozen candles, spaced around the room, and their flickering light now lent a soft and romantic glow. A bottle of red wine— some of the best the French had to offer—sat open on the sideboard, two thin-stemmed goblets next to it, just waiting to be filled.

He'd seen to all of the details himself, and he was satisfied with the outcome. He'd set the stage perfectly, every detail gleaned from the script.

He heard her swift intake of breath when she entered. "Colin?"

Her tone held a question, but then she walked past him to the table and brushed her fingers across the glossy petals of the tulips that spilled from a crystal vase. Five more vases filled with the same pretty spring-time blooms were scattered about the room.

"Oh, this is lovely. Tulips are my favorite," she said softly. "I didn't think you would remember."

A smile trembled on her lips when she looked at him. She appeared so young, so vulnerable just then. Colin frowned. *Remember?* Hell, no. He'd forgotten all about the tulips he'd once sent her. But the recollection rushed back now, including the way Tempest had greeted him at the door that evening, with a single yellow bloom tucked into her fiery hair. The flower had been the full extent of her attire.

He swallowed hard, ruthlessly shoving the memory aside. But desire stayed, taunting him, torturing him.

"Actually, I was going for a certain look here," he said meaningfully.

Still Tempest didn't get it. Her expression remained almost hopeful. And he knew a panicky moment of regret.

"I have tulips on the terrace of my penthouse in New York. I planted them myself," she murmured.

"Tempest—" he said evenly, wondering how best to open her eyes. But she misunderstood his tone.

"No, really. I know it's hard to believe, but I have a green thumb. When I was growing up, one of my nannies had an interest in horticulture and I guess she passed it on to me. It certainly wasn't as if my mother ever deigned to get her hands dirty—unless it was in a mud bath."

She laughed after she'd said it, but Colin heard only pain, and his conscience gave another sharp kick because he had her inadvertently walking down memory lane when that was hardly his intention. He didn't want either one of them starting on *that* rocky path.

And yet some things were inevitable, he decided, as he watched her pull a cheery yellow tulip from the vase and rub it against one of her smooth cheeks. The color reminded him of the dress she'd worn the night before. Not many women could pull off that color without winding up looking sallow. She'd been nothing less than radiant.

And she still was, her luminescent green eyes glancing about the room as she said wistfully, "My tulips are blooming right now, but by the time I get back to New York they'll be done. They don't last very long."

"A lot of things don't," he said.

"Especially beautiful things." Her expression turned sad. "We didn't."

"Tempest," he said again, this time adding a little more edge and urgency in his tone for both their sakes. "There's no going back. That's not why I did this."

"No. I know." But then she tucked the tulip behind one ear and the years seemed to rewind despite his words.

"Thank you for all of this, Colin. And I accept your apology for last night. This is... This is—"

She broke off suddenly, and glanced around again before her gaze swung back to his. Her expression was one of disbelief, then embarrassment, and finally unmitigated rage.

"This is the setting for one of the scenes from *Flights of Fancy!*"

Colin nodded. Why did he want to apologize? He was only giving Tempest a taste of her own medicine. And he was being generous on top of it. He was at long last allowing her exactly what she'd been seeking for the past several days.

"You said you wanted an audition," he reminded her.

"An audition?"

Colin folded his arms and settled onto the arm of one of the room's generous sofas, determined not to start second-guessing his decision.

"That's right. That's what I'm offering you." Raising one eyebrow in challenge, he added, "Right here, right now, heiress. What do you say?"

"But..." She moistened her lips. "This is the big love scene between Roxy and Cole."

"If you can't do it, just say so." He shrugged.

"Who'll read the other part? Surely not you?"

"Do you see anyone else here?"

Her eyes narrowed. "Which is I'm sure why you picked this part for the audition."

Indeed he had. Why should she be the only one to fight unfairly, using sex when on the offensive? *Paybacks are hell.* That was all this was about, he assured himself. That and the need to get her out from under his skin once and for all.

"It's a pivotal scene and, given the myriad emotions

Roxy experiences during it, it's also the best gauge of your range as an actress."

"And the side benefit is that you'll get to see me naked," she added dryly.

"I've seen you naked before." He kept his expression nonchalant, but his mouth had gone dry.

"This is different."

Yes, it was, he reminded himself. Besides, he didn't plan to let the scene progress that far. Of course, he wasn't about to share that nugget of information with Tempest. He wanted her uncomfortable and off-kilter, since that was exactly how he was feeling at the moment. In fact it was how he'd felt since he'd walked out the door of Stan Dartman's office a week ago and seen her sitting on that bench, looking so lost, looking so lovely.

Even so, he made his tone bland when he asked, "Does doing a nude scene bother you? If you get the part, Roxy won't be making love to Cole with her clothes on, you know."

"Are you saying I have a shot at this?"

"I'm a fair man."

And he meant it. He could afford to be, he figured, since he doubted she could act—lessons with the famed Celia Church and a couple of well-done impromptu scenes notwithstanding.

Feeling on firmer footing, he said magnanimously, "Impress me here, heiress, and I'll arrange another audition with Stan when we get back to the States."

Tempest licked her lips again and nodded excitedly. "Okay. Thank you. Just give me a minute to get into character."

She pulled a compact from her handbag and frowned at her reflection for a moment, before reaching back in for eyeliner and a tube of lipstick. A few quick swipes of each added drama to her eyes and had her lips looking as wet and red as dew-drenched strawberries.

She glanced down at her clothes then, and shook her head.

"This dress is all wrong for Roxy. She'd go more for Spandex than silk. And these flat shoes…" She sent him a rueful smile. "I'd have worn red patent leather stilettos if only I'd known you were going to give me this shot."

He swallowed thickly, picturing a pair of lethal heels adding several inches to those already mile-long legs, and he wondered whether it was disappointment or relief that had him wanting to sigh.

"Let's just work with what you've got."

And they did.

For the next fifteen minutes they ran the dialogue. He offered her a script, but she had no need for it. She knew the lines by heart, and her delivery was impressive. No, Colin admitted, flawless.

Tempest had him believing she was a down-on-her-luck prostitute, eager for a way out of the life and yet dragged back into it time and again by circumstances beyond her control. Everything about her seemed different and distinctively Roxy—until the part where she sidled up to him for the kiss.

This Colin remembered.

The meeting of their mouths was not so much a reunion as an explosion of desire. He felt her fingers, greedy for skin, tear at his white shirt until the last button gave way and she could force the fabric over his shoulders. Her mouth, hot and hungry, stole over his chest and had him sucking in a breath. Then she stepped back, smiled mysteriously, and began to work her dress up over her well-toned thighs, exposing the stingy scrap of lace that covered her. Colin felt the blood drain out of his head to pool elsewhere.

Need raged inside him, as powerful and unexpected as a flash-flood. It swept him away, swept him over the edge of sanity. In that moment he forgot his own name. But he knew hers.

"Tempest," he whispered on a ragged sigh. "God help me, but I want you."

She went still.

"It's Roxy. *I'm Roxy.* And that line's not in the scene," she said at last.

He was so lost in her that it took him a moment to surface. "Wh-what?"

"I said, that line's not in the scene. Cole doesn't tell Roxy he wants her. In fact, he *doesn't* want her. Not really. He's just using her."

"Using her?" Colin repeated inanely, his brain still too wrapped in fog to function properly.

Tempest laughed harshly. "So that's what this is about. Using. And you had the nerve to tell me once that a part in your movie wasn't for sale."

"It's not," he protested, coherent at last. "This is an audition."

"No, it's not. This is nothing but a sham and a way to boost your ego. My God, why not just bring back the casting couch and complete the cliché?"

Now he was angry as well. "I'm more professional than that."

"I used to think so," she shot back.

"Well, you're the one who started this—sliding a thigh along my leg that first day at the Palais, and then spouting lines of dialogue in Bar des Célébrités last night."

"And now we're even? Is that it?"

She adjusted her clothing, slipped her feet back into her shoes. When she looked at him again, he glimpsed hurt beneath the anger.

"I wanted this part, Colin, I really did. I have since I first read the script. But do you honestly think so little of me that you believed I would prostitute myself in order to get it?"

"Tempest—"

"I'm a good actress." She nodded vigorously to punctuate her words. "I've worked hard at my craft. I take this seriously, damn you. *Seriously!* What will it take to make you see that?"

She opened the door and stepped out into the late-afternoon sun. Turning on the other side of the threshold, she was limned in light, and she regarded him as he stood in the shadows. Something about their positions seemed suddenly apropos.

Her voice was quiet, but it cut as neatly and deeply as a scalpel on flesh. "I've done a lot of things in the past that I regret. God knows, half of those things wound up on the cover of one tabloid or another. But I never used anyone, Colin, least of all you. I may have gone too far in trying to get this part, but I never set out to make you feel...cheap."

Her voice broke on a sob that tore at his heart. She had committed other sins, he knew, but he was man enough to admit that what she said now was true.

"It wasn't like that."

"What was it like, then?"

Colin recalled the way he'd all but gone up in flames a moment earlier. He had no answers. For either of them.

"Hell if I know," he murmured, rubbing a hand over the back of his neck.

Tempest slammed the door in his face, but not before

he saw the glimmer of tears shrouding her emerald eyes. He didn't follow her. She needed time and space to regroup. He did as well.

He paced to the sideboard, poured himself a glass of the 1989 St. Emilion and drank half of it while he mulled over a reasonable excuse for his behavior. The one that sprang immediately to mind had him dropping down onto the sofa, unmindful of the wine that sloshed over the glass's rim and stained the knee of his jeans.

Had he spent the past three years lying to himself? Conveniently denying that he'd fallen in love with Tempest Herriman when in truth he had?

If he accepted that as fact, then things just got a whole lot messier, he realized. Because, despite all that had happened between them, despite everything she had done, he wasn't over her.

Not by a long shot.

Lost in this revelation, he took a few seconds to register the whir of the dinghy's motor. When he finally did, he scrambled out onto the deck in time to watch Tempest pilot the small craft in the direction of the shore.

She'd left him stranded on the yacht, but he couldn't work up much outrage. This time, Colin knew, he deserved what he'd got.

CHAPTER SIX

TEMPEST SLEPT FITFULLY and woke early the next morning. A glance at the clock had her groaning. At this hour the last of the previous night's parties had barely ended, and the street cleaners were probably out, hosing the worst of the excess from La Croissette. She wanted nothing more than to remain buried beneath the silk-covered duvet on the oversized bed in her suite. Most of the thousands of people in town for the Festival would be asleep—including Audra, wherever she had passed the night.

Colin forced his way into her thoughts. She'd left him on board the *King's Ransom*. Well, he could rot out there for all she cared. Although she knew she wouldn't be that lucky. All he had to do was pick up a cell phone or the ship-to-shore radio and he would be rescued. In the meantime, it felt as if it was her heart being held captive.

How could she have been so stupid? How could he have been so cruel?

Okay, she could admit that for a couple of minutes, locked in his embrace, she'd had a hard time distinguishing between Colin the mouth-watering man and Cole the fictional character, but she'd used that as part of her motivation for the scene.

Used.

Anger had her throwing back the covers and getting out of bed. And she wasn't just angry with Colin. She was angry with herself for allowing him to hurt her again. Spitting mad because the fact that he could still wound her made Tempest realize that the deep well of feelings she had for Colin McKinnon had hardly run dry.

Damn him, but no man before or since had ever gotten to her quite the way he did. It was a bitter pill to swallow that he still had the power to twist her into knots emotionally.

Well, she wouldn't just lie in bed feeling hurt and helpless. She would...do something.

Since it was barely past dawn, she settled on ordering Room Service and drawing a bath. While she waited for breakfast to arrive, she pulled her hair into a simple ponytail, scrubbed her face and brushed her teeth.

Maybe after indulging in a long, hot soak she would play tourist and venture into the Marché de Forville. Or leave the glitz and glamour of the harbor area entirely and head up into the narrow streets of the old town. Assuming she could outwit the faithful paparazzi camped outside the Herriman, she could enjoy her walk, browse through the quaint shops of Le Suquet, and find a nice restaurant for lunch on what she had decided would be her last day in Cannes.

She wasn't running away, but she *was* going home. She'd had enough.

Tempest had just turned off the tub's faucet when she heard the knock. That would be Room Service, she thought, grabbing some money for a tip. When she opened the door, however, the man holding the tray was Colin.

"What are you doing here?" she asked, pulling the lapels of her robe together and wishing to God she hadn't washed every last speck of make-up off her face. She already felt too exposed and defenseless where this man was concerned.

"I've been up all night thinking. I need to talk to you."

He looked like hell; she'd give him that. Golden stubble shaded his jaw and shadows lurked under his eyes. But, since she had passed an equally sleepless night, she was fresh out of pity.

"This is a private floor." She stepped around him into the hallway and glanced toward the elevator. "Who let you up?"

Colin took the opportunity to walk into the suite. Setting the tray down on the narrow entryway table, he said, "A nice young man named Henri. It turns out he's a fan of both my work and earning a little extra cash."

"The Herriman chain prides itself on security. Your being here uninvited in my suite represents an inexcusable breach—especially since you bribed your way up." The haughty tone made her sound like her mother, but she pressed ahead. "This floor is supposed to be accessible only to certain guests and others with the proper authorization."

She stalked to the telephone, intending to pick up the receiver and have a word with the management, but Colin placed a hand over hers.

"Come on, Tempest. The guy did me a favor, that's all. If you want to be mad at someone, be mad at me."

She pulled her hand away, raised her chin. "I want you to leave."

"I won't stay long," he promised. "But I think we need to clear the air about a few things."

"I'm not really dressed for conversation."

No, she wasn't. She stood before him, dwarfed by the fluffy white robe that bore the hotel's insignia on its breast pocket. All her fiery hair had been tamed by a simple rubber band at the back of her head.

He liked it better down.

The memory of the passion that had erupted between them the previous afternoon reminded him why he had come.

"I want to apologize for my behavior yesterday. Things got...out of hand on the *King's Ransom*."

Tempest nodded curtly in acceptance and then glanced meaningfully into the hallway. He wasn't going to leave now, though. That wasn't all he had come to say.

He dipped his hands into the pockets of his jeans and rocked back on his heels.

"Seducing you...using you," he said, settling on her term for what had passed between them. "That wasn't why I asked you to meet me. I didn't plan to take advantage of you or the situation. The fact that I did was inexcusably unprofessional of me, but it says a lot about your skill as an actress. I was...lost in you."

He saw the surprise on her face. She blinked slowly, as if not certain she'd heard him right.

"Thank you," she said at last.

"If you're still interested in the role of Roxy, I'll give Stan a call when I get back to the States and set up an audition."

If she got the part—and he had little doubt she would after her performance aboard the yacht—Colin knew it would be pure torture to work with her and to have to watch her making love to another man, even if only for the camera. Still, he figured he owed her that much.

There was no mistaking her surprise now.

"Do you mean that?" she asked.

With one word he could discourage her. As angry as he'd been with her at times for her poor judgment and for the incident with Will, he was not heartless. Nor was he a liar.

"You're a much better actress than anyone in Hollywood has given you credit for being, Tempest. And that includes me."

"I've worked so hard," she murmured, half to herself.

"Then I'd say those lessons you've taken have paid off."

She smiled. No sultry temptress lurked in the quick quirking of her lips. Instead, Colin glimpsed joy and a kind of gratitude that left him feeling humbled.

"Thank you for saying so."

He gave a jerky nod, backed up a step. "I'm going to leave the final decision on casting to Stan, but you'll have your shot."

"That's enough. I'll do the rest," she promised.

"Okay."

Silence ensued as they regarded one another. Something had shifted in their relationship, Colin realized. A kind of peace had been brokered at last. And, even as he told himself the past no longer mattered, he discovered that he had to know—especially now, since it was a good bet they would be working with one another.

"That night three years ago..."

"After the Oscar party?"

"Yes." He scrubbed a hand over his face and exhaled sharply. "Will is my best friend, Tempest."

She wasn't sure where he was going with this, but the opening was there so, she took it. The past needed to be laid to rest once and for all if she was to move on.

"I know that. And, believe me, I didn't mean to put him in the middle."

"Then maybe you shouldn't have stuck your tongue down his throat," he said sharply.

"My tongue... What are you talking about?"

"Forget it." He turned and stalked down the hall toward the elevator, nearly plowing into Audra, who had just stepped off it.

"Hey, Colin," Audra said. Then, "Uh-oh. I'll just leave the two of you to your arguing. Keep in mind that making up is the best part."

Tempest brushed past her friend without a word and ducked through the brass doors behind Colin, depressing the open button to keep them from sliding shut.

"What did you mean by that?"

"Let it go. It doesn't matter any longer."

But clearly it did.

"Even if I believed it didn't matter to you, it matters to me. I need to know. What did Will say happened that night after you left Morton's?"

Colin turned the question around. "Why don't you give me *your* version of events?"

She'd waited three years for this chance, and part of her, the part that still felt so wounded by his abandonment, wanted to tell Colin to go to hell. Still, something in his gaze told her a lot more than her future as an actress was riding on her answer. His respect. And she realized she wanted that even more than she wanted the role of Roxy.

"Will helped me into the limo after the dress fiasco. He was very kind about it. He told me he would explain everything to you before you saw and read about it in the tabloids. I really didn't mean to flash the paparazzi. He knew that. I assumed you did, too. But then I went to the restaurant later that week and...you never showed up."

She looked so earnest, so innocent. But then she had proved her acting skills to Colin aboard the *King's Ransom*. Was this another kind of performance? One intended to win his approval? He'd already told her she had the audition. What more did she have to gain?

"Will told me you came on to him in the car. He said you kissed him and suggested that the two of you go back to his place for the night."

Her shock was unmistakable. Her hand dropped away from the control panel, allowing the doors to close.

"No. That's not true. That's simply not true."

"That's what he said, Tempest."

That was what Colin's best friend had told him. For the first time in three years, however, he began to question it. Just as he had begun to understand the reasons it had been so easy to believe it in the first place.

It was galling to admit that fear topped the list. He'd been falling in love, and feeling as helpless as he'd imagined his father had felt all those years before. When confronted with Tempest's alleged infidelity, he'd glommed on to it as an excuse to cut her loose and end things fast.

The elevator lurched and began its descent, but that wasn't what had Colin feeling so unsteady. What a fool he'd been. And, like his father, what a coward. They had both taken the easy way out.

Tempest stood in front of him now, blinking and shaking her head in disbelief.

"But Will's always been nice to me. I mean, I know he doesn't exactly like me, and he made it clear three years ago that he thought I wouldn't be good for the new reputation you were cultivating for yourself as a serious director with an eye beyond Hollywood, but... My God, why would he lie about something like that?"

Colin knew. He knew exactly. Will was at the helm of Colin's political ambitions. Sometimes he thought his friend wanted the Senate seat even more than he did. As Colin's friend, and now campaign adviser, Will had often talked about the need to make sacrifices in order to get ahead. Tempest Herriman had been one of those sacrifices.

"You didn't kiss him and try to entice him to spend

the night with you?" It came out as a question, but it was more of a statement.

"Is that what you thought? That's what you've believed all this time?"

"He's my best friend."

"And I was just…what?" she asked on a shaky whisper. "The woman you were sleeping with?"

That was what Colin had told himself at the time. He'd been a liar then. He couldn't, wouldn't lie now.

"No. I…I loved you."

Tears filled her eyes before she closed them on a moan. "I loved you, too."

Colin rested one palm against her cheek, giving in to his need to touch her, to offer comfort and to receive absolution. "I'm so sorry, Tempest."

"You didn't trust me."

"That's not it." The sound he issued was harsh and directed inward. "The person I didn't trust was myself."

He kissed her in apology, but need hurtled well ahead of contrition when she melted against his chest and opened her mouth under his. He wanted all of her, needed all of her. Now. Always.

"Tempest," he sighed against her lips.

He leaned back far enough to watch her eyes widen as he tugged the rubber band from her hair. That wild mane of red tumbled free. He fisted his hands in it and held on as he kissed her again in earnest.

And then the elevator jerked to a stop.

Colin was coherent enough to shove Tempest behind him just as the doors opened onto the lobby. He'd hoped only the bellman would see the pair of them before the doors finally slid shut again, but he caught a glimpse of Benton Landry standing several paces away, talking to another man. He was shaking his head, the expression on his face an odd mixture of disgust and delight.

When the elevator began its ascent, Tempest said, "I think he saw us."

"I know."

And yet it surprised Colin to realize he wasn't upset. He had just been discovered by one of his party's biggest contributors snuggling in an elevator with the very woman he'd been warned to stay away from. In the space of time it had taken for the doors to close, Colin had provided Benton Landry with proof positive of his so-called Hollywood values. Yet he couldn't care less.

"Will this hurt you politically?" Tempest asked.

He turned to face her. "I don't know. I'm only certain of one thing right now."

"What's that?"

He eliminated the space between them, settling his hands on her hips and pulling her forward until their bodies were touching from chest to thigh.

"Do you still need to ask?"

When he lowered his head for a kiss, however, Tempest pulled back. "I want to make it perfectly clear that this has nothing to do with the part of Roxy Remington."

"Not a thing," he agreed. "Not a damned thing."

His hands were big, and capable of gentleness, but there was nothing gentle or patient about him now. And Tempest was glad. She didn't want either at the moment. He backed her up until her shoulders rapped against the rear wall of the elevator.

"God, I can't get enough of you. I can barely wait until we get back to your suite."

"Audra's there," she reminded him on a strangled sigh.

"My rooms at the Carlton?" he suggested.

"With Benton Landry downstairs and the paparazzi

waiting outside? I'd rather not run that gauntlet in my bathrobe, thank you very much."

He closed his eyes briefly, swore. "I want to be alone with you. Now."

"I have an idea," she said.

Her smile turned wicked and she reached past him and hit the red emergency stop button on the control panel. The elevator lurched to a halt between floors four and five and an alarm blared.

"What are you doing?" he sputtered, raising his voice to be heard over the din. But he thought he knew, and he hoped the incredibly detailed fantasy already teasing his libido would prove possible.

"I'm improvising," she replied. "A useful skill, wouldn't you agree?"

"Oh, yeah. Very useful. I'll follow your lead."

But it was Colin who forged ahead. She moaned when his teeth nipped at her earlobe, and sighed as he trailed kisses down her neck to her collarbone. Reaching between them, he untied the sash of her robe and parted it to reveal the perfection he remembered. The garment slid to the floor and was joined by his shirt a moment later. Just as she had aboard the *King's Ransom*, she had ripped half the buttons off this one, too. He didn't mind. Nothing mattered.

Colin had never experienced this kind of urgency, this brand of desperate need. She had beguiled him three years ago. She consumed him now.

"This is insane," he murmured against her temple, pushing her fumbling hands away from his belt buckle. But then he unfastened it himself, and groaned as she worked jeans and jockey shorts down over his hips.

Insane or not, he couldn't stop. He couldn't deny either one of them the passion or satisfaction that had been withheld from them for so long.

She moaned when he drew one of her long legs up around his waist. She held on desperately, nails digging into the flesh on his shoulders, when he picked her up completely. And when he entered her Tempest cried out as shrilly as the elevator's alarm.

Her name said it all. She was wild in his arms, a storm of need as powerful as a category five hurricane breaking shore. He gave and she took, and then returned the favor until he thought his lungs would burst, his legs would give out. Finally, she sobbed out his name and went limp against him, and Colin allowed himself to be leveled.

CHAPTER SEVEN

THEY SPENT THE REST of the day in Tempest's suite. Audra had taken one look at their glazed expressions when they returned from their encounter in the elevator and, after making one bawdy yet accurate comment, had packed some things in an overnight bag and left for Trent's hotel room without another word.

"We probably should get out of bed," Tempest said, noting the time. It was nearly four o'clock in the afternoon.

"Why?" Colin used his index finger to trace a lazy circle around the nipple of her left breast. "Give me one good reason."

She shivered, amazed that she still had enough energy to want sex after the day they'd had.

"We should eat. Aren't you hungry?"

"Starved." And, as if to prove it, he placed his mouth where his hand just had been.

Half an hour later, however, he was the one swinging his legs over the side of the bed.

"I guess we *should* have dinner. We need to keep up our strength," he said with a lazy grin.

"I'll order Room Service."

"We can go out if you'd like," he offered. The paparazzi would be seeing them together at some point anyway, he decided. If not in Cannes, then back in the States.

But she shook her head. "Let's eat in. I don't feel like sitting in a crowded restaurant right now. That would require clothes."

And, because he admired her practicality, he leaned over and kissed the corner of her mouth.

"Okay. I'll go call in our order. What do you want?"

"Whatever you're having is fine. I think I'll hop in the shower."

She turned back at the door, lips curving seductively. "Why don't you join me when you get off the phone?"

Colin ordered two steaks, because he figured they both needed the protein, and a bottle of champagne because he felt like celebrating. As he waited for Tempest to join him in the main room after their shower, he decided to further set the mood. He pulled the heavy draperies to block out the late-afternoon sun and used the dimmer switch on the lights to shroud the room in intimacy. He'd created a similar ambience aboard the *King's Ransom* the day before, using candles. Today, though, his motives were far different.

Tempest loved him. Or at least she had when they were together three years ago. Neither one of them had spoken the words again, after admitting their past feelings in the elevator, but Colin felt pretty confident that, despite the way he'd hurt her, she still had strong feelings for him. With time and care he could make her love him again.

Love makes you weak.

In his mind, he heard the echo of his father's voice, his speech slurred from too much to drink just hours after discovering Colin's mother with another man. For the longest time that had been Colin's mantra as well. But he didn't feel weak now.

More than twenty years after the morning he'd dialed

911 to report his dad's suicide, he'd finally realized it wasn't his mother's infidelity that had doomed Michael McKinnon, nor his father's seemingly obsessive love for her. Colin could look back now and see plenty of other problems in his parents' marriage. Neither one of them had been perfect. Yes, his mother had cheated, but was the action his father had subsequently taken any more honorable?

Lost in that thought, he was startled by the sound of a key turning in the door's lock.

"Everybody decent?" Audra asked as she poked her head into the suite.

"Hello, Audra. Come in."

"Colin." She smiled, apparently feeling as awkward as he. "I just came back for something I forgot. I won't be long. Where's Temp?"

"Putting on lotion. We, uh, *she* just got out of the shower."

"Oh." She glanced around the dim room. "It looks very cozy in here, even romantic."

"Yeah, well." He coughed, embarrassed.

Her voice was surprisingly sharp when she said, "Don't hurt her again, Colin."

"I'm not planning to."

"Good." Audra tilted her head to one side. "A lot of people sell Tempest short—her parents, casting directors, half the people in Hollywood."

"Me," he added softly.

Audra nodded. "She's done a lot of changing in the past few years. Enough to make me proud of her and maybe even a little envious. God knows, I still grab my fair share of bad press, and then some. But my point is that Tempest has a lot more going on inside her head—and her heart for that matter—than most people give her credit for."

"I know."

Clearly Audra wanted to underscore the point, and so she continued.

"She's not just some air-headed heiress out blowing her billions on whatever strikes her fancy."

"I don't care what she spends her money on," Colin replied patiently. Recalling the recent tabloid story, he added, "If she wants to buy sapphire-studded shoes, that's her prerogative. It doesn't make me question her intelligence. We all have our little quirks."

Audra shook her head. "You still don't get it."

"Get what?"

"Ask her about Ellen sometime."

"Ellen?"

"Just ask Tempest about her, and then maybe you'll understand what I mean about her being misjudged and sold short."

Audra retrieved the item she'd come back for and left without another word.

The meal arrived and Tempest joined Colin at the table a moment later.

"I thought I heard Audra," she said, settling into the seat across from him.

Her hair was still damp, and she was wearing it down. A sheer black robe concealed about as much of her ripe figure as would an open window. He found the view even more mouth-watering than the perfectly cooked *filet mignon* on his plate.

"She came back for something she forgot, took one look at the low lights and decided not to stay long."

"Very perceptive."

"Yes." He filled her champagne flute and then his own, which he lifted in a toast. "To perception."

Colin was too caught up in the way the see-through

fabric of Tempest's robe rubbed against her skin to immediately realize the double meaning of his words. When he finally did, he had more pressing needs than conversation.

COLIN WOKE IN AN empty bed. A glance at the clock on the nightstand told him it was not quite midnight—although it seemed much later, given their activities before drifting off to sleep. A sliver of light slipped through a crack in the door that led to the main room of the suite and he could hear Tempest talking to someone. Audra? Maybe she had come back again.

Curious, Colin rose, hunted for his jeans in the tangle of clothes on the floor and pulled them on. Then he slowly opened the door.

Tempest was seated at the suite's table, a laptop computer open in front of her, a pair of glasses perched on her nose and the telephone receiver tucked between her shoulder and chin. He'd never seen her look businesslike before.

Sexy, he decided. Very sexy.

"That won't do," she said, her voice brisk and professional. "I've read their grant request, Marge. I can't understand why the rest of the board is balking at this. We're talking about an after-school program in one of New York's roughest neighborhoods, for heaven's sake."

She drained the contents of her coffee cup while the person on the other end of the line said something that Tempest apparently didn't agree with. She set the white porcelain cup back onto its saucer with a smart click.

Her tone was impatient when she replied, "I know he missed the grant application deadline, and I know we've already given the green light to a similar project in Brooklyn, but I think this one deserves funding as well."

She tapped on the keyboard of her laptop. "I'll be back in New York early next week. We could—"

She slipped off her glasses and rubbed her eyes. "I see. No, no. I'll tell him. Do you have his home number? I'll call him myself now." She jotted it down. "Thanks."

After she hung up, she typed something into the computer.

Colin prepared to make his presence known, but Tempest picked up the telephone again and began dialing. And so he stood where he was, too curious to consider the rudeness of his blatant eavesdropping.

She sipped her coffee again as she waited for someone to come on the line.

"Larry? It's Tempest Herriman. Sorry to call you at home, and I'll apologize if I've interrupted your dinner. But I have some good news that I knew you'd want to hear immediately. The Foundation has reconsidered your grant request...yes, isn't it wonderful? Listen, since you missed the deadline, and we're actually bending Foundation rules here, you'll need to keep the identity of the funding source quiet, okay? Just say it was an anonymous donor." He said something that had her smiling broadly. "You're welcome. It's a good program, Larry. I think—as does the entire Herriman Foundation board, of course—that it's going to make a difference in the lives of some of the city's most at-risk children."

She glanced up then, and caught sight of Colin. He swore she blushed, although why he couldn't have said.

"I have to go, Larry. I'll call the bank and have the funds routed to your organization's account early next week. Thanks. You, too."

She hung up, and logged off the computer as well.

"I didn't realize you were up," she said, stuffing papers and file folders back into a slim briefcase. "I hope I didn't wake you."

"No." He pointed to the papers. "Foundation business?"

"Yes."

"A little late for that now, isn't it? It's well after regular business hours back in New York."

"No one minds being bothered at home when the news is good. I was just letting a grant applicant know he'd received funding."

He nodded. "I didn't realize you did any hands-on work for the Foundation."

"Just the fun stuff," she replied. "It's great public relations to have a member of the Herriman family actually call the applicants with the news."

A few days ago he would have accepted her explanation. But now, even if he had not overheard her telephone conversation, Colin would have had his doubts. Three years ago she hadn't been what he'd expected. And he was beginning to realize, as Audra had said, that there was much more to this woman than anyone knew.

"So *you'll* be routing the money? You handle those details?"

"Just a formality." She shrugged. She crossed to the bar and took a bottle of sparkling water from the small refrigerator tucked into the paneled wall. "Want one?"

"No, thanks. So, are you a voting member of the Foundation board?"

"Yes."

"But your vote doesn't carry any more weight than that of the other members?"

"No. Of course not."

"That money you'll be routing is your own, isn't it?"

She blinked in surprise.

"I overheard both conversations," he said. "I wasn't trying to eavesdrop, but..."

He spread his hands wide and watched her face cloud. Once again, she seemed embarrassed.

"Yes, it's my money."

"Why?"

"It's a good program," she said simply, as if that explained everything. And, in a way, it did.

"Yes, but you could have told the man you just spoke with that the Foundation turned him down and you were going to fund the program yourself."

"It's really not important that he knows the exact funding source," she said, and took another sip of her water.

"Or that he reveals it to anyone else?"

He'd hit on the truth, he was certain.

"What good would that do?" she said defensively.

"It might help repair your public image—force more people to take you seriously."

"You sound like my parents," she said, blowing out a breath in frustration. "Be generous, but make sure everyone knows it. That's not true generosity, Colin. It's a publicity campaign."

"Some might consider it simply a matter of *quid pro quo*."

"That's the politician in you speaking," she said, and he thought she sounded a little disappointed.

"Perhaps, but what would it hurt? Why not take credit for recognizing a good program and seeing to it that it gets the funds it needs?" he asked.

"Larry Kendall and a group of hard-working volunteers have a great idea to keep at-risk kids off the streets after school. Studies show that more kids get high, have sex and are victims or perpetrators of violent crime between three and six o'clock in the afternoon than at any other time of the day. But if the media get wind of my involvement in this program then it gets turned into a bored heiress's project *de jour*. The focus needs to be on the kids, not me. I don't need the limelight, Colin."

"I know." But he was beginning to realize how much she deserved to have it shine on her—for the *right* reasons.

A question nagged at him.

"Who's Ellen?" When she just stared at him, he said, "Audra told me I should ask you."

"Why do you want to know?"

"I'm not sure," he replied honestly. But it suddenly seemed important. "Who is she?"

He didn't think she would answer. She was quiet for so long. Finally she said, "A funny, sweet, amazing young woman who had her whole life ahead of her."

Past tense, he realized. Whoever Ellen was, she was gone now. And still he had to know.

"How did you meet her?"

"That's not really important."

"Please," he said simply.

She fiddled with the label on the bottle she held in her hand. "She had an inoperable brain tumor and she wanted to see Paris before..."

"She died."

"Yes. A friend of hers wrote to the Herriman Hotel there and asked if it would be possible to get a discount, given the circumstances and the fact that Ellen didn't have much money. I found out about it and got involved."

There was more to it than that, Colin was sure.

"That was a nice thing you did."

She shrugged. "I got back as much as I gave." A sad smile softened her features. "We had a wonderful time shopping on the Champs-Elysées."

The puzzle pieces fell into place then.

"The sapphire shoes."

"She got such a kick out of them. I bought her the matching handbag, too."

"You took a dying girl to Paris, pulled out all the stops, and even bought her gem-encrusted shoes. Yet the tabloids reported it as another Tempest binge. And that day outside Stan's office, I said..." He closed his eyes briefly, remembering his harsh words and regretting them. "Why didn't you say something?"

"What should I have said? Look at me—I'm so generous. I'm such a philanthropist. Is that what you would have done, Colin?"

"No. Of course not. I'm sorry," he said.

She gestured with the bottle of water. "I have a lot of money—money that I never had to work for—so plenty of people make assumptions about me and my character, regardless of my motives. It's enough for me to know I'm not as shallow or self-absorbed as they claim. Or," she admitted quietly, "as I used to be."

He'd been one of those people. "I'm sorry for thinking the worst of you, Tempest."

She looked away. "I made it easy. I've done a lot of stupid things over the years that exposed me and everyone around me to ridicule."

But underneath it all she had a good heart. He'd sensed that three years ago, which was why, unlike all of the other women he'd dated casually and left easily, she had proved impossible to get over.

I love you. The words were on the tip of his tongue. He decided against saying them just now. It was the curse of being a director, he supposed, but Colin had the perfect setting in mind for giving voice to those feelings. Of course he could *show* her what was in his heart.

"Are you coming back to bed?"

"I'm not really that tired."

He stepped toward her until she stood within arm's reach. "Me either."

"Oh?" One neatly arched eyebrow rose.

"You could put on those sexy glasses again and..." He leaned in and nipped at her earlobe, before whispering a suggestion that would have made Roxy blush.

"When you get to Washington, you'll have to sponsor legislation to make sure that's legal in all fifty states."

He grinned. "Count on it."

CHAPTER EIGHT

THEY SLEPT WRAPPED IN EACH other's arms, and, even though he didn't want to leave her, the following morning Colin decided to return to his suite at the Carlton. He had a lunch meeting with a potential foreign distributor for his film, and he'd promised interviews to a couple of reporters in the afternoon.

First, however, he needed to speak to Will. He'd phoned his friend and asked him to come to his suite at ten o'clock. After showering, Colin decided against breakfast—he felt too keyed up to eat—and ordered coffee instead. He was downing his third cup when Will knocked at the door.

Colin wasn't sure what he would say. Will had been a good friend for more than a dozen years. Still, the betrayal cut deeply, and the issue went beyond Tempest. What other unilateral decisions had Will made or did he intend to make on Colin's behalf because he felt they were in the best interests of the candidacy?

Sucking in a deep breath, he opened the door, ready for the confrontation even as he dreaded it. But Will wasn't alone. A smiling Benton Landry strolled in behind him.

"Hello, McKinnon."

The older man's expression set Colin's teeth on edge. Turning to Will, he said, "I didn't ask you here to talk politics. I told you on the phone that the matter was personal."

"Tempest Herriman?" Landry asked, smirking around the stump of his unlit cigar.

Colin reined in his temper. "That's none of your business."

"I'm afraid it is," Will said grimly.

"I have a little movie I'd like you to view." Landry held up a videotape. "Quite a performance, I think you'll agree."

He walked over to the suite's entertainment center. Even before the grainy black and white images came up on the television screen Colin knew he was being blackmailed. His back had been to the security camera for most of that encounter in the elevator at the Herriman, but Tempest was easily recognizable. Colin switched off the television just before his celluloid counterpart parted her robe.

"What do you want?"

"A little more cooperation than what I've gotten so far, son," Landry replied, with a serpent's grin.

That didn't surprise him, but he turned to Will. "Are you in on this, too?"

"No, of course not. I wouldn't do something like that."

"Wouldn't you? What about three years ago, when you fed me that pack of lies about what went on in the limo?"

"I don't know what you're talking about." But he swallowed visibly and his gaze cut away.

"Leave acting to the professionals, Will."

"Okay, fine." He swiped a hand over his face. "But let me explain."

"Yeah, you do that," he snapped, too irate to care that Landry was there as a spectator. "Tell me why, when Tempest never kissed you or suggested sex, you told me she had."

"I did it for your own good, Colin. One of us had to think clearly. God knows, you weren't."

He seemed so sincere, and that only made it all the more painful. Will wasn't apologizing even now. In fact he was still as single-minded as he'd been three years ago, Colin realized, when Will added, "I think you should hear Landry out. Your candidacy can be salvaged."

"Is that what's most important to you?"

"Colin." Will's voice brimmed with patience. "Step back and look at the big picture."

"I am. Believe me. And I'm not liking what I see. You are—were—my best friend."

"Yes, and I did you a favor. Tempest was trouble then and she's trouble now," he said, pointing toward the television. "Don't tell me she didn't know that scene in the elevator would be caught on tape. The Herriman is famous for its security."

A couple of days ago Colin might have taken the bait. But he *wouldn't* believe Tempest had planned for their very spontaneous encounter to be caught on tape, much less viewed by strangers. Personally, and professionally, she had just as much to lose as he did.

"Don't try to shift the blame, Will. She did nothing wrong three years ago. She did nothing wrong last night."

Will snorted, impatient now. "You're right. She *didn't* do anything wrong last night. I watched the tape with Benton this morning and she looks like she's very accomplished at that sort of thing."

Colin reacted before he could think better of it. His fist connected with Will's chin, sending the other man to the floor.

"Don't ever speak about her that way again. Do you hear me?"

Landry's laughter shattered the tension.

"There you go again, McKinnon, thinking with

what's in your trousers rather than what's in your head. You should be thanking your friend here, not trying to beat him to a pulp. He has your best interests at heart."

More than mad, Colin felt sick. "And I suppose you do, too?"

"Not at all." The older man's expression turned ruthless. "I have my own interests to worry about. And I find it will help tremendously to have another friend in the Senate. Someone who will see things my way and vote accordingly on legislation that affects my business holdings."

"What about Stowman? Why not just back him and be done with it?"

"He wouldn't be quite so neatly in my pocket as you will be," Landry replied baldly.

"So, if I don't do what you want after the election you make this tape public?"

"I'll make it public today if you don't start toeing the line." Landry fired up his cigar and blew a stream of foul-smelling smoke directly into Colin's face. "Well? What's it going to be, son?"

Colin didn't need to think about his answer. He'd wanted this shot at the Senate for more than a decade, carefully plodding a path toward his eventual candidacy. But he wouldn't go into politics as a puppet, allowing someone as dirty as Benton Landry to pull his strings.

"I'm not your son, Landry. Go to hell."

The other man's face turned purple with rage. He pointed the glowing red tip of his cigar at Colin. "I told you once that you wouldn't want me for an enemy. You're going to regret this."

He stormed out, and Colin turned to Will. The two men had been best friends for more than a dozen years.

He'd trusted Will's judgment, sought his advice. Now Colin could barely stomach the sight of him.

"You can leave, too. There's nothing I want to say to you right now."

"I can't believe you're going to throw away our friendship and your political future over some woman." His tone was laced with disgust.

"She's not just *some* woman. And I think you figured that out three years ago—which is why you lied to me about what happened after the party."

Will stopped at the door and turned to face him. A bruise was already blooming on his chin. Colin was sad that it had come to this. But if he was sorry about anything, it was that he hadn't taken Tempest's side three years ago.

"She's not worth it," Will said.

"She is to me."

COLIN HAD HELD OUT HOPE that Landry was bluffing, but within the hour the older man made good on his threat. The video was leaked to the media, and by evening portions of it were being played for television audiences from one end of the globe to the other. Making matters worse, it was also well on its way to becoming one of the hottest downloads in Internet history.

History. That was what Colin's Senate bid most likely was at this point. Already people from the national party had left blistering messages on his hotel voicemail. Yet that didn't bother him as much as the fact that Tempest was once again making headlines for all the wrong reasons. And this time he was partly responsible.

Colin had tried to warn her after Landry left his suite. He'd called her number at the Herriman half a dozen times without success.

It was too late. She was ambushed by legitimate journalists and tabloid paparazzi on her way to the Majestic to meet Audra and Trent for lunch.

TEMPEST WAS SHELL-SHOCKED by the ensuing blitz. To her horror, it seemed the original *Are they or aren't they?* question had finally been answered to everyone's satisfaction.

A bellman at the Herriman was summarily dismissed for selling the tape to Landry, who had gone to him with a fistful of money after spying Colin and Tempest in the elevator the previous day. Landry had taken a chance, after seeing their disheveled appearance, that things between the pair would heat up to the flashpoint.

He'd certainly gotten a lot of bang for his buck, Tempest thought wryly now as she paced the length of her suite.

She hadn't heard from Colin other than the messages he'd left on her answering machine. In them, he sounded worried, angry. At her or the situation? She could only wonder what he thought of this mess. It was, as one television reporter noted, "vintage Tempest." Three years ago, when Colin had loved her, he'd still found reasons to leave. Now he had so much more at stake. Would he stick around this time?

I love you. She'd whispered those words in the dark last night, after he'd fallen asleep. And no matter what happened, she wouldn't regret the past twenty-four hours.

Tempest reminded herself of that resolution when her parents called. She supposed she should be flattered that they had actually picked up the telephone and dialed it themselves, but the reason behind both phone conversations was hardly pleasant.

Her mother rang first.

"My God, Tempest! We thought you had finally begun to settle down. And now this."

Frances Herriman sighed heavily, and Tempest knew better than to interrupt. "When are you going to stop being such a disappointment? When are you going to stop hurting your father and me this way?"

"I didn't do this to hurt either of you. I lo—"

"Your father and I would like to be able to hold our heads up high in public. But your escapades make that all but impossible. And this latest one. Do you have any idea how sordid it all seems? In an elevator, for Chrissakes!"

"I haven't actually seen the video," Tempest murmured.

Her stomach lurched when her mother replied, "Well, I have—and so has your father. *Your father!*"

It was official. Tempest wanted to die. People—everyone from perfect strangers to her parents—were watching her have sex with Colin. Of course none of them would understand that it went far beyond a mere physical act. Her mother's next statement underscored that fact.

"If you *have* to have those kinds of base urges, can't you please be smart enough to satisfy them in private? At least Colin had the good sense to keep his back to the camera almost the entire time. He's hardly recognizable."

Tempest didn't try to defend herself, or to explain that, as foolish as making love with Colin in an elevator had been, it *had* been *making love,* not the lurid need for sexual gratification her mother implied.

She hung up, exhausted emotionally. And then the phone rang again and her father's voice, vibrating with fury, spilled from the receiver as painful and poisonous as snake venom.

"I didn't think you could top that stunt outside Morton's, young lady, but I was wrong."

"I'm sorry for all the embarrassment this is causing you," she said dutifully. She wouldn't apologize for her relationship with Colin, but she'd never meant to hurt her parents or sully their reputations.

"If I could cut you off—disown you—by God, I would! But you've got the trust fund your grandparents left you, and you'll no doubt continue to spend it as freely as you please, making a mockery of the Herriman name. But I want you off the Foundation board."

"Off the board?" She sagged against the side of the sofa. Staggered. Other than acting, it was the one thing she truly enjoyed. "But, Father, I—"

"Fly back tonight. We'll hold a press conference outside our offices in Manhattan tomorrow, announcing your resignation. You can make a full apology at that time for the embarrassment your appalling lack of dignity and decorum has caused the Foundation and the other members who sit on its board."

"You won't reconsider this?"

"You're off, Tempest. I want you gone. I hope that cheap thrill was worth it."

"It's not like that. Colin—"

"I don't want to hear about him. The only good news in all of this is that his political future is in the toilet—right along with my good name."

After hanging up, she sat on the sofa and willed her roiling stomach to settle. For a while, during the past few years, since she'd joined the Foundation board, she had enjoyed a tenuous sliver of respect from her parents. Now that was gone as well, proving as conditional as their love. They were distancing themselves from her, trying to step clear of the splatter as the dirt began to fly in earnest.

Maybe they had the right idea, Tempest thought. She

had little doubt that if they could claim no relationship to her at this moment they would.

   She sucked in a deep breath as an idea came to her. She couldn't spare her parents, but maybe there was a way to protect the man she loved.

CHAPTER NINE

NEWS CONFERENCES WERE common in Cannes during the Film Festival. Hotel lobbies and poolside lounges boasted scads of televisions to accommodate the closed-circuit events. Even so, Colin nearly bobbled his bottle of water when he glanced up from the newspaper he was reading on the Carlton terrace and saw Tempest standing behind a bank of microphones on the TV monitor.

She wore a conservatively cut suit, with her hair pulled back into a severe twist. Her make-up was subdued and minimal. Colin could see the strain in the tight set of her mouth and he ached to soothe her. Since the tape had surfaced, however, he hadn't been able to reach her.

"Your girlfriend is on television," a man seated nearby said with a snigger.

Colin ignored him. He had refused to hide out in his hotel room since the story had broken. He hadn't granted any media interviews, but neither had he kept a low profile. He wouldn't have anyone assuming by his absence that he was ashamed of his relationship with Tempest.

Now he saw that she had decided on a similar course. No, not similar at all, he realized as she started speaking.

"I won't be taking questions," she began. "I'm going to read my prepared statement, after which I will be leaving Cannes, and I ask that you respect my family's privacy, even though I have given you every reason to invade it.

"First, I am stepping down from the Herriman Foundation board effective immediately. My presence there can only bring the wrong kind of publicity to a worthy and worthwhile organization. I am extremely sorry if I have, through my inappropriate actions, made it more difficult for the Foundation to carry out its noble mission.

"Second, I wish to apologize to my family. My thoughtlessness has harmed them and their good name on several occasions, none more so than now. I very much regret that."

He watched her take a deep breath, and then she looked dead into the camera. He swore she looked right into his soul.

"And, finally, I wish to apologize to Colin McKinnon. He is the real innocent party in all of this. I know from the grainy video that has been circulating that everyone assumes he is the man I am..." she cleared her throat "being intimate with on the tape. In fact, he is not."

A chorus of gasps went up from the reporters, who then began shouting out questions in several languages. Tempest held up a hand to silence them, and continued in English.

"The truth is I hired an actor to impersonate Mr. McKinnon in the most intimate segment of that tape. It sounds absurd, I know. But I desperately wanted a part in the Stan Dartman movie Mr. McKinnon recently signed on to direct. Unfortunately, Mr. McKinnon would not even give me the chance to audition. Knowing his political ambitions, I foolishly thought I might be able to use a sordid video as leverage to coerce him into giving me the role of Roxy.

"I had no intention of having the tape made public, but it fell into the wrong hands, and—well, the rest is history. I would take it all back in a heartbeat if I could. I wanted something I couldn't have and I went too far to get it. Now, someone who doesn't deserve to be hurt has had his reputation tarnished.

"I wish Mr. McKinnon the best of luck in his upcoming race for the U.S. Senate, and I offer my sincerest apologies for any personal embarrassment or professional harm my ill-advised stunt has caused.

"Thank you."

With a nod toward the reporters, she gathered up the papers laid out on the dais in front of her and, amid a shower of shouted questions, hurried out of range of the cameras.

"You ought to sue that bitch," a man near Colin called out. "She could have tanked your career in politics before it ever got off the ground."

Listening to him, Colin knew Tempest's ploy had worked. A lot of people loved a good conspiracy theory. Of course, not everyone would be convinced of his innocence. Still, it was possible that enough people would buy in to Tempest's explanation that Colin might be able to resurrect his candidacy.

The woman so many people had long pegged as shallow and self-serving was magnanimously offering Colin a face-saving out. She had just fallen on the proverbial sword for him. But that wasn't why he felt so amazed. Tempest had sacrificed everything. He knew what her position on the Herriman Foundation board meant to her. He knew how desperately she wanted the role of Roxy. And she was good enough to play it. She was not only passing on this chance; her announcement all but ensured she would be a pariah in Hollywood for years to come. She'd sacrificed it all for him, and he knew why. He knew *exactly* why, and it had his heart soaring.

It was time he returned the favor.

Love makes you weak? Hell, no. Quite the opposite.

"So, are you going to sue her?" the guy asked again.

Colin was grinning when he stood.

"No." He tucked the newspaper under his arm. "I'm not going to sue Tempest Herriman. If she'll have me, I'm going to marry her."

TEMPEST WANTED TO LEAVE Cannes immediately after her press conference, but Audra insisted they stay.

"You really need to go to the awards ceremony tonight," she told her. "Show your face and even publicly ask Colin for forgiveness in order for your story to look remotely legit."

She had a point, but Tempest still wanted to turn tail and run.

"He hasn't called," she said. She lifted the arm that covered her eyes and boosted herself up on one elbow on the bed in her suite.

"What are you talking about?" Audra said. "He left half a dozen messages."

"But nothing since my news conference this afternoon."

"Well, you've made it pretty difficult for him to contact you without blowing your story to bits."

Tempest nodded. "I guess maybe his silence means he's pleased with the way I handled things."

"And why wouldn't he be? You saved his ass," Audra replied pointedly. She eyed her friend. "Was it worth it, Temp? And obviously I'm not talking about your elevator escapade."

"I think so. Yes." Slumping back on the bed, she whispered, "I want him to be happy, Audra. I love him."

"I guess that's what matters, then."

Audra leaned over and grabbed Tempest's hands, pulling her to a sitting position.

"But, for tonight, you need to look your absolute best." She rubbed her hands together and walked to the closet, where she thumbed through the array of designer originals hanging there. "I think scandal calls for something bold, don't you?"

She pulled a skimpy silk charmeuse dress the same shade as Tempest's eyes from the closet. "Mmm. This will do. And wear your hair down. It should be loose and wavy, unapologetically sexy."

"I thought the point was to look contrite," Tempest said dryly.

"Uh-uh. Not now. Besides, in-your-face has always been more your style. If you continue to act all wimpy and subdued, you'll be sure to arouse suspicion."

There was some bizarre logic in that, Tempest decided as she got up to take a shower.

Audra helped her get ready afterward. She brightened Tempest's make-up when Tempest would have toned it down, and fussed with Tempest's hair until it framed her face with all the subtlety of a raging wild fire.

"It's going to take all of your considerable acting talent to make people believe you don't care what they think," she said, giving Tempest's arm a squeeze as they arrived at the Salon des Ambassadeurs for dinner.

The crowd was small, exclusive. Just three hundred people were gathered, and yet somehow Audra had managed to get the two of them seats at a table midway to the staging area. A hush fell as they entered the large room. People turned, whispered. Tempest wanted to die. She smiled instead, inclined her head regally as the murmurs reached her ears.

Across the room, she caught a glimpse of Colin. He had his back to her, and he was seated with some of the biggest names in the industry. She knew a moment of hope. He wasn't being shunned here, but then movie people were a tolerant crowd. The proof would come when he returned to California and had to deal with the press and political party hierarchy.

She choked down dinner with the help of a glass of Piper-Heidsieck. She was hardly in a celebratory mood, but the champagne helped quell her nerves. And then she was on her feet, applauding with as much enthusiasm as the others in the room, when Colin won the Palme d'Or.

He stood, head held high as he walked to the dais, and Tempest wanted to believe that her earlier press conference had something to do with his confident demeanor. It had been the right thing to do, the best thing possible for the man she loved, but her heart ached all the same. Just last night she'd run her fingers through that blond hair and had been caressed by the hands that now held the Festival's coveted award.

"I'm proud of this film, and pleased to have been presented with the Palme d'Or. But what I want to say as I stand here before you is a little off topic. I hope you will bear with me.

"Everyone in this room is undoubtedly aware of the most recent scandal involving Tempest Herriman. She and I have been linked in a video, which Miss Herriman has gone on the record as saying she concocted as a way to blackmail me into casting her in what will be my last movie."

Colin looked right at her then, and enunciated as clearly as possible, "I want everyone to know that Tempest Herriman is nothing but a liar."

She sucked in a breath and felt her face heat to the same shade as her lipstick as the people around her openly gawked and wrinkled their noses, as if they had just found a fly floating in their bouillabaisse. Audra gripped her hand under the table, and that small show of solidarity was the only thing that kept Tempest from fleeing the room and this newest, and by far most painful, humiliation.

"Here's the truth. I had already told Miss Herriman she could audition for the part of Roxy Remington in *Flights of Fancy*. I have little doubt she will be cast once Stan Dartman, the producer, watches her audition. She is a good actress. That much should be clear to everyone after today's Oscar-worthy performance at her press conference."

Her head felt light. Her ears were buzzing. But over the sound she heard him say, "That *is* me in the video. I *was* with Tempest in the elevator at the Herriman and...well, the video speaks for itself as to what we were doing.

"But, as someone I greatly admire and respect once told me, pictures don't tell the whole story. So, that's what I'm doing right now."

He smiled at her then, and her eyes filled with tears.

"A lot of people have warned me that Tempest Herriman is all wrong for me. And I will admit that she tends to make the kind of headlines a person in my position would prefer to avoid. But I know the real Tempest. She is kind and caring, smart and funny. She goes out of her way to help people who need it and deserve it. But you'll never hear about the good deeds she does because taking credit and garnering favorable publicity for herself aren't high on her list of priorities."

She had just managed to dry her tears when he announced, "As I said, I was in the elevator with Tempest Herriman. I was there because I can't seem to stay away from her. I was there, ladies and gentlemen, because I love her."

She muffled a sob with her hand, crying even as she wanted to shout with joy.

"It's oddly fitting that I was in an elevator when I figured out that she's the one for me, because our relationship has already had its share of ups and downs."

The crowd laughed, as did Colin.

"The Herriman Foundation is foolish to let her step down. Just as I would be foolish to let her get away."

He set down the microphone then, and began to weave through the murmuring crowd. When he stopped at the table, he winked at Audra.

"I owe you for getting her here tonight."

"You?"

"Thank me later." Audra grinned, and then reached out to grab the handkerchief from Colin's breast pocket. She handed it to Tempest and said, "I think you're going to need this, honey."

"Why are you doing this?" she whispered to Colin. "I had it all worked out for you."

"I know you did. But you missed one key point."

"What?"

"How can I spend the rest of my life with you if I let you claim we're not involved?"

"Colin, I love you so much."

"I love you, too. Which is why I won't let you do this."

She closed her eyes briefly. "But your political career—"

He shrugged. "I'll run as an independent if I have to. Let the people decide. That's what's great about our democracy. If all else fails, I can fall back on this direct-ing thing. Word on the street is I'm not too bad at it."

She laughed. What else could she do when he was smiling at her with that sexy half-grin that had all the women in the room sighing in envy?

"What do you say, heiress? Are you going to make an honest man out of me?"

It seemed as if every person in attendance leaned in to hear her reply. But this was a private conversation, Tempest decided. And, God knew, so little of their re-lationship was private as it was.

Standing, she took Colin by the hand and tugged him toward the exit as the room's occupants began to chatter in excitement.

"Where are we going?"

"You'll see."

After leaving the Salon she headed straight for the nearest elevator.

Tempest and Colin smiled when the doors slid open. They grinned madly when they stepped inside the lift's tight quarters. And they laughed outright when the doors began to close on the crowd of astonished spectators gathered outside.

"Ask me again," she told Colin, winding her arms around his neck.

"Marry me, heiress?"

She hit the emergency stop and the alarm screamed as she pulled him close for a kiss.

She never actually said a word, but Colin McKinnon had his answer.

EPILOGUE

ARE THEY OR AREN'T THEY?

Tempest McKinnon, Academy Award nominee and wife of newly elected United States Senator Colin McKinnon, tossed down the glossy celebrity magazine and heaved a sigh of disgust.

"Can you believe they're still harping on that question?" she said.

Colin glanced up from the speech he was preparing and smiled indulgently. "Cut them some slack, sweetheart. They just want to know."

"But it's none of their business."

He shrugged. "True, but why not indulge them? They're going to find out eventually anyway."

"I suppose." Then she straightened and grinned brightly. "Oh, my God! Come here, quick!"

"What? What is it?"

He was on his feet in an instant, rushing to her side. Tempest grabbed his hand and placed it under the hem of her blouse on the small mound of her stomach that made it impossible to snap her favorite pair of jeans.

"Wait...wait. Right there! Did you feel it? Did you feel that kick?"

"I did!"

Colin kissed her. In his excitement, he picked her up

and actually spun her around, before dropping down with her onto the sofa in their Malibu estate.

"Are they or aren't they?" He laughed. "Just wait till the media find out that not only *are we*, but it's twins!"

Everything you love about romance...
and more!

Please turn the page for Signature Select™
Bonus Features.

BONUS
FEATURES
INSIDE

Fiona's Corner
by Fiona Hood-Stewart

BONUS ARTICLE

I first went to Cannes as a little girl: my father
kept his yacht a few miles down the coast, in
4   Juan les Pins, so we were frequent visitors.
Since then it has changed quite a bit, but still
retains its charming Riviera atmosphere. I
would definitely recommend spending at least
some time there if you are in the South of
France. It's a good base if you are thinking of
visiting other places in the area, such as Saint
Paul de Vence, where many famous artists
such as Picasso lived, and the perfume town of
Grasse, up in the hills.

Cannes has an interesting history. In 1834
Lord Brougham, the former English Chancellor
of the Exchequer, discovered the then small

fisherman's port when it consisted of nothing more than a few village houses set around what is now known as the old port. Lord Brougham liked Cannes so much that he decided to stay and build a villa for himself, where he invited his aristocratic friends. Many of them also built homes there, and within a few years the town had become a playground— filled with rich hotels and restaurants, a holiday destination for much of the world's royalty. By the turn of the twentieth century Cannes had grown to almost half its current size.

Elaborate and luxurious hotels were built on the Croisette, Cannes's seafront promenade, the most famous of these being the Carlton, which was built in 1912. Its white façade is seen on televisions around the world during the Film Festival in May. The Palais des Festivals, with its famous red-carpeted steps, is also home to the tourist office and one of the busiest casinos in the world. The immaculate Croisette is maintained by one hundred and thirty gardeners and has retained its elegance, despite the hordes of tourists who traipse up and down it every year. Fast food restaurants and souvenir shops have not been allowed to spoil its glamour, which is still maintained by designer boutiques. The hotels all have their own immaculate private beaches, which are open to anyone prepared to pay. There are also two public beaches in Cannes, but they are small and crowded and it's better to go to the Plages du Midi, west of the old town.

The area around the old port is probably the most interesting part of Cannes. The fishermen in their little wooden boats still go about their business, despite being overshadowed by a plethora of enormous private yachts. The old town, known as Le Suquet, rises steeply from the port, crowned by an eleventh-century tower. The Rue Saint Antoine leads up to the top of Le Suquet and is lined with restaurants. Many of them are excellent, but I recommend the views from the top of the street in the Place de la Castre, which are breathtaking. From here, one truly appreciates the glorious setting of Cannes. As for the best places to eat, the Rue Félix Faure is definitely one of the best places. All the restaurants here specialise in fish and one of the most respected is Astoux et Brun.

I hope that you will enjoy my story, and that it may inspire you to visit one of the world's most glitzy and fun places. Who knows? Maybe there's a prince lurking there for you!

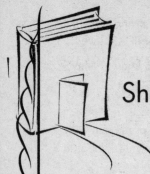

Sharon Kendrick's
Travel Tale...
About Cannes

BONUS ARTICLE
ABOUT CANNES

8   *Cannes is set on the glittering coastline known as
the Côte d'Azur, amid some of the most expensive
real estate in the world...the fabled and beautiful
South of France.*

*It is also home to the annual Cannes Film
Festival (which is where my story is set)—an
internationally renowned event which features the
age-old sirens of temptation. Sex. Power. Youth.
Beauty. And of course we mustn't forget fame—
perhaps the most heady of them all—with its
sometimes terrible karma which sweeps up the
impressionable to unimaginable heights, only to
smash them down again without a care.*

I first went to Cannes when I was twenty. I
was working as a waitress in the nearby
mountain village of Plan du Var, and on my

weekly day off I used to visit all those places whose very names used to evoke such magic. Nice. Juan les Pins. Cap d'Antibes. And of course, Cannes.

I had very little money with me that day—or any other day, for that matter! I stepped from the bus beneath the beating heat of the sun with nothing but a couple of apples and a large bottle of water in my bag. I might have been hungry but I didn't notice...I was too busy wandering up and down La Croisette—staring up at the ornate hotels and the tall palm trees which lined the wide road. I watched as expensive open-topped cars with leather upholstery purred by—and their occupants looked equally expensive, their eyes hidden behind dark shades.

Beyond La Croisette were shops spilling over with designer goods, frequented by skinny women with costly jewels gleaming against their brown skin.

But the town's riches paled into insignificance against the living treasure which is the Mediterranean Sea. Impossibly blue, it twinkles like a star-strung sapphire ribbon against the golden sand.

On this beach lay the oiled and perfect bodies of young women, sometimes watched over by their partners—elderly men whose shirts failed to disguise the paunch of easy living and whose faces were tired and jaded. And it was then that I realised that this place had a dark under-belly...with unsettling currents which seethed beneath the apparent calm of the surface.

I have to say that it was with mixed feelings that I went back to Cannes to research this book. Because going back is often dangerous. It reminds you of time, and how quickly it passes. It makes you nostalgic, and nostalgia can be dangerous too—since it colours memory and sometimes makes it seem more perfect than the present.

But surprisingly little had changed—except maybe me! This time the fashion police could breathe a sigh of relief, since I wasn't wearing a thigh-skimming dress with stripy socks and blue clogs! And this time I was able to afford a proper lunch—a delicious salade Niçoise.

I ate the unforgettable combination of tuna and green beans and hard-boiled egg and anchovies (who would ever have thought that such a mixture could be so delicious?) and around me French people were talking in that passionate, almost urgent way they have—gesticulating elaborately and elegantly with their hands and reminding me of how much I love this country.

After lunch I went to the Festival Theatre—the steps of which I had seen featured in countless glossy magazines with all the great European and Hollywood film stars standing on them as they posed for photographs.

Now, what the hell was I going to write about?

The steps leading up to the theatre itself seem to go on for ever, covered by a red carpet which is there all year round—a scarlet snake that slithers the entire length of the staircase. What must it be like to walk up there with the eyes of the world's press upon you? I wondered.

Pretend, I thought. Pretend it's *you*.

So I hooked my straw bag over my shoulder and began my slow ascent. Instead of a sundress and sparkly flip-flops I imagined that I was wiggling my way up there in a skin-tight gown of silk-satin and high-heeled shoes—dripping with diamonds, or sapphires, or emeralds.

And by doing that I began my story. In my imagination I had found my heroine...the woman who had it all—or at least looked as if she did. But inside, the story was very different. The glossy exterior was nothing but a sham—a mask—because inside the woman's heart was breaking with the kind of heartbreak that most people have felt at least once in their lives. Being a famous movie star offers you no protection against the pain of living.

And then I tried to put myself inside her skin (as I do with all my heroines). What must it be like to have to always present a certain image to the world? To smile as if you haven't a care in the world even though you feel as if you just want to crumble and go under? How can you possibly make yourself look like a goddess when your eyes are rimmed red with crying?

So why had she been crying?

Well, you wouldn't need to be Einstein to work *that* one out! It had to be a man...and not just any man...but a truly *magnificent* man.

Maybe it was because at just that moment I heard the lazy and mellifluous accent of an Italian behind me—but I just *knew* that my hero would have to be Italian. Controlled and yet passionate. The kind of man who had exuded an irresistible, lazy sexuality since he'd first started to shave. I could see his black hair and dark eyes—and an olive skin which seemed almost luminous, lit from within. I could picture his hard, lean body, too—and imagine the thrill of being enfolded in his arms.

And I knew that other women would have fantasised about him, too...that this man would be famous...head-turningly and heart-stoppingly famous.

Later still, I sat in the swanky bar of the Majestic Hotel, sipping at a cocktail as I watched the setting sun sinking into the wine-dark sea. And for a moment it seemed as if Cannes herself was laying on an evening to inspire my story—for on the beach a wedding was taking place.

There they were—the beautiful people. The men were clad in soft linen and the women in silk. Against the magnificent backdrop they sipped champagne while chefs prepared lobster and beautiful salads. The bride wore a deceptively simple ivory dress, her blonde hair loose over her shoulders, a leaf-green pasmina clutched between her fingers, where her brand-new and shiny wedding ring shone out like a beacon.

I watched as they lined up in groups for photographs and thought that I had never seen a more perfect wedding, and I knew that one day I would use it in a book.

But it doesn't feature in Matteo and Jennifer's story.

You see, they are already married.

Or rather, they were.

Soon they are going to be divorced.

And that is why she has been crying...

The Writing Life
by Jackie Braun

BONUS ARTICLE

Even though I have worked as a journalist both full time and freelance for nearly two decades, I can't claim ever to have met someone like Tempest Herriman, my larger-than-life heroine, who has an unfortunate knack for making the wrong kinds of headlines.

Still, my background did come in handy when I was fleshing out both her and the story's leading man, Colin McKinnon, an action hero turned director who is getting ready to run for the United States Senate. Colin can't afford a scandal and, of course, with a name like Tempest, my heroine can't help but create one.

As I said, I've never met anyone quite like Tempest, but during the eleven years I worked as an editorial writer for a daily newspaper in Michigan I had the privilege of meeting all manner of elected officials and influential people. They came before the editorial board, of which I was a member, seeking the newspaper's endorsement for their candidacy or their cause.

Afterward, the other board members and I would discuss the issues or candidates, reach a consensus, and then either I or the other editorial writer would pen an opinion piece.

I was in my midtwenties when I was invited to become a member of that board. I think I may have been the newspaper's youngest editorial writer, and I'm told I was the first female one in its more than one-hundred-year history. I was green enough to be nervous the first time I met a powerful, publicly elected official, and then a little disappointed when I realized he was just a man—not as tall as I'd imagined he would be, based on the pictures I had seen, and he had coffee breath besides.

That was when it hit me that the people we see on the television and read about in the newspapers are in many ways ordinary folks, no matter how extraordinary the circumstances in their lives. Whether they are heads of state or chief operating executives of multimillion-dollar corporations, federal law-makers, judges, governors, mayors, city council members, university presidents, lobbyists, etc., if you strip away their polish and purpose they are not all that different from you and me.

They all have good days and bad days—and they can all use a breath mint from time to time.

I believe that applies to celebrities as well.

We see them gliding glamorously along the red carpet and tend to think that's how they live their lives—ferried about in limousines while they sip champagne and wear *haute couture* gowns. But, while their wealth may keep them from having to schlep the garbage to the curb or run to the grocery store for a gallon of milk, it does not make them immune to some of the everyday travails the rest of us experience—including bad hair days or cases of halitosis.

No matter what the size of their bank account, they have insecurities and idiosyncrasies. They might not have to wait in line at a trendy nightclub, but they can and do make mistakes.

Tempest certainly makes her share of mistakes, which are then magnified by the media's glare. I wanted to provide readers with a peek underneath her public façade to the flesh-and-blood woman. No, I didn't give her stinky breath—but, despite her wealth and privilege, or perhaps *because* of them, Tempest comes from a very dysfunctional family. When her story begins, she has finally accepted that fact and is trying to make over her life—not only to win back the man she loves and to gain the respect of her peers, but so that she can respect herself. A lofty goal indeed.

Some readers will probably assume I based Tempest and Colin on real celebrities. Certainly Colin's political ambitions are reminiscent of those of another former Hollywood action hero who went on to become the governor of California, and Tempest is not unlike a real-life hotel chain heiress who has had to live down her own risqué videotape and tabloid headlines.

When the idea for this story first began to germinate, however, I did not have those two celebrities in mind. In fact, particularly in Tempest's case, I wanted to make her more of an amalgam of all celebrities and red carpet divas than merely to base her on one actual person.

I decided to make her extremely wealthy, and famous for that wealth, because I believed that would cause a lot of people to sell her short on her acting ambitions. Let's face it. We all do this. We assume that if someone is born with great gobs of money she won't have either the talent or the determination to earn her way in life.

Also, about the time I began to write this story, a couple of other female celebrities suffered what are now commonly referred to as "wardrobe malfunctions". The media, especially the sleazier elements in the press, had a field-day. The resulting photographs are still buzzing around the Internet, there in the cyberspace equivalent of a photo album for all eternity.

As someone who lives in fear she will leave a ladies' room with her dress tucked into her pantyhose, I could not help but feel horrified on their behalf.

As a journalist, however, I know that celebrities and public figures often want to have it both ways. They court publicity when it suits their needs, and then complain about the lack of privacy when it doesn't. Still, I do feel sympathy for some of them. What would it be like to live one's life under such constant scrutiny? What would it be like to make mistakes that are so well documented they are all but impossible to live down?

In answering those questions I came up with Tempest and Colin, and a love story that would certainly set tongues wagging if it were to occur in real life. Within the pages of this book, I hope it will leave readers smiling...and sighing.

Enjoy!

20

IN BED WITH THE BOSS
by Sharon Kendrick

PROLOGUE

HE STARTED WITH HER ANKLES, which were the most delicious ankles he had ever seen, then his eyes traveled slowly to her knees, and beyond. From across the room, he made a leisurely appraisal of slim hips and a tiny waist, exquisite breasts and hair the color of fire. He saved the face until last, and when at last his gaze reached the huge emerald eyes and pouty pink lips, he almost choked on his glass of champagne.

"Josephine?" he silently mouthed in incredulous question, and because she hadn't moved, he walked over to where she stood. "Josephine?"

Josephine's heart was racing and her hands felt clammy, but not just because he was the most devastating man in the room—he had always had precisely that effect on her.

"Of course it's me, Blake," she remonstrated. "Surely you recognized me?"

There was a pause. "Not really." Last time he'd seen her, she'd had braces on her teeth and freckles. The little girl next door. In the tiny village they'd lived in he had watched her grow from toddler to teenager. And now? He swallowed, even though he was no longer drinking. "You've...you've grown up all of a sudden."

"But I'm 23 years old now, Blake," she said softly.

"And you live in London now?" he guessed.

"That's right. You, too?"

"Mmm." God, she was beautiful! More than beautiful. "How long since we've seen each other?"

She stared into the ice-blue eyes. She could have told him to the exact minute. "Oh, must be about seven years," she said casually. "Not since you moved away."

He couldn't take his eyes off her. "What kind of work do you do?" he questioned casually.

"I'm a model."

A model. Yes. That would explain the sudden transformation from duckling to dazzling swan.

"A successful model?" he questioned.

She gave a modest smile. "Kind of." She sipped her drink and smiled at him. "How about you?"

The smile beguiled him. "I'm a venture capitalist."

"Sounds like a bandit!"

He laughed. "Does it?" A bandit might have carried her straight off to bed with him, something he—uncharacteristically—felt *just* like doing.

"Do I look like a bandit?"

Kind of, she thought, but shook her head. "No, you look like a venture capitalist!"

"How about another drink?" His lips curved in a smile. "Or would you rather dance?"

There was no choice! But she managed to shrug her shoulders, as if she didn't mind either way. "I love dancing," she admitted.

Normally, he could take it or leave it, and he couldn't remember the last time he had danced with a woman who wasn't Kim. But the opportunity to hold her was too much to miss. "Me, too. Come on, then."

The gods must have been looking down on her, because at that moment the music slowed, and he took her in his arms and she felt almost dizzy, achingly aware of the hard, lean strength of his body.

"I—I like this song," she said, rather shakily.

"Mmm." He liked the drift of her scent even more. He absently pulled her closer and buried his lips in her hair and Josephine was unprepared for the shimmering of heat that skittered such debilitating sensations across her skin. Blake felt the sudden jackknifing of desire as her slender curves melted against his flesh like butter, and he had to stifle a moan. Maybe he'd better just take her home and say good-night.

Sooner, rather than later.

But he was seduced by the moonlight and the way she walked, the way she made him laugh. And a shared past could produce nostalgia...and nostalgia could be pretty potent stuff. He accepted coffee. And then another, and her eyes mesmerized him with their dazzling green fire.

"Guess I'd better think about leaving," he said reluctantly.

"I guess so. It's been...fun."

"Yeah."

She was lost in the light of his eyes. "Goodbye, Blake."

"Goodbye, Josephine."

24

She wondered if she would ever see him again, and when she reached up on tiptoe to kiss him goodbye, her lips somehow collided with the faint rasp of his jaw, and it felt so earthy that she shivered against him in unstoppable response.

Something inexplicable exploded inside him and he turned his head and captured her mouth with his, knowing without a shadow of a doubt that this was heading for the bedroom.

"I don't usually do this kind of thing," he groaned, as the kiss got hotter and harder.

Neither did she, but once again his mouth had hungrily covered hers and her words somehow got lost on his lips.

It was the best night of Josephine's life, but in the morning he had left without asking to see her again, and much later she heard that he had gone back to Kim and that they had become engaged. And soon after that she had met his cousin Luke, and within three months they were married.

LUKE HAD GONE.

He hadn't even taken his toothbrush, but she knew he had gone. That fact hit her with a certainty even more intense than the blade of lightning that illuminated the bathroom with its harsh blue-white light. Josephine momentarily shrank from its impact, and winced. The toothbrush was still there, yes, but further investigation showed that her husband of just one year had cleared the rest of the house like a locust. Gone were the rows of designer suits and the handmade Italian shoes. Gone, too, were the priceless objets d'art which he had always insisted they buy.

Or rather, that *she* buy, Josephine reminded herself bitterly.

The lightning was followed by a thunderbolt that could have deafened the hounds of hell. And then the rain began—a rain so heavy and remorseless that the loud banging on the front door didn't register straight away. And when it did, she froze with a sinking feeling that felt almost like disappointment.

Had he left, only to return?

She ran into the hall and pulled open the door and the sight of the tall, drenched figure made her heart

BONUS FEATURE

briefly suspend its frenzied beat. For it wasn't Luke who stood there like a dark avenging angel, but his cousin Blake. Blake. The man she had not seen for over a year—not since he had stormed round to her flat and told her that she would be a crazy fool to marry a man like Luke.

"B-Blake!" she gasped, but the word dried to sawdust in her mouth.

"Disappointed?" he drawled, but at least she was here. And she seemed to be okay. "Expecting your husband, were you, sweetheart?"

She shook her head, wishing he wouldn't use that word, not when he didn't mean it. "He's taken all his clothes. He's gone."

"I know he has," he said grimly.

Her eyes narrowed. "How can you possibly—"

But Blake wasn't listening. He had unceremoniously pushed his way past her, to stand dripping raindrops onto the beautiful, polished wooden floor.

"Shut the door!" he commanded, his eyes raking reluctantly over her skimpy evening dress. A pulse began to beat at his temple. So she still dressed to kill. "Or were you hoping to freeze to death? Just shut the door, Josephine! *Now!*"

Mutely she obeyed him. There was something about the tone of his voice that was impossible to ignore. But maybe if she had listened to him the last time around, she wouldn't be in this situation.

She stared at him. They said that time healed, but

time didn't always change the way someone made you *feel*. She hadn't seen him in over a year, but the sheer force of his personality was devastating as ever. As were his looks. The blue eyes were as vibrant as a summer sky and the hard, lean body as formidably gorgeous as it had ever been. Lucky Kim, she thought, forcing herself to remember in the most painful way possible that he had a fiancée.

"What are you doing here?" she whispered. "And how on earth did you know that Luke had left, when I've only just found out myself?"

He gave a cynical smile, which iced over her. "Because he rang me from the airport."

"The airport?" she repeated dully. "Where was he going?"

"He didn't say."

"I don't understand," she breathed, and she heard him swear softly beneath his breath.

"I think you're just about to," he gritted. "He's with someone called Sadie." The blue eyes bored into her questioningly. "Know her?"

Josephine nodded. "Yes, I know her," she said dully. Best friends weren't all they were cracked up to be, were they? And yet, deep down, he wasn't telling her anything that she hadn't already guessed.

But despite the fact that Luke had gone, only one question nudged at the edges of her mind.

"So just why are *you* here, Blake?"

Blake shrugged. "I guess I've come to pick up the pieces."

Still feeling as though she was in the midst of some nightmare, Josephine stared at him uncomprehendingly. "And what's that supposed to mean?"

His eyes moved over her, noting the angular line of her collarbone and the way her hipbones jutted against the filmy material of her dress. As a model, she had always been slim, but now she looked as though a breath of wind could blow her away. Had marriage to his cousin turned her into a mere shadow of herself?

"How the hell can he afford to take off like that?" he demanded.

Josephine stared at him blankly, because his words didn't make sense. Come to think of it, nothing made sense right now. "What?"

"I think it might be a good idea if you took a look at your accounts," he ground out.

All she could see was his blue eyes burning into her. "Accounts?" she echoed.

It was only a hunch, but Blake knew his cousin well enough to suspect that he had taken more than his clothes with him. "Just do it, will you?" he said quietly. "I doubt whether Luke has financed his trip with the fruit of his own labors."

The rising sense of panic she felt was making her blood run cold, and though she shook her head in denial, she couldn't stop herself from suspecting the worst. But he wouldn't have taken her money, surely? Bad enough that he had walked off with one of her supposed friends—surely it couldn't get any worse than that?

She could feel Blake's eyes on her as she walked to the bureau to find the telephone number of the bank. She picked up the phone and punched in the numbers and when it was answered she said, shakily, "I'd like to know the balance of my current account, please. And could you check my savings account, too, please?"

The sums quoted took her breath away and her fingers were trembling as she turned round to meet the piercing brilliance of his eyes.

"Both accounts are empty," she said in a dead, flat voice. "He's taken everything."

His mouth twisted, ruing an aunt who had showered everything on his pretty, petulant cousin. "It seems that your precious Luke is nothing more than a common thief."

The rising panic was fast turning into a swamping tide. "Oh, my God," she breathed. "He can't have done!"

"Well, it looks as if he damned well has!" He let out a low sigh of frustration. "I told you that you were a fool to marry him, Josephine! I've known the guy for most of my life—I *knew* what he was like! You should have listened to me!"

Yes, she should have listened to him, but how

could she have done, when her perception of him had been tainted by the night she had spent in his arms? And the fact that he hadn't wanted her afterward.

"Does it make you feel better to say 'I told you so'?" she questioned, her voice shaking with a sense of anger and outrage.

He shook his head. "You know, you're going to have to contact the police."

"The *police*?" It was unthinkable, surely, to report her husband to the police?

"Of course you will!" he stated impatiently. "Your precious Luke can't be allowed to get away with bleeding you dry! I presume that most of it was *your* money?"

Of course it was. Luke's "acting" career had dried up around about the time she'd married him. They had lived off the small fortune she had earned as a model. And when she had decided to study for an alternative career, her fees at business school and the fact that neither of them had been earning had eaten into a fair bit of it.

"Yes," she said dully. "It was mine."

"Well, surprise, surprise," he murmured.

And then, with threatened tears making her mouth taste salty, she turned to stare up at the impassive man who stood before her. "Oh, Blake," she whispered, because he might be forbidding, but at that moment he looked so damned strong. "What the hell am I going to do?"

"You could always go back on the catwalk," Blake murmured.

But Josephine shook her head. Her days of hanging around the cattle market, of being judged by the length of her legs and the swell of her breast were long gone. "I'm through with modeling."

Blake's eyes glittered. "You could always come and work for me."

"You?" Disbelievingly, Josephine stared at the to-die-for face. *"You'd* give me a job? Just like that?"

"Well, no, not just like that. Didn't I hear that you'd gone back to school? That you were planning to make your mark in the world of high finance?"

She wasn't sure if it was sarcasm she could hear in his voice, but now was hardly the time for nit-picking about his attitude. "But I know virtually nothing about venture capitalism."

Now the blue eyes gleamed. "Oh, so you remember what I do for a living, do you, Josephine?" he questioned softly.

She remembered a whole lot more besides, but that was a trip down memory lane that she did *not* intend taking. "Like I said, it's not something I'm familiar with."

"Well, it isn't exactly brain surgery," he drawled. "And you're a fast learner, aren't you?"

Her cheeks flushed as she wondered whether he was referring to the things he had taught her in bed, but she pushed the thought away. "Why?" she whispered. "Why would you go out of your way to help me?"

His mouth curved. Did she think that if she turned those big, green eyes on him, she could twist him around her little finger like she'd done once before, and make him act in a way that was alien to him? Because before Josephine, he'd never had a one-night stand in his life. Never.

"Oh, don't flatter yourself that it's because your plight is making my heart bleed for you," he murmured. "You got yourself into this situation and part of me feels like telling you to get yourself out of it, but—"

"But?"

"Luke may be a worthless airhead," he mused. "But the fact remains that he happens to be related to me—and his behavior leaves a rather nasty taste in my mouth."

"And the scandal wouldn't do your reputation any good, I suppose?"

He gave a cool smile. "Oh, I wouldn't worry your head about that. My reputation speaks for itself—and some two-bit marital breakdown wouldn't affect it. No, I'm in a position to offer you a job, that's all. I will give you a job, until you decide what you want to do."

She eyed him warily. "A job doing what?"

He elevated the elegant curve of his eyebrows. "Why, doing what you do best, of course—being decorative."

Some women might have taken that as a compliment, but not Josephine. Men always took her at face value, and never saw beneath the pretty face, until sometimes even *she* wondered if she were all superficial glamour, with no real substance beneath. "Decorative in what way?"

His eyes narrowed. Did she think he was going to demand that she use the potent weapon of her sensuality to please him? Lie draped around his office, half-naked, perhaps? He felt the jerk of desire.

"My receptionist, Sallie, is going on maternity leave and I need someone to replace her. Someone to sit behind a desk and answer the phone and smile prettily at all the visitors. Using you might work out better than employing a temp. Think you could manage that, Josephine?"

A receptionist! Not exactly what she'd had in mind when she'd sweated over management strategies and long-term projections! But Blake Devlin ran a highly successful company—and wouldn't a foot in the door, however lowly, give her the entrée she needed?

"But your business is in central London," she said haltingly. "And this is much too far to commute." Not that she felt she *could* stay here, not with Luke's ghost haunting the half-empty rooms, mocking her with the knowledge of what a sham their marriage had really been. "So where do I stay?"

"Why not come and stay with me?" He shrugged his broad shoulders, although the beat of his heart queried the wisdom of his next words. "I have a large apartment—there's plenty of room."

Her stomach tied itself up in knots. Once she would have given the world to hear him say those words. "I could always ask one of my girlfriends to put me up—" But her voice trailed off. Most of her girlfriends were cozily cohabiting—could she really just land on one of their doorsteps like Cinderella? While Blake lived slap-bang in the center of London, just a short distance from his offices.

And didn't the thought of sharing with Blake make her heart beat faster with a delicious, illicit kind of pleasure? "I'm not sure," she said uncertainly.

His cool smile mocked her. "You think I'm offering you the other half of my bed? Is that what's worrying you?"

Josephine's cheeks flamed as her mind cruelly conjured up a forbidding sensual memory. "Of course I don't! And anyway, what about Kim?" she questioned, forcing herself to say the name without her voice shaking. "Won't she object to another woman living in your flat?"

"What I do is not Kim's concern."

She stared at him. "What do you mean?"

"Not anymore." There wasn't a flicker of emotion to disturb the shuttered features. "You see, Kim and I are no longer engaged."

Josephine stared at Blake in disbelief. "You're not engaged to Kim anymore?"

His mouth tightened. "That's what I said."

"But why?"

Blake stared at her, thinking that she ought to give a little more attention to the mess of her own life before she started enquiring about *his*. "I don't think that's any of your business, do you? Now why don't you pack a suitcase, and we'll drive to London?"

Still dazed by the speed of what was happening to her, Josephine threw together the most suitable clothes she had, leaving Blake standing grim-faced in the sitting room.

"I can easily let this place out," she offered, once her packing was done. "That way I'll be able to pay my way." And at least that would give her some kind of financial independence, along with the salary he would be paying her.

He nodded. "Shall we go?"

He took her case from her while she locked the door of the house and settled herself into the leather-lined luxury of his car.

He shot her a brief look as he turned the ignition

key, but forced his eyes back onto the road imme-diately, his hands tightening around the wheel.

He had persuaded her to change out of that ridiculously provocative little evening dress, but jeans and a sweater were proving almost as dis-tracting. How had he allowed himself to forget what a knockout of a woman she was—with her long, rangy limbs, which once she had wrapped so ea-gerly around his neck?

Forget that, he told himself doggedly. *Forget* it.

JOSEPHINE TRIED TO DOZE on the journey to London, but nothing could stop the thoughts that whirled around her aching head. Luke had stolen her money and her friend and delivered the ultimate slap in the face.

"I can have him traced, you know," said Blake carefully.

She opened her eyes and turned to look at the hard, dark profile. "How?"

"There are ways and means."

She supposed there were, if you were rich enough. "I don't know." Could she bear to see him? What would they have left to say to one another?

Blake looked at the stiff, uptight set of her shoul-ders and wondered what had happened to the life and the fire that had once burned so brightly within her. Had Luke stamped that out completely? And why the hell had she allowed him to?

"Maybe you're hoping that he'll come to his senses and come running home to you?" he ground out. But he didn't wait for an answer, just drew up in front of a large and elegant apartment block. "We're here," he said shortly.

But once inside the luxury of his home, reality began to hit home and Josephine realized just where she was, and with whom. Had she been out of her mind to agree to live in such close confines with a man who had once made love to her all night, and then walked away without a backward glance?

She looked around her, longing for the escape of sleep. "Where will I be sleeping?"

His mouth hardened. As far away from him as possible. But the pert thrust of her breasts reminded him of something very elemental indeed, and he felt the hardening of desire.

"I'll show you." He beckoned for her to follow him to the guest bedroom, where a huge bed seemed to dominate the entire room, and as he slung the suitcase down, he wondered what she wore in bed these days.

Josephine looked around, anything to avoid the sudden hectic glittering in his eyes. "This is lovely. Thank you."

"Do you want to go to bed right now?" he questioned silkily.

Caught in the cross fire of his eyes, Josephine stared across the bed at Blake as fantasy and reality spun her mind into confusion. "B-bed?" she gulped, and felt her heart accelerate.

Was she always this compliant? he wondered furiously. So at ease with her own sexuality that she would turn on for any man who made a move on her? Would she resist him if he pulled her into his arms and began to make love to her right now?

"Yes, bed," he responded mockingly, as he turned to walk away. "It's getting late, and I'm bushed. Good night, Josephine—I'll see you in the morning."

And he shut the door very quietly behind him.

After a largely sleepless night, Josephine was up early the following morning, pulling on a demure sweater and skirt with an unexpected feeling of liberation, despite the situation she found herself in.

She realized how heavy Luke's influence on her had been. He always insisted on vetting her clothes—and the ones he liked had been designed specifically to show off her reed-slim figure to advantage.

Why had she let him dictate to her so?

Because she had wanted to make their partnership work. Because she wanted a marriage just like the one her parents had had. Revealing clothes had seemed a small price to pay for a harmony, which had never quite happened.

She walked into the sitting room and Blake

stilled momentarily when he caught that first sight of her—a Josephine he had never seen before.

She was wearing a knee-length skirt in soft, heathery colors of purple and green, with a green sweater, which brought out the color of her eyes. Her hair was scraped back in a chignon that sat neatly on the back of her long neck, but the most surprising thing of all was that she was wearing a pair of wire-rimmed spectacles.

She looked neat and sweet and—astonishingly enough—extremely *efficient*.

"Glasses?" he exclaimed.

She was having a bit of difficulty concentrating—but then she had never seen Blake in an exquisitely cut three-piece suit before, a suit that seemed to make his long legs go on forever. "Men never make passes at girls who wear glasses" was her one irreverent thought before meeting the question in his eyes.

"You don't like them?"

"I didn't say that," he responded steadily. "I just didn't know you wore them, that's all."

"I prefer them. Luke used to like me to wear contact lenses, so I did."

That figured. Glasses made her look almost prim. Aloof. And so at odds with the passionate woman he knew lay beneath. Blake swallowed. Though no less attractive for looking aloof. No way.

"There's coffee in the pot. And some muffins in the basket."

"Th-thanks."

She forced herself to eat something, though it wasn't easy, not with Blake's long legs stretched out underneath the table, only a whisper away from hers.

She wondered just what kind of reception she was going to get at his company, but she waited until they were in the car before she asked him. "What exactly have you told your employees about me?"

He shrugged. "Just that you're an old friend, and that you're standing in for a while."

Friend? He didn't make her feel like his friend. "Not that I was deserted and duped by my ex-husband?"

He shook his head impatiently. "Wouldn't that rather risk you sounding like a victim, Josephine? Or maybe that's how you see yourself?"

"Maybe in the past I allowed myself to be," she said slowly. "But not anymore."

"Good," he murmured, but he was struggling to keep his eyes on the road. With her knees pressed decorously together, he noted that she still had the best pair of legs he had ever seen on a woman.

"You probably *could* walk back into modeling, you know. If you really wanted to," he observed, thinking that maybe it was a crime to deny the world that much beauty. There was a pause. "Did you resent it when Luke asked you to stop?"

Josephine shook her head. She had been so busy trying to see the wisdom in Luke's objection to her work taking her away from him that there hadn't been the time or the inclination for resentment. Then it had seemed a good idea—only now was she beginning to get an idea of how little she had asserted herself. And only now it occurred to her that Luke's demands might have been motivated more by jealousy of the fact that her career was eclipsing his. "Not really," she sighed, wondering how she could have been so *blind*.

She didn't elaborate, which Blake thought was curiously loyal in view of what Luke had done, but which might also mean that she was still in love with him. Though if she was, then why describe him as her "ex"?

"So are you still in love with Luke, Josephine?" he drawled, as the car glided into the underground car-park.

It was a question that brought painful memories in its wake and Josephine stared into the steely gleam of Blake's eyes. Just what *did* she feel about Luke now? "I don't know," she said flatly.

He wasn't prepared for the sharp slam of jealousy in his gut. "Come on, Josephine, you can do better than that."

She shrugged. Maybe she could. "You've already

guessed that the marriage was a disaster—a fact confirmed that my husband sought to leave me so suddenly."

"That doesn't answer my question. A woman can still love a man, even if he treats her badly."

He didn't appear to have noticed the irony that *his* behavior toward her had hardly been textbook perfect. With a sudden growing sense of resolution, she put all her energy into a smile. "I hope I have a little more pride than that, Blake. I've never really been a fan of masochism. Now, hadn't we better get going?"

He noticed how neatly she had avoided answering the question. "Sure." He watched the way she walked up the stairs in front of him and forced himself to stifle a groan. Demure the skirt might be, yes—but it did absolutely nothing to disguise the high, hard curve of her bottom.

He followed her into Reception and willed the aching to subside. "This is Sallie!" he announced, smiling at the glowingly pregnant blonde at the desk. "Sallie, this is Josephine—who's going to be filling in while you're away. Will you show her the ropes?"

"Yes, Blake. Of course."

He gave a ghost of a smile. "I'll see you later, Josie," he said softly.

Then he was gone, and Josephine found herself watching his retreating back almost wistfully. She

42

was on her own now—and it was up to her to show not just Blake, but everyone else in the company, that she wasn't just a pretty face, but could do the job properly.

Sallie gestured to a chair. "So you know anything about venture capitalists?" she asked.

Josephine shook her head. "Not a thing! But I'm ready to learn!"

"You'll need to be," said Sallie.

It was a long time since Josephine had put in a full day's work, and she had never worked in an office before, so by the end of the afternoon she was absolutely dead on her feet.

But by going-home time, she had learnt to use the complicated phone system and got to grips with the computer terminal.

She was also beginning to get an inkling of just how vast Blake's empire really was...and how hard he worked...and the contrast between him and his cousin couldn't have been more marked.

"So you're a *friend* of Blake's, are you?" Sallie asked carefully over afternoon tea. "Not a girlfriend, or anything?"

Josephine shook her head. One bout of passionate sex 15 months ago certainly didn't put her in *that* category. "No. Why?"

"Oh, nothing. He hasn't gone out with anyone since he split with Kim, you know," Sallie confided. "We all reckon he's still carrying a torch for her."

"Oh." Stupidly, Josephine felt her heart lurch with disappointment.

So maybe Kim wasn't completely out of the picture. But at least Sallie's comment reinforced the fact that entertaining any false hopes about a man who despised her was a complete waste of time. It was just extremely bad timing that after working nonstop, a shadow should fall over her desk just as she was repairing her lipstick. Josephine blinked as narrow hips swam into her line of vision and she looked up into a pair of ice-blue eyes.

His gaze was cold and distinctly unfriendly—but then, why should it be otherwise? She was just someone he saw as a loser, someone he was reluctantly doing a favor for.

44

And Josephine realized that she might never have his affection, but that she was damned well going to have to earn his respect. The question was how?

WEEKENDS WERE GOING to be the worst, Blake decided. At least during the week, the days were filled by going to the office and evenings spent catching up on the million and one things he needed to do. But Josephine's first Saturday in his apartment had him feeling like a caged tiger with nowhere to go.

He almost collided with her outside the bathroom and his blood pressure shot through the ceiling. No glasses or prissy little skirts and sweaters now, he thought furiously. Just long, pale limbs still

glistening with tiny beads of water, and hair streaming in rivulets over her shoulders to cling erotically
to her breasts.

"Can't you put something on?" he snarled.

"I was just on my way to do exactly that!" she
retorted, but her cheeks went very hot. She hadn't
missed the sudden darkening of his eyes, nor the
fleeting look of hunger that had crossed his face. "I-
if you wouldn't mind letting me pass."

"Delighted," he said sarcastically, but even
though he pressed himself against the wall, he could
still feel the warmth emanating from a body clad
only in a large bath sheet.

"Thank you," she said, the close proximity making her only too aware of his raw masculinity, the
rugged features, and the muscular shafts of his
thighs, which rippled through his jeans.

She shut the bedroom door behind her with a
shaking hand, feeling the guilty sting of blood to her
breasts and realizing that he wasn't immune to
her—nor she to him. But deep down she could tell
that he hated himself for wanting a woman he despised so much.

He was drinking coffee in the sitting room when
she finished dressing and he looked up as she
walked in, wondering where she had acquired the
knack of always making him want to drag her off
to the nearest bed. He fought for something conventional to say, and fixed her with a bland smile.

BONUS FEATURE

"So how has your first week at work been?"

She narrowed her eyes suspiciously. Was a criticism about to come winging her way? "I've really enjoyed it."

"Not quite modeling, though, is it?"

"No. But it's rather refreshing to be judged on what you do, rather than how you look."

He frowned. He'd never thought of it that way. "But the pay isn't as good."

"Pay isn't everything," she said, with a touch of defiant pride. And she would show him just how hard she had been working! "Er, Blake?"

"Josephine?"

46 How she wished he wouldn't always adopt that horrible sardonic tone! "I...er..." She met his cool, quizzical stare. "I have a proposition to put to you. Well, sort of."

His mind played out an aching sexual fantasy. He could think of a few propositions he wouldn't mind putting to her. "Really? About what?"

"About work actually."

He gave her a look of barely concealed amusement. "I can hardly wait," he murmured.

"Do you remember Giuseppi Rossi?" she blurted out, seeing his hateful smile.

He frowned as he flipped back through his memory bank. "The young Italian horticultural chemist?"

"That's right. He's called by the office a few times now."

"And you've had a chat with him, am I right?" His mouth twisted. He could imagine—the Italian looked as if he should be starring in the movies, not bent over a test tube in a laboratory.

"That's right." She drew a deep breath. "Blake, he says you won't see him—"

"Because there's no point," he butted in impatiently, instantly recognizing where this conversation was headed. "I have no intention of bankrolling his company, Josephine—so if that's what you're about to ask me, then you can save your breath."

"But he's *brilliant*!" she argued, ignoring the dangerous light in his eyes. "This organic weed killer he's working on sounds absolutely revolutionary!"

"So, a week into the job and already you're an expert?"

"Please don't patronize me, Blake!"

"I'm trying to tell you how it *is*, Josephine—and it's just not the kind of scheme I involve myself in!"

"So my opinion counts for nothing?"

"Why should it?" he questioned arrogantly.

"What about the fact that I came away from business school with a distinction?"

He was impressed, but he didn't show it. "That's theory, not practice!"

"Or that they told us that sometimes—just some-times—we should go with our instincts, and my in-stinct is telling me that this is a brilliant idea."

"I said *no*, Josephine," he growled. "My experi-ence overrules your instinct. Believe me, I'm right."

It felt like being kicked in the teeth. Not just the way he had dismissed her idea out of hand, but his zero lack of faith in her judgment.

"Then I'll just have to prove you wrong, won't I, Blake?" she challenged hotly.

"SO ARE YOU GOING TO carry on sulking at work, as well?" Blake murmured, leaning over the reception desk only to be punished by the mesmerizing vision of her breasts gloriously outlined in pure cashmere.

Josephine looked up and frowned, and wished he would stop wearing that gorgeous aftershave, or stand farther away. Or something. "I am not sulk-ing."

"Wrong. You've been off with me ever since you asked me about Giuseppi." In fact, she had sub-jected him to a polite freeze whenever he spoke to her, and infuriatingly, it was having the effect of making him *want* her to talk to him. He wasn't used to women giving him the cold shoulder, he was used to them eating out of his hand. "Are you still mad about *that*?"

She gave him a chilly stare. Of course she was! "It wasn't so much that you failed to look at his proposal in full—it was the fact that you obviously credit me with no intelligence or imagination at all."

The jury on the intelligence part was still out—an intelligent woman wouldn't have rushed headlong into marriage with a man like Luke, surely? But of her imagination, he was in no doubt—she had certainly been as imaginative as a man could want the night he'd made love to her.

"Let's just say I'm giving it some thought," he said placatingly.

And she was supposed to fall to her knees and thank him, was she? Her chilly look didn't waver. Josephine had been working her socks off at Devlin Associates—and while *he* might not have noticed it, the others certainly had. Why, just this morning, his second-in-command had told her that if her people skills could be marketed, then none of them need ever work again!

"And I'm supposed to be grateful for that, am I, Blake?"

"You could try," he answered flippantly and thoughtfully fingered a bright petal of one of the flowers that stood on the desk. He hadn't really noticed flowers there before. "Did you put these here?" he questioned suspiciously.

She nodded. She had jettisoned the rather ugly and very dusty rubber plant. "I thought it added something to the atmosphere of the room. Do you have a problem with that?"

BONUS FEATURE

He shook his head. "Just make sure that you use money from petty cash, that's all."

"I did." She smiled, steeling herself against the sheer potency of his appeal. "Was there something else you wanted, Blake?"

"Have you eaten lunch yet?"

"No," she answered repressively.

"Want to grab a sandwich with me?"

It wasn't the most alluring invitation she had ever received, but her curiosity was aroused. He had never asked her to lunch before, so why start now?

"Why not?" She shrugged.

50   His irritation at her noncommittal response was only increased when the proprietor of the Italian deli around the corner danced besotted attention on her request for beef on rye. He narrowed his eyes as he watched her accept the sandwich. Was she *flirting* with him? He had to say that she wasn't. Maybe it was just some unconscious message she sent out that had most red-blooded men fawning all over her.

They sat down. "This is very sweet of you, Blake," she murmured.

"Not really. I've got some news for you, and I thought it best if I broke it away from the office."

There was something darkly ominous about the way he spoke, and the hand that held the sandwich froze halfway to her mouth. "What news?" she whispered.

"Just that I've managed to trace your husband," he said. "I've found Luke."

Josephine's hand shook uncontrollably. "You've *found* Luke?" she whispered. *"Where?"*

Blake was watching her face carefully. "Your husband is on a beach in Bali." He shrugged in distaste. "He certainly decided to leave you in style!"

Using *her* money. Josephine's ego, which she had been slowly building up all week like a convalescent patient, now collapsed like a day-old soufflé. She let her gaze drop to her half-eaten sandwich, unwilling to meet Blake's eyes, reluctant to see the mockery there—or his triumph at seeing her neatly slotted back into the role marked "victim."

"I can get him back to England, you know."

She did look up then. He looked so sure of himself. So confident. So strong. "How?"

"I could threaten him with the police—"

"That would make him want to stay, surely?"

"Not if I told him you *haven't* yet reported him—but that you damned well will if he doesn't get back here and give you what he hasn't spent."

Josephine shook her head tiredly. Had Blake tracked him down deliberately to undermine her? To force her into contacting the police, as he thought she should? She had been doing okay before this latest bombshell—not great but okay—and part of the reason for that was that Luke's absence had made her feel free. Unburdened by the nagging weight of a marriage on the rocks, a relationship in dire trouble.

"Do you want him back?" he demanded.

"No, of course I don't!"

"I don't mean back with *you*, Josephine," he said, in a voice which for Blake could almost be described as gentle. "I mean to sort the whole business out to some kind of satisfactory conclusion."

She tried to imagine what the reality would be like. Luke back in England. Seeing her living with Blake and putting two and two together to come up 105. She shuddered. "Not yet," she prevaricated.

He stirred his coffee, allowing himself to ask the question that had been bothering him for a long time now. "Why did you marry him?" he asked quietly.

"For the same reason that everyone gets married, I suppose. Because I thought I was in love!"

He silently registered her use of the word "thought". "But you weren't?"

"How could I have been? I barely knew him—it all happened so fast." She had been hurting and vulnerable—her one-night stand with Blake having eaten into her already precarious self-esteem. People thought that models had everything most women wanted, but what no one seemed to realize was that beauty often went hand in hand with a crippling insecurity. Because people wanted you for all the wrong reasons. Luke certainly had—and maybe Blake had, too.

"He rushed you," said Blake slowly.

But Josephine shook her head violently, and a strand of bright-red hair came free of the constricting chignon. "I must have wanted to be rushed," she explained carefully. "And he was fun. Everything with Luke was carefree. He made me laugh." At a time when laughter had been in drastically short supply in her life.

"Did you marry him on the rebound from me?" he asked quietly.

Josephine had rarely experienced such a pure and blinding rage as she glared at Blake across the table of the coffee shop. "Of all the arrogant and insufferable things I've ever heard, that really has to take first prize, Blake! Is your ego so overinflated that you think one night with you—*one night*," she repeated in disbelief, "would lead me to marry the first man who asked me?"

"So the fact that Luke was my cousin had nothing to do with it?"

She opened her mouth to say something more on the subject of his ego, then shut it again. For wasn't there a tiny kernel of truth in his assumption? She had been swept off her feet by Luke, yes, a handsome actor who could have won an Oscar for his use of manipulative charm. But hadn't the fact that he had been related to a man she had spent her formative years pining over, made her feel a certain sense of *triumph*? And *power*?

Particularly when Blake had come blazing round to her flat and urged her to postpone the marriage. She had decided that he was motivated by sour grapes, nothing more, and certainly not out of concern for her. *He* didn't want her—he had made that abundantly clear—but he was damned if anyone else should have her, either. Hadn't her indignation at his request that she put an end to it only fueled her determination to marry Luke?

"Maybe just a little," she admitted.

Blake expelled a long, low breath, realizing that one-night stands were never as straightforward as they appeared to be at the time. Which he guessed was why he'd only ever had one in his life. You felt good for a while, and then you just felt empty. He had hurt Josephine by the way he'd behaved toward her. He recognized that now.

He sighed, wanting to put a smile back on her lips—and heaven only knew, there had been precious few of those in the past couple of weeks. "Listen, Josie—let's forget about Luke for a minute. What if I told you that I had another look at Giuseppi Rossi's scheme—and you were right—it *did* show potential? Maybe it's time for me to move in different directions." His eyes gleamed. "I think I'm going to back him."

54

Josephine stared at him, recognizing the sweetener for what it was, but knowing that she could not accept this attempt at an olive branch on Blake's terms alone. She leaned across the table toward him. "I want to help back him, too. I want to put some money in!"

He frowned. "You don't need to—"

"But I want to!" she interrupted passionately— because it had been her hunch, *her* hunch—not Blake's.

"Why?"

"Because if it's the success that I think it's going to be, then I want part of it. It's my baby, Blake— not yours."

A smile played at the corners of his mouth. "How much money?"

"Enough."

"How much?" The sum she mentioned made him raise his eyebrows. "But you haven't got that kind of money, Josephine. Not unless you're planning to sell the house?"

"No, I don't, but I can get it."

"How?"

"I have a necklace I can sell." A necklace given to her by Luke in the first few heady weeks of their relationship. A garish piece, bought more as a symbol of how much he had been prepared to spend on her than because of any intrinsic beauty. She had never really liked it.

* * *

"You're willing to gamble that much on the basis of *what*?" he demanded incredulously.

"I told you. Instinct," she answered slowly and fixed him with a curious look. "Don't you ever act on instinct, Blake?"

"Not usually."

Something unsaid hovered in the air between them. "Ever?" she persisted.

There was a pause. "Just the once."

"When was that?" But even as she asked the question, she knew what the answer was going to be.

His mouth flattened. "The night I slept with you, sweetheart."

Josephine forced herself to remain impassive. "I thought you'd forgotten all about that night," she said quietly.

"*Forgotten* it?" Blake echoed, in disbelief, because since she'd moved in he'd been remembering it about every two seconds. "Why on earth should you think that?"

"Because you never mention it."

"Well, neither do you," he accused softly.

She didn't look away. "No."

"And *anyway* it isn't the easiest subject to bring up, is it?" He adopted a mocking voice. "Josephine, do you remember the night when we tumbled uninhibitedly into bed together?"

She pushed a piece of bread around the plate. "But that's exactly what happened," she said baldly.

"And you badly regretted it, didn't you?"

She looked up. "Not as much as you obviously did!"

His eyes narrowed. "Meaning?"

"You couldn't wait to get away the next morning, could you?"

How honest to be? Totally, he decided. He owed her that, no matter how hurtful his words might be. She had endured enough subterfuge with Luke.

"I thought that we both understood the situation for what it was," he said softly.

Josephine blinked uncomprehendingly. "What was to understand?"

"That sometimes these things happen. A man and woman end up in bed together, even though they hadn't planned for it to happen."

"And it doesn't *mean* anything—is that what you're saying?"

This was proving even harder than he had anticipated and the look of confusion, which was blazing from her eyes, only added to his discomfiture. If he had ever wondered whether there had been other one-night stands in Josephine's life, then she had silently and implicitly answered it by the look on her face.

"I'm saying that it provided a great deal of pleasure at the time." A pulse beat insistently at his temple as he remembered just *how* pleasurable. "But sometimes that's as far as it goes."

Josephine swallowed. How eloquently he had put it, but no less wounding for that. "And you ran straight back to your relationship with Kim, didn't you?"

He shook his head. "I didn't go straight from your bed to Kim's, if that's what you're implying. I wasn't with Kim at the time—"

"For which I suppose I must be grateful."

"But, yes," he sighed, and stared into her hurt and angry face, "I *did* get back with her. We went back a long way and I felt I owed it to both of us to give it one last shot. It wasn't the first time we'd split up. That's the way our relationship was at the time."

58

And now? she wondered, but pride would not let her ask him that. Just because the girls at work thought he had never gotten over Kim didn't mean anything, did it? There had certainly been no sign of her since Josephine had moved in with him. And Blake himself had told her that the engagement was broken.

As they stood up to leave, she decided that it had been a painful and difficult talk, but maybe it had cleared the air between them.

And their one night of hot sex could now be consigned to history.

BLAKE SLAMMED INTO the flat at just gone eight, his face dark as thunder, to find Josephine grilling chicken, her sensible skirt stretched tight over the cups of her buttocks as she bent to take two plates out of the oven.

"Everything okay?" she asked.

Blake sucked in a breath of frustration. She had taken to cooking dinner some nights, so that he had the torture of watching her move around his kitchen. An exquisite torture, he decided, just as she smoothed her hands down over her apron, emphasizing the washboard-flat stomach.

He threw his briefcase onto a chair and averted his eyes. "Yeah, sure," he agreed sardonically. "Perfect as pie! I spoke to your friend Giuseppi this afternoon, who now seems to think he's died and gone to heaven!"

"You told him the good news? That you were going to back him?"

Good for whom, he hazarded, wondering whether she had hopes of her own for the sexy young Italian. "Yeah, I told him."

He sounded as though he had had second thoughts. "You don't seem very happy about it," she ventured.

More than one kind of frustration began to simmer into a boil. "What do you expect, Josephine?" he demanded. "I tell him one thing, and on the strength of what a cub receptionist says—I go back on everything I said and agree to back him! What do you think that says to him about my professional judgment? My reputation?"

"Your *pride*?" she teased.

His *pride*? Maybe she was right. And maybe the absence of pride might give him the freedom to ask her what had been bothering him.

"Like a drink?" he questioned.

Something in the darkening of his eyes was making her heart beat a little faster, and she switched the grill off with a shaking hand. "Sure."

He handed her a glass of wine and watched her while she drank some. "You never did answer my question," he said slowly.

She guessed from the deepening of his voice that this was nothing to do with work. "What question was that?"

"About whether you regretted what we did that night?"

"Didn't I?"

"You know you didn't."

"For what it's worth—then, no, I didn't regret it—not really. Just the way it fizzled out, I guess."

"But you recovered pretty quickly—fast enough to marry Luke within three months of meeting him."

"And you went back to Kim," she pointed out. "You had a pretty speedy recovery yourself."

He nodded, and he felt the stir of longing deep in his groin. "But things have changed now, haven't they?" He put his glass down.

She saw the way his eyes had darkened and something deep inside her began to melt. "Wh-what?" she whispered, as he walked across the kitchen to face her.

"You're no longer with Luke." He stared down at her. "And..."

"A-and?" Her lips trembled, and he traced their shivering outline with the tip of his finger.

"I'm no longer with Kim. Which makes us free agents, doesn't it?"

He moved his finger to smooth the curve of her jaw, and from there to her neck, and then farther still to the swell of her tiny breast, and shaking uncontrollably, she let him.

"And free agents can do what the hell they please, don't you think?"

"Blake." She swallowed, because his face was ablaze with hunger.

"And this will please both of us, sweetheart," he murmured huskily, his fingers beginning to undo the buttons of her blouse.

"Blake!" Josephine gasped, as he impatiently freed the last button and the air washed over her breasts.

He seemed to have been waiting for this moment all his life. "What?" he growled, and bent his dark head, suckling the nipple through the lace of her brassiere and her head jerked back, her eyes closing with helpless pleasure as he pushed one hard thigh between the unprotesting softness of hers.

She gripped his shoulders as the fierce promise of his body began to send sensual messages singing through her blood. "Don't you like what I'm doing?" he murmured.

He brazenly asked this particular question just as he was impatiently pulling the zip of her skirt down, so that moments later it had pooled in a whisper at her feet.

"Do you?" he demanded.

Since *this* question was accompanied by a provocative finger wriggling all the way up her thigh, she could do little other than make a shuddering little sigh, which became a moan when he found what he had clearly been seeking.

He felt the jerk of desire—sweet and sharp and potent—as he delved beneath her lace panties to find her honey sweet and turned on, and he sucked in a disbelieving breath. This was how he remembered her—so instantaneously responsive to everything he did to her.

"Do you know what I want to do to you?" he whispered huskily.

She shook her head, and raised her mouth to nip her teeth at the lobe of his ear, hearing his half-stifled murmur of delight.

"Everything," he breathed. "I want to do everything to you, Josephine, and then a little bit more."

She knew before he began to tug at her panties that he wasn't planning on taking her to the bedroom. Through half-shielded eyes she sneaked a look downward, where his desire could have been daunting if she hadn't wanted him so much. She doubted whether he would even *make* it to the bedroom, not in that kind of aroused state.

She flicked open the belt of his trousers and unzipped him and she heard his sigh of pleasure as he sprang free into the palm of her hand.

"Oh, sweetheart," he ground out unsteadily as he raised his head to look down at her, his blue eyes dazed. "Sweetheart."

His mouth grazed hers, explored it and licked it until she was on fire with him, and when he impatiently shoved aside the supper plates and bent her over the kitchen counter, she felt a wild and dizzying sensation of elation.

God, but she made him crazy! He kicked away his trousers and stared down at her, silhouetted against the countertop. Her hair had worked its way free, and was wild and messy—tumbling over the lace-covered strain of her breasts, while her cheeks were pink and her green eyes glittering.

He felt her syrupy moistness as he pushed against her, and then he thrust into her with an exultant kind of groan.

Josephine was unprepared for the sensation of completeness, of this being so *right*, but then, if her thoughts went out of control so did her body, because almost immediately the fiercest, most elemental orgasm had her shaking in his arms just before she heard his own soft, disbelieving sigh.

So the first time had not been an exaggeration. It was always this good with this man. She lifted her lips to his ear. "Thank you," she whispered softly.

He was about to ask her what she was thanking him for when the telephone began to ring, and in her disorientated and sleepy state of fulfillment, Josephine automatically reached out her hand to pick it up.

Blake groaned. "You should have ignored it," he whispered, but she smiled.

64

"Hello?" she yawned, and then stilled as she heard the voice at the other end, a cold, clammy sweat breaking out on her forehead. She handed him the receiver. "It's for you," she said, in a voice that was a hairsbreadth away from shaking. "It's Kim."

Blake took the receiver and tried to plant a kiss on Josephine's lips along the way, but she was busy wriggling out from underneath him, her face like thunder and her naked breasts brushing tantalizingly against his chest.

He sighed. "Kim? Hi!" He listened for a moment. "Well, it's not exactly the best time—" Kim was speaking rapidly now and he watched helplessly as Josephine flounced across the kitchen, her bare bottom wiggling. He heard her open the bathroom door and slam it shut with an almighty bang.

He listened to what Kim was saying.

"Yeah, okay. I'll see you there," he said. "But it'll have to be quick."

He replaced the phone, pulled on his jeans, and then went and hammered on the bathroom door.

"Josephine!"

"Go to hell!" she yelled.

"I need to talk to you!"

"Go and talk to *Kim* instead, why don't you?"

And then she turned the shower full on to drown out the sound of his voice and the sound of her tears.

SHE STOOD BENEATH the hot jets for a long time so that her skin was pink and wrinkled by the time she emerged, and, though she stood and listened for several minutes—there was no sound from the rest of the apartment.

He had gone.

Gone? Where? To *Kim*?

Like an automaton, she dressed in jeans and a sweater, but she did not bother drying her hair—she couldn't care less what it looked like—and her hands were shaking too much to be of any use.

It hurt, she realized. It hurt like crazy to think that Blake was still so close to Kim that he would rush straight off at her bidding, especially at a time like *that*.

And she realized something else, too.

That somewhere along the way she had fallen in love with her boss. So where did that leave her? Vulnerable and open to all kinds of heartache if all he wanted was a willing bed-partner.

Trying to dull some of the pain, she finished her glass of wine and didn't hear the front door close, didn't register anything at all until she saw Blake standing there in the kitchen, his face not guilty, but full of a quiet suppressed rage.

"I'm surprised you're still here," he said quietly.

She lifted her chin, her eyes glittering but defiant. "I don't have a choice, do I?" she returned. "Where else would I go at this time of night?"

He gave a bitter smile as he poured himself a glass of wine and drank it, before turning to face her, his features set. "And that's the only reason you stayed, is it, Josephine? A kind of emotional prisoner?"

"A *physical* prisoner," she corrected icily. "There was precious little emotion involved in what just happened."

"So, history has repeated itself," he mused. "There was precious little emotion involved the last time, if my memory serves me well."

She turned her face away, afraid that he would see the sudden leap of tears. No emotion? Maybe not for him, but for her, it had been overwhelming. The stupid and indiscriminate kind of emotion that made you love a man who would never love you back.

"How's Kim?" she asked flippantly. "Has she forgiven you your infidelity *this* time? Or has she grown a little tired of your wayward libido?"

Blake glared at Josephine, his breath coming quick and fast. "Kim rang me up to tell me that she's pregnant!"

There was a long, awful pause and Josephine very nearly passed out. "Oh, my God," she moaned.

Blake understood immediately and stared at her, his eyes glittering furiously. "It isn't *my* baby!" he roared.

"It isn't?"

"Of course it isn't! She's living with a lawyer! She has been for months! She rang me on her mobile to say she was just passing in a taxi, and I went downstairs to congratulate her. And do you really think that I would have made love to you—"

"Oh, please don't dress it up!" she snapped. "Having the minimum amount of clothes removed and being bent over the kitchen counter is hardly what I would call making love!"

Arrogantly, he raised his eyebrows. "I didn't hear you objecting at the time."

Her cheeks went pink. "That was because...because..."

"Because what, Josephine?" he prompted softly.

Because she had been in the throes of a physical response so intense that it had threatened to rock the foundations of her world. But hadn't it always been like that with him?

"I was as carried away as you were at the time!"

It wasn't any kind of loving declaration, but he nodded, badly needing to control his indignation and his fury, because if he wasn't careful then things would get said that they would regret. Or more important, things *wouldn't* get said—things that maybe he should have said a long time ago.

"Do you really think I would go straight from your arms and into Kim's?" he asked again.

She bit her lip. "How should I know? You never talk about her, do you? And you bit my head off when I asked. But the girls at work mention her."

"And what do they say?"

"Just that you never got over her—and that you've never been out with anyone since you split up."

He sucked in a breath. "Well, one part of the equation, at least—is true." He met the wary question in her eyes. "I haven't been out with anyone since Kim."

The other fact penetrated her befuddled brain. "Does that mean you are over her?"

"Of course I'm over her!" he exploded. "I'm not

the kind of man who can make out with two women at the same time—it's not in my nature!"

Her voice was low. "What about the night of the party?"

He shook his head. "I told you, my relationship with Kim was off at the time. That's how it was—on and off—sometimes for great chunks of time." He could see from the question in her eyes that she wanted maybe *needed* some kind of explanation. "She was the kind of woman I thought would make a good wife—"

"What kind of woman is that?" she asked, thinking how coldly dispassionate he sounded.

"Someone steady, logical, calm—"

"The 'right type'?" she put in sarcastically. "As opposed to the type of woman who would leap into bed with you without even being asked out for dinner first?"

"Don't put yourself down, Josephine."

"Why? Are you going to do that for me?"

"And stop being so bloody defensive and *listen* to me for once!" he stormed, and then controlled his breathing with an effort. "Kim thought the same about me—intellectually, she could imagine us settling down together—two people with a lot in common who would make good companions."

"So what happened to change your mind?"

He shrugged. "Relationships aren't like a mathematical problem—you can't punch in all the right numbers and come up with the perfect partner. I went back to Kim soon after that night with you, but I discovered—" He wondered whether what had happened between him and Josephine had made him view the world differently. "I discovered that there was no real spark between the two of us, although there was a good deal of respect and affection. And the spark is what keeps a relationship alive."

Josephine stared at him, realizing that things really *were* over between him and Kim, but realizing something else, too.

"Isn't this going to change things at work?"

He frowned. "What things?"

"Do you think we'll still be able to work together now that we're having sex?"

"Have you worked out the answer to your question yet, sweetheart?" Blake drawled.

Josephine blinked. He had just rung through to reception saying that he needed to see her urgently, and here she was, in the dauntingly large room of his penthouse office. "What question?"

"About whether we'd be able to carry on working together now that we're having sex."

"What a horrible way to put it!" she said crossly.

"It was *your* choice of words, Josephine," he pointed out and then he gave a slow smile. "I think it's working out just fine, don't you?"

"Yes," she said cautiously. But only by making the huge effort of separating the cool Blake at the office with the hot and passionate Blake at home. Her mouth dried. And if she wasn't careful, she was going to break her cardinal rule of not linking the two men. "Is that what you called me in here to say?"

He rose to his feet, thinking how beautiful she looked when she was trying to be angry with him. "No, I called you in here to ask two things. The first is why you've started sending the press releases round in an email to everyone in the company."

"Because it's instant and because it gives everyone a buzz. And it makes *everyone* feel involved!"

"It's not how we usually work it, Josephine."

She heard the faint note of authority in his voice and decided to ignore it. She stared him out. "So? If we always did things in exactly the same way, we'd never progress, would we, Blake?"

"Are you arguing with me?"

"No, I'm trying to make you see sense!"

"Like you did with Giuseppi, you mean?"

"Exactly," she said smugly.

"Except that it's too early to say if his scheme will take off."

"I'm confident," she answered.

"I know you are." He walked across the office and stared down at her. What a difference a month could make—because the Josephine who sat so

BONUS FEATURE

glowingly before him was a million miles away from the deflated woman he had brought back to London with him. "Everyone here thinks you're pretty wonderful!"

"And what do *you* think?" she flashed back.

His voice was slightly unsteady. "I think you're pretty wonderful myself."

"Why, *thank* you, Blake," she said demurely, then hastily stood up. Praise was all very well and good, but there was something in the darkening of Blake's eyes that was making her feel distinctly un-professional, and she had vowed never to be *that*.

"What was the second thing you asked me in here for?"

72

He raised her hand to his lips. "A kiss."

She shivered and tried to take her hand away, but he had it locked fast in his. "Blake—we mustn't."

"Mustn't what?" he murmured, as he bent his head to nuzzle his mouth against the long line of her neck.

"*You* know!" She tried to wriggle out of his arms, but unfortunately just at the same moment he pulled her against him, so that the wriggle became a sinu-ous writhe against the hard length of his body.

"Mmm. I know everything," he teased, and bent his head to kiss her.

"Blake, this is going to get out of hand," she protested.

"I intend it to," he said, sliding his hand underneath her skirt.

"I won't be able to resist unless you stop it," she begged.

"Then don't."

There was a moment when she pretended to struggle, but it was as fainthearted as could be, because she wanted him as much as he wanted her.

He made love to her very swiftly and very beautifully on the floor of his office.

"Lock the door!" she gasped, just as he began to unzip his trousers.

"I already did!" he gasped back.

"Oh, my," sighed Josephine afterward, languidly stretching her arms above her head. "That was just *heaven*!"

Blake looked at her where she lay on his office floor, her eyes closed, her clothes awry, an expression of satiated bliss on her face, and he realized that he needed some kind of closure with her past. Hell, they *both* did.

"Fix your clothes, Josephine," he said suddenly. "We're going out."

Josephine opened her eyes. "Out where?"

THE CAR CRAWLED ALONG the busy London streets, and *Josephine* tried to take in the facts. Luke was *back*. Here in *London*!

"How long has he been back?"

"A couple of weeks. I guess he thought that he

BONUS FEATURE

could lie low and not be discovered, but I found out as soon as he had set foot in Britain."

"But you didn't bother telling me?"

Blake shot her a look. "You claimed not to be particularly interested."

And she hadn't been. That much was true. But then her heart and her mind and her body had been full of the man beside her.

"Besides," he gave a tight smile, "you seem to have blossomed pretty well without him. You've become some woman, Josephine."

It was probably the sweetest thing he had ever said to her. "Why, th-thank you," she responded shakily.

74

THE DOOR TO LUKE'S APARTMENT was opened and Josephine was shocked by the sight of her estranged husband, wearing just a pair of trousers.

He had gained weight and his face was tanned but puffy, with a faint sheen of sweat, his eyes dark-rimmed. In his hand he held a glass half-full of whiskey, and his eyes narrowed with sly perception as he stared from one to the other.

"Well, well, well," he sneered. "So my powerful cousin finally got what he always wanted, did he? Hope she's a bit more responsive in *your* bed, mate, than she was in mine."

Resisting the urge to smack him in the face, Blake looked across at Josephine. Was *that* why she had thanked him after her orgasm, she wondered? He gave her a tender smile. "We've no complaints in that department, have we, sweetheart?"

Luke scowled. "What do you want?"

"Can we come inside?" asked Blake quite calmly.

"If you want," came the ungracious reply.

Inside, the flat was a shambles and the first thing that Josephine saw was a discarded pair of women's high-heeled shoes and a crumpled pair of panties.

Blake stood watching her frozen expression, then turned to Luke.

"So you're still with Sadie, are you?"

"God, no! I traded her in for a newer model, actually." Luke gave a glassy grin. "So what can I do for you, Josephine?"

The unplanned words came tumbling out all by themselves. "I'd—I'd like a divorce please, Luke—just as soon as possible."

He stilled, and a calculating look came into his eyes. "Why, so you can get it together with Mr. Megabucks?" He stared insultingly at her neat, navy suit. "He'll never marry you, you know, Josephine—however much you try to turn yourself into the woman he wants you to be, with the frumpy clothes and the glasses!"

"On the contrary," interjected Blake smoothly. "I love Josephine very much whatever she's wearing—or not wearing—and I intend to marry her as

BONUS FEATURE

soon as possible—if she'll have me. Oh, and one more thing, Luke."

Luke stilled, as if something in Blake's tone was more than a little threatening. "What?"

"I imagine that even *your* profligate habits haven't been able to blow all the money that you stole from Josephine—"

"For richer or for poorer," mocked Luke. "Those are the words of the wedding vows—"

"Shut *up*," ground out Blake. "I'm telling you that if the remainder of the money isn't in her bank account by the end of the week, then you will be hit with the full force of the law. And I want everything that you *have* spent paid back. In full. Understood?"

76

Luke lasted the blistering blue stare for only about ten seconds, and then his eyes dropped to his bare feet. "Yeah," he agreed sulkily.

Her heart was pounding so hard that Josephine could barely breath and she clutched at Blake's hand. "C-come on. L-let's j-just get out of here," she stumbled.

They made it back to the car and she sat there with tears streaming down her cheeks.

"Why are you crying, sweetheart?" he asked gently. "Did it upset you to see him looking such a mess?"

She shook her head. "Wh-what did you have to say that for?" she sobbed.

"Which bit in particular?" he asked, smiling.

"The love and flowers bit! To hurry the divorce along? Or to salvage what's left of my pride?"

"Neither. Because it's true. It's always been true—only I was too blind and too stubborn to admit it to myself before. You're the spark I've been missing—the spark that I need. You make me feel *alive*, sweetheart—more alive than I thought it was possible to feel."

She stared at him, knowing deep down that he would not say these things if they were not true.

"So will you marry me?" he murmured silkily.

"I can't marry you."

There was a pause. "Would you mind telling me why? It isn't because you don't love me, I know that."

It was an arrogant declaration, but at least it was honest. "You're so confident that I love you?" Josephine questioned quietly.

He wondered if she was blind to the way that she looked at him sometimes when she thought she wasn't being observed. Like the sun had suddenly come out. "But you do, don't you?"

What point was there in denying it anymore?

"Yes. Very much."

"So why won't you marry me?"

Josephine let out a long, low sigh. "Because it would be too easy."

"Marriage is *supposed* to be easy," he said gently. "Not difficult."

BONUS FEATURE

"Yes, but don't you see, Blake—I've already had one failed marriage. I don't want to rush into another—like a woman crossing a stream and leaping from one emotional rock to the next. This has all been like a roller coaster—"

"What has?"

"The closure with Luke. The relief. The closeness with you—but what if it's all an illusion? What if six months down the line we find it's all played out?"

He shook his head. "It won't be."

"But how can you know that?" she demanded, her voice rising, knowing that she was heaping pain on herself by not giving in to what she wanted more than anything in the world, but knowing, deep down, that she needed the courage to see it through. "You thought that you wanted to marry Kim—you were with her for *years*, and yet in the end you acknowledged that it wasn't right."

"Because I feel differently about you than the way I felt about Kim," he said simply. "With Kim I just felt that I was playing a part—a part I wanted to play, it's true. But none of it felt real, the way it does with you. You're everything I thought I *didn't* want—you're stubborn and fiery. You make me want to make love to you in the most unsuitable of places."

She blushed, remembering them working late

last night, and the protracted pleasure of the ride in the lift.

"You make me *respond*," he continued passionately. "And I don't just mean sexually, I mean emotionally, too. You engage me at a level I didn't think I had in me. I broke every rule in the book the night I took you home from that party. Don't you understand, Josephine, that we *belong* together—in a way that Kim and I never did."

"Oh, darling," she whispered.

"I must have been mad not to have admitted it to myself sooner. I risked losing you—hell, I *did* lose you! I'm just thanking God that your marriage failed and that I had the chance to try again."

It was hard to reconcile Blake—her passionate but contained Blake—coming out with such unequivocal declarations of need and love. She wanted to get on the mobile phone and to demand that Luke give her the quickest divorce in history so that she could become Mrs. Josephine Devlin at the first opportunity.

But she owed it to him to apply the brakes just a little.

Hell, she owed it to *herself*.

She reached for his hand and kissed the tip of each finger in turn, and she thought that she could read a certain sense of victory in the ice-blue eyes. But his words surprised her even more than his wry smile.

"You aren't going to give in on this, are you, sweetheart?"

"How can you tell?"

"I just can." Like he seemed to be able to tell most things about her, and his knowledge of her grew day by day. He sighed, knowing that she was right and respecting her for it, even as it irritated him that she would not bend to his will.

But wasn't that one of the reasons why he loved her?

EPILOGUE

"SO HOW DOES IT FEEL to be a millionaire, sweetheart?" Blake asked softly.

Josephine smiled. "Huh! You tell *me*—you should know!"

He laughed. Giuseppi's revolutionary organic weed killer had been launched to ecstatic worldwide response and the shares had been floated on the stock market last week, leaving him with his biggest ever success on his hands.

No. Not his.

"You know, it's your success, sweetheart. All yours." He leaned over to plant a kiss on her lips. "If it hadn't been for your stubbornness and determination—I would never have backed him. I should have listened to you from the outset."

"But why should you have done?" she asked him. "*You* were the expert—"

"Supposedly," he interjected dryly.

"It was just an instinctive feeling that it was all going to come good."

As they had done together. More than good. Blake had once said that Giuseppi had looked as though he had died and gone to heaven—well, he now had a pretty good idea of how he must have felt!

"And yet you ruthlessly refused to be instinctive about marrying me," he mused, "when I knew you wanted to. We keep acting out-of-character around each other, don't we, Josie?"

She considered this. "Or maybe it's just that we bring out the best in each other," she said seriously. "Exploring the sides of ourselves that we'd never really looked at before."

82   He smiled. "Happy?"

"Ecstatic would be an understatement!"

"That's a 'yes', is it?" he teased.

They were sitting outside on Blake's roof garden in the glorious, golden summer sunshine, just contemplating whether to eat in or go out for supper.

And contemplating other things, as well.

Josephine's divorce had come through and Luke had paid back most of the money. She was now financially more than solvent and well respected within the company—more important, she now respected *herself*. She sighed. It didn't get much better than this. The board had just agreed to promote her, and she was living with the man she loved.

"It's been well over a year since I first moved in

here with you," she observed, a note of surprise in her voice. "Hard to believe, isn't it?"

In some ways, yes—in others, not at all. Time was immeasurable when you were happy, Blake realized, and he was happier than he had imagined it possible to be.

He kissed her again, just for the hell of it. "You know, maybe you were right, sweetheart, maybe we *don't* need a wedding ring to be committed to one another."

Josephine frowned. "I don't remember saying *that.*"

"Not in so many words, perhaps." He shrugged. "But marriage to Luke scared you off, I know that, and the last thing I want is for you to enter into an institution that makes you uneasy. I'm not going anywhere, honey—and we don't need a wedding to prove it."

The frown grew deeper. "Are you saying that you no longer want to marry me?"

With great difficulty, he bit back a smile. "That's not what I'm saying at all," he corrected smoothly. "Just I'm perfectly happy with the status quo. Aren't you?"

Suddenly, no, she was *not*! "I *do* want to get married, actually," she said sulkily, but the soft blaze from his eyes teased a smile out of her. "I've been waiting for you to ask me again!"

He shook his head and a mischievous light

glinted in the blue eyes. "Oh, no—we've done it that way round and you said no. So in the spirit of our wonderful and very equal relationship, I really think you ought to ask me, Josephine."

"I'm not getting down on one knee, if that's what you think!"

"Why not sit on my knee instead?" he suggested gravely.

She did as he asked, perched herself comfortably and erotically over one hard, muscular thigh and looked deep into his eyes. "Will you marry me, Blake?"

"I'll have to think about it."

"For how long?" she cried, trying to keep the alarm from her voice.

He enjoyed the moment. "Oh, for about—say— five seconds." He grinned. "Of course I'll marry you, Josephine—though I thought you'd never ask, you stubborn woman!"

He kissed her for a very long time and as she kissed him back her last rational thought was that Blake knew exactly how to handle her.

In more ways than one!

THE END

*ORIGINALLY PUBLISHED ONLINE AT
WWW.EHARLEQUIN.COM

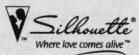

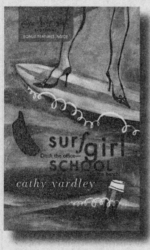
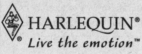

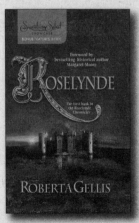

If you enjoyed what you just read,
then we've got an offer you can't resist!

Take 2 bestselling love stories FREE!

Plus get a FREE surprise gift!

Clip this page and mail it to Harlequin Reader Service®

IN U.S.A.	**IN CANADA**
3010 Walden Ave.	P.O. Box 609
P.O. Box 1867	Fort Erie, Ontario
Buffalo, N.Y. 14240-1867	L2A 5X3

YES! Please send me 2 free Harlequin Presents® novels and my free surprise gift. After receiving them, if I don't wish to receive anymore, I can return the shipping statement marked cancel. If I don't cancel, I will receive 6 brand-new novels every month, before they're available in stores! In the U.S.A., bill me at the bargain price of $3.80 plus 25¢ shipping & handling per book and applicable sales tax, if any*. In Canada, bill me at the bargain price of $4.47 plus 25¢ shipping & handling per book and applicable taxes**. That's the complete price and a savings of at least 10% off the cover prices—what a great deal! I understand that accepting the 2 free books and gift places me under no obligation ever to buy any books. I can always return a shipment and cancel at any time. Even if I never buy another book from Harlequin, the 2 free books and gift are mine to keep forever.

106 HDN DZ7Y
306 HDN DZ7Z

Name	(PLEASE PRINT)	
Address	Apt.#	
City	State/Prov.	Zip/Postal Code

Not valid to current Harlequin Presents® subscribers.

Want to try two free books from another series?
Call 1-800-873-8635 or visit www.morefreebooks.com.

* Terms and prices subject to change without notice. Sales tax applicable in N.Y.
** Canadian residents will be charged applicable provincial taxes and GST.
  All orders subject to approval. Offer limited to one per household.
® are registered trademarks owned and used by the trademark owner and or its licensee.

PRES04R   ©2004 Harlequin Enterprises Limited

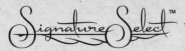

COMING NEXT MONTH

Signature Select Spotlight
IN THE COLD by Jeanie London
Years after a covert mission gone bad, ex-U.S. intelligence agent Claire de Beaupre is discovered alive, with no memory of the brutal torture she endured. Simon Brandauer, head of the agency, must risk Claire's fragile memory to unravel the truth of what happened. But a deadly assassin needs her to *forget*....

Signature Select Saga
BETTING ON GRACE by Debra Salonen
Grace Radonovic is more than a little surprised by her late father's friend's proposal of marriage. But the shady casino owner is more attracted to her dowry than the curvy brunette herself. So when long-lost cousin Nikolai Sarna visits, Grace wonders if *he* is her destiny. But sexy Nick has a secret...one that could land Grace in unexpected danger.

Signature Select Miniseries
BRAVO BRIDES by Christine Rimmer
Two full-length novels starring the beloved Bravo family.... Sisters Jenna and Lacey Bravo have a few snags to unravel...before they tie the knot!

Signature Select Collection
EXCLUSIVE! by Fiona Hood-Stewart, Sharon Kendrick, Jackie Braun
It's a world of Gucci and gossip. Caviar and cattiness. And suddenly everyone is talking about the steamy antics behind the scenes of the Cannes Film Festival. Celebrities are behaving badly... and tabloid reporters are dishing the dirt.

Signature Select Showcase
SWANSEA LEGACY by Fayrene Preston
Caitlin Deverell's great-grandfather had built SwanSea as a mansion that would signal the birth of a dynasty. Decades later, this ancestral home is being launched into a new era as a luxury resort—an event that arouses passion, romance and a century-old mystery.

The Fortunes of Texas: Reunion
THE DEBUTANTE by Elizabeth Bevarly
When Miles Fortune and Lanie Meyers are caught in a compromising position, it's headline news. There's only one way for the playboy rancher and the governor's daughter to save face—pretend to be engaged until after her father's election. But what happens when the charade becomes more fun than intended?

FIONA HOOD-STEWART

Scottish author **Fiona Hood-Stewart** has led a cosmopolitan life from the day she was born. Schooled in Switzerland and fluent in seven languages, she draws on her own experiences in the world of old money, big business and the international jet set for inspiration in creating her books. She now lives in Europe with her two sons, with whom she shares her life.

SHARON KENDRICK

Born in west London, **Sharon Kendrick** now lives in the beautiful city of Winchester, U.K., and can hear the bells of the cathedral ringing while she works. She has had zillions of jobs, which include photographer, nurse, waitress and demonstrator of ironing board covers. She drove an ambulance in Australia and appeared on television in Tehran, but writing is the only job she's had that feels just right. Her passions are many and varied, but include music, films, books, cooking, gazing at the sky and drifting off into daydreams while she works on steamy new love stories!

JACKIE BRAUN

Jackie Braun earned a degree in journalism from Central Michigan University in 1987 and spent more than sixteen years working full-time at newspapers, including eleven years as an award-winning editorial writer, before quitting her day job to freelance and write fiction. She is a past RITA® Award finalist and a member of the Romance Writers of America. She lives in mid-Michigan with her husband and their young son. She can be reached through her Web site at www.jackiebraun.com.